# Good Man
# *Hunting*

## By Lisa Landolt

GOOD MAN HUNTING

# Good Man Hunting

## Lisa Landolt

**A V O N**

*An Imprint of* HarperCollins*Publishers*

HarperCollins books may be purchased for educational, business, or sales promotional use. For information please write: Special Markets Department, HarperCollins Publishers, 10 East 53rd Street, New York, NY 10022.

FIRST EDITION

*Interior text designed by Diahann Sturge*

Library of Congress Cataloging-in-Publication Data
Landolt, Lisa.
 Good man hunting / Lisa Landolt.—1st ed.
  p. cm.
ISBN: 978-0-06-134039-0
1. Single women—Fiction.    2. Women—Societies and clubs—Fiction.
3. United States. Federal Bureau of Investigation—Fiction.    I. Title.

PS3612.A54836G66      2008
813'.6—dc22         2007034824

08  09  10  11  12      OV/RRD      10  9  8  7  6  5  4  3  2  1

*For Diana*

# Acknowledgments

I would like to extend my deepest appreciation to the following people for their inspiration and assistance with the creation of *Good Man Hunting*.

To my mother, and best friend, Margaret Landolt. You read and edited every version of my manuscript, listened to all of my ideas and gave me your own, kept me laughing, and always made me feel like I could accomplish anything.

To my other family members for their support, including my twin sister, Laura Landolt; my father, Bob Landolt; my brother, Rob Landolt; my grandfather, Bob Landolt; and my aunt Mary Landolt. To Haylie and Joshua for keeping me company and entertained.

To our dear friend Joyce Fielding for her support and humor. The book wouldn't be the same without your inspiration.

To my friend Sharon King. You are the most talented writer I know, and your feedback has been invaluable.

To my agent, Janet Benrey, of Benrey Literary Agency, who sold my manuscript so quickly and made the entire publishing process enjoyable.

To Lucia Macro, my editor at HarperCollins, for bringing *Good Man Hunting* to life.

*Before they were desperate housewives,*
*they were desperate singles.*

# Chapter One
# The Airport

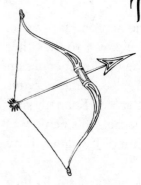

I wonder how many people's lives have been changed at the airport. It happened to me at LAX, on the other side of the scanning machines. Sitting down to put back on my white Reebok tennis shoes, I remember thinking these tennis shoes are supposed to be safe—the kind you won't have to take off to be scanned. At that moment, I realized that we can never be sure our actions are safe anymore.

"Excuse me," an airline employee—security it looks like—says to me. "Ms. Sandra Greene?"

"Yes?" I look up at the two security guards wearing black shirts and black pants, making them clash in the sea of brightly dressed tourists.

"Can you come with us please?" The shorter one gestures for me to stand up.

"What's the problem?" I tie my left shoe a little too tightly.

"Security matter."

My mind races. Was there something in my purse the screeners didn't like? But I have my purse; wouldn't they have taken it? Maybe they didn't like something in my checked bag?

"If you would just come with us," the first one says again. I stand up and pick up my purse, glancing over to the other side of the screening machines and then at the people on this side. People are staring, and that makes me as nervous as the security guards do. Flashes of Senator Kennedy and how he wasn't able to board a plane because his name was on some terrorist list go through my mind. I wonder if my name is on that list, too.

"In here, please." The first officer leads me into a small office that has the typical desk setup and two guest chairs. "Have a seat." I sit down in one of the government-issue brown chairs. The security guards leave just as another man walks in.

"Sandra Greene." A balding man, with several file folders under his arm, shuts the door. I can't tell if he's asking if I'm Sandra Greene or telling me that I am. He looks pretty harmless: short-sleeved button-down shirt, thin black tie, black pants, and multiple pens in a pocket protector. He sits down behind the desk, and I'm suddenly feeling better. This little guy obviously has an administrative error or something he needs to address.

My opinion changes, however, when another man enters. He's wearing a heavy dark blue suit when it's ninety-something degrees and humid outside.

"Ms. Greene, I'm Senior Agent McFarland with the FBI,"

he introduces himself and pulls the extra guest chair around to the other side of the desk next to the little guy.

FBI? Okay, something is really wrong, I tell myself. A million cop-show reruns go through my mind, and I'm reminded how you're not supposed to say anything at all except your name until an attorney shows up. You just know the FBI hates all the crime shows, letting the simple folk like me know we have rights.

"Do you know why you're here?"

"Yes. To catch a flight back to Dallas." I play the dumb-blonde card without even thinking and hug my purse in my lap. I wonder if my checked bags are still on their way to Dallas.

"No. Do you know why the FBI wants to speak with you?" He looks exactly like you would expect an FBI guy to look like, so if he's an undercover agent, he's not a very good one.

"No, and, um, I'm sure there must be some mistake." In the twenty-one years I've been alive, I've never been in serious trouble; I've never even gotten a speeding ticket. People like me just do not have meetings with the FBI.

"There's been no mistake. We've been investigating you for some time now, and if you will cooperate with us, you will find the consequences will be less severe. We've been working on a series of murders that we believe you can help us with."

"*Murders?*" I repeat it as if I've never heard the word before. "I don't know anything about murders." My mind goes over the events of the past week. Was there anything out of the ordinary with the passengers on the boat in Hawaii? No one got pushed over or anything. I did think that Dick guy was kind of weird. But not a murderer. Did I miss something? Chris Rock was right; police officials can make you wonder if you've stolen your own car. Have I done something wrong that I don't realize?

"The murders involve women between the ages of twenty and thirty-seven," he continues. "The last victim may be someone you know. A wealthy supermodel." He slides a black-and-white photo across the desk toward me, and I don't even want to look at it. This really can't be happening to me.

"I'm sorry, I can't help you. Would it be possible for me to, you know, go now? I'd like to catch my flight." I feel my fingers trembling.

"It's okay if you want to go, since you're not under arrest. Yet. We were just hoping you'd be willing to help us so such an arrest could be avoided."

"Why would y'all want to arrest me?" My heart sinks. I would never be involved in killing; I don't even kill spiders in my apartment. Everything in my life is going so great now . . . I don't want anything to interfere with it, especially something like a murder investigation. I feel like I'm about to break down and do the "ugly cry," but then I remember my mom always said that crying makes you look guilty.

"Let's put it this way. . . ," he pauses for effect. "If you refuse to help us, it will appear you are hiding something. You might then be considered a suspect."

"I, of course, want to help you any way I can. It's just I don't think there's anything I can do." I wish he could understand that I don't want to be involved in any of this. Like, it's just not a good time right now for me to help the FBI with a murder investigation.

"Do you belong to a group called the Hunt Club?" he asks, opening another file that the little guy brought in with him. I'm tempted to say no, or it's none of his business, or that I want my attorney, not that I have one. But I'm guessing he may know I'm a member. I mean, it's not a secret or anything. I have tons of stuff with the Hunt Club name on it and the number *five*.

"Yes, I am a member. I joined a few months ago. What does that have to do with anything?"

"We believe you can help connect the dots between the murders and the Hunt Club members," he says matter-of-factly, flipping through the file folder until he finds the page he's looking for.

"That is ridiculous. The ladies in the Hunt Club would never hurt anyone." I shake my head. "I've never met more compassionate, kind women in my life."

"Okay, great. If you're so sure they haven't done anything wrong, then you won't have a problem talking to us about them."

"I'll tell you anything you want to know." I nod, feeling determined that I can clear this whole thing up. "Because I know they aren't involved with murder or anything else."

"Give us all the details you can about the Hunt Club," he says, reaching for his pen. "How did you first get involved with them?"

"I first learned about the Hunt Club through a friend of mine. When she sent me an invitation to her wedding." I relive the events for Agent McFarland as he takes notes on his yellow legal pad.

# Chapter Two
# The Rush

I have my face scrunched up in my rearview mirror as I assume the position to roll my mascara wand over my lashes—mouth open, eyes looking upward, tongue almost out. Sitting with my car idling in the middle lane of Central Expressway, I remember again how much I hate rush-hour traffic in Dallas. But at least it gives me a chance to do my makeup and flip through my mail on my way to work.

A formal white envelope embossed with a gold number *five* on it sits next to me on the passenger seat. It's a wedding invitation from Annette Rodacker. Good for her, I think to myself, signaling to take my exit when the traffic finally moves. I can't help but smile. Sometimes it feels as if my whole life is stuck in traffic, but I know if Annette can find a husband, that means there's still hope out there for me.

Before going in to work, I look at the other contents of the envelope. There are instructions to the reception at a place called Gleneagles, along with another little matching card. I have to laugh at Annette's joke—she always did have a great sense of humor. The card reads:

*The Bride and Groom are registered with*
*Bloomingdale's, Saks Fifth Avenue,*
*Barneys New York, and Harrods*

"Okay, the next time I'm in New York or London, I'll be sure to stop by and get them both wedding gifts," I mumble as I stop the engine and step out of my Hyundai.

"We're having a rush for some reason," Jerry, my flour-covered manager says when I walk in the door. He quickly shovels a pizza out of the oven and throws it on the cutting board. "Must be a game on."

"Forty-five," a driver yells, running out the door with a pizza carrier held out in front of him.

"Fifty-three." Another one goes.

"We need to get these times down, people," Jerry yells to the brightly lip-glossed teenagers on the food line who are giggling and sticking pieces of ham into their mouths. "Nicole," he yells to another of them, "why aren't you slapping?"

I tie my orange apron around my waist and hurry to the pizza-prep line. It's already extremely hot in the store, and everyone is sweating. The damn AC never works right, overwhelmed with the heat from the pizza ovens and the Texas sun shining through the front windows.

"Pull your pinks!" Jerry yells again from the cutting board on the upper level, hovering over us like he's on the bridge of the starship *Enterprise*. The girls pull the pink order slips off the small rack in front of them and stick each one under a different pizza. It's the only way to keep them from making the same pizza more than once.

"Okay, what do we need?" I ask, washing my hands before I begin slapping.

"Four sixteen inches and two twelve," Nicole tells me, the hat on her head almost falling off. The hat is supposed to meet health regulations by keeping her hair out of the pizzas, but these teenagers think it's more fashionable to have it touching their heads as little as possible.

"Is Chris working tonight?" Brenda asks in her perpetually high-pitched-giggle voice from where she stands, doing nothing, next to Nicole. They have a dozen pinks waiting for them, and all they care about is when the cute drivers will be in. Sometimes, I think Jerry might be right . . . firing them and just doing it all myself would be faster.

"Thirty-seven," another driver yells as he runs out of the store with his pizza. I can't believe the pizzas are still going out the door over thirty minutes old.

"Hey, Paul, would you please come over here and help on the line?" I pull one of the phone people to help because we're quickly descending into pizza chaos. Paul hesitates for a moment, rolls his eyes in typical teenager fashion, and then drags his feet as he walks over to the pizza-prep line.

"I NEED A REMAKE!" Jerry practically sings in a tone that says, "See, Sandra, I told you it was stupid to hire sixteen year olds who've never worked before." The phones are ringing off the wall.

"First ring! First ring!" Jerry yells to the phone people. "Put them on hold! Put them on hold!"

"What do you need on the remake?" I holler back at him, getting the different-sized pizza screens ready. I smile to the girls on the line, as if to let them know everything is okay. Jerry always panics during a rush.

"It's a sixteen inch, PMH. And it's already seventeen minutes old, Sandra."

"Nicole, which one are you making?" I laugh for a second as I lean over her shoulder, my sixteen-inch circle of dough in mid-slap. "Slide that one to Paul. Make the pepperoni, mushroom, and ham from that one. And Brenda, you have waaaay too much cheese on that one."

"Remake in!" Nicole slides the remade pizza in the oven and blows a bubble, even though she knows she shouldn't have gum on the line.

The rush slows down, and I can finally take a breath. My pizza makers are supposed to be cleaning the pit, sorting through food that has fallen beneath the metal bars on the line and then putting it back in the proper bins to be used again. Instead, they're whispering and giggling at Chris Myers, one of the college-age drivers who just now decided to show up for work. In truth, part of me wishes I could be over there with them. But I know they see me as just some geeky assistant manager. I wish I had grown up in that world of family money, designer clothes and haircuts, and to work just for something to do or because there's a cute guy who works here.

"Ladies, if there's time enough to lean, there's time enough to clean." Jerry interrupts their giggling and gossiping. Then it's time for more yelling: "Drivers up! Let's go, people!"

As I stand over the food line, picking the dried food out from under my fingernails, I think I would rather dig ditches for the city of Dallas than spend another night working in this place. There's got to be more to life than this.

Driving home to my apartment after work, I take off my hat and run my fingers through my matted hair. I carry in the leftover slices from one of the many remakes from tonight, walk into my kitchen, and put my stuff on the counter. I flip through the bills and late notices again until I come across Annette's wedding invitation.

My routine is always the same. I walk over and plop down on the couch as I turn on the TV—nothing is ever on this time of night, so I put in an old VHS tape of my favorite show: *It's My Life*. It's a show that has been off the air for a while, but I still love watching it. Homely high school girl who has a crush on amazingly hot high school guy, and amazingly hot high school guy doesn't know Homely Girl even exists. I haven't seen the actor who plays the hot guy—Michael Something— in anything since. As I fast-forward through the commercials, I open Annette's invitation again.

I guess I should go to the wedding. I haven't seen Annette in, gosh . . . how long has it been? A year, maybe? We used to work out, or attempt to, at the ladies' gym together. That was back before my shift change and promotion when I became a pizza vampire who rarely sees the light of day.

Annette and I always did share the same goals: marry a nice husband, have two kids—one boy and one girl, with the boy born first—and have a big house with golden retriever puppies playing in the backyard. I know I should be there for her. She doesn't have that many friends—she's so much like me, kind of awkward and shy.

According to the invitation, the ceremony is going to be

held at the Methodist church downtown. It's a huge church.
They're having it in the sanctuary, not in the chapel. I laugh
for a moment, thinking I definitely need to go; I need to spread
myself out on the pew to make it look like more people will
be on her side.

I'm not really a dress-wearing type of gal, but it's not by
choice. I just don't get a chance to wear them very often. On
occasions like Annette's wedding, I revel in the opportunity
to have makeup on my face without a coating of flour on top
of it and to actually smell like something other than pizza
sauce. Wearing a blue skirt and white blouse, I climb the steps
up to the church. The parking lot is almost packed, so I figure
they must be having several events going on.

"Good afternoon, are you a friend of the bride or the
groom?" I am greeted by a gray-haired gentleman in the foyer,
who hands me a program.

"The bride. Annette Rodacker."

"The usher will be right back to escort you," he tells me.
"Why don't you sign the guest book?" I smile at him and walk
over to a table to sign the big white book with the big white
pen with the big white fluffy feather.

"Welcome, how are you?" A woman says, who is wearing a
pin with a big *five* on it made of diamonds. I sign the book and
notice the pages are filled with names. Maybe Annette has a
lot of relatives or something.

"Or 'something' is right," I mumble to myself as the usher
comes back and escorts me into the sanctuary. The pews
can hold almost five thousand people, and they are almost
all filled. Five thousand people. At a wedding for sweet little
unemployed, still-living-with-mom-and-dad Annette. I guess
I won't be spreading myself out in the pew, after all.

"Are you a friend of Annette's?" An elegant sixtyish woman asks me once I'm seated. I am in a row about a dozen pews from the front, squeezed into a spot just big enough for one more person. Or a woman's purse.

"Yes." I smile.

"Oh, we just LOVE her," the woman says, nodding to me and then to the woman on the other side of her, who also nods. All the sudden, I'm nodding, too, and wondering who "we" is.

"Oh, do you go to this church, too?" I ask, although I'm not sure if the church in which we are sitting is Annette's church.

"No, no, she's at the Hunt Club with us."

The Hunt Club? I can't see Annette *hunting* anything. I look at the wedding program, and I notice Annette is marrying William Michael Rutherford. The Third.

"Do you know her fiancé, too?" I ask the Hunt Club lady.

"Oh, yes. He's of the Kennebunkport Rutherfords, you know."

"Ah, yes, of course. The *Kennebunkport* Rutherfords." I have no idea what she's talking about, and I'm now wondering if I'm at the wrong wedding. Maybe there are two Annette Rodackers. Our conversation is cut short by the entrance of the groom and the groomsmen at the front of the sanctuary. There must be a dozen or more ushers. It appears Annette's colors for the wedding are white and gray. Who chooses gray for a wedding color?

When the organist begins, and all the flower girls and dozen or so bridesmaids slowly proceed down the center aisle, the colors make more sense. Each of the girls is wearing a taffeta silver gown with just a hint of purple. Annette's colors are white and *silver-purple*, not *gray*. How lucky for the bridesmaids that they have beautiful dresses they might actually wear again.

We stand at the sound of the wedding march, and I almost

don't recognize Annette as she walks down the aisle. She looks amazing in a slinky white wedding dress and veil, like right out of a *Modern Bride* magazine. I recall her telling me that her dad manages a Home Depot and her mom works part-time as a perfume sniper at the mall. I'm impressed at the extravagance they went to for the wedding.

Rose, the Hunt Club lady I sat with during the ceremony, keeps me company during the reception as well, which turns out to be a good thing because I would have been lost without her. The reception is held at the Gleneagles Country Club, and it is a gorgeous place: lavish halls lined with trees, elegant chandeliers, horse statues, and beautiful flowers everywhere. It's hard for me to picture Annette marrying someone who would have connections to a place like this and to a world like this. Rose and I walk through the receiving line together, and it feels weird that I don't know anyone except for Annette.

"Sandra! So good to see you." She hugs me, and she's suddenly the same old Annette again.

"You look wonderful! Congratulations."

"Thank you. This is Will. Will, this is Sandra." Will is probably one of the most handsome men I have ever seen— almost breathtakingly handsome. Handsome beyond what you think exists anymore outside of movies. *How did she end up with him?*

"Nice to meet you, Sandra." He waves at me instead of shaking my hand, and I notice he does that with everyone. "You will have to come over when we get back from our honeymoon." He flashes a sweet orthodontically straightened smile.

"I don't want to lose touch again. Promise." Annette hugs me again.

"I promise. Congratulations again." I'm embarrassed at how

I've held up the line. I shake hands with Annette's parents and then move around with the rest of the crowd.

"There you are. Come sit with us." Rose puts her arm around me like we are longtime friends. I bet she's like someone's rich aunt, only with her, it would be pronounced, "ont," and she would always know every man in the room on a first-name basis. I walk over and sit at the reception table with her and other ladies whose names I've already forgotten. "You must try the marinated asparagus spears. They are wrapped with Parma ham." Rose practically pounces on a nearby waiter with the hors d'oeuvres.

"So, what do you do for a living, Sandra?" A woman in a silver-gray suit asks me, and a quiet hush falls on the table as the six ladies wait for the answer.

Damn, I think to myself.

"I'm the assistant manager of a pizza place. I'm, um, trying to save up money for college." I can't believe I am still employed at the pizza place. It was supposed to be a temporary thing, and now I've been there almost three years. As much as I'd like to go to college, I wouldn't know what to study even if I could afford to go.

"That's lovely. You must come to one of our Hunt Club meetings," one of the other ladies—Charlotte, I believe—says.

"Definitely. I think you would really like it." Rose starts her contagious nodding thing again, and all of the women join in. It seems a bit strange; why would these well-off, sophisticated ladies make an effort to hang out with an assistant manager of a pizza delivery franchise?

"I'm not really into hunting." I love all animals, and I can't imagine being in a group that sets out to kill them.

"Oh, no, dear," Rose says, and she and the other women laugh. "We don't hunt animals."

"You don't? But I thought it was called the Hunt Club?" My question goes unanswered as the women are now busy taking turns complimenting the food. I join in with the chorus of "Yes, yes, you are so right, this is delicious."

"You must come to our club. We meet on Sunday evenings and Wednesday mornings," Charlotte says and then follows the trend of announcing the food she is eating before putting some in her mouth, "This is a goat cheese phyllo tartlet, with sun-dried tomatoes, peppers, and herbs!"

"I have to work on Sundays." I cut my turkey breast and think about saying, *This is honey-roasted turkey with whatever-the-heck-that-is on top* but then decide against it. I scrape off the sauce, determining that I'm not very good at playing "name that food," and put a bite in my mouth.

"You'll come on Wednesdays, then?" Rose takes a pink business card out of her purse and hands it to me. I notice it has a huge *five* on it in the background and has her name and the title *President* on it. "All of our meetings are held at Miriam Ellington's house. The address is on the bottom there, and if you need help finding it, just give me a call." She takes a big drink of champagne and acts as if a lifesaving idea comes to her in the middle of it: "In fact, why don't I pick you up?"

"That's okay." I'm not sure it's really for me. I'm not really a "joiner" to start with, and I'm wearing one of my few good outfits. I'm not even sure I can find something to wear to the Wednesday morning meetings.

"Annette comes to the Wednesday meetings," Charlotte tells me and then laughs. "Of course, she'll be in Aruba this Wednesday. But when she gets back, she'll be at the Wednesday meetings."

"Just come to one meeting. If you don't like it, you don't have to come back."

"Okay, I guess I will. But I'll need to drive in case I get called into work or something."

"Great. It's settled then."

"Rose," I lean toward her and whisper, "Is there a cost? For the club?"

"Yes." Rose then turns to the ladies across from us and asks loudly, "What is it now, Joyce? Five hundred dollars?"

"I believe so." The red-haired lady on the end holds up her glass as if she'll toast to the five hundred dollars.

"I believe it is five hundred dollars for each hunt, but we'll have to check," Rose says finally.

"Ah, I'm not sure this is something I can afford right now," I whisper again. It's not something I can afford ever, really. And it's probably better to be up front with them from the beginning.

"Oh no, Sandra, we'll sponsor you. Don't you even worry about money," Rose tells me.

"No, really, I couldn't." I am interrupted by William's best man, who is preparing to make a toast to the new bride and groom. I don't get another chance to speak to Rose privately because she gets up to dance once the toasts have been made.

# Chapter 3
# Checks

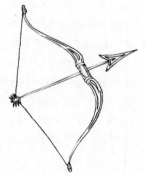

I have no business being at a place like this, I say to myself as I climb the steps of the huge Highland Park home. It looks like a house out of *Gone with the Wind*: large white pillars leading from the porch on up to at least three stories tall. The front door is big enough for a giant to get through. I am glad I parked my silver Hyundai down the street, so hopefully no one else at the Hunt Club meeting will see it. Very carefully—as if I'm afraid I might break it—I ring the bell.

"Sandra, so good to see you!" Rose gives me a big hug and takes one of my hands. "Take off your shoes here, dear." She gestures to an antique bench in the entryway. I notice other pairs of shoes are already set aside next to the bench. It never dawned on me that I would have to take my shoes off. I hope they don't notice how worn they are. Even my poor shoes stand out among the designer labels, and I feel as if I'm breaking the law when I place my Payless sandals next to the Prada mid-heel pumps.

The carpet in the living room is white and plush. No wonder we have to take off our shoes. Rose leads me into a large adjacent living area—a sitting room, she calls it—where I am introduced to about twenty other women. They are all ages, from twenty on up, but the most interesting are the ladies in their fifties and sixties. They are the ones drenched in diamonds and pearls. I know they probably spent more at their hairdressers' this morning than I make in a month. But they are all so nice to me. I keep waiting to hear what the catch is.

The hostess, Miriam, serves us mimosas and teeny-tiny banana-nut muffins as Rose finishes introducing me. Miriam appears to be in her forties, but her eyes seem to hint that she might be older. She's one of those women whose age is difficult to discern, thanks to the aid of modern medicine. I notice she has a stack of papers in her lap as she sits on a couch across from me.

"Did everyone get my e-mail about the hunt requests?" Miriam asks, her blood red sculpted nails fingering the edges of the stack of paper. "I didn't really see anything for the Dallas area, but if any of you notice something you can help with, please let me know."

"I think I can help with the architect. My husband's old roommate from Texas A&M owns an architectural firm in Richardson," a blond woman says from behind me. She's sitting in an oversized chair and has a mimosa in each hand.

"That's wonderful, Sharon." Miriam writes something on the top piece of paper. "Can I have Missy contact you directly?"

"Of course."

"Now, where are we with our current hunt?" Miriam asks, causing the women to bend and reach for notebooks they brought with them. They look like scrapbooks, and for an instant, I wonder if this is one of those ladies scrapbooking clubs you hear about. "Amber, are you getting excited?"

"Nervous is more like it," a girl about my age says from the chair next to Miriam's. She's got short brown hair, no makeup, and is wearing jeans and a short-sleeved sweater. Her casualness makes me feel more at home.

"Oh, don't be. This is where the fun begins." Rose opens her scrapbook. "We're on Week Four, right?"

"Yes, and I have some more pictures and information from the PI in Washington," Elizabeth, with her perfectly bobbed hair and professional mannerisms, tells us. The women almost cheer at the news. "It looks like you've chosen an excellent prospect." She passes out an eight-by-ten picture of a sweet-looking, handsome man, whom I think I recognize but can't seem to place. She also hands everyone a small stack of papers that are stapled into groups.

"You'll get one when you join officially," Charlotte whispers to me. I recognize her huge number *five* pin made of diamonds from when I saw her at the wedding. "In the meantime, you can look on with me." The stack of papers looks like it is mainly statistics, and it has CONFIDENTIAL stamped at the top of each page.

"As Miriam mentioned at the last meeting, Brantley is now working for a Senate advisory committee. Before that, he was on the Sub-Committee on Energy and Power. Been in the D.C. area for five years. Graduated Harvard with a 3.7 in political science. No outstanding school loans. Parents are Harriett and Brant Sr.; Harriett is a retired nurse. Brant Garnier

Sr. is a real estate developer." Elizabeth is reading over the information, and I notice several of the women circling different items.

"Look at his total income: $175,900 a year." A red-haired woman—Joyce, I think her name is—pulls her designer glasses down her nose to use them as a magnifying glass. "Does this really sound worth it? Remember our motto: 'You can fall in love with a rich man just as easily as a poor one,'" she says in a sweet, lyrical voice, and I notice she has diamonds on every finger.

"Yes, but it's fine, Joyce. You'll notice farther down on the sheet it shows he has investments estimated at over six hundred thousand dollars. That's adequate for Amber," Miriam says, and the others agree.

"I've never thought about having that much money before." Amber looks embarrassed.

"Well, you will now, honey," Charlotte says, and everyone nods in agreement. "Your life is about to change forever."

It still isn't clear what these women are doing, but I get the feeling they are about to either kidnap Brantley or scam him. It's kind of creepy that they have so much information on him. I flip through the pages of Charlotte's packet. His gym membership is listed. Where he goes to church—mainly just on Christmas Eve and Easter Sunday. His dentist. His doctor. His hairdresser. The grocery stores and gas stations he goes to. Where he shops online, like SharperImage.com.

"How are you feeling about relocating?" Miriam asks the shy Amber, who is fidgeting with the edge of her sweater.

"Okay, I guess. If that's what I have to do. It just seems like Washington, D.C., is such a big place."

"We'll be there with you for a while, and we'll introduce you to other Hunt Club members in the area. Not to worry."

Miriam pats Amber on the knee. "You won't be in this alone, remember."

During a short break in the meeting, fresh croissants are brought out. Rose makes sure she's at my side to introduce me, and everyone goes out of their way to make me feel welcome.

"Rose, I hate to sound dumb, but I'm not quite getting what is happening here," I whisper, as Rose hands me a small china plate with a croissant on it.

"What do you mean, dear?" She gives me another mimosa. I never did finish my first one, which is still in the sitting room.

"With Amber? And the plans for Brantley?" I wish I could ask if they are going to rob the guy or something.

"Oh, of course, I apologize. Let me introduce you to Amber." She leads me into the other room.

"No, it's not that. I was just wondering, um, why or what is she doing? What's going on, exactly, with the Hunt Club?" I stop her midway to the sitting room.

"Come sit down," Rose smiles and gestures to the couch, where she sits on the very edge of it and balances her plate on her knees. "I should have given you the background at the wedding." I join her on the couch and notice several other ladies sit with us.

"Would you like some fruit, Sandra?" Miriam holds out a silver tray on which there's a rainbow of fruit in the middle with croissants all around it.

"No, thank you."

"It was common, when I was a little girl, for the grandmothers and mothers to get together to try and figure out ways for their granddaughters and grandsons to meet their proper prospective spouses. They called it *matchmaking* in those days, but that term has taken on a slightly different meaning now, so we don't call it that.

"Hunt Club was founded by Dorothy Mae Roberts back in the nineties. She was a lovely woman, but she never met the right man for her. So when she got older, she was determined that there must be a way in this modern society for the . . . *lovely* girls to meet handsome, successful, wonderful men." Rose takes a sip of her mimosa.

"We can no longer really rely on relatives, and the type of girls we all were, or are, just don't do well in clubs or bars or even formal parties. We're not the glamorous, sexy, articulate, savvy women who get the rich, good-looking men," Charlotte explains. I glance casually around the room, and I guess I never noticed, but they're right. The women here are dressed in expensive clothes and have their hair and nails done, but none of them are drop-dead gorgeous women. And neither is Annette, which makes me laugh, because she is actually the opposite. So how did Annette end up with someone as good-looking as she did?

"So, like with Annette and William?"

"Yes, we helped Annette and William find each other. William was an excellent choice, a distant relative of the Kennedys," Rose tells me, and I'm almost shocked. William would never be the type of man Annette could get. It may sound mean, but it's just being realistic. She doesn't have the background, the education, or the connections. I've never even heard her use a complex sentence.

"But there's got to be more than just introducing them, right?" I'm still trying not to sound harsh.

"Of course." The women laugh. "It takes all the help they can get. And that's why we're here." Rose smiles at me. "We've made it into a game. Hubby hunting."

"We can help you get any guy you want. Anyone." Charlotte adds, "As long as he isn't married. The more handsome and rich, the better. We enjoy a challenge."

"We enjoy helping our girls meet the men they've always dreamed about. And, like the matchmaking our grandmothers did, the love will come later," Miriam says and sits down in a chair across from me. "Our goal is to share in the joy as the girls walk down the aisle on their wedding day."

"We would like to do the same for you. If you would like to join us," Rose tells me.

Any guy I want. No matter how good-looking or rich. Marry him. It sounds too good to be true, and in my case, it really is. What rich, good-looking guy would ever be interested in plain old me? Assistant manager of a pizza delivery. Forty or so pounds heavier than I should be. Only a high school education. Daughter of a single mom who lives paycheck to paycheck and often has to rely on food stamps. Not exactly whom the world's top bachelors are looking for.

"I think it's great what you're doing. But I doubt it would work with me," I finally say.

"Why not? Don't you want to get married?" Rose asks, and I'm suddenly feeling lonelier than I've ever felt in my life.

"Those type of men. They would never want me." I wish I could tell them how I've been wondering lately if there is anyone out there for me. I've never even really had a serious boyfriend. Or even a nonserious one.

"Oh, honey, that's not true. Not true at all," the women seem to say in unison. "They just need the right circumstances to get to know you. Give us a chance, and you'll see."

"What do I have to do?" I might as well hear more about it, even though I doubt they could help me.

"Just join us and play the game. Right now, we're doing

Amber, who's probably a lot like you are. She's been working at a day-care center for several years, barely making ends meet. She was living with a boyfriend until one day he just took off with her money and left her with nothing. Her only family is her dad, who lives up north, but she hasn't seen him since she was a kid," Rose tells me.

"So, now the Hunt Club has become like her family. After we get things going on her hunt to get the husband she wants, we'll draw another name, and if it's your name, we will help you meet and marry the man you want. And, if it is another girl's name, then you can help us with the hunt. It's all laid out in our Game Books." Miriam holds up one of the scrapbook-looking things.

"Rose, didn't you say there might be a cost for all this?" I tear off a piece of a buttery croissant and put it in my mouth, where it practically melts.

"Yes, but as I mentioned, we would like to sponsor you. What that means is if you can pay, great, but if not, we'll cover the game fees. All you have to do is be willing to meet the right man and agree to marry him within five months. You can pay us back after you get married and have the money." Rose smiles at me.

"What happens if he doesn't ask me to marry him in five months?"

"He will," Charlotte says. "It never fails. We set the five-month goal because it's just enough time to figure out if he is the one. It also keeps the game interesting."

"See, part of the game is that everything is kept a secret. Everything. He will just think he's met the right girl for him. Within five months of your first meeting, he should propose. Otherwise, he might start suspecting a setup or something if it drags on too long." Miriam sips from her almost-empty glass of mimosa.

"But, what happens if he finds out after the marriage and gets mad about the setup?" I hesitate to ask, but I can see something like that happening.

"It's important that we keep what goes on here from the husbands as much as possible. Of course, you would try to save the marriage, and explain to him that we were just trying to help you find you your soul mate. A few husbands have found out about what we're really doing and actually want to help us. But if something happens, and the marriage doesn't work out, then . . ." Rose pauses and shrugs her shoulders . . . "so what? You can get a divorce and even play again if you want to."

"I've done it four times." Charlotte touches me on the arm. She almost seems proud.

"The most important thing, Sandra, is you will never have to worry about money again. It's a way to improve your station in life. Your status. Even if you get divorced, you can get half of his assets and estate. Maybe even alimony, depending on the state," Rose says as the rest of the group returns to the sitting room to reconvene the meeting.

I'm not sure what to say, which is unusual for me, since I always have an opinion. Part of me thinks these women seem like a bunch of bored, rich people with nothing to do but play Cinderella-matchmaking games with homely girls who don't have a chance at Mr. Right. Another part of me thinks *How can I possibly say no to this?*

"Just give it some thought. We'll talk again when the meeting is over," Rose tells me. She and Miriam help collect the china plates, and then Miriam continues talking about "week four."

"If you look over the information I passed out, I think you'll see Brantley might actually have all twelve of the qualities listed on Amber's preferences sheet," Elizabeth says. "He's not only good-looking and rich, but we've also discovered he wants a family. Having kids definitely has been a deal breaker in his former relationships any time they discussed marriage. He appears to be looking for the right woman to settle down with."

"That's great," Amber says. "I had a feeling he had a big heart."

I study Amber for a second—she's really not unlike me. Kind of average looking, nice, but nothing extraordinary. She'd never get a guy like Brantley on her own, and I am dying to see if they can pull this off. I reach over and pick up the eight by ten of Brantley. He has dark hair and brown eyes. A strong jaw. Very good-looking. Nice smile that makes him seem warm and maybe a little funny. Amazing what you can glean from a photograph.

"It's time to integrate further into his life, and see if they're compatible." Miriam looks through her notes. "Where are we on the stake-out party?"

"I contacted the D.C. Hunt Club and arranged to speak with Sabrina, the senator's wife who I told y'all about last time. Her husband has professional connections to Brantley and his colleagues. Right now, she is looking into possible dates for the party so we can all check him out," Elizabeth says, and it's obvious she's the brains of the bunch. She looks like an accountant or something. Someone good with numbers.

"Great, Liz." Miriam is writing it down. "Who is in charge of the H Team?"

"I am," Rose says and raises her hand. "Selma, Beth, and Teresa are with me."

"How was your trip to D.C.? Were you able to confirm the information we have on Brantley so far?" Miriam is flipping pages in the information sheets.

"We had a wonderful trip to D.C.! I'm passing the info sheets around to you now. We met with the PI to review the new data, and then he actually took us to Tosca, where Brantley routinely has lunch. At first, it seemed like he wasn't going to show the day we were there—wasn't it Friday? I think it was Friday—but then Brantley came in with two other colleagues. Oh, Amber, you picked a GOOD one." Rose pauses as the women giggle like junior high girls.

"Oh, you got to see him?" Amber seems the most excited. "What was he like?"

"Verrrry nice. Tall, but not too tall. Very masculine, and he just reeks of power. Yet, we noticed he was very polite and solicitous of the waiters and the people around him. At one point, Selma and Teresa talked me into going over to his table."

"It was your idea first, though," Teresa points out, slapping her lap like she still can't believe Rose did it.

"I didn't quite know what to say to him, but I wanted to hear his voice. So, I decided to pretend like I recognized him as being someone else. We were sitting two tables over from him, and when they finished eating and were waiting for the check, I stood up and just walked right up to him." She pauses for effect. "I said, 'Hello, aren't you George Stephanopoulos?' He started laughing because, aside from the dark hair and eyes, he looks nothing like him."

"Who is George Snuffalufagus?" I whisper to Charlotte, but I don't think she hears me.

"Then Brantley looks up at me with the warmest brown eyes and says in a deep voice, 'I wish I were, but I'm sorry,

I'm not George. I'm Brant Garnier.' He shook my hand, and Amber, he does have nice big, warm hands." Rose smiles and holds up her right hand.

A round of *oooooooohs* begins from the ladies in the room.

"He's a wonderful, charming man. He reminded me of you because he's quiet and reserved. Very sweet. You two will be great together."

"Thank you." Amber has tears in her eyes.

"We also got some great information about his apartment building." Teresa holds up pictures of the multistory building and then passes them around.

"Rose, y'all didn't, like, break in his apartment, did you?" I ask quietly.

"No, of course not." She laughs loudly. "A girl from the D.C. Hunt Club made friends with a guy in his building, and they showed us around. One of our rules is we don't break the law."

"We also don't believe in actual stalking." Charlotte leans over toward me. "But what he doesn't know won't hurt him." She smiles deviously.

Teresa is still going over their findings. "He belongs to the Capitol Hill Squash & Fitness Club, and we hit all his usual places: his dry cleaners, grocery store, and hair salon."

"Oh, and his hairdresser, Samantha, was very helpful." Selma jumps in. "Teresa actually made an appointment, and we all sat in Samantha's station while Teresa got her hair highlighted."

"It looks . . . good," someone behind me says, and laughter follows. Teresa's hair color appears to be a combination of reddish blond and even a little purple, at least in this light.

"Thanks. I really don't like the color. Or the cut. But at least it gave us three hours with Samantha."

"You did great, y'all. Very impressive information," Miriam says, flipping through the pages. "Okay, let's hear from Team U." She continues methodically reviewing each of the four teams—H-U-N-T—and each team presents their report to the group. I can't believe how organized their system is and how much information they were able to get on Brantley.

"Do we have corroboration for his income yet?" Rose asks.

"Yes, it's on page seventeen," Liz announces, and papers shuffle. I glance over at Charlotte's sheet and notice there are copies of bank statements.

"How do they get the information?" I ask Charlotte.

"We have private investigators who work with us. They do all kinds of background checks. We make sure all the bases are covered so the game will work."

"What if something happens, and it doesn't work?"

"It always works. But if it doesn't, then another guy is chosen and the game begins again."

"Everyone," an older lady says from the corner of the room. "Please don't forget to ante up for the game, if you haven't already."

Several of the ladies get out their checkbooks.

"Does everyone pay five hundred dollars?" I ask Rose, as we stand up. She puts all the papers inside her scrapbook.

"Yes, for each game, everyone who is still single pays five hundred dollars. Or we sponsor you. For those who are married, they will pay five thousand dollars per game. It helps cover costs for travel, the private investigators, and other such things."

"Five thousand per game?" I repeat as Rose leads me into the dining room.

"It sounds like a lot, but really it isn't," she waves her hand as if to say "don't be silly." "Believe me, the money is no big deal once you're married—especially when you marry well. All of the high-society women's clubs have activities, parties, and charity events, so the husbands and outsiders don't think twice when they hear we require five thousand dollars every six months or so. All women's groups do the same thing." She pauses as four other women join us. "The other groups just don't have as much fun as we do." The women laugh. They do seem to have a lot of fun. I smile at the ladies as Rose introduces me once again. "This is the Membership Committee." I notice the women all have the number *five* set in some type of diamond pin on their dresses.

"We are so happy to have you here," Joyce tells me. "Do you have any questions for us?"

"Rose has been answering them for me, but I was wondering, how many members are there?" I glance at the women around the table, who all seem so nice.

"Nationwide, I'm not sure what our numbers are. But this particular group has, what Martha, fifty?" Miriam turns to the white-haired lady next to her.

"Let's see, at the Sunday meetings and Wednesday meetings there are, I'd say, fifty active members. About half are our single girls, like you," Martha says.

I pause to do the math. Fifty active members. Twenty-five of them married. Twenty-five times five thousand equals a hundred twenty-five thousand dollars. Then there's twenty-five not married, which makes twelve thousand five hunded. That's a lot of money to spend on each game. A hundred thirty-seven thousand dollars.

I sigh for a moment. "I guess I have to ask why me? Why would you want to help me?"

"You seem like exactly the type of person we are here to help," Joyce says. "When Dorothy Mae started this group, she wanted to make a difference for the girls who were kind of lost out there. The 'pizza people,' struggling to make their way, who need . . . a little help getting the man they want."

"I'm afraid I'll need more than just a little help."

"We'll take care of everything, don't you worry. Do you think this might be something you'd be interested in?"

"Yes, I think so. What would be the next step?"

A stack of paper suddenly appears on the table in front of me.

"We just need you to fill out the membership application, and then we'll do a background check. That's it," Rose tells me. The application must be over fifty pages long. "Do you think you can bring it to Sunday's meeting?"

"I'm sorry, I have to work on Sunday evenings."

"No reason at all to apologize. We understand. What about bringing it by sometime?" Miriam suggests.

"Sure, of course."

# Chapter Four
# Application

I arrive home and put the Hunt Club membership application on my kitchen table. To my relief, a few minutes of flipping through the pages reveals half of the application is really a survey of my preferences for the man I want. Another section wants information from my résumé. That part won't take long, since I've only worked at the pizza place and as a games attendant at Six Flags Over Texas. I wonder how I'll be judged on my background?

I flip ahead in the application to start filling out the questionnaire about what I want in a husband. There are fifty-seven questions in the questionnaire, and it seems surreal to be designing what kind of man I want. This should be the fun part. I like the attitude of these women. The instructions read as follows:

These questions involve characteristics that will help you develop a connection with the right man for you. Don't be afraid to be honest. The more honest you are, the more help we can be to you.

*Question 1. Rank in the order of most important (number 1 would be the most important, and 12 would be the least important) for your potential husband:*

___Love of Children and Family        ___Time to Spend with Me
___Physical Appearance                ___Movies, Music,
___Financial Wealth                        Tastes in Entertainment
___Education                          ___Love of Sex
___Career & Ambition                  ___Sense of Humor and
___Kindness                               Friendliness
___Charity                            ___Religion

I put kindness as my first priority, followed by charity as number two. Then I scratch out both of them. As much as I would like to be the type of person who would value those qualities most in a potential husband, it wouldn't be honest. At all. I'm embarrassed that my true priority seems to fluctuate from physical appearance to financial wealth and then back. The Hunt Club members seem to stress we can fall in love with a rich guy just as easily as a poor one, so hopefully they'll understand my choices. I can't help it. My dream guy is a gorgeous, rich guy. Like the one Annette ended up with or like Brantley. All my life, guys like that have always overlooked me. Like I'm invisible. I would love for that to change.

I also don't want to work at a pizza place, or places like it, the rest of my life, living from paycheck to paycheck. To never know what it's like to have extra money or to be able to buy things I want rather than what I need. I'm dying to know what it's like to shop at those fancy stores without the salespeople looking at me like I don't belong there or the security guards following me around like I'm going to rip something off. It would be nice to be able to pay both my phone bill and my electric bill on time every month—instead of having to delay one or the other until my next paycheck, while hoping those pink disconnection notices don't get here first.

If I married someone with money, then we could actually go out places, and I could dress up in beautiful clothes and not have to use a blue Magic Marker to fill in the scratches on my one pair of blue pumps. And most of all, I want—I need—to marry someone with money so I can spend enough of it to where the pain of not having it will finally fade away. To erase those horrible years when I was little, when it was just Mom and me having to move from place to place, skipping out on rent, trying to move to the state that issued the most food stamps, putting up with my mom's creepy boyfriends just so we could live with them, and she could borrow—or steal—money from them.

My next choice on the list is tied between sex and religion. What does that say about me? How would they know how he feels about sex, anyway? I guess that's where investigating the ex-girlfriends comes in handy.

Once I'm finished with the fifty-seven questions about my ideal husband, I flip back to the questions about me. My grades in school were pretty good. And I did get raises and promotions at both Six Flags and the pizza place. I can't believe I'm actually proud of that. Who am I kidding? My application has nothing going for it. I wish I had a college degree or exciting jobs to put down, but they've never been an option for me. The Hunt Club members will have their work cut out for them, and I can see me being their "ultimate challenge" or something.

The time flies by, and all of a sudden I need to get dressed and get out the door to work. For a split second, I consider taking the completed application by Miriam's house on my way, but then I kick myself. Like I'm really going to ring her doorbell in Highland Park wearing my pizza uniform.

On Central Expressway, it's bumper-to-bumper traffic, barely moving once again. Time to apply the mascara and touch up my makeup, as if I'm heading for somewhere nice instead of work. When I finally arrive at the pizza place, the heat hits me the second I'm opening the door. It's got to be 95 degrees outside and probably hotter inside. The makeup I just put on will be running down my face in a matter of minutes. I wonder why I even bother in the first place, except that it's the last thread of femininity I have when I'm in my work uniform.

The drivers are all standing around the phone counter, and it looks like the place is pretty dead. I don't know which is worse, a rush where I'm pulling my hair out or afternoons like this when the phone isn't ringing, and we're paying people to just stand around. Jerry isn't here, which means I have to be the tough one. I hate confrontations.

"Brenda and Nicole, remember, if the phones aren't ringing, we need to be cleaning," I say quietly and then turn to face the drivers. "Can y'all, please, help fold boxes or do the dishes in the back? We all should be working on something until orders come in." I tie my orange apron around my waist and wash my hands so I can prep the dough for the evening. I know I shouldn't expect the others to find work to do if I'm not obviously working, too.

"Why don't you send me home?" Chris Myers walks around the stack of gray dough trays over to where I am standing.

"But, didn't you just get here?" I look up at his cute face and can't believe how unmotivated he is. Glancing out in the parking lot, I notice Chris's Mustang parked right in front. "You don't even have a car-top sign on, yet."

"It scratches the roof of my car."

"I wish you could blow it off, but you know you have to use car-tops if y'all want to deliver pizzas. It's company policy for your own safety, so you'll be easier to see." I start restocking the bins over the line. Brenda, Nicole, and the other phone girl, Erin, are laughing at us. I know the real reason the drivers like Chris don't like the car-tops. They don't want to be seen driving around town with a neon pizza sign on their nice cars. I don't blame them; I wouldn't want to put one on my Hyundai, either.

"So, are you going to send me home?" Chris is just standing there. Looking at me. It seems weird for a second that he isn't trying to be cute or flirting with me. For guys like Chris, flirting is an unconscious act like breathing. They can't talk to a girl without putting on the charm. But I know I'm invisible to guys like him, so they don't even bother.

"I really can't send you home yet. We need to see if there's going to be a rush. Please go put a car-top on, okay?" I try to sound professional somehow. Chris calls me a colorful name under his breath as he walks to the back of the store to get a car-top. I have no choice but to ignore it. I'd love to write him up and send him home, but Jerry isn't here, and I'm too chicken to do that on my own.

"Sandra," Brenda stands there with her mouth open. "*Um-mmm*, can you believe what Chris just called you?" she says sarcastically, her bright pink lip gloss reflecting off the florescent lights.

"Yes, I heard him." I use the dough knife to open another packet of ham to put in the bins, knowing full well that the reason we go through so much is because the girls are always eating it.

"You're just going to let him get away with that?" The pitch of Brenda's voice gets higher with every word she says. I look over at the phone girls. Nicole is laughing, and her loose hat almost falls off her head.

"Would one of you mind grabbing the spray bottle and putting the coupons on the boxes, please?"

Brenda mumbles something under her breath, but it's not difficult to guess what it was. She walks to the counter to get the water bottle. I try not to let it bother me; they're teenagers who don't really need or want this job, anyway. Like with Chris, I can't send them home until the rush is over.

The phone rings. There are two girls standing right next to the phones, and no one moves.

Two rings.

Three rings.

"Please answer the phone," I finally say. "First ring, remember y'all?"

Jim, one of the drivers, runs over and answers the phone.

"Gosh, Sandra," Nicole says sarcastically, "I can't believe you're going to let us get away with that."

Chris walks by carrying a car-top sign, and Brenda shoots him with the water bottle.

"Nicole and Erin, you need to be busy, please." I pick up the pizza screens from the cutting table and take them back over to the line so we can use them again.

"Bitch," I hear Nicole and Erin say.

I hate this job.

# Chapter Five
# Getting In

I am a little out of breath from hiking up the hill from where I left my Hyundai parked down the street. I dressed up just to come by and drop off the application, but now that I'm here, I'm not really comfortable being social with Miriam. Everything about her intimidates me. Staring up at the white, carefully carved pillars, I realize even her house makes me feel small and insignificant. I climb the steps and ring the doorbell, carefully again, and wait as the chimes play.

Miriam answers her door wearing a black leotard and tights. "Sandra, how nice to see you. Please come in. I'm just waiting for my Pilates instructor to get here." She waves me into the foyer and takes the application from me. I step inside and begin removing my shoes, trying not to choke on the perfume in the air.

"Don't worry about that. I only have people do that during meetings when there are so many of us. The maids come this afternoon anyway." She leads me into the sitting room, and I notice her hair is perfectly styled. Obviously, she has spent a great deal of time spraying and shellacking it in place. Her makeup is applied heavily, as if she's going out or something. I don't think I've ever seen anyone so primped for Pilates.

She plops down hard in one of the chairs, then looks at me as if she has forgotten something. "Can I get you something to drink?"

"No, thank you." I sit across from her and watch as she opens the application.

"Did you have any questions about it?"

"No, not really." I smile. "Although, I have to be honest, I don't really have a lot of background to put down in there."

"That's perfect. No problem. It gives us more of a clean slate to work with." She actually seems happy.

"And the part about my parents, I'm embarrassed to admit, but I don't know where my dad is." I watch as Miriam flips to the page about my parents and siblings.

"No brothers or sisters, *um-hum*." Miriam is almost humming. "My, you moved around a lot."

"Yeah." I don't know what to say. I feel myself sink deeper into the chair and wish it would somehow suck me into it so I won't actually be facing her. My stomach does flip-flops, and for a second I wonder if they will actually let me in the club.

"I see here your mom works as a checker at Kroger?"

"Yes."

"That's wonderful."

"It is?"

"Absolutely. I worked as a cashier for Luby's for nine years. And you know Rose? She ran the cash register at a deli. She also made the sandwiches there." Miriam closes the application and sets it in her lap. "Kind of like you making pizzas."

"Right." I laugh, trying to imagine Rose working at a deli.

"Speaking of which, how are things going with your job? You don't seem to talk about it very much," she asks, and I'm touched that her interest seems sincere.

"I guess it's okay. Some of the time. I don't know. I manage mostly teenagers, so . . ."

"That is a challenge, I'm sure. My last husband had two brat teenagers, and what a nightmare that was."

"Really, it's just one in particular—Brenda—who gets the others going. She's like some teen beauty queen, you know? Her parents are really rich, and she doesn't need to work, and I'm not really sure why she's even there. Except for attention from the delivery guys. And to drive me nuts." I try to laugh, but my depression is probably obvious.

"We all here have been in that situation before." She nods, and her face is solemn. "I know how girls—and women, for that matter—like Brenda can really ruin the dynamics for the rest of us in a workplace. Or in a social environment, for that matter."

"I don't talk about it much because I'm trying to block it out. I'm not exactly proud of working there."

Miriam is staring at me. "I'm so sorry to hear you have to put up with that. You won't be there much longer once we can get your wedding arranged, and I promise you'll never have to put up with a Brenda again." She smiles at me, and I have a strong feeling she knows where I'm coming from.

"And never be embarrassed about what you do; it's just a job, not who you are."

"It's a helpless feeling because it does feel like what I am. I think I'm turning into one big pizza," I tell her. I can't remember the last time I didn't smell like pizza or have dried food and sauce under my fingernails. "I don't know how I ended up there or managed to stay there so long."

"We all come from similar backgrounds with similar jobs, and many of us come from divorced families or single-parent homes. It is nothing at all to be ashamed of. You have just the background we want, and I'm confident you'll be admitted with no problem."

"Thank you." Her words almost leave me teary-eyed. "Y'all are so nice, here."

"I can't wait for you to be selected for the hunt. Just wait till you see the options out there for you." We are interrupted by the doorbell chimes. "That must be my Pilates instructor."

"I need to be going, anyway." I stand up as she does and then follow her to the door.

"If you have any questions or anything, don't hesitate to call." She opens the door to reveal a very tan, very good-looking guy wearing sweats. I wonder if I should start doing Pilates. . . .

"Do you know how long the application process usually takes?"

"A few days. We have a PI who handles it for us, and he's pretty fast. We'll give you a call with our decision as soon as it's complete." She smiles. I say hello to the "Pilates instructor" and say good-bye to Miriam.

Walking back to my Hyundai, I'm still a little concerned about a private investigator doing a check on me. I hated having to put my Social Security number on the application. I guess he'll confirm where I've worked and my credit. Not that I have any.

I continue with the daily grind of my pizza job and then rush home every night to check my messages. Just having the hope of something changing in my life somehow makes the days better. It is several days before Rose calls with the results of my membership application. She leaves a message for me to call her back, and it's hard for me to wait till morning to call her.

"Congratulations, dear, you're an official member," she tells me when I finally call her.

"Thank you, Rose, that's wonderful."

"Can you come to the meeting tomorrow night? We'd love to get you started on reading the materials and signing the paperwork."

"I'll see if I can arrange to get off work." I need to call in sick because I'm sick of that place.

"That would be great. We meet at Miriam's at seven thirty."

"Okay, no problem."

When I get off the phone, I want to dance around the room. I've never been so happy to join a club. I'm not crazy about giving out so much personal information, but I know anytime you join a club there will be paperwork.

Jerry throws the traditional fit when I tell him I'm sick and can't work. I get the extended version—all about how the rush is going to be bad because the Texas Rangers are playing; how the girls drive him nuts because they stand around gossiping and eating off the line; and how the drivers must be doing something "extra" on deliveries because their tips are astronomical. I try to shake it all off and focus on the meeting. I even run by Wal-Mart to buy a new outfit.

I'm getting used to the brisk walk I take when parking my car down the block from Miriam's house. It's exciting to think I'm a part of something like the Hunt Club, although I hate to get my hopes up about them finding me my "dream man."

The routine is similar to the Wednesday-morning meeting I went to. Come in, take off my cheap-ass shoes and place them with all the designer ones, and meet with everyone in the sitting room. Rose is there, and she does the introductions again. Hors d'oeuvres are served along with a choice of wine, champagne, or mimosas. Tonight there are about twice as many people, and I'm having a hard time remembering names. After introductions, I am whisked off to the dining room, where the Membership Committee is waiting.

"Congratulations," Martha says, hugging me to begin the official hugfest.

"Here is your Game Book." Miriam gives me the white notebook. "You can decorate it any way you'd like. In it, you'll find a list of the rules for the game, tips on how to play, and summaries of former rounds."

"We have some basic paperwork for you to fill out." Martha hands me a small stack of paper. "Just basic information for our files. Did you bring your driver's license with you?"

"Yes, right here," I open my knock-off Dooney & Bourke purse and hand her my license. She disappears from the room as I read over the forms. One of them says CONFIDENTIALITY AGREEMENT along the top, and it's written in legalese. I believe I get the gist of it: don't tell anyone anything. No problem. Who would I tell? I sign the form and move on to the next one. It asks for emergency contacts and medical information.

If they travel around like they do, I can see where this would be necessary.

The last form says HUNT CLUB AGREEMENT on the top. It talks about the different ways I can reimburse the Hunt Club for "game fees." I guess this is only fair. There is also a line that talks about agreeing to pay the Hunt Club the equivalent of 10 percent of my husband's and my first-year's salary "to ensure the longevity of the club for future members." They are going to be the ones bringing my husband and me together, supposedly. I think they deserve something for that. And 10 percent of our first-year's salaries doesn't sound like all that much.

I flip through the form. If a member has any problems getting the equivalent of 10 percent of our salaries to give to the Hunt Club, there is a two-page list of "helpful suggestions." It includes everything from explaining the money is for Hunt Club "teas," "formal speakers," and "shopping sprees," to "charity tennis matches," and even "book clubs." While I understand about some of the more drastic stuff the Hunt Club does, I feel funny thinking I will have to keep so much information about the Hunt Club a secret from my husband. I laugh at just the thought of "my husband." Deciding not to worry too much about it, I skip over to the next pages. It still sounds unbelievable that they can get me a husband, much less a rich one.

The only other clause on the form says that I

1. agree to play the game and follow the rules set forth in the Hunt Club Game Book;

2. agree to say yes to the wedding proposal from the man I have chosen within five months of

the introduction; or in the event I decide not to marry the man I have chosen, I agree to continue the game until another husband is found;

3. agree that in the event of divorce from or death of a husband, I will give 50 percent from all monies I actually receive as separate and community property, real or personal, except any court-mandated child support, to the Hunt Club. A Hunt Club attorney will be provided to secure the best possible terms in the divorce or in the event of any type of dispute after the death of a husband; and

4. agree that all terms of this agreement will be held confidential.

"The second one makes it sound like I *have* to get married." I look at Rose next to me. None of the women look surprised that I point this out.

"Oh, don't worry about all that legal mumbo-jumbo. Basically, we put that in there to make sure the girls are really serious. The last thing we want to do is invest time and money to help a girl find the perfect man only to have her back out because she doesn't really want to be married."

"That makes sense." I smile at everyone and decide to just sign the paperwork as Martha returns with my driver's license. We stand and go back to the sitting room with the other ladies. I notice Amber is there, still looking shy, but happy and excited at the same time. Liz has more pictures of Brantley today, and everyone is passing them around.

"Okay, let's look at Week Six." Miriam picks up a glass of champagne before sitting on the couch across from me. The women pull out their scrapbook-notebooks. I open mine and go to the tab that says "Week Six." There, I notice the packet of statistics that was passed out in Week Four, as well as the packet for today. I missed a whole week of meetings, so I'll have to go back to Week Five to catch up.

"Amber, what are your thoughts now that we're getting to know Brantley on a more personal level?"

"I think he's wonderful. The more I learn about him, the more I can't wait to see him."

"You'll have to wait a little longer before you can see him, but we'll do what we can to get all the information you could want on him in the meantime." Miriam smiles. "Okay, let's hear from our teams. Is everything in place with Sabrina for our stake-out party in D.C.?"

"Sabrina has been really great, along with Constance in the D.C. Club. They suggested a formal reception for his office. That way, since Sabrina knows his colleagues, they will be able to make sure Brantley comes to the party," Liz tells us.

"Sabrina?" I whisper to Rose.

"She's the senator's wife who has professional connections to Brantley."

"Great. How soon can we have it?" Miriam writes the information down in her book.

"She said one of the guys from Brantley's office has a birthday coming up on, let's see," Liz says, shuffling some papers. "Actually, it's next Sunday. We could have the party around that."

"That sounds perfect. Let's shoot for Friday afternoon? We'll fly up Thursday and make sure everything is in order, then fly back Saturday or Sunday," Miriam announces, and everyone writes the information down. I'm not sure I can actually go. Even if the cost is covered, Friday nights are our busiest night at the pizza place. I don't know if I could use my vacation time this next week. I guess it never hurts to ask Jerry.

"All right, I'll get that set up with Sabrina." Liz switches gears. "Now, on to the other stuff. If y'all will pass these around." More pages start circulating. "This is just some more information about his personal habits and his medical records."

Medical records? That seems a little too private. I wonder how they got those.

"Everything looks pretty good. No sign of heart trouble, cancer, or real physical problems," Liz tells us, and we look over at Amber, who looks pleased.

"What's this about a 'swollen,'" Joyce pauses to clear her throat. "What is that word?" Joyce asks, giggling.

"That means his airway, silly," Liz tells her.

"It says his lips and tongue swell up, too?" a girl behind me says, reading the notes on his records. Papers are shuffling as the women are trying to find where the details of the swelling are located.

"Read farther down."

"What page?"

"Third page. See?" Liz holds up the page, and the ladies continue flipping through their copies. "He's allergic to strawberries."

"Looks like he blows up like a balloon." Joyce laughs so hard her papers slide off her lap onto the floor.

"I bet he still looks cute." Amber giggles.

"Otherwise, he appears to be a healthy one," Liz announces. "That's all I have for the medical records. I think Joyce—don't y'all have the dental ones?"

"Yes, that's us." Joyce has picked up her pages off of the floor and appears eager to make her report.

"Okay, then, go ahead T Team." Miriam looks over at Joyce.

"We did some investigating on our own about Brantley's girlfriends." A girl about my age whose name I don't know jumps in and starts telling us. She has a grin on her face, which indicates they enjoyed their work. "He's had quite a few girlfriends, but none really serious." She has a stack of pink pages she is passing out that has names of girls on it and a brief description of each. "Right now he's dating a White House intern."

"Oh no!"

"No, it's not like that. The girl is fresh off the farm. Jodee Margaret Orkester. She's from Indiana, and it's her first job after college," Jackie tells us. "I don't see any problems with her, since they aren't that serious."

"Good." Miriam is reading over the pink sheet. "Who exactly is this Cami person that you've listed on here?"

"Camille Monique Tarrell. She's just a good friend. They went to Harvard together. She's a political journalist. Single. Brantley and she dated for a short time in college, but nothing came of it."

"How good of a friend are we talking here, Jackie?" Martha from the corner speaks again as she taps her cane on the floor.

"*Mmmm*, they play racquetball. Meet for lunch. That kind of thing."

"We may want to relocate her, too. Circle her name for me, will you Miriam?" Martha says, making it suddenly obvious who is really calling the shots in the Hunt Club.

"Relocate her?" I ask Charlotte.

"Yes, we'll have one of our sister Hunt Clubs find her a

better job with great pay, so she'll move away from Brantley," Charlotte whispers back and then turns to the group.

"I was able to talk to his prior girlfriend Jennifer Tomlinson. You'll see her on the top of page two." Joyce waits while everyone catches up. "She and Brantley dated for about six months. Even though he broke it off, she still didn't say too many negative things about him."

"That's what we like to hear."

"There was only one little thing the girls reported, which is why we pulled his dental records," Joyce continues, and I wonder if there may be some dental problem that could throw a wrench into the game. It is amazing how much background checking and data gathering these women have done. Talk about thorough.

"He apparently is supposed to sleep with a blue appliance thing in his mouth. For TMJ."

Miriam is looking at the dental charts. "It doesn't appear that serious."

"Aw, the poor dear has headaches," someone says from behind me.

"Speaking of girlfriend information, did you get any indication of how many sexual partners he's had?" Charlotte asks.

"We haven't been able to tell from the girlfriends yet. We know Jennifer is one and likely Jodee. But I'm sure there are others."

"We'll need a report on that, too," Martha adds. "Liz, why don't you get the PI going on that." It seems kind of creepy that we're getting that type of information. What are we going to do? Give all the girlfriends a scorecard to fill out? I don't dare ask that because it wouldn't surprise me if they did.

"Okay, is there anything else? I believe we've covered everything. I'll send e-mail confirmations for the flights and hotel. Be sure to touch base with Liz if you have a preference for going to the party or doing other research while we're in D.C." Miriam checks her list. "Are there any questions?" She waits. No one says anything. "Great, let's eat."

# Chapter Six
# D.C.

I know it is a big risk to my pizzeria-management career to take vacation time with such short notice *and* to miss a Friday night. However, the opportunity to visit Washington, D.C., go to a fancy party, and practically stalk a good-looking guy is just too much for me to pass up.

Rose and I arrange with Miriam to share a room at the Four Seasons, so Rose can make sure I'm doing everything I'm supposed to, since it's my first Hunt Club event. I've never stayed in such a beautiful hotel before. I hate to think about the cost so far. Rose keeps saying not to worry about it because my husband and I can always pay it back down the road. It's still too far beyond anything I can imagine to have a husband.

Rose helps me by zipping up my new black dress we bought for the party, and I finish up by applying mascara and lipstick. I really do feel like a princess when we climb into a limo downstairs and head over to Brantley's office building on the Hill. Rose and I requested to attend the birthday party instead of doing "surveillance." The party is supposedly for a twenty-nine-year-old associate of Brantley's named Greg.

"Who are all of us supposed to be?" I ask Rose as we climb into one of the elevators in the lobby of Brantley's office building. "Isn't it going to be strange when so many of us show up, and no one in the office knows us?"

"That's how D.C. parties are. And we've invited all the Advisory Committee members and everyone our PI could find who knows Greg. Brantley's friends will be there, too. No one will think twice about us; just remember we're friends of Sabrina's." Rose smiles. I notice she is wearing her diamond brooch again, the one with the number *five* in the center of it. The doors to the elevator open before I have a chance to ask her what the *five* means.

"May I help you?" the receptionist asks, with her formal appearance dictating the atmosphere in the office: hair in short no-nonsense cut, thick glasses, dark suit.

"Yes, we are here for the Greg Madison birthday party," Rose says to her. The expressionless receptionist stands and leads us to a large reception room. There are chairs and small tables strategically placed around the room, with more being brought in as we stand there.

"Rose, great to see you!" Another lady wearing a *five* diamond pin hugs Rose, and I notice there are about a dozen people—all women—already here, even though it's about an hour until the party. At the opposite end of the room, there is a white draped table where a caterer is laying out napkins and cocktail forks. Another caterer is very carefully stacking different kinds of cheese cubes, one by one, into a tower. On a table next to the cheese tower, there are wineglasses and bottles of wine.

"Constance, you look wonderful," Rose tells the woman, and they link arms to walk to the opposite side of the room where there are chairs. "I want you to meet one of our newest members. This is Sandra Greene. Sandra, this is Constance Richmond, the president of our D.C. Club."

"Nice to meet you." We shake hands. I suddenly feel a million miles away from pizza, flour, sauce, and snotty teenagers. It's almost surreal to think I'm standing in a party room in D.C.

My heart is racing as Rose and I try to mingle with the other guests. I have a glass of white wine in one hand, and I've already had a sample of the different cheeses. By far, the number of "undercover" Hunt Club members from Dallas and D.C. outweighs Greg's real guests. I notice the ladies are doing their best to get to know Brantley's friends and coworkers. The guest of honor, Greg, has already arrived with a pretty girl on his arm. Now, we Hunt Club girls are waiting—hiding our excitement—for Brantley to come in at any moment.

The double doors open and several of Greg's friends come in, holler at him, and shake his hand. Behind them, a well-dressed dark-haired man enters, talking on his cell phone. I recognize him as Brantley, even though his hair is a little different from the photos I saw. There is no reaction at all from the women in the room, although I know most of us want to jump up and down, singing, "He's here! He's here!"

Brantley seems to be scanning the large reception room while still talking on the phone. He walks over to Greg and shakes his hand and then greets some of his own friends who are talking near the wine tables. Rose and I get a better look at him as he walks by. He's about six feet tall, or maybe just under that, dark charcoal suit, nice shoes, dark stripped matching tie, white button-down shirt—Rose says it's heavily starched. Should I be taking notes, I wonder.

"He has a sweet face," I say quietly to Rose. And he seems almost like a different person when he smiles because his face lights up. His cell phone is put away somewhere now, and he's laughing with his coworkers—his laugh reminds me of Jay Leno for some reason.

"He is darling, isn't he?" Rose glances over at him, nonchalantly. I notice Miriam approaching us.

"I'd call this a success," Miriam whispers to us and smiles from behind her wineglass.

"Definitely." I'm impressed with how casual our Hunt Club group is. Everyone seems to look like actual D.C. businesspeople.

"Try to engage in small talk with some of his friends. See if you can find out anything." Miriam turns to walk toward Charlotte.

Rose takes my wine out of my hand. "Why don't you go down there and get a glass of wine? Maybe talk to the bartender there about the different kinds. Try a red one."

"Okay, why not?" I smile at her, take a deep breath, and tell myself I can do this. I walk past Brantley and his friends to the wine table, and, out of the corner of my eye, I notice them watching me as I walk past. That's not something that happens very often: good-looking guys noticing me. I walk up to the wine table and ask the bartender what he recommends. When I finally have my glass of red wine, I turn for a moment to look at Brantley and his buddies, who are just a few feet away.

"Hi," one of them says. I almost turn around to see if he's talking to someone else.

"Hello."

"I haven't seen you around." The circle of guys splits in half, and they turn to face me. I come eye to eye with Brantley. He is gorgeous.

"I'm a friend of Sabrina's." I take a sip of wine, praying I don't drop it.

"Sabrina?" The tall blond friend of Brantley asks me.

"You know, Joel's wife," Brantley tells him. He has a nice voice. I glance across the room over at Rose, who mouths the words *introduce yourself* and holds out her hand.

"I'm Sandra Greene." I take a step toward the guys and extend my hand. They start introducing themselves. I notice when I shake Brantley's hand that Rose was right; he does have a warm hand. I can't help but wonder, what if Brantley recognizes Rose from the restaurant when she approached him? I guess it won't matter. It's a small world and everything. No wonder she is spending so much time at the other end of the room.

"So, what do you do?" The guy named John asks me.

I don't know what to say. I can't tell him I'm an assistant manager of a pizza delivery in Dallas. I take a sip of wine to stall while I make something up.

"I'm FBI. Undercover," I finally say with a grin. It's one of the few things that come to mind when I think of Washington, D.C. It was either that or saying I work for the president.

"Oh, you are." The guys laugh.

"I'm actually undercover CIA," John tells me.

"CIA doesn't work domestically, dumb ass," the other guy—Eric I think—says. You can tell Eric probably left home with his suit in pristine condition; but now, the jacket is not quite sitting on his shoulders, it's unbuttoned, and his tie is coming off by itself. A little too much wine, perhaps?

"I'm with the NSA," Brantley says, and for some reason, I notice he has long eyelashes.

"Right. The NSA." John practically elbows him. I assume he's referring to what the president is always talking about. The National Security Something.

"Yes. The National Shellfisheries Association. We're pretty interesting. Once you get past OUR SHELL." Brantley laughs at his own joke. I am wondering if he learned about shellfisheries when he worked for the advisory committee or sub-committee or whatever.

"Attention everyone," Greg says and holds up his glass in the middle of the room. "I just want to thank you all for coming to my birthday party. Especially Lana, here, who has made the day certainly more enjoyable." He kisses the blonde, long-legged Lana very aggressively, and it's apparent that Greg has already spent a good amount of time at the wine table.

"Yeah, I wonder what his wife would think about Lana?" John laughs quietly, and the others join him. How nice, I think to myself. Our little circle breaks up as the guys go for more cheese, and Brantley walks by me for a glass of wine.

"Sooo . . . ," Brantley claps his hands and rubs them together. "What are we drinking?" He asks, to no one in particular, which is funny, since I'm the only one standing there.

"Um, what am I drinking?" I ask the bartender because I forgot, and for an instant, Brantley smiles at me. Nice smile. Natural, I'm guessing. No four years of braces for this guy.

"I believe you have the Rioja," the bartender says to me, "nineteen ninety-five Bodegas Roda."

"I'll have the white." Brantley gestures to a glass of white wine near him.

The bartender hands him a glass, and he turns to watch Greg, who is still speaking to the room. I am not really one for small talk, and I hate that my mind has gone blank.

"Is he always like this?" I ask and then realize I'm probably supposed to know Greg, since it is a party for him.

"He's kind of going through a marriage thing." Brantley is scanning the room now. Like he's looking for someone better to talk to.

"A marriage thing, huh? I hear those can be brutal."

"Marriage can be brutal." He nods and drinks another sip, not looking at me.

"You sound married?"

"Nah, not me. I'm not really into marriage." He smiles a little, though more in the direction of the room instead of at me; his tone is detached. "But I guess that would change if I met the right person."

"Brant, give me your phone." John has returned.

"It was nice talking to you," I say as sweetly as I can, feeling like if I stay any longer it will be weird.

"Yeah." Brantley halfway nods at me as he's pulling the cell phone back out of his pocket and arguing with John about whom he is calling.

I walk casually back over to Rose. "That was so fun," I tell her.

"How was he?" Rose and I turn to see that Christine and Teresa have already made their way over to Brantley for their shot at getting to know him better.

"Hot. Really hot." I sip my wine. "Though not as friendly as I thought he would be."

* * *

Rose and I meet up with the other Dallas Hunt Club ladies for dinner at Tosca to discuss what we've discovered. I've never done anything like scoping out someone to see what they're like. This trip has made me absolutely love the Hunt Club. Being "undercover." Meeting people. Practically stalking people. Fancy parties and fancy clothes and fancy people. I love it.

"What a great party," Teresa says, sitting down next to me.

"Mission accomplished," Miriam agrees. "Now, who wants to report first?" Before arriving at the restaurant, Rose helped me to write down some notes—impressions, dialogue, everything—about what took place for me at the party. I notice everyone else has taken notes, too.

"I've added new data about Brantley's friends. Who they are and where they hang out. If we want to do some setups with them, I think we're good to go." Liz reads over her list of Brantley's friends. She seems to have formed a positive opinion about them. I'm not sure I agree.

"They reminded me a little of the guys at my high school," I say, opening the menu. The different options are in Italian with the English translations underneath. *Insalata mista organica delle fattorie al condimento d'aceto balsamico e olio novello. Mixed organic local greens salad, with balsamic vinegar and olive oil dressing.*

"Really? How so?"

"Just the way they joked around. The guys are all in their late twenties on up, but when they got together," I say, pausing when I realize everyone is listening to me closely. "They just seemed like a bunch of schoolboys joshing around."

"That's important to note." Miriam writes it down in a small spiral notebook that she has taken out of her purse. "The last thing our Amber needs is to be around a bunch of rowdy frat boys."

"It's fine. We'll just have to prepare her for how to handle them." Charlotte studies her menu, too.

"Sandra has the notes, and she'll pass them out at the next meeting," Rose tells them. The next meeting is Sunday, and I have to work. I'll have to arrange for Rose or someone to pass out the information. "She was able to actually speak to Brantley."

"Yes, I noticed you integrated quite nicely." Miriam smiles. "What did you think of him?"

"I think he's a good guy. Probably even better when he's away from his buddies. Although, Greg's speeches did give me a chance to ask him about marriage a little. Brantley says he's not really 'into' marriage, but he might be if he met the right girl. I guess that means that he's not that serious about Jodee or whatever."

"Exactly." Liz is writing. "That corroborates what the PI told us. Good work, Sandra."

"So, did you get the impression he's nice?" Charlotte puts her menu aside. I notice she's still wearing her huge number *five* pin made out of diamonds. "Do you think he'd like Amber?"

"I'm not sure how to answer that." I try to choose my words carefully. I know how much Brantley means to Amber; I'm just not sure they'd be a good match.

"Just be brutally honest about him. That's the best way." Miriam looks up from her notes. I look over at Rose, who nods at me.

"He's very good-looking. VERY. And he has a nice voice, nice eyes, and long eyelashes." Several girls laugh. "But I didn't really sense a warmth from him, you know what I mean? Maybe it was just me. Guys are cold around me all the time."

"What you're saying is important. If he was cold to you, he'll likely be cold to Amber," Rose tells me.

"Maybe if we get Brantley in a different atmosphere?" I ask.

"Right, I think it's best if we make sure Amber meets up with Brantley in an environment that isn't a social event. Somewhere where he's more himself and tuned into his real emotions would be better. The birthday party had him with his buddies. That won't work for Amber. At least not until she gets to know him better." Liz looks out over the other tables in the restaurant. Looking for any sign of Brantley, no doubt.

"Excellent. I agree." Miriam nods and writes something down.

"One-on-one, alone," Charlotte says.

"Maybe not one-on-one," I say. "I don't know if Amber would be able to keep a conversation going with him at the beginning. I had a hard time with that. Maybe just a more, you know, caring atmosphere somehow? Quieter. Where Amber's friends can be around for support?"

"Quiet and caring," Teresa says, squinting her eyes and trying to come up with something. "Something at church?"

"His own wedding?" Selma jokes.

"We can create that type of environment. Your instincts are right on. Ladies, let's start brainstorming the right setup: where, when, who, and how." Miriam smiles as she switches gears. "All right, where are we with Jodee and Cami?"

"We found some more information about them," Christine says. "They each spend a great deal of time at his apartment."

"Why are they spending so much time at his apartment?"

Christine shrugs. "They just seem to like hanging out there. Sometimes just one of them. Sometimes both."

"Amber isn't going to like that very much."

"They're pretty outgoing and assertive, too," Liz adds. "Brantley could barely get a word in when we saw them this morning. They just went to Starbucks and back, and the girls were walking him like he was a puppy or something."

"He does seem to like strong women," Christine says. "All of his girlfriends have been like that."

"Okay, we need to go ahead and help Amber's confidence and get her more versed in conversations with men. Get her past her shyness a little bit." Miriam looks directly at Liz, who is nodding. "We'll just have to make sure Jodee and Cami won't be a problem." She closes her little notebook as the waiter comes to take our order.

We leave D.C. the next morning, and I'm left with the feeling that I hope something can work out for Amber and Brantley. I am really curious to see how the Hunt Club can bring them together. They seem worlds apart.

# Chapter Seven
# Worlds Apart

Like Cinderella, my D.C. limo has turned into a Hyundai, and my cocktail dress has changed into a pizza uniform and bright orange apron. My hands may be in pizza dough, but my mind is in Miriam's sitting room. It's hard to be standing in a hot store, elbow-deep in pizza fixings when I know I could be at the Sunday meeting, drinking mimosas and helping to plan the next stage in Amber's hunt. My motivation is pretty much zero for supervising the crew and making sure the pizzas are made correctly. Jerry has barely spoken to me since I walked in the door. I know he's ticked off because he didn't have his assistant manager here to help during the Friday-night rush.

Dumping sauce on another circle of dough with my blue sauce cup and then swirling it around, I'm trying to think about what Brantley and Amber have in common. So far, I haven't been able to come up with much except they are both nice people. How can the Hunt Club bring together two people like this and expect them to fall in love—especially long enough for Brantley to propose?

"Gee, I wish I could take a Friday night off," Brenda says from the line when I slide the pizza down to her.

"Really. We'd probably be fired if we missed a Friday," Nicole says loudly.

"Brenda, please slide that pizza down to Nicole, and start the next one." I ignore their comments and walk over to the dough trays to see if we have enough pulled for tonight.

My heart is so not into making pizzas or being around these people. Jerry is making me stay late to close, which means I'll be out past 2:00 a.m. Working this late always means there's no time for a social life—except for one with other similarly situated late-night workers. Since I joined the Hunt Club, I've noticed more and more how my vampire hours are not going to cut it, especially when it's my turn for the hunt.

I can't wait for Wednesday to arrive, and I'm almost running to Miriam's house from where I park my Hyundai. I feel more comfortable around the Hunt Club members, but I'm still not comfortable enough to let them see the Hyundai or where I live. I'm out of breath by the time I climb the steps. To my surprise, Annette opens the door and greets me with a big hug. I didn't realize how much I've missed her friendship until I saw her again at the wedding.

"How was your honeymoon?" I step inside and remove my shoes.

"It was so beautiful. I've never seen such blue water," she

tells me, her skin glowing with a mix of tan and sunburn. "Big lizards though. Real big."

"Sandra, how are you? Glad to see you." Rose waves from the edge of the sitting room. I wave back as Annette and I move in that direction.

"How do you like the Hunt Club?"

"Love it. I never knew stalking could be so much fun."

"Just wait till it's your turn. Talk about exciting!" Annette laughs and leads me to the small table with the mimosas. I notice the gorgeous diamond wedding ring on her hand—it must be several karats. We walk over and get our notebooks out. Annette's is decorated with pictures and looks like a scrapbook, while mine still has its plain white cover. I guess I need to get moving on decorating it.

"Week Seven, everyone." Miriam sits down on the couch. "It's setup time. Everyone read the section for today? We need a good environment for Brantley to get to know how sweet and wonderful our Amber is. Let's hear what you think. Amber, what about you? How do you think this should be cultivated?"

"I'm not sure." Amber is so quiet and sweet that I really can't picture her in the fast-paced D.C. environment. "I don't know if working with him would be good. I think I'd be too nervous. And what could I do for a Senate Committee member or whatever?"

"What about having her become friends with that Cami girl?" Joyce suggests, gesturing with her mimosa.

"She gave me the impression of being kind of territorial. I'm not sure Cami is the way to go," Liz says from her chair next to the drink table. She always seems smart to me, and I'd be tempted to trust her opinion.

"And we've seen his office now. It's pretty . . . what's the word I'm looking for?" Rose asks.

"Boring?"

"Depressing?"

"Stiff?"

"Yeah, it's a pretty strict environment. Even if we got you set up there, it may be hard to get close to Brantley. We don't know if you'd get a chance to see him very much."

"What about his gym?" Charlotte suggests. "I had a lot of success that way."

"I think there's a lot of competition there, as well. D.C. is a big image kind of town. They use the gym as a place to show off. You go there after you get in shape," Liz says.

"*Hummm.* Remind me about his church." Charlotte opens the statistics package of notes again. "Okay, I see. Methodist. Same one as George Bush. The church is huge. And, with all the security and everything, I'm guessing it would be hard for her to get close to him."

"What about an elevator arrangement?" A girl behind me suggests, causing everyone to laugh.

I have to ask. "What's an elevator arrangement?"

"That's where we set the couple up in an environment where they're trapped together. It actually works out pretty well," Rose says.

"We do that one a lot." Annette smiles. "Remember the big New York blackout?"

I have to think for a second. "You mean the one where something bizarre happened to one little power grid in, like, Cleveland, and several states including New York had blackouts?"

"Yep. That was us."

"August 13, 2003. Started at 4:00 p.m. We had no idea it

would affect so many cities, though." Miriam laughs. "I was just shooting for Manhattan."

"That was one of my favorite setups."

"Mine, too!" Christine says.

"Well, of course, Christine. It was for your hunt." Rose holds up her mimosa glass to her.

"George and I were stuck on the eighty-eighth floor. All alone. In the dark. It was hilarious."

"But it worked, didn't it?" Miriam says.

"Very well."

"We really can't do that in D.C., though. If we start messing with the grids again . . . I can see the feds showing up," Martha mentions from behind us.

"NSA," I mumble.

"Exactly. We'd be front-page news. Maybe on a smaller scale? The elevators in his apartment building?" Liz asks.

"How does that sound to you, Amber?"

"Trapped in an elevator with him? That might be fun, I guess. But what would we talk about?"

"See, I think that's what we need to focus on. Putting Amber in her best setting, where there won't be any awkward silence or anything," Annette says from next to me. I know she's speaking from her own experience. When I met her at the gym, she was even shyer than Amber. "Especially on the first encounter."

"What about an accidental encounter on a vacation trip?" Rose asks.

"They'd still be alone, and it would be up to her to carry most of it," Annette says, shaking her head. "Can we get a more intimate setting? See if we can address a core connection? Maybe like at a special relative's house. Dinner?"

"True, that was a good idea in your case." Miriam points at Annette with her pen. "What about Brant Sr. and Harriet? Any ins with them?"

"They are in Boston." Liz flips through the information. "Brantley does see them pretty often, since they're such a close-knit family. Especially Brantley and his dad. We'd have to find a way to get close to the family."

"My only concern," Rose pauses to make sure she's not cutting Liz off, "based on what we've seen in the past, is that it would take some time for us to forge a relationship with the family to get as close as we would need to be. Months maybe. And if we do anything less, you'll just end up with a dinner or something. It might only give her one shot, really. I think it would be great if she could have more time than that."

"Okay, this is obviously our priority. All teams focus on the right setup for Amber. Have something ready for us for next Wednesday's meeting," Miriam says, then turns to look at me. "Sandra, Rose has asked that you be on her H Team. Sound okay?"

"Sounds good." I smile.

As the meeting comes to a close, I feel kind of bad for Amber because I know the circumstances would be the same for me. I don't know how they'd ever get someone that good-looking and powerful to be attracted to me. And I know I'd never be able to handle the pressure of being by myself and trying to get to know someone like that. It would be a disaster.

"Sandra?" Rose touches me on the arm. "Can you stay for a few minutes? I'd like to get you up to speed on our team."

"Sure." I turn to say good-bye to Annette. "I guess I'll catch up with you later?"

"You have to come over and see the house. Soon."

"I will."

Rose sits down next to me. "We are the H Team, which means we handle the checking of Brantley's background on a bird's-eye level." She shows me a sheet of paper, and I recognize it as one from the statistics packet. It has the list of all of Brantley's hangouts. "We've visited almost all of them, and now we just need to have the information available in case we need to help with a setup or relocation."

"Miriam and Liz, where are we with the relocations?" Martha asks from where she stands directly behind my chair. I didn't even realize she was there. "Did you give me the list?"

"Yes, Martha. I left it for you in the dining room. So far, it's Jodee, Cami, Amber, and we've discussed Brantley." Miriam and Martha walk into the dining room.

"I want you and Liz to start working on the plans for Jodee and Cami right away." Martha can be heard from the other room until the door is closed behind them.

"Why would they relocate Brantley?" I ask Rose. "I'm sorry to eavesdrop."

"No, that's no problem. The Relocation Committee considers all possibilities, including relocating Brantley to another job or situation where Amber will have a better chance."

"If you did relocate him, would he come here?" I can't imagine what an adviser to a senator would have to do in Dallas, Texas.

"Anything is possible. That's what makes this game so much fun." Rose smiles and flips through our team's notes to make sure I have copies of everything they've done so far.

"So, what happens next with Amber?"

"Well," Rose says, sitting up straight in her chair. "We will run some sims on the computer to see if they are really compatible. See if she and Brantley fit each other's likes and dislikes. We'll look for some type of core connection between them. Then, we'll present her with the best options for a setup with Brantley. Relocate people if we need to. Get everything set up for them to meet, and once Amber is poised and ready to go, let nature take its course."

"I worry a little about her. You know, Brantley just seems so—"

"Worldly?"

"Yes. I don't know if I can really picture them together."

"It's always like that. But, just wait until we move closer to the setup date. You will be surprised how well it all comes together. If they are meant to be, it will happen."

"But we only have five months, right?"

"No, honey, the five months is the courtship time. It starts when Amber actually meets Brantley." Rose smiles. She and I start walking out together. "I think that's it for now for H Team. Do you have any other questions?"

"No, thank you for all your help."

"See you at the next meeting." Rose hugs me and climbs into her burgundy Cadillac.

Sitting in traffic again, I wonder on scorching-hot days like these if my poor Hyundai is going to make it. I pick up the game manual off the passenger seat and start flipping through it until the Silverado pickup truck in front of me finally moves. It's rare that I go anywhere without the Game Book; although I keep it pretty well hidden.

I love looking through the different weeks. I think Week One is my favorite—that's when we get to narrow down our choice to pick a future husband. The Week One section includes things like the latest list of philanthropists or the richest people from *Fortune* magazine, with a little blurb about each man who is single. They also have websites listed where we can go to look at models, college frats, and even the Bar Association Web sites for the different states so we can look up lawyers if that's what we want. There's a sheet that gets filled out on the guys we pick, and then Jeremy, the PI, can start doing a check on them.

I can't wait until it's my turn!

# Chapter Eight
## Connections

"Welcome, everyone," Miriam says, doing a *Sound of Music*–type of spin around the room, with a mimosa in her hand. "Today we're still on Week Eight, and the teams were to come up with setups for Amber."

All of the ladies seem very excited, but then I glance over at Amber, who looks a little worried. I would be, too; in the back of my mind, there will always be a doubt as to whether the club can help me. She must feel the same way, and the longer it goes on before she can meet up with Brantley, the more the suspense must be killing her.

"Amber, let's start with you." Miriam flips open her scrapbook and takes out an expensive pen.

"I've been working with Liz on my presentation and confidence." Amber points to Liz. "The heads of the teams have been helping me brainstorm to see if we can come up with something setup-wise. And I appreciate all y'alls help. I just don't know." She looks down. "I wonder if this is going to work with Brantley and everything. He's so busy and knows so many people."

"It will work. Trust us. That's why we're here. The whole goal of the game is to come up with the perfect setup for you," Rose tells her, and she has a voice that makes you want to believe anything she says. "We're not about to give up, and neither should you."

"We've done a lot harder hunts than this one, believe me. You have nothing to worry about," Charlotte says, and I wonder if she's referring to one or more of her own.

"Can she move into his building?" I suggest.

"It's an option." Miriam looks at me. "But usually we find it doesn't pan out because the guy ends up taking her for granted. There's no urgency to be with her, since she's only right upstairs or around the corner. Too likely she'll end up just being his friend."

"I think we talked about an elevator arrangement, too," Rose says, sipping her mimosa.

"That was mentioned, but let's talk some more about it. While a 'traditional' elevator situation might be out, what if we staged something else that would have them together but with one or two of us there for reinforcement?" Joyce asks.

"I like that idea. What do you have in mind?"

"Car trouble? Stage it so he'll come to her rescue?"

"Nothing better than a good ol' flat tire to bring two people together," Charlotte says.

"Good for a quick interaction, but I can't see that working

into anything long-term with Brantley," Liz says. "Besides, we can't be sure he'd be the one to stop."

"Hey, we can't even know for sure if he knows how to change a tire. Or if he would even if he knew how," Teresa says.

Someone behind me sighs, and there is silence in the room.

"It sounds so hopeless," Amber says sadly. I have to agree with her. I don't see how we can get the two together.

"Maybe it's time we start focusing more on the core connection," Miriam says.

"I think I may have already uncovered it," Martha says. She is tapping with her cane, and I wonder if she is even aware she's doing it. "Liz and I studied the information we got from the PI about the Garnier family. I believe I may have come up with something."

"Somehow, you always manage to come through." Miriam laughs.

"It may sound a bit tricky at first, but bear with me." Martha clears her throat before she continues. "According to Brant Sr.'s medical records, he is hearing-impaired. Almost totally deaf, except for some hearing on his right side. Has been since childhood."

"I don't understand," Christine mumbles. "Does Brantley have that, too?"

"No, it doesn't appear so." Martha holds up one finger as if to say "give me a minute." "Since Brantley is so close to his father, I had a feeling that maybe his dad's disability might have influenced him in his everyday life. So, we did some checking to see if we could find anything, and it turns out my hunch was right on. Brantley does volunteer work. There's a Center for the Deaf in Washington, D.C., where our young Brantley works with the deaf children."

"And since Amber loves children and works in a day-care

center, she and Brantley have that in common already. That's wonderful, Martha!" Rose says. I look over at Amber, who is staring at Martha, fascinated.

"So, we can have Amber volunteer at the same place?" I ask.

"Would that be enough, though?" Tammy asks. "She'd be in the same boat where she'd have to initiate the conversations and get him interested. How would she stand out from the other volunteers?"

"Good point." Several ladies say, sounding defeated.

"No. They need to be thrown together somehow. So he'll be focused on her and only her," Miriam says. She turns once again to look at Martha, who is smiling.

"Actually, what I was thinking was setting up a sign language conference. American Sign Language, I believe they call it—have it be a boot camp intensive training program. Have him be awarded a free scholarship to it because of his volunteer work. According to Jeremy, the director of the D.C. deaf center said Brantley has been working on learning sign language. He learned a modified family version of sign language from being around his dad, so he's had to learn standard sign language practically from scratch. It's been hit or miss, according to Jeremy, and Brantley never has taken an official course to advance him beyond beginner. What do you say we help him out with that?"

"Great idea. That's great, Martha!"

"I even know a little sign language. I learned it in junior high." Amber says and signs "I love you."

"You are about to learn a lot more." Miriam laughs. "We'll need to set you up as a sign language expert who works with children. I believe that is Brantley's soft underbelly. Let's attack him that way."

"Okay, that's great and everything, but even if we have them meet, is having sign language in common enough to make them actually fall in love?" Tammy still sounds skeptical, and I'm not sure what more she could want. Put the two of them together in an environment where they share the same interests and see what happens.

"You bring up an excellent point, Tammy." Martha doesn't miss a beat. "Brantley meets attractive, interesting ladies every day that he has things in common with. How can we be sure Amber will be different?"

Silence in the room as Martha looks around at each of us.

"Thankfully, I'm not finished. I think we should explore Brantley's interest in his dad's disability a little further and see if Amber can use that to have a more serious connection with him," Martha continues. "According to the articles we found from several years ago about Brant Senior's accomplishments, he has overcome a lot in his lifetime. His parents couldn't handle a deaf child and had to give him up. So he grew up as a ward of the state of Massachusetts, living in orphanages and even mental wards, since that's what they did with orphaned deaf kids in the forties."

"It sounds like he went through hell," Amber says. "I remember my teacher saying that it used to be in some states that deaf kids couldn't be adopted at all."

"There are still obstacles now for deaf children. Which is probably why Brantley volunteers with the kids at the deaf center," Martha tells us. "So, we'll have Amber set up as someone who works with deaf foster children. It should be exactly what they need to establish the core connection. We'll just have to be careful to handle it subtly."

"That is so great," Joyce says, almost standing up in her excitement.

"Isn't that kind of like manipulation, though?" Lexi asks. "See, this is exactly the type of thing I hate about these hunts. I don't want to have to trick the guys into liking us and marrying us."

"But we wouldn't be tricking him because I am truly interested in that," Amber speaks up, and I don't think I've ever heard her so determined. "I would love to help the deaf foster children."

"There you go. That sounds like a great connection to me." Miriam writes the information down in her book.

"I think it is a WONDERFUL idea," Rose says. "Thank you so much, Martha. And Liz." Others quickly join in, and the women are so excited they are practically applauding. I have to admit, I'm impressed. I didn't think anyone was going to be able to find a common thread between Brantley and Amber.

"So, we'll need to form a nonprofit organization for the deaf—maybe go under the umbrella of an existing one." Miriam is reading her notes out loud as she writes them. "So it can sponsor the conference."

"My husband is an attorney for several nonprofits. I'm sure he can get us affiliated with one of them," Tammy says.

"Good." Miriam writes that down. "See if you can set that up. We'll then need a meeting facility, like a nice hotel. Have formal literature about our nonprofit created. And learning materials about the deaf as well as curriculum made for the American Sign Language classes. Team H, can you start on that?"

"Absolutely." Rose smiles.

"We should have a bunch of us be in the conference, too. To help Amber and also make sure Brantley doesn't veer off with some other attendee," Charlotte says.

"Right, in fact, all conference attendees should be Hunt Club members or people who work with us," Liz says. "Get some of the husbands in there, too."

"Husbands, yes, as long as we keep the actual hunt details confidential from them," Miriam says. "Anyone know of a husband with an interest in a sign language conference?"

"Jeff might do it," Tammy says.

"Oh, my George loves that kind of thing." Christine practically stands up. "He already thinks we do matchmaking and thinks it's great. He won't have a clue what we're really up to."

"Have them help bring up how great Amber is with kids," Liz says.

"Where is the N Team? Christine, can you also start developing a background for Amber? We'll need papers showing her credentials. References, those kinds of things. Jeremy can help you with it, because we need it to be foolproof in the event someone checks."

"I'm on it," Christine says.

"Who do we know that teaches ASL?" Joyce asks.

"I think there's a deaf center here in Dallas where you can take lessons," I tell them.

"That's good, but it might take too long. We need an individual who can work with us. And with Amber. A superintensive course in signing." Miriam puts her hand under her chin. "Isn't there a girl in—I'm trying to think. I believe there's a girl in the Chicago Hunt Club who is fluent in ASL. I'll contact Maria and double-check. If so, we'll fly her down to help us."

I glance casually over at Amber, who is writing all this down. It's so great to see her smiling again.

"The best part is our Amber really does love children. Once

he sees that side of her, along with her ability to work with deaf kids, that will seal the deal," Martha says.

"We'll also need to coordinate their likes and dislikes." Liz pulls out a stack of paper. "I made a list of what Jeremy came up with on that." She starts passing the list around.

"Amber, can you start working with Liz on getting in line with those qualities?" Miriam asks.

"Sure. No problem." More smiling. The fact Amber is so sweet and genuine makes me even more excited for her. She deserves a guy as good-looking and rich as Brantley Garnier.

"We'll continue with the make-over, too, now that we have his likes and know what the setup will be," Liz says. "I'll call Daireds in the morning and see if I can get an appointment set up."

"Sounds great." Rose is writing information in her notebook. "I am so pleased. Martha, you have come through once again."

"I told y'all. It's just a matter of being creative."

I, too, am impressed, and the more I hear about it, the more I think it just might work.

"Okay, everyone, I'll get ahold of an ASL instructor who can teach us. It may mean more meetings for those of you who can. If you have to work and can't make the sessions, it's okay. We'll need to have some beginners in the class, too," Miriam tells us. "In the meantime, everyone go get a book on ASL, or look it up on the Internet."

"Start with the alphabet," Amber says. "Then basic signs, then sentences. You know, the latest trend is to teach babies how to sign before they can speak."

"I read that somewhere, too. How interesting," Rose says. I'm tickled that Amber is contributing. Up until now, she hasn't really spoken at all unless someone asked her a question. I think learning sign language sounds like fun, too.

"Next meeting, I'll have the details about the ASL training. The trainer will also be able to help with the curriculum. Tammy, let me know as soon as you can what Jeff says about the nonprofit. We'll need to file the paperwork with the state of Texas I think, even if we go as a subordinate."

"I think Jeff can handle all of that for us," Tammy says.

"We also have attorneys who can do it. We don't want Jeff too involved. Just touch base with me tomorrow." Miriam is still writing. "U Team, can you get with Jeremy, and see about the questions we still have regarding Brantley's background? Did we hear anything about the mental health issue?"

"Liz and I looked into that when we checked the family medical records," Martha says. "We didn't see anything to indicate a depression or other problem. But to be sure, let's have Jeremy see if he can find a copy of a check or something made out to a psychologist."

"Great idea," Liz says. "I'll call him later this evening."

"I think that covers the bases until our next meeting," Miriam says, finally. "Are there any questions? Suggestions? Comments? Complaints?"

The women laugh. Once again, the mood is festive in the Hunt Club.

"Thank you, everybody," Amber says.

"Okay, let's eat." Miriam officially adjourns the meeting. I say my good-byes quickly and have to head home to change. I told Jerry I would be "late" to work but that I would definitely be there. He's going to start thinking something is up if I continue to take off so much. I have the vacation time saved up though, so he really can't hold it against me.

\* \* \*

"I'm sorry I'm so late," I yell to Jerry as I rush in the door of the pizza place. I grab my apron and tie it, then run around the ovens to the sink. "Where is everybody?" I ask, noticing that Erin is the only other inside person.

"Some of the drivers are out on runs. The others are in the back." Jerry pulls a pizza out of the oven and tosses it onto the cutting table.

"What about my pizza makers?" I lift up the gray trays to check the dough.

"Nicole called an hour ago from the hospital. She said she was on her way." Jerry looks at his watch. "So, I don't know where the hell she is."

"Hospital? What's up with that?" I check the food bins to see if anything needs to be refilled.

"Oh, you weren't here, so you don't know." Jerry puts the cut pizza into a box. I am assuming his comment is to high-light the fact I haven't been in as much as I should.

"The other one, what's her name—Brenda. She was in a car accident earlier today. Nicole went to visit her." Jerry walks around the corner to tell one of the dishwashing drivers that a pizza is ready for them to deliver.

"Is she okay?" I yell to Jerry, and it echoes through the store.

"She's pretty banged up," Erin says from the phone counter. "She hit a tree over on Forest Lane. Which is kind of funny, if you think about it."

"Twenty-two," the driver yells and runs out the door with the pizza.

"Her mom said something about plastic surgery," Jerry tells me. "She has some deep cuts on her face from the windshield and a broken arm. Apparently, there was a witness who said she was weaving out of her lane. All over the road."

"She's lucky she was wearing her seat belt," Erin adds.

"I'm glad to hear that. I remember having my first accident. It really shakes you up." As much as I dislike Brenda, I'm sorry to hear she's hurt. Teenagers tend to feel invincible. When I wrecked my mom's car at sixteen, it stuck with me for a long time, even though I wasn't hurt. "We should probably send her something."

"You mean, like a pizza?" Jerry asks.

"No, like flowers or something." I laugh.

"Duh!" Erin yells, and for once I agree with her sentiment.

# Chapter Nine
# Training

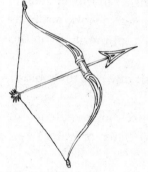

I'm having my usual nightmare about pizzas when I suddenly hear the sound of someone banging on my front door. At first, my mind just incorporates the banging into the dream, but once I have one eye open, the knocking is clearly happening in real life. I glance at the clock: 11:30. To most people, this would be midday, but to vampire workers, like me, this is actually too early to get up. I grab my robe and stumble into the living room, anyway.

"Sandra?" The person banging at the door seems to know my name.

"Annette?" I greet her as I open the door. "Is everything okay?"

"Yeah, I'm sorry, did I wake you?" She's laughing, probably

at my hair. "I brought you lunch and thought I could fill you in on last night's meeting."

"Call it breakfast, and you've got a deal." I open the door. Annette has been to my tiny apartment before, so I don't bother making the standard excuses about it. "Make yourself at home while I change, okay?"

"I hope you like lasagna." She puts the plastic bins on my kitchen table and helps herself to the dishes in the kitchen. It reminds me of old times, back when we were work-out buddies at the gym and used to pig out after our mornings on the treadmills.

"Sounds good." I gesture for her to sit down at the table in one of my mismatched chairs.

I change clothes quickly and walk back in the kitchen to the fridge. "Would you like some Coke, water, or water?"

"I'll take water."

"So, what happened with Amber's hunt at the meeting last night?"

"It was the usual, you know, with all the teams giving their reports and stuff. They should know by the next meeting which hotel we'll use and what the dates of the conference will be. Oh, and Miriam brought in an American Sign Language instructor—Nancy Kitener or something like that. She's from the Chicago Hunt Club. They are getting everyone involved with the training, not just Amber."

"That might be fun to learn." I sit back at the table and hand her a glass of ice water.

"Not at the pace Nancy has us going. But I can see where we need to know it in order to make the conference look believable. It's just hard to imagine us learning ASL that fast. Sign language isn't as easy to learn as many of us thought it would be. You should have seen everyone running for the mimosas when the training session was finally over."

"What about Amber? How is she doing?"

"I think she's the only one who's actually getting it. She said she took it in junior high, so really it's a refresher for her. She'll be ready."

"I would be so nervous if I were Amber. Meeting Brantley and everything." I take a bite of the lasagna and decide it needs a little microwaving. "I'm popping this in the microwave. Want me to do yours?"

"Great, yes." She hands her plate to me, and I walk over to the microwave and take turns heating the two dishes. "You've got to remember we've been working with Amber for over two months. It's taken a lot of baby steps to get her where she is now, confidence-wise."

"I really like her. She seems genuinely sweet, you know?"

"She is. Oh, and Liz and Christine have started on her makeover. Last night, she showed up to the meeting, and *get this*! They got her blond hair extensions! They look really good."

"So, she's a blonde now?" I hand her plate back to her.

"Thanks. Yep, with long hair." She laughs loudly. "We know from Brantley's friends that he's a sucker for blondes. Amber said she's always wanted to see what it would be like to be blonde, and I guess the hair experts at Daireds agreed with the idea."

"Won't it be kind of obvious at some point that her hair isn't real?" I can't help but laugh at the image in my mind. Amber—with her dark, short, kind of mousy hair—all of a sudden having long blond hair.

"Liz said it all depends on how it is done, and the stylist

at Daireds said there was no problem. Amber got the kind that is actually fused to your hair, rather than a hairpiece or something. And they're teaching her how to maintain it all. Brantley won't have any reason to know unless you tell him they're extensions." Annette takes another bite of lasagna.

"That is hilarious. And bizarre! I can't wait to see what she looks like now."

"Apparently, hair extensions are no big deal. Everyone has the attitude that Brantley could have just met Amber on the street when she had extensions, so why not give them to her now? They've also got her the professional spray-on tan stuff and wearing new makeup."

"Talk about an extreme makeover. What else do they have her doing?"

"A lot." Annette laughs. "But it's fun, and Amber seems really interested in the ASL stuff. She's working with Nancy for two hours in the morning and four hours in the evening. Then she'll have 'homework' for that. Liz is helping her with her appearance and losing some weight, as well as still helping her build confidence with speech lessons and stuff. And I think Miriam is the one who's teaching her all about D.C. and how the legislature works."

"That should keep her busy." I sip my Coke.

"They had her quit her job at the day-care center."

"I thought she liked working there, and the whole kid thing was part of the connection between her and Brantley?"

"I guess it is a major change for her. I bet it's weird for her not to go there. But, she's supposed to be meeting someone from the deaf center here in Dallas to see about the new job. As soon as she is fully trained in ASL, she'll start a whole new career."

"I'd still be kind of overwhelmed if it were me." I don't like change very much, especially when it happens so fast.

"Not if you were about to meet your dream guy. I think you'd be really excited."

"I don't even know if there is such a thing as my dream guy." I decide to just be honest with Annette. "And even if he does exist out there, why would he want someone like me?"

"I used to think the exact same thing. But, now I know for a fact there is someone out there who is wonderful and who is just waiting to meet you. You'd be surprised what you can achieve when you have so many people believing in you."

"They did say something about how, regardless of what happens with the guy we meet, at least the game will help us raise our status."

"That's it exactly. Like with Amber. She's working with a stylist and makeup artist at Daireds, as well as a fashion coordinator and speech coach named Morgan from the Apparel Mart in Dallas Market Center. Liz set it all up for her. And Amber says she feels like a princess."

"What's the plan for her moving to D.C.?" I take a slice of garlic bread that Annette brought with the lasagna.

"That won't happen for a while. Although, last night, one of the teams said they were already working with the D.C. Hunt Club to find a nice, safe apartment for Amber. It will be sad to have Amber leave our group, but there are a bunch of really nice ladies who are just waiting to help with the hunt up there." Annette obviously has tremendous confidence in the Hunt Club, and I guess I can understand why, since she met William through them. "But don't worry. We'll still send a few of us with her to D.C. to get settled in."

"Then the D.C. Club will take over? And that will be it?"

"Pretty much. Although we will get updates. Oh, and get to go to the wedding, of course." She's finished her lasagna. "And we'll also start over with a new hunt. Maybe it will be you next time."

"I love the idea of finding the right guy, believe me. But I would kind of like to see how things go with some other hunts first, before I jump into it." I guess I want to make sure they can really help me before I put myself out there.

"Oh, you've got to do it. It will change your life. Just think of it. Getting any single guy you want. Someone hot. And even if it's one of the other girls whose name is picked, it's still fun to play the game. Lots of opportunities for travel. And learn new things like ASL."

"That is true," I tell Annette. "And that was great lasagna, by the way. You know, I've missed our lunches. I haven't missed the workouts we used to do, but I've missed us getting together."

"Me, too. Only, I finally did get used to working out. It was with Joseph, Miriam's fitness guy, when I started hunting for Will. I have managed to stick with it through sheer willpower. So far. When I was a kid, my parents had me take years of dance lessons, you know, ballet, tap, jazz." She stands up for a second and performs a quick tap routine, and then she falls back in the chair laughing. "See? I wish I'd stayed with it. Dance always seemed like more fun than the Pilates and aerobics I have to do now."

"I probably should ask Miriam about her fitness people. I did meet her Pilates instructor once at her house. Talk about a hottie."

"That must have been Joseph. He's certainly a motivating factor to continue with the workout sessions." Annette hangs out with me, talking about the Hunt Club and how things are going in married life, until it's time for me to leave for work.

I am so tired that on my way to work, sitting in traffic, I almost fall asleep. To my surprise, work isn't exactly terrible today. Things actually run smoothly, without any squabbles or countless remakes. As much as I hope Brenda recovers quickly, I'm not eager to have her back at work. Nicole and Erin are much more easygoing—I'd almost say *professional*, but they are not quite there yet—when Brenda is not around. Even Chris has been less of a jerk to me.

# Chapter Ten
## Amber's Setup

Miriam's sitting room is filled with ladies cheering and laughing with Amber, who looks the happiest I have ever seen her. I never would have thought we could have prepared her for meeting someone like Brantley, but I have to admit, she is ready. Probably the biggest change that has taken place with her, besides the long blond hair, is in the way she carries herself. Shoulders back, chin up, and a big smile on her face. There are occasional shy looks, but she can now hold her own in a roomful of people.

Her makeup looks professionally done, like a model, and her nails are sculpted. Nancy and Miriam have been drilling her all day on ASL, and I think she's proficient. We have accomplished a lot in the past two weeks.

"Okay, let's get started. Tomorrow is the big daaay," Miriam sings.

"I can't believe I'm finally going to see him face-to-face," Amber says, giddy like a little kid.

"I think the blond hair is what's gonna get him," Annette says from next to me. "Lexi talked to Cami in D.C., and she confirmed that's Brantley's biggest weakness."

"How did she manage to find that out?"

Annette laughs. "Lexi just called Cami out of the blue and acted like she was interested in what Cami does for a living. Political journalist or whatever. Once Lexi mentioned that, Cami couldn't stop talking."

"I'm guessing Cami would be pretty ticked off if she knew what Lexi was up to."

"Oh, it's great. She had no clue what was really going on."

"H Team," Miriam begins, and people finally stop talking among themselves. "Where is Brantley right now?"

"He arrived at DFW airport at 2:00 this afternoon, and a limo was waiting to take him to the Hilton Anatole. I believe he will be quite impressed with his accommodations." Rose passes out a copy of his itinerary.

"We didn't put him in the Mansion?" Martha asks.

"We originally planned on that, but then Miriam pointed out that a nonprofit probably shouldn't be spending that kind of money to put him up at the Mansion at Turtle Creek. The Anatole is fine, and that way he's in the same hotel as the conference," Rose says. "Amber was going to stay at the hotel, too, but we decided it would be too easy that way. When they hit it off, he can ask Amber to meet him for dinner or drinks at Nana's on the twenty-seventh floor."

"And Amber, you've gone over the rules?" Martha turns to her.

"Yes. Don't be too eager. Don't talk too much. Let him come to me. No sleeping with him before the engagement." The women in the room laugh.

"Get that ring before the fling," Joyce sings from her seat at the end of the couch.

"Are you all moved in to your new place?"

"Yes, and it's gorgeous. We found out that Brantley has always loved high-rise condos." Amber sounds animated. "They don't have high-rises in D.C., did you know that? So, anyway, Rose arranged to get me moved into one. The owners are in Europe, but it will look like I own it until they get back."

"It's just lovely," Rose adds. "It's on the eighteenth floor of the Vendome over on Turtle Creek."

"What about his likes and dislikes? Are you up on all that?" Annette asks her.

"Oh yeah. Liz and Rose have been grilling me on the John Grisham books Brantley likes and the movies, and oh, the music." Amber makes a funny face. "Seventies stuff, mostly."

"Our goal is to make him think fate has brought him the perfect woman," Martha says.

"What time does the first session start tomorrow?" Miriam asks for like the hundredth time.

"The welcome breakfast is from eight to nine. The hotel will provide a breakfast buffet every morning in the conference room. Brantley will get his first look at Amber at the breakfast tomorrow, but she will not really notice him," Liz says. "Then the Deaf Culture and Innovation session is from nine to noon, with two breaks. This session also covers the current trends seen in children. We've been able to arrange for some impressive speakers. I believe our Brantley will be impressed."

"Catering service ready?"

"Yes. Then lunch has been arranged in the restaurants

downstairs. There are actually a number of restaurants inside the Anatole, but our attendees will be encouraged to eat at the Terrace or La Esquina. Of course, Nana's will be available for dancing and dining when Brantley and Amber want a romantic setting," Liz says. "The afternoon will continue with the seminar, where the boot camp will officially begin."

"Nancy, your team ready?"

"We're set. It should be a great conference." Nancy nods from the end of the couch. "Where are my other attendees?" Over half the room raises their hands. "Brantley will be in the beginner group, and Amber you will be helping me with that session. I will arrange for you to teach him when we break into smaller groups. You will also be assigned as his practice partner."

"I'm ready."

"Just remember how to say coffee," Teresa says and laughs loudly. "Yesterday, instead of asking if we wanted coffee, she asked if she could 'drill' us." Amber shows them the sign for coffee.

"Where are our advanced attendees?" Nancy continues, and several people raise their hands; some I have never seen before. "Good. We'll have you meeting in the second room we have reserved. Even though Brantley won't be in that class, it's important that we stick to the schedule and do the work. One little slip up is all it takes for him to see we're up to something. So come prepared to work just like it was any conference."

"Will there be any attendees who aren't one of us?" Annette asks.

"No, everyone is either a Hunt Club member from here, my group of signers from Chicago, or husbands of your Hunt Club members. There are forty attendees for the beginner group, and seventeen for the advanced." Nancy flips through her notes. "Everyone knows how to make Amber stand out without being obvious. And, in the event Brantley veers toward another female attendee, he'll be surprised to find that she is married—whether she actually is or not in real life."

"Memorize the battle plans, ladies. I don't want to see your Game Books anywhere around the conference," Miriam says.

"Liz, is there videotaping capability?" Martha asks.

Liz shuffles through paper. "Yes, they have that in both conference rooms. I think it's like an eye-in-the-sky kind of thing."

"Can we get a tape of the seminar and Brantley? At least for a few days."

"Absolutely, what a great idea!" Liz writes that down. "There will be a reception every evening after the conference is over, and we'll have excursions scheduled so Brantley can see the sights if he wants to. The only one I think he'll be sure to go to, with or without Amber, is the Ranger game on Wednesday night. Amber, are you up to speed on that?" Liz asks. "Apparently, our Brantley is a big baseball fan."

"Yes, I've been studying baseball enough to sound like a Ranger fan, and I'll make sure I go. I just wish it wasn't so hot. I hate sweating."

"No, no, honey." Joyce waves a finger at Amber. "Remember, we don't sweat. We *glisten*."

"That's the downside to the games, but if you wear shorts and drink lots of water, you should be fine." Miriam flips to the next page of her notes.

"For goodness' sakes, Miriam, why didn't we get them box seats with the air-conditioning?" Martha asks.

"Liz and I looked into that. But we figured, since we're supposed to be a nonprofit organization, that it's another situation where going to such expense wouldn't be realistic."

"Are you all ready with your wardrobe, dear?" Rose changes the subject.

"Yes, and Liz will be with me every morning to make sure everything looks right. The Daireds stylist will be there, too. To make sure my long hair looks natural."

"It looks beautiful. You can't tell it's fake." The girl next to Amber plays with the back of her hair. Amber flips her hair and then pushes it behind her shoulders. You can tell she's been practicing.

"Tomorrow night, we'll meet back here at 10:00 p.m. sharp," Miriam reminds us. "Amber, if Brantley asks you out somewhere, I don't want to see you here. Got it?"

"Got it."

"Are there any questions?"

"Yes, I was just thinking. What if Brantley recognizes me in the beginner class? I was just talking to him a few weeks back at the birthday party," I ask. The ladies kind of look at each other, and for a minute, no one says anything.

"It's been our experience that the guys usually don't remember seeing us," Rose finally tells me. "Unfortunately, to guys like Brantley, we are invisible."

"That's the truth," Teresa says.

"Remember, if anything goes wrong, call me or Liz on our cell phones." Miriam is sitting on the edge of her seat, like she's the one who is about to meet Brantley instead of Amber. "I think we're ready."

"Who do we have shadowing Brantley?" Martha asks from her throne behind me.

"Joyce was at his gate and baggage claim when he arrived. Tammy was standing by when he checked in the hotel, and she also confirmed with the management offices to make sure everything is great at the hotel for him. Liz will be there as one of the event coordinators this week, and she'll be introduced to him as such. He'll either be shadowed by her, Tammy, or, of course, Amber, with me and Rose as backup," Miriam says. "Anything else? Anyone?"

"Okay, then, let's go over the signing exercises again," Nancy says, and with a round of groans, we pull out our packets of material.

I feel so nervous for Amber as I pull into the parking lot of the Anatole Hotel. I don't bother with the valet—I can't see him parking my Hyundai after he's been parking Mercedes all morning—so I park in the side parking lot. I'm a little intimidated walking into such a large hotel . . . It has something like sixteen hundred rooms. Miriam gave us specific directions to our two conference rooms, and I head toward the elevators. The sign next to it says NANA RESTAURANT in big letters. I hope I get a chance to see that. It's a five-star restaurant with reportedly fantastic views.

"Good morning," Liz says to me at her seat behind a table draped in a burgundy cloth. "Are you here for the ASL Boot Camp?" she asks, pretending that we don't know each other.

"Yes, I'm Sandra Greene." I tell her and proceed with the check-in process. Liz gives me my packet of the beginners materials and a name tag, and I walk in the large conference room. There are tables lined up to form a *U* in the room, and I sit down on the opposite side from the doorway next to Annette. I notice most of the chairs are still empty. Brantley isn't here yet.

"Hi, I'm Annette."

"Nice to meet you." I shake her hand and can't help but grin a little. "I'm Sandra."

"Do you want to get some breakfast?" Annette stands up. I follow her over to the breakfast buffet, and we both keep an eye out for our special guest. Annette and I put fruit on our plates and return to our seats. We look through our materials, acting like we've never seen them before. A man in a suit walks up to the podium and checks the materials next to it, and several other attendees arrive. Still no sign of Brantley.

Amber finally walks in, and she looks wonderful. We can't help but stare at her as she and Nancy walk to the podium. She's wearing a sapphire suit that has kind of a mini skirt showing off her legs, and she's wearing high heels. She looks sophisticated, like she doesn't know she's beautiful. Her long blond hair is straight down her back, and the different highlights reflect the light. I am amazed at Amber's transformation from the kind of dumpy, dark and short-haired, no makeup, jeans and tennis shoes girl she used to be.

Nancy is still showing Amber something at the podium, and she doesn't look up when Brantley finally walks in. She is so well trained, I almost laugh. He's wearing khaki pants and a light blue button-down shirt that shows off his nice build. He is breathtakingly handsome, and his eyes seem to look right through you. After a moment, Amber glances around the room casually, but her face remains expressionless. Brantley sits across from me in the U, and it's obvious he's seen Amber. He greets the guy next to him—Christine's husband, George, I think—and then starts flipping through the educational materials.

I watch Brantley over the edge of my folder and want to cheer when he looks over at Amber several times. She turns around—most likely to let him see how long her hair is—and picks up an armful of study packets. She then walks back over to Nancy, says something we can't hear, and then proceeds in my direction to start passing out the new packets. This way she'll get to see Brantley up close.

"Hi, we'll be getting started in a few minutes," Amber tells me.

"You look beautiful," I whisper, and she smiles, careful not to break character. She continues around the room, and we're all watching discreetly as she gets to Brantley.

"Hi, we'll be getting started in a few minutes," she tells Brantley and George. "Please have something from the breakfast buffet."

"Thank you," Brantley says and looks at her closely, and I wonder if Amber is still breathing. She walks back over to Nancy and hands her the extra packets.

The rest of the "attendees" stagger in and introduce themselves to their neighbors.

"We deserve Oscar nominations," I say to Annette, who just smiles. Most people are eating something from the buffet, and I watch as Brantley finally gets up and walks over to it. Several people greet him and comment on the different food choices. I never thought I would find a guy scooping scrambled eggs onto a plate so fascinating.

"Good morning," Nancy says, as well as signs, from the front of the room at 9:00. "Welcome to the ASL Boot Camp. I'm Nancy Kitener, and I will be your lead instructor for the next five days. We also have some guest speakers. I'd like to turn your attention to Mr. Rick Sorenson, at the buffet table there. He is with the National Association for the Deaf. He will be speaking to you in just a few minutes about Deaf Culture and current trends. Mr. Sorenson is deaf himself, so you will need to look at him when you speak, so he can read your lips." Mr. Sorenson waves at us with his fork.

"We will have a series of guest lecturers and other instruc-

tors helping me, and as they arrive, I will introduce them to
you. You can also read a little bit about them in our nonprofit
profile in your packets." Nancy holds up one of the green and
yellow folders.

"Next, I'd like you to meet Amber White." She gestures to
Amber, who is looking through some stacks of paper, turned
sideways with her hair falling across her shoulders. Amber
smiles and waves. "Amber is with the Metroplex Center for the
Deaf, where she works with deaf children. She has graciously
agreed to assist us with the training, and she will be working
one-on-one with some of you on your ASL. She is also the
person most directly involved with the curriculum we will be
using this week, and we're very lucky to have her here."

Nancy is doing such a great job that for a moment I forget
this is a setup for Amber, and it feels like a real conference.

Mr. Sorenson is an interesting speaker, but my thoughts are
completely on Brantley. Not much interaction so far. I would
be getting anxious again, if I were Amber.

"We'll break for lunch now. Your meals are paid for if you
would like to eat at the Terrace or La Esquina," Nancy tells
us, and we pack our things to go. I can tell everyone is taking
their time because they want to see what happens with Amber. She walks over to Brantley very casually.

"Brantley," she says sweetly, tossing her hair behind her
shoulders, and he watches closely. "If you go anywhere else,
let us know, and we'll reimburse you." Big smile.

"Oh, Mexican sounds fine. I'll probably just go to La Esquina."

"Okay." Amber nods.

"Where are you going?" Brantley stands up, and I notice
George is quick to leave the area so Brantley won't be tempt-

ed to invite him along. I'm holding my breath to hear what Amber says. People are starting to leave the room, which is good; otherwise it might be obvious we're here to watch.

"Probably La Esquina."

"Would you like to eat together?" Brantley asks, and I exhale. "If you aren't already meeting up with someone?"

"It's the long hair." Annette leans over to whisper to me.

"Sure, I'd be glad to eat with you," she says, kind of awkwardly, but it works. Annette and I look at each other, and I want to give her a high five. Our group is so well orchestrated; no one is around them, and it looks like it just ended up that way. Of course, that means we won't be able to hear everything that is happening, which is a downside.

We know the rules; we can't be obvious, but it's difficult. We stay far enough away so we're not noticed as we head to La Esquina. It's just Brantley and Amber at the same table, and Brantley is laughing. I'll take that as a good sign. Liz has been working with Amber on her conversational skills, but I notice Brantley is doing most of the talking.

"I'm going to have to get to work," I tell Liz and the rest of our group.

"That's okay. We're glad you came to the morning session."

"I'm just mad because I'll miss the show."

"Can you come to the meeting tonight?" Annette asks. "We can fill you in then."

"I'll try my best."


I am completely frustrated as I sit in traffic on Central Expressway. I want to be back at the Anatole helping Amber, not up to my neck in damn pizzas. The afternoon and evening drag by at a snail's pace. The lack of orders makes it easier for me to leave early, though, for which I am thankful. I rush home, change clothes, and get over to Miriam's house. The meeting is already under way in the sitting room as I take off my shoes in the foyer.

Lots of laughter coming from the room. Amber shrieking with laughter.

"He was so attentive," she tells the room filled with women. "It was so weird. He hung on every word I said. And you were right, Liz. He loved hearing about the kids, and I didn't really have to make anything up off the top of my head, since I just talked about my day-care kids. Oh, I added in some Colloquial Implant stuff and listening tests, but the rest came naturally. And he just ate it up." More laughter.

"You did great, Amber. I'm really proud of you," Martha says. I've never seen Martha so happy. I quickly sit down in a chair toward the back.

"Sandra, good to see you." Rose and some others greet me, and I wave.

"I asked him about the kids he works with, and you could tell he really cares about them. My heart melted when he told me about one little boy in foster care. He's been passed around so much and can't get along with other kids his age. It looks like he'll be in the foster system until he's eighteen. And he's only six now."

"Did you have a chance to mention your interest in adopting deaf children?" Rose asks. "I know that's not scheduled until at least date two, but if the topic came up?"

"I didn't bring it up, but when he started talking about Aaron, I felt I had to mention it. I told him the stuff I learned about how some deaf kids can't be adopted in some states because there aren't enough parents who are trained in ASL. And since Lexi found out how much he loves kids, I told him it would be a dream of mine to have a house full of them.

That I'd like to have some of my own but also adopt hearing-impaired children."

"What did he say?"

"He was just like a sponge. Sucking it all up. He was almost speechless, and I could tell I got him good." She throws her head back and laughs. "It was so fun."

"Did he say anything about your hair?" I ask. "Sorry if you already mentioned it, but I just got here, and I've been dying of curiosity." Several women laugh.

"Yes, he kept saying how pretty it was. Of course, I acted like it was no big thing. And at one point there was an older lady who approached us and told me how beautiful she thought my hair was."

"That was Isabelle, dear." Rose laughs. "She's one of us."

"Oh, I didn't recognize her. Anyway, she did a great job getting him to notice how other people love my hair. When she walked off, that is when he started really complimenting it."

"Long blond hair is like a man magnet," Martha says and laughs.

"Okay, tomorrow, you'll continue with the seminar. Don't try to rush this, Amber. Let him make the moves. You want him to work a little," Miriam reminds her.

"He already asked me about the Ranger game on Wednesday night," Amber says. "You should have seen his sweet face when I told him what a big Ranger fan I am."

More laughter. Everything seems to be going better than we planned.

"I know it's difficult, especially when he's being attentive. But you must be neutral for a little bit. Be there for the attendees, devoted to your cause," Liz says.

"Since the conference is going on, we aren't going to have our usual Wednesday morning meeting. Instead, let's plan to meet while Amber and Brantley are at the Ranger game. Say seven? George, Christine, and Tammy should plan on going to the game, too, and Liz, you should go, since you're the coordinator. Make sure George keeps the conversation going. If things look like they are going smoothly, Tammy, you, and Christine should make an excuse to leave, and Christine, tell George to be focused completely on the game so our love-birds can talk," Miriam says, and she looks like she's directing an imaginary orchestra with her pen as she points to the different people. "If Amber gets stuck though, be sure to move in closer and make her the star of the conversation."

"No problem."

"I guess we're done then. Y'all are welcome to stay and watch the video from today's conference. Otherwise, see you Wednesday evening."

I walk into the other living area with Rose, and she starts the VCR. The ladies are hilarious—they bring in popcorn and soft drinks, and watch the video like it's a movie or something. They keep the sound turned down until Brantley or Amber say something.

"*Mmmm*, look at him. He's staring right at Amber." The ladies cheer.

"Now he's reading something. Pay attention, Brantley. This is important." Tammy talks to the TV and eats her popcorn.

"What's that he's reading?"

"*Mmmm*, the material for later in the afternoon, looks like," Liz says.

"I guess he doesn't find Mr. Sorenson that interesting?"

"He's not paying attention, that's for sure," Rose says.

"*Boooo!*" Several ladies say together.

"Watch this part, watch this part!" Tammy practically stands up. "He's staring right at her!" More cheering. The ladies continue cheering and booing different things in the video, often replaying the parts where Brantley watches Amber. Those are my favorite parts, too.

I have to work, so I miss the conference again on Tuesday, and I have to work Wednesday morning if I want to be able to go to the seven o'clock meeting. I'm not the only one with a job who has to miss much of the conference, but it still feels like I'm a bit out of the loop. This is the most exciting part of the game, and everyone is having so much fun. Especially Amber.

# Chapter Eleven
## Games

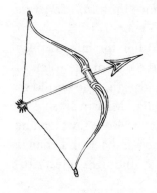

I rush up the sidewalk to Miriam's house, and Annette greets me at the door, smiling. "I can't believe how well this is working."

"Me, too," I step out of my shoes and put them with the others. We grab our mimosas and head to the sitting room. It's weird not having Amber there, but we all know she's at the Ranger game with Brantley.

"Our Amber is doing great," Miriam tells us.

"You can tell he's really taken with her," Martha says from her corner chair. "We were just watching the video from today. The poor boy's hooked."

"Well, of course he is. He's just met the woman of his dreams, who shares all of his interests and is the picture-perfect person he's always wanted." Liz laughs.

"How is Amber holding up under the pressure?" Annette asks, taking another sip of her drink.

"Marvelously. I'm really thrilled," Rose says.

"She's playing it cool. Staying focused on the training like he's just an afterthought," Liz adds.

"You can tell she wants to just pounce on him," Christine says. "I hope she can hold off on that."

"We've talked to her and prepared her for him to push things, especially since we're hitting the end of the week. If she'll keep stringing him along until Friday, then he should go all out to make sure he can see her again," Miriam says.

"He's already asked her to Nana's later," Rose says, leaning back in her chair. "They're going to each go back and change clothes and then meet up at Nana's at midnight. Pretty romantic."

"She has a list of the rules. She knows we ran the computer simulations on this, and she can't even show Brantley her condo until after the conference ends on Friday," Miriam tells us. "And she knows she can't spend the night in his hotel room, either."

"She's got to get home to walk her dog." Rose laughs. "It's an Akita I borrowed from a friend of mine. Still a puppy. I'm afraid it's eating the condo as we speak, but Akitas are Brantley's favorite."

"I think it's wonderful for her." Liz smiles. "She called me before they left for the game—I think she was actually in a bathroom stall—and we talked about the outfit she'll change into to go to Nana's. Black minidress of course, black strappy heels. Hair down, since that's what he likes. They'll go to the bar where Nana's always has a jazz band playing—it's beautiful up there—and order a mimosa and cheesecake."

"Did you work on Amber's dancing?" Martha asks, tapping away with her cane.

"Actually, she picked it up pretty fast. She's a natural once she gets going."

"How are things in the conversation department?" I ask.

"She's doing fine, so far. They share a common love of children, a desire to help deaf foster children, and I think Brantley is convinced she loves baseball now. She says they talk constantly and never run out of things to say," Rose says. "Liz, you did a great job on this one. You should be commended."

"It's been really fun. I'm going to be sorry when it's over."

"I called Constance this afternoon to let her know where things are. The girls in the D.C. Club are already preparing for Amber's move to the area. And—" Miriam flips through her stickies that are on top of her scrapbook. "Jeremy told me yesterday he has already arranged for a supervisory position to come up at the deaf center where Brantley volunteers. He was going to make sure the director calls Brantley to ask him to keep an eye out for anyone at the conference who might be interested."

"Wouldn't it be great to get Amber set up in that?" Joyce holds her glass up as if to toast Amber.

"The plan should work. We just need to leave it in Brantley's lap, and see what he does," Martha says. "We're hoping Brantley will insist Amber move up there, help her get moved, and want to show her everything."

Miriam closes her game book. "We'll meet again on Saturday morning to hear our reports from Amber, Liz, and Nancy. Other than that, we have the conference video we can watch."

We head into the other living room while Miriam makes the popcorn.

Torture does not describe having to wait to hear what happens with Amber and Brantley. The Friday night rush at the pizza place isn't as bad as it has been in the past; Brenda is still out with her car accident injuries, and Jerry isn't sure if she'll be coming back. My motivation level is still at an all-time low, though. I don't even care whether Chris puts on a car-top sign or if the phone girls stand around doing nothing. I even make a personal call, from the phone counter, while I'm on the clock.

"I just had to call," I say to Annette. "Have you heard anything?"

"I'm glad you did. I had to help Will with his work today, so I wasn't up at the conference, but I talked to Rose last night. Everything is fine."

"Am I wrong, or do you sound concerned a little?"

"Well, we *think* it will be okay."

"Oh no. What's happened? Tell me, Annette." I glance over at Erin and Nicole, who can't believe I'm on a personal call. I never do this.

"Amber spent the night with Brantley after the game and going to Nana's on Wednesday night. Probably last night, too."

"So? Isn't that good?" I would think the ladies would be thrilled.

"No, not really. It's too soon. The computer sims that Miriam has done on this type of thing show if they sleep together too soon, there won't be a reason for him to see her again after the conference. The fling will have flung, so to speak."

"That's not true. Is it?"

"I'm afraid so. The sims are never wrong."

"Damn, after all our hard work."

"I know. And Brantley still hasn't said anything about the position in D.C. We were hoping that would be the shoe-in."

"You haven't heard anything at all today, though, right? Maybe he talked to her about it today?"

"Maybe. I hope." She sighs. "I guess we'll find out in the meeting tomorrow morning."

"Yes, I'll be there. I should probably get back to work now. Thanks for the info, and I'll see ya tomorrow."

Damn. Amber better not blow this. Why did she have to sleep with him so soon? I walk back over to the food line and start picking through the food in the pit.

"Gosh, I wish I could make personal calls." Nicole starts in with the sarcasm. "Especially on a Friday night."

"Make all the personal calls you want, Nicole. Help yourself," I tell her, not looking up.

"Sandra," Jerry yells from his perch overlooking us. "Can I see you in the office?"

"*Whoooa*, Sandra's in troooouble."

I walk past the phone people and drivers as I go back to the office.

"What is up with you?" Jerry leans against the blue desk, his apron covered with pizza sauce that he always splatters as he cuts the pizzas. "You just gave Nit-wit Whatshername the green light to make personal calls." He gestures at Nicole with the pizza cutter.

"I know. I was just joking. Sorry."

"Get your shit together. I told you, I need an assistant manager who puts her job as first priority, and I thought that was you."

"It is first priority." I lie, picking at the food under my nails and looking down at the layers of flour on the front of my apron. "I'm just not feeling so hot tonight, Jerry. Just ignore me, okay? I came in even though I wasn't feeling well. Doesn't that show you I'm dedicated?"

"I suppose." He looks at me. "Just don't let the phone girls go wild making personal calls."

"I'll talk to them."

We walk out of the office, and I head over to Erin and Nicole.

"Hey, y'all. I was just kidding about the personal calls. I'm not feeling so hot right now."

"We figured something was up," Erin says.

"Can y'all help me with cleaning out the pit?" I know they are far more likely to do what I ask if I am doing it, too. Without a word, Erin and Nicole come over to the line. At least they're listening to me, I think to myself. Things are much better now without Brenda leading the riots.

I realize I must not get distracted by the Hunt Club. It isn't a job. It is just a game. And it's a game that can go on for a while, especially if Amber screwed up her chances with Brantley. I was hoping things would work out, and sooner rather than later maybe I would have a shot at the next round. Or, at least be able to get more involved in the next round. But it's just a game, not my life. Pizza is my life.

Taking off my shoes in the foyer of Miriam's house, I guess I am early because Annette hasn't shown up yet. I walk through the main living room to the sitting room. Most of the other members are there, including Amber. She's wearing a nice pants outfit, and her hair is up in a French twist. Very sophisticated. Several people wave as I walk in and sit down.

"The limo dropped him off at the airport about an hour

ago," Liz tells us, turning off her cell phone. "They say to be there two hours early for check-in."

"Overall, the training was a success," Nancy says. People are being quieter than usual. Either that, or it's my imagination.

"Okay, let's get started." Miriam opens her notebook. "Liz, is everything taken care of at the hotel?"

"Yes, the bill is paid, and all of our stuff is back in the office." Liz gestures with her pen toward the back of the house.

"Good. And did Brantley ever suspect anything wasn't legitimate about the conference?"

"Not at all. He seemed to get a lot out of it."

"His ASL skills improved tremendously," Nancy tells us. "In fact, all of your skills improved."

"Now, let's hear from Amber. How did last night go?"

"It was pretty wonderful." She seems really tired. "We went back to the condo, and he loved it. He also loved Sake."

"You served him Sake?" Christine asks, and we all look up at Amber and then at Liz.

"No, Sake is the dog." She laughs. "And Brantley *loves* Akitas. He was able to train him to do a few tricks. Sit. Stay. Don't eat the drapes."

"Did Brantley spend the night with you, dear?"

"Yes. And I know y'all are worried about that, but I know he likes me. A lot. I am sure I'll hear from him any minute."

Silence in the room.

"Did he ever say anything about the job in D.C.?" I ask.

"Yes, he told me about it last night. He said I should look into applying and that maybe I'd like living in D.C."

"Well, that's great news!" I sit up on the edge of my chair and notice Annette is here. "Isn't that great news?"

"It is good, Amber. You did just fine," Liz says, and it's obvious she's trying to be nice.

"It's just . . . We were hoping he would practically drop to his knees and beg you to take the job," Rose says, "but it's okay that he didn't."

"The problem is, he also told George about the position in D.C.," Christine says.

Nancy sighs. "And me. Saying I should announce it." It's obvious everyone is disappointed.

"So, is Amber going to apply? Is that the next step?" Annette sits down in a chair nearby.

"We haven't decided about that one yet." Miriam looks down. "We need to see what Brantley's next move is. See if he contacts her."

"Maybe by not applying for it, it will make Brantley more likely to contact her and try to talk her into it?"

"What if he doesn't contact her?" I hate to ask, and I can tell Amber practically flinches.

"He will. Trust me, y'all. I can tell he likes me."

"How can you tell?" Martha asks.

"Because he *slept with me*." She suddenly sounds just like the teenagers who work for me. I'm surprised when she doesn't say, "Duh!"

"That . . . doesn't necessarily mean he likes you as in *likes* you, dear," Rose says gently.

"I hope we didn't do all this work for a one-night stand." Christine sighs loudly.

"It wasn't a one-night stand."

"Well, now, looking at all the facts here. Maybe it's not so bad." I try to find something positive. "What happened when he left this morning?"

"That's the problem. He took a cab back to the hotel so he could pack. He left earlier than he needed to," Liz says. It does sound like there was no urgency to see her again.

"You didn't go with him to the airport?"

"I offered." Amber looks down at her sock feet. "But he said there was no need. I was kind of looking forward to riding in the limo, you know?"

I think everyone is looking at her feet now.

"Let's not get discouraged, now. It's all part of the game to overcome obstacles," Martha says. "What fun would it be if it was easy?"

"I can still move to D.C., right? And just keep running into him or something?"

"No, that would be you doing all the work. And you know how the game works. If we want him to propose, he has to struggle to get you."

"There's got to be something." I can't believe it can just fizzle out like this. Everything seems to be coming to a screeching halt. They spent an awful lot of money for a one- or two-night stand.

"He could still call her. Any minute. So, let's not overreact here." Liz tries to sound positive.

"That's right." I smile at Amber. "He'll probably call, anyway. I can tell he really liked her."

"Where are we with the other girls?" Martha wants to know. "Cami and the other one? Jodee."

"We were waiting to see how the conference went."

"Well, let's get Jeremy in place. So, if Brantley is interested in still seeing Amber, we can at least have them out of the way."

"Relocation Committee, we should meet after this."

"What else can we do, Miriam?" Liz asks.

"We move forward, anticipating that Amber will hear from him. But if he doesn't call . . . Then Amber, it's your decision if you want to move on to the next candidate for you."

"I want Brantley." Amber shakes her head. "Y'all said I could have him."

"If there's a way to get him, then you'll have him. But just keep in mind that you have other options out there."

"In the meantime, do we move on to the next hunt?" Annette asks.

"Absolutely." Miriam's mood instantly lightens, and she shuffles papers. "The games must go on. While we're waiting to hear from Brantley, we'll draw for the next round at Sunday's meeting. Be sure our single girls who aren't here today are notified so they can get their names in."

"I'm on it," Liz says. It's obvious that everyone's spirits have improved at the news of a new game starting.

"How long will we give Brantley to contact Amber?" I whisper to Annette.

"I don't know. It's up to Amber, I think. Miriam and Martha will help her decide when it's time to pick someone new. Until then, at least we get to start another round. It could be YOU this time!"

"Let's go ahead and break for today. We'll meet at our usual time tomorrow night." Miriam closes her book. "There's a buffet being set up in the dining room."

I notice Martha and Miriam are quickly at Amber's side, and I can't help but wonder how Amber will handle it if Brantley doesn't call her. That would have to be the worst thing that could happen to someone like her. And someone like me.

Annette and I follow the other ladies toward the formal dining room. The table is set with fine china and crystal. Annette and I sit together at the far end of the table, next to the large picture window.

"I never thought I would be attending so many formal functions in my life," I whisper to Annette as we move toward the buffet. "And the funny part is, I actually really like them."

"I don't think I'll ever get used to it." She laughs and gestures to the three forks next to the place settings. "Just months ago, I never knew desert forks even existed."

"Desert fork? What's a desert fork?" I elbow her.

"How is married life treating you, dear?" Rose asks Annette as we sit back down with our food.

"It's wonderful. Will and I are truly soul mates, and he's my best friend."

"How did y'all meet? I mean, what made you decide to hunt him in particular?" I'm probably the only one in the room who doesn't know the answer to that question.

"Oh, I had a pretty tough time with my hunt, as anyone here will tell you. I had to have a kind person who loved me for *me*, and for a while it looked like there wasn't a guy out there that was like that." She takes a sip of her drink. "But then Rose knew someone who had connections to the Rutherford family. She showed me a picture of Will, and from the instant I looked at it, I knew he was special. Something about his eyes."

"He is a nice-looking guy." I think to myself what an understatement it is to say he's "nice-looking."

"It's more than that, though. He's beautiful on the inside. The Maine Hunt Club helped me slowly get used to the society girls up there, so I could get to know his world a little bit. It turns out he felt out of place just as much as I did. We finally met when I had dinner with his family. It was like magic or something, because once we started talking, it felt like we'd always known each other."

"They have a special connection," Rose nods. "We knew almost immediately that they were destined to be together."

Several of the women are listening to Annette tell her story, so I decide to save my more personal questions until later. There's got to be more details. I'm still dying to know how the homely, shy Annette I knew and still love ended up with someone like Will? What made her special to him?

"I hope Brantley and I have that," Amber says.

"Oh, you will," several of the ladies seem to say at the same time.

"Tell us some more about your time with Brantley, Amber," Joyce says, and Amber begins describing the romantic dinner they had at Nana Restaurant overlooking the Dallas skyline.

"She has come a long way," Annette tells me quietly. "When I first met her, she wouldn't even look up long enough to make eye contact with me." We glance over at Amber, who is completely animated as she describes dancing with Brantley.

"You'd never know that from looking at her now."

"She really deserves to be happy. She's had a hard life. Her dad abused her, and then she moved down here and ended up living with a boyfriend who did the same thing. It's taken a long time for her to overcome all that to get to the point where she is now."

"I'm glad we've done such a thorough background check on Brantley." I take a bite of my salad. I've never really liked salads, but these fancy ones always seem to taste pretty good. "At first, it seemed a little, you know, creepy how much we were able to find on him."

"Some of the details we learn about people can be really interesting." Annette laughs. "You'd be amazed what we've seen on some of the hunts. The crazy things people do, and they think no one will ever know. I, too, am really glad we have the private investigators and so many Hunt Clubs working together."

"I can't wait to start the new game tomorrow," Cheryl says from across the table. "I'm dying to see who'll be chosen next."

Rose turns to look at me. "And Sandra, wouldn't it be fun if your name was chosen?"

"Isn't it too soon for me? Since I haven't been a member that long?"

"Oh no, it's never too soon," Charlotte jumps in. "We would love to have you be the next bride."

"Definitely. You'd love it," Annette tells me.

"Annette, when I filled out the preference sheets," I say, lowering my voice so hopefully the others can't hear, "I was afraid they wouldn't like what I chose."

"Why? What did you put? Your first priority is sex, right?"

"No." I laugh. "That was third. But, my first priority was looks, followed by the money one. What kind of person are these ladies going to think I am?"

"Don't worry about it at all." Joyce overhears us. "We want you to put looks and money first. Everyone always puts those. Or, they would if they were being truly honest. Remember our motto, dear: 'You can fall in love with a rich man just as easily as a poor one.'" Joyce smiles and drinks her mimosa.

"Based on what you told me about what you and your mom have been through, no wonder you would choose those. But, no matter what our motto says, I don't think you'd be happy with some rich good-looking guy who has the personality of a shoe or who is a workaholic or something. We'll help you find looks, money, AND other qualities you really truly need in a husband."

"Don't be silly, Annette. All you need are looks and money. Everything else will come in time." Charlotte laughs. I guess she is the expert, since she's played the game four times.

"I hope so. I'm just not sure he's really out there. Or that he'd really like me."

"I felt the same way. Just wait and see. This game really works," Annette whispers to me as Miriam stands up.

"Ladies," Miriam begins, "I would like to propose a toast to our Amber. The future Mrs. Brantley Garnier." Everyone toasts Amber and smiles, and our thoughts are all on one thing: Brantley making the next move.

After the lunch, I have to rush off to work again. I find myself feeling completely agitated as I sit in traffic on Central Expressway. I want to be back at Miriam's house supporting Amber in her waiting and joining in with the other girls as they discuss the next hunt. The afternoon and evening drag by at a snail's pace. My heart is no longer in my job. Not that it ever really was. My heart and my mind are now on my future and the possibility of a husband.

# Chapter Twelve
# The Next Hunt

My heart is racing a million miles a minute as I drop the tiny slip of paper with my name on it into the large crystal bowl. How exciting it would be to be able to pick out the man I want and marry him. Someone rich and gorgeous like Will or Brantley. I could barely sleep last night just thinking about it.

"Everybody in?" Miriam is walking around the room one last time with the bowl.

"I absolutely love Week One," Rose says taking a sip of her mimosa.

"I do, too. Everyone is so excited." Joyce says and can barely sit still.

Miriam sticks her hand in the glass bowl and swirls the

names around and around. "Now, before we draw our next bride, let me go over some club business."

"The suspense is killing me," Annette whispers to me, and I nod in agreement.

"Has everyone been reading the hunt requests that were sent to you?" Miriam asks, and people are just staring at her. "Tammy, did you see the one about the lawyer?"

"Yes, but they're looking for mergers and acquisitions. Jeff doesn't do that kind of law. I can ask if he knows anyone, though."

"Please do. They should also check with Robin Whatshername. Kruber? Ruber? Down at the Austin Hunt Club," Martha says.

"Ruber. When will she be back from her honeymoon in Barbados?"

"In about another week and a half," Miriam says, swirling the names in the bowl again. "Okay, are there any questions or comments, then, before we draw?"

Nobody moves or says anything.

"All right then. Martha, if you would draw for us." Miriam stands up and walks over to where the white-haired Martha is seated, cane lying across her lap.

"Let me get a good one." Martha sticks her hand in and starts digging.

*Please let it be me! Please let it be me!*

"And our next bride will be . . ." Miriam opens the slip of paper. "Lexi Donaldson!" The ladies applaud, and several people hug Lexi. I almost want to cry, but I figure it's okay. I need to probably play a few rounds, so I'll know what my options are out there.

"Sorry," Annette whispers to me.

"Actually, Miriam, I've been thinking about this, and I think I need to pass this time around."

"Oh no, Lexi. Why, dear?"

"It's the man I want. You know, the one I would like to go after, he's kind of married right now."

"What does 'kind of' married mean?"

"They are fighting and talking about divorce, but they haven't filed yet."

"We can't go after a married man, Lexi," Rose tells her. "You know the rules."

"I know. I know. And that's why I need to pass on this round. Maybe by the next time I'm picked he'll be divorced, and we can go after him. I'm sorry, y'all."

"You're doing the right thing, honey. If he's the one you want, then you should wait till he's available," Martha says, which sets the mood for how people respond to her decision. "Let's draw again, shall we? Miriam?"

"Okay, let's see who our next bride will be." Miriam swirls the names around several times and then walks back over to Martha.

"Give me a good one," Martha says again, digging her hand in deep. I'm afraid to even get my hopes up.

"And our next bride will be . . ." Miriam opens the slip of paper. "Sandra Greene!" The ladies cheer and start hugging me.

I can't believe it. Now I really am about to cry.

"Congratulations!" Annette hugs me and shakes me by the arm, singing, "This is going to be soo great!" Several other people hug me, too, and I try to get myself together.

"Somebody get her another mimosa." Liz laughs. Another drink appears in front of me, and I take a sip.

"Wow, geez, are you sure you want to do me? I mean, I'm so new and all."

"Absolutely. You deserve it. Any single guy you want. Just name him," Charlotte tells me, and everyone nods.

"Did you get a chance to look at the Week One materials? Lots of good ones in there," Rose tells me, opening her book. I notice others do the same, and pages start flipping.

"We added a new Physician Collection, did you see, Sandra? How about a nice, good-looking doctor?"

"A surgeon?" Someone else asks.

"Pediatrician?"

"OB-GYN?"

"No OB-GYN. We don't want a guy who's been looking at hoo-hoos all day."

"Or, you can have a lawyer. The Bar Associations have pictures you can look at on their Web sites."

"No, she needs a loving husband, not a shark," Teresa says, and I notice Tammy shoots her a dirty look.

"Annette, are there any other Kennedys available?"

"No, not that I can think of. I think I got the last single one for a while." Annette laughs. "What about a professional athlete?"

"Lots of other politicians, though. And good guys at the Highland Park churches, too."

"Let's look at your preference sheet, shall we?" Miriam pulls out the questionnaire I filled out with the membership application. I hold my breath, not sure how she'll react when she sees my answers. "Good girl, just like me. Physical appearance is priority one. Then financial stability."

"What kind of personality do you typically go for?" Lexi asks from across the room.

"Who cares about personality?" Joyce asks, and laughter fills the room. "For Pete's sake, why don't we get some choices that have the looks and the money. Then, once we've got those, we can narrow it down based on their positive characteristics when it comes to values and whatnot?"

I knew I always liked Joyce.

"I'm afraid she'd end up with a good-looking rich jerk," Lexi says.

"But, looks and money are what Sandra chose on her preference sheet." I notice Miriam glances over at Martha, who is nodding. They share a smile between them. "Let's do looks and money first, then we'll determine his virtue."

"*Oooh*, I like that. So, who do we know that is rich and drop-dead gorgeous?" I hear Tammy say from behind me.

"She deserves an extremely good-looking one. Here, let me look," Joyce says, flipping through the pages of her notebook.

"We have a nice collection of male models you can choose from," Tammy touches my shoulder. "Some of them have bodies that are ab-so-lute works of art."

"*Mmm-hum*, let's look at those models," Selma says.

"Need to be rich though, too. No starving models for our Sandra," Rose adds. It feels so weird to have the women scrounging for the best men for me. Like they're picking out expensive dresses or maybe puppies out of a pet store. I can't seem to stop laughing.

"Do you have anyone particular in mind you'd like to have, honey?" Joyce asks me.

"No, not really. I need to think on it."

"Okay, now, do y'all want to designate new teams and team leaders?" Miriam asks.

"No, let's just stay with our current ones. I think we worked pretty well last time," Liz says, and others agree.

"I think our teams did fantastic last time with Amber," Rose says.

"Okay, then, all teams, here's your assignment for next time. We need to pick out the best candidates for our Sandra. Leave no good-looking, rich stone unturned!" Miriam says excitedly. She turns to look at me. "If it's okay, I'm going to pass around copies of your questionnaire so everyone will know your preferences."

"Sure, I don't mind at all." I'm still laughing.

"Can you come to the meeting on Wednesday morning?"

"Yes, absolutely." I think I'm in shock. Any single guy I want. Any of them. Like I won the lottery or something. The groom lottery.

If I was out of it and lacking motivation before, my work ethic is even worse now. I've even made a mistake on a pizza, which I never do. Instead of a pepperoni, mushroom, and sausage, I made a pepperoni, ham, and beef. Of course, the teenagers will never let me hear the end of it. Then again, they don't really complain, since they know they'll be able to eat the mistake.

All I want to do is go home and start reading the Week One material again so I can pick out my husband.

Around two in the morning, I finally get home from work. I'm wide awake. Not just because I've been working, but also because of the semitrucks that are back, parked right next to my apartment building. It's hard to sleep with them idling and making that "chugging" noise all night.

So, I do what I always do. Plop down on the couch and put in a videotape of my favorite old show, *It's My Life*. It always makes me laugh, even though I've seen it a zillion times. It reflects the way my high school was so accurately that I half expect my old teachers to appear any second. No one in my high school looked like Jake, however. Jake is the hot senior who doesn't know the homely sophomore even exists. I'm glad there wasn't a Jake at my high school; if there were, I would never have gotten any work done because I'd be spending all my time writing notes to my friends about how cute he was.

Opening the Hunt Club notebook to Week One, I try to determine my ideal mate. The whole doctor idea is okay, but I'm not sure I really want to spend the rest of my life with someone who has to put the health of others over the priority of spending time with me. They also seem kind of detached emotionally—I know they have to be because of their job—but I don't want that. It's the same kind of thing with the lawyer. Why marry someone who is trained in how to win arguments? How fun is that?

Picking a good-looking guy out of a lineup isn't as easy as I thought it would be. They are all so good-looking, but they are also the exact type of guy who would be cold to me under normal circumstances. How many times have hot guys like these not even stooped to acknowledge my existence? That's what I see when I look at some of the pictures. Maybe I'm just tired, and I don't even realize it. I close the notebook and focus back on the video. I wish I could have a guy like Jake. Or, rather, the actor who plays him. Michael Something.

Hey, wait. Why can't I have him?

He is my ideal man. Tall, dark, and sexy. Great body, great blue eyes, great smile, great laugh, and did I mention great body? He has a way of looking at people that seems so sweet and caring. I wonder what he is like in real life.

# Chapter Thirteen
# Week Two

I arrive at Miriam's house a few minutes early, hoping I might be able to ask about Michael Something and the chances of me—of us—going after him. But everyone else seems to have the same idea about getting there early, too. They are so excited about the prospects they've uncovered for me. Rose ushers me to the sitting room while Liz brings me some juice and muffins.

"Just . . . wait . . . till . . . you . . . see who I brought for YOU!" Liz says, sitting next to me on the couch. "This is Dan Gilliam, and he's an attorney here in Dallas. Look at those eyes and that smile." She hands me his picture.

"He is very nice looking," I tell her. I am a big sucker for blue eyes, and he definitely has those.

"He practices in the area of criminal defense. Now, that's

not necessarily a bad thing. He is AV Rated," Liz starts talking about how everyone deserves a fair trial, blah, blah, blah. In truth, I don't care about the area of law he practices.

"I'm not really into lawyers, Liz. I'm sorry." I almost tell her that I've never met an attorney who wasn't an ass. I decide not to, since Tammy is sitting behind us, and her husband is an attorney.

"No, don't be sorry. You can have anyone you want. And if you don't want an attorney, hey great. It just helps us narrow down the search a little."

"Good morning everyone," Miriam says, sitting on the couch across from me. "How are you doing, Sandra?"

"Good." I smile, feeling a little nervous, and the game hasn't really gotten rolling yet.

"Amber, honey, have you heard anything from Brantley, yet?" Rose asks, and everyone gets quiet as we wait to hear the answer.

"No, nothing yet." Amber barely looks up at us.

"He'll call. Don't worry," Liz tells her.

"He's just busy getting back to work after being gone that whole week. I'm sure he'll call," I say.

"We've got some good stuff to show you," Charlotte says and sits down next to me. I was hoping Annette would be here, but so far, no sign of her.

Miriam opens her book. "We're on Week Two. It's hubby selection time."

"We've got one you might want, Sandra." Rose jumps in and holds up an eight by ten of a very tan, very cute blond guy. "He's in medical school at Harvard. Top of his class. Wants to open a family practice."

"Wow, he is cute. How much more school does he have?" Liz asks as Rose passes around the pictures.

"I think he's got several more years at least. But that doesn't really mean anything, does it? He can still be married and be in medical school."

"What do you think, Sandra?"

"He's very good-looking. But I think I'd like to consider several before I make my decision."

"Good plan," Annette says, walking in the room and pulling up a chair on the other side of me. Several people wave to her, and I'm relieved to see she finally made it here. "With that much more school to go, won't he, like, be in debt?"

"Depends on who's paying for his schooling," Rose says.

"We've already ruled out attorneys, by the way," Liz announces to everyone, and I'm still not sure she understands my decision.

"Oh no. Why?" Tammy asks.

"I'm just not interested in law, really." I turn to explain to her, trying to be nice about the fact I think I'd die of boredom if I had to live with a lawyer. She nods but still looks at me like I'm crazy.

"Well, how about this one? The yummy Tom here?" Teresa holds up a picture, and people pass it down to me. Dark hair, mustache, glasses.

"I'm not really into mustaches either."

"That's okay, neither was I," Annette says, reaching for a muffin off the dish on the end table.

"Okay, let's scratch off mustache men," Liz says.

"See, this is why we should focus more on personality, intellectual interests, and traits the couple have in common." Lexi looks over at Miriam. "You can't find a soul mate based on photographs and financial statistics."

"It's still a workable place to start. I honestly believe this will work," Joyce says. "Okay, so, who's got another one?"

"I'm sorry, y'all. I guess I'm pretty picky." I'm embarrassed about my priorities again.

"No, don't you be sorry at all. You can have anyone you want. We're just here to make suggestions. Whatever you do, don't decide on a guy just because we like him. We're not the ones who will have to live with him," Rose says, and the other women start nodding.

"Hey, I must have gone through a hundred prospects before I decided to have them get William for me," Annette says.

"There are four pretty decent-looking men who made *Fortune* magazine's list of richest people. Don't know if you saw that, Sandra, so I circled them for you, here." Liz hands me a sheet with names and financial data on it. I'm always impressed with her research skills.

"We still have Richard." Christine passes a picture down to me. "He's in Texas Oil. Owns his own oil and gas company in Houston. Big bucks. He knows EVERYBODY and has been around the world. You would never be bored with him."

"Nice smile," I say.

"He has been married before, but he's divorced now."

"Any kids?" Annette asks as she takes the photo from me to get a better look. "He looks kind of old."

"Yes, he has kids, but at least they aren't little. I think they're in their teens, which means they can pretty much fend for themselves."

"And drive Sandra nuts," Miriam says. "I don't think Sandra needs to be worrying about teenagers right now."

"Right, I'd prefer if the guy is divorced that he either doesn't have kids, or the kids are still young enough not to hate me. Or life in general." I look over Annette's shoulder to glance at the picture again. He is nice looking, that's for sure. "How often does he have the kids?"

"Holidays and summer, most likely," Christine tells me. "Or maybe every other weekend, depending where they live."

"Let's keep his photo with the doctor, though, and come back to him," I suggest.

"Let me show you what I've picked for you." Cheryl walks from one of the chairs behind me. "Look at this guy. Isn't he gorgeous?" She makes me laugh because it sounds like we're shopping for dresses or something.

I take the picture from her. "Yes, he is striking." I smile. This one has dark hair, dark eyes, and a great smile. And a wonderful body. "What does he do?"

"Fireman."

"No, Cheryl, there's no money in that," Joyce says. Even I roll my eyes when I hear Joyce say that.

"I think he'd make enough. And besides, you won't find a guy with a bigger heart than a fireman." Cheryl looks at me and then over to Joyce.

"True. But he'd also be gone for days at a time." Rose looks at his picture. "Although, he is darling."

"Rose, pass Joyce his picture," Charlotte says. "You'd better check out his picture before you say no, Joyce."

"My concern would be if he got hurt on the job or something. I think I would always worry about him. But I do appreciate your finding him for me, Cheryl." I smile at her.

"No problem, there are a lot more men out there for you." She walks over and sits down again.

"Sandra, I have the perfect guy for you. This is Shawn. He's a model for one of the agencies here in Dallas. I was kind of saving him for myself, but I think I want you to have him. Very successful. Look at those muscles." Selma hands me a professional eight by ten. He looks almost like a painting; he's lying down on concrete, no shirt, and his eyes are partly closed. Hair all messed up.

"He's a hottie, that's for sure." I don't really feel anything for him other than physical attraction. There's got to be more interest. I'm not really feeling anything special about these guys. "Let's keep him with the others," I say finally.

"None of these are quite right, are they?" Annette seems to read my thoughts.

"No, not really."

"Okay, let's go beyond the looks and money a little bit," Annette suggests. "Have you thought any more about what kind of personality you like in a guy?"

"Someone funny, I guess. Easygoing. Nice. Not too into himself, you know? At least not to the point of being a jerk."

"We've run into a lot of jerks like that," Rose tells me. "So, we know exactly what you mean. You need a nice guy, not an egomaniac."

"No lawyers, then. That's for sure," Teresa says, and Tammy almost chokes on her muffin.

"No real estate people, either," Christine says. People look over at her for a moment.

"What's wrong with real estate people?"

"They just seem like jerks. And pushy."

"No way. Real estate people are usually nice." Teresa rolls her eyes.

"Someone who I can be my goofy self around, who cares genuinely about people. And about animals," I tell them.

"And you want good looks, no mustache. What about weight and height?" Joyce is changing the subject back to looks again. And taking notes.

"I'd like him to be taller than me, at least. Which should be easy, since I'm just five feet four inches. As for weight, not too skinny. Well, not skinnier than I am."

"That's the rule I go by, too," someone says from behind me.

"I don't care if he's heavy as long as he's healthy, and he falls into the good-looking category."

"What attributes do you look at to consider if a guy is really good-looking?" Miriam asks me.

"That's a hard one."

"Yeah, usually it's just a matter of knowing him when you see him," Annette says.

"That's because you are considering more than just his looks," Miriam tells us.

I think for a moment. "I usually like blue eyes. Deep, dark blue eyes. Dark hair more than blond. Not into bald guys at all. Nice smile. Broad shoulders. Nice butt."

Several women laugh when I say that.

"Actually, I don't care about butts and that kind of thing. I just say it because everybody else does." I laugh, too. "I guess I just want someone who is smart but who doesn't make me feel stupid. Someone who can have a good time in the toothpaste aisle at Kroger, you know what I mean?" I hear the scratching of pens writing down what I'm saying.

"You like romantic men. Candlelight restaurants, flowers, that kind of thing?" Martha asks from behind me. "Maybe you're an old-fashioned romantic?"

"Maybe. I don't know. He doesn't really have to buy me flowers or anything."

"Give us an example of a guy you think is cute. Married or not." Miriam suggests. "Just to give us an idea of what you like."

"Actually, I do have one particular guy in mind who is like

the yardstick I use to gauge other guys. Y'all are going to laugh, though."

"No, we won't. Who is it?"

"Maybe he's the one? Does he live around here?"

"I don't think so. He's an actor, so I guess he's out in California."

"An actor? That's perfect. What a fun hunt that would be!" Christine sounds excited, and she hasn't even heard who he is yet.

"That would be a challenge we haven't had before," Liz says. "I agree with Christine. I think it would be fun to get you an actor."

"His real name is Michael, and I'm not sure about his last name, but he used to play Jake on the sitcom called *It's My Life*."

"Oh, I know exactly who you're talking about. That guy is GORGEOUS," Annette says. "Those eyes, and those lips and—"

"What else has he been in?" Rose asks, trying to figure out if she's seen *It's My Life* before.

"I haven't really seen him in anything else."

"He did a made-for-HBO movie I saw just a few weeks ago," Tammy says from behind us. "I think his last name is Warren."

"Yeah, that's it. Michael Warren."

"Liz, would you get on the Internet real quick and print off a picture? And bio if you can find one."

"I'm on it." Liz walks into another room.

"Do you think Michael Warren would be good husband material for you?" Martha asks me. "If you want him, we can help you get him."

"I don't know. He's so gorgeous. And funny. And interesting. And, I guess I can't even imagine him liking me."

"But he's your dream guy, so to speak?" Annette asks.

"Yes. He is my idea of the perfect man."

"Then, let us get him for you!" Charlotte says, and the others cheer along with her.

"We can help y'all get together; that's no problem. The actual problem is that actors can be jerks sometimes," Martha says. "Not to discourage you, because I think it would be a successful and exciting hunt. But just keep that in mind. You can always switch if you end up finding his real personality is nothing like what you've seen on TV."

"Okay, here we go." Liz is back, and she sits down in the straight-back chair again. "Is this him?" She holds up a color printout of a picture of Michael.

"Yeah, that's him." I laugh. She passes the picture around so everyone can see it.

"Wow, I've never seen anything that good-looking in my life." Teresa stares at his picture.

"Talk about yummy." Selma looks over her shoulder.

"Here are some basic stats I found. His full name is Michael Edward Warren. He's twenty-seven years old and lives in Malibu, California. It says he's not married, but he does have a girlfriend he's been seeing for over a year."

"Ah, we'll take care of her. Not to worry." Martha winks at us.

"Get this, y'all. He grew up in Houston and arrived in Hollywood the day after he graduated from high school. He took acting lessons, but he never finished college."

"I don't have college, either."

"He's been in several sitcoms and made-for-TV movies, as well as some off-Broadway plays."

"Is he into charity work?" Cheryl asks.

"Volunteer at a deaf center, perhaps?" Teresa jokes.

"It doesn't say. We'd have to check with Jeremy."

"What do you think, Sandra?"

"He sounds interesting. I'd like to know more about him."

"Liz, let's get Jeremy started on a full background check. Including criminal and financial. Also find out what his interests are outside of acting. That may be a good lead for us," Martha says.

"I'm filling out the fax request as we speak."

"Security is pretty tight around actors," Miriam tells me. "But he's not on the A-list, so maybe he's still approachable. I agree with Martha. If we can connect with him through his hobbies, that might be the fastest, most direct way."

"Find out some more about the girlfriend, too," Martha adds.

"Sandra, he is a nice choice for your husband." Rose looks at Michael's picture. "He is stunningly good-looking."

"That's why I can't imagine him liking me."

"Leave that to us." Charlotte laughs. "He will like you, don't you worry."

I wonder how she can sound so sure.

"I'm happy for you, Sandra. You deserve someone like him." Annette looks at his picture.

"Let's get our teams going." Miriam flips to another page in her notebook. "Team H? Rose, can y'all start researching his public appearances? See if you can narrow down where he goes, how he dresses, who he hangs out with. Jeremy can help target the location of his gym and things like that, but I also think you can get a lot off the Internet."

"We'll need corroboration, though."

"Right. On high-profile guys like Michael, we'll have to confirm facts before we act on them."

"Also check to see if he still has family in Houston and how close they are. Maybe there's an avenue in that way," Martha says.

"Okay, U Team," Miriam moves on. "Statistics. Let's get them. Work with Jeremy and find out as much as you can. He's probably used to getting girls, so we need to narrow down his likes and especially dislikes." Liz is writing it down.

"And N Team. Christine, can y'all focus in on any charity work he does? Who is he connected with? What does he care about really strongly? Does he like art or music? Let's start thinking in terms of a good setup venue."

"What kind of auditions does he go on?" Someone asks from behind me.

"We might see if he'd be interested in doing an independent film. Like in Texas, perhaps." Martha starts her tapping with her cane.

"A movie deal. That would be so cool." Teresa laughs. "Las Colinas has studios, doesn't it?"

"Yes. Isn't *Barney* filmed there?" Annette asks.

"Lets hope he'll be interested in more than a *Barney* episode."

"Texas has other actors who do projects here. Mathew Mc-Conaughey, Sandra Bullock, Chuck Norris, Jamie Fox," Martha says. "Miriam, who was that entertainment attorney we used a few months back? He has an office here and in Austin. Let's call him and find out who the independent directors are who like to use Texas locations. See if we can get Michael out of Hollywood and the red tape out there."

Miriam nods. "I'll also check to see who his agent is."

"Do you think we could really stage a production of some kind?" I laugh, because it sounds unreal to think we could stage a movie or theater production.

"Sure, it happens all the time. Even if the movie never

makes it to theaters or Cannes, we can at least look into production costs and try to get Michael here to be in it," Tammy says. "It doesn't sound like it needs to be that big of a project for him to do it. Maybe get you in the movie, too, Sandra."

"Maybe we all can." Christine laughs. "Regardless, though, we'd need a good script to draw someone like Michael."

"The directors will already have plenty of scripts to consider. Let's see if we can get a hold of Tom Hanks's wife. She loves to help small productions."

"I'm on it," Liz says.

"T Team," Miriam moves to the last team. "Y'all are on girlfriends. Get all the scoop you can on everyone he's dated and been with. Find out what he's like up close and personal. And help Liz compile his likes and dislikes so we can see if he and Sandra are compatible."

"I love getting the good stuff on the relationships." Joyce laughs.

"How soon can I—" Lexi pauses. "I mean, we, us. How soon can some of us go to Malibu?"

Miriam laughs. "Let's wait and see where we are first. But likely within the next few weeks, so you can start researching that. You might as well study the city and know your way around."

"This is going to be one of our most exciting rounds so far. I can feel it," Tammy says.

"Teams, you all know what to do? Okay, are there any questions? Comments?" Miriam closes her notebook.

"I almost forgot." I reach down into my tote bag. "I brought an old VHS tape of the show he was on, in case y'all want to see him in action. It's from a few years ago, though."

"That's a good idea. Let's go in the living room and put it on." Miriam leads us into the other room, takes the tape from me, and puts it into her VCR. We have to wait a few minutes for him to appear on-screen.

"That's him." I pause the tape with the remote for just a second and then play it so they can hear him talk.

"He seems like a nice enough guy," Lexi says.

"Oh, I think he's darling," Rose adds.

"Selma!" Teresa says, laughing. "Stop making yummy noises."

"Just think, Sandra. There's your future husband right there," Annette says. I watch Michael sit down in one of the high school desks and lean over to talk to the girl next to him. Never in a million years would someone like him like someone like me.

# Chapter Fourteen
# Week Three

Jerry allows me to have Sunday evening off so I can go to the meeting at Miriam's house, as long as I agree to open for him Sunday morning. It isn't as painless as I thought, considering I didn't get home until after 2:00 a.m. when I closed the night before. In the back of my mind, I am always hopeful that my days making pizza are numbered. I would love for the Hunt Club to move me into a really cool job for the sake of getting Michael. I mentally write my letter of resignation with every pizza I make.

"Hi, Sandra, how are you?" Rose hugs me when I finally arrive at Miriam's house. Everyone seems so excited about the hunt, and I still can't believe it's all for me. We walk into the sitting room and join everyone else. I notice Amber isn't here.

"How are you holding up so far?" Liz brings me a glass of white wine.

"Fine, I think I've watched every episode of *It's My Life* twenty times so I could see Michael."

"We've got some good stuff." Liz sits down in her usual chair.

"Okay, Week Three, everyone," Miriam calls our attention. "Where are we? Team H?"

"We've been working with Jeremy, pretty much like everyone has. And he's given us some leads on Michael's personality, or 'persona,' I guess we should say," Rose tells us as she passes out some information. "He absolutely loathes the press, which is why you don't see much of him in the tabloids. He actually punched a photographer last summer and almost got arrested."

"So, be careful with your cameras if you end up going to stake him out," Miriam says. "Make sure he sees us as possible fans and not paparazzi."

"He has a house near the ocean, and he likes to hang out at the little surf shops. Outdoor cafés, that kind of thing. He's basically a beach bum, more or less."

"I actually like that," I tell them. I wish I could hang out at the beach all day.

"His primary choice for clothes seems to be T-shirts and shorts. Dressing up to him means wearing shoes, I'm afraid." Rose looks at me. "I don't know if you'll get a lot of formal evenings out with him."

"No, that's okay with me. I like T-shirt-and-jeans-type guys."

"Then you'll definitely like him. He likes to go to the clubs along the beach, but the casual ones, of course. His favorite drink is beer. Doesn't smoke, and in fact he's donated money to help clean up the beaches. Smoking is now prohibited at most of the beaches, thanks to people like him. He's into heath and fitness," Rose continues. "And he runs five miles a day along the beach and loves to surf."

"Can you surf, Sandra?"

"No, the only thing I've ever done at the beach is stand there in the ankle deep water."

"You may get to learn, then. He seems pretty protective of his privacy, so it's hard to know what he does with his time. His best friend is Sammy Blankman, who was also in the HBO movie with him. That's about all I have so far."

"That's good." Miriam writes the information down. "And the U Team?"

"Here is some more personal information we've come up with so far." Liz passes out a small stack of paper to each of us. "He's from an Irish Catholic family. Grew up in Houston, like we said last time. His friends call him Mike, and in his younger days, the girls called him Mikey. It's just plain Mike or Michael now. His parents, Nick and Christina, are divorced, and his mom remarried a guy named Harold, or 'Hal.' His mom is a schoolteacher in Clear Lake. His stepdad owns a car repair place—not your usual mechanic though. He's actually the owner of the chain. Mike has two older brothers, Nick Jr. and Jason, both who attended college at the University of Houston. They help their stepdad with his business."

"How close is he to his family?"

"It's hard to tell because of the press machine out there, but I'm guessing not that much, I don't think. There are no articles that talk about or show him back home in Houston,"

Liz says. "When Mike got to LA after high school, he lived with his mom's brother until he got his first acting gig. A local production of *Fiddler*. From there, he took bit parts in sitcoms. Landed an agent a few years later, who got him the leading role on *It's My Life*. He reportedly loves acting, but hates all the hoopla that goes with it. Loves his fans but from a distance, mostly."

"That's interesting. We need to keep that in mind for when Sandra meets him. It may be she'll need to act like she doesn't know who he is." Miriam looks at me. "Definitely don't want to seem like his biggest fan. Did you get more likes and dislikes?"

"Yes, but unfortunately, not much corroboration yet. Mostly just fan stuff. Pretty typical. Loves fast cars, hates the press, his favorite color is blue, boxers instead of briefs, favorite food is popcorn, and he is into acting for the 'art' and not the money."

"Is that last part true?"

"Who knows? I haven't been able to get information from people close to him yet."

"Maybe one or two of us should buddy up with the best friend, Sammy?" Lexi asks.

"Are you volunteering? It may not be a bad idea." Miriam looks over the statistics. "Teresa, you and Lexi get with Jeremy on this. Find out where Sammy hangs out, and see if you can get some info out of him. Can you do it this week?"

"I can leave for Malibu right now." Lexi laughs.

"Me, too." Teresa stands up like she's ready to go.

"I contacted Monica in the L.A. Club. She doesn't know Michael, but she said there are some girls in their group who have connections to actors. I don't know if he hangs out much with actors other than Sammy, though. But you might check. Lexi, be sure to check in with Monica and see if you can get some guides while you're out there. We need a good lead," Liz says.

"N Team. Christine, did you find out anything about charity work?"

"Just the 'Kick Your Butt' campaign to stop the smoking and littering on the beaches. He also was pretty active with 'Friends of the Bay,' but that may also have been for the same campaign. He's not into working with deaf kids—I checked. His music tastes seem to vary. He likes the alternative rock scene—retro bands mostly. As far as art goes, he doesn't seem to care much. At least that I've found out yet."

"What about the auditions he goes to?" Martha asks.

"He likes the local stage productions." Christine flips to the next page of her notes. "He also seems to like indie films, kind of like what we talked about last time. I think he would go for doing a movie here in Texas, even a smaller independent film. Jeremy told me he's even funded a few projects in the past."

"Where is he financially? Liz did you and the PI find anything?" Joyce asks, and several people laugh. "What's so funny? It's important that we know these things."

"If you'll see page four of the handout I passed out." Everyone turns to the page. "He has substantial investments in alternative fuels, such as the French Fry grease bio-diesel thing Darryl Hannah is into. Energy conservation may be his niche, although I'm not seeing any connection to a group. Probably because he hates publicity."

"He only made two hundred thirty thousand on the HBO movie," Tammy reads.

"Yeah, but look at his salary for the sitcom. One hundred

thousand an episode." Joyce points out excitedly. "How many episodes did he do, Sandra?"

"The show was on the air for almost five years. And it was a weekly show."

"Some of those sitcoms only tape twenty-six episodes, and I'm sure he didn't make that much starting out," Tammy says.

"Okay, even so. That's twenty-six episodes a season," Charlotte says. "That's what? Two million six hundred thousand a year?"

"Sound workable to you, Sandra?" Miriam asks as people laugh again.

"Um, gee, I think so."

"We don't know if he still has that, but if he invested it, then you should be set," Rose says.

"Damn, I'm going for an actor when I get picked." Selma stands up to get another glass of wine.

"How many houses does he have, and where are they?" Martha asks.

"He has the one in Malibu. A three-bedroom, two bath near the ocean but not right on the beach. Again, likely for privacy reasons, since people can come right up to your house if it's on the beach. He skis in Aspen about once a season, but other than that, I am not seeing indication of another house." Liz flips through the information packet.

"I bet he uses another name. Miriam, can you have one of the PI's find out if he uses an alias?"

"Good idea. I did contact an entertainment attorney in Austin, by the way, who knows some film projects we might be interested in."

"And I have the info for Mike's agent. She's out of L.A.," Liz says.

"T Team. Where are we with his girlfriends?"

"He's been linked to some Hollywood actresses, but for the past year or so, he's been seeing a perfume model named Sofia Elon. She's originally from Helsinki, I think," Joyce tells us and passes out some information. "Naturally white-blonde hair, really tan, super-thin. We basically hate her."

"*Hmmm*. Not so good." Miriam looks over the fact sheet. My heart sinks. How in the world can I compete with that?

"What have his other girlfriends been like?" Teresa asks.

"Same kind of thing. Models or actresses. At least that is what we've found so far. It could be that since he hates the spotlight, we're seeing the models and actresses because they want the spotlight. If he dated other people, they may be in the shadows."

"How serious are he and Sofia?" Martha asks. "Are they living together?"

"No, she has an apartment in New York and spends a lot of time there, since the perfume line she is modeling for is out of Manhattan. She seems like she's independent."

"Who do we have in New York that can get more of a scoop on Ms. Sofia?" Miriam asks Martha.

"Ronita is with the Hunt Club there. We should start with her."

"Teams, keep up the good work, and let's all dig a little deeper. I want to know how this boy spends his time. There's got to be something that can be used as a setup."

"What about the indie film?"

"That's an expensive way to go. And I checked with our attorneys. We'd have to be careful because contracts will be involved. The industry is pretty sensitive to scams. If they think we've set up the project in order to get Mike and Sandra together, we might be facing a fraud lawsuit," Miriam says. "It's still a possibility, but we'll have to be very careful."

"What about a smaller production? Like a play?" Tammy asks.

"I don't know how we'd get him here for a play."

"Can we get Sandra to California? Have her meet him in a play out there?"

"That might be a possibility, too. What draws him to projects?" Miriam asks.

"*Umm*, being able to use his skills for the sake of 'art.' Lack of publicity." Liz is reading from her notes.

"Do we know if Mike is working on any acting projects at the moment?" Martha asks.

"Not according to Jeremy," Liz says. "He's officially between projects, according to his agent."

"So what are your thoughts, Sandra?" Miriam asks me, and I don't quite know what to say. It seems like things are going pretty fast.

"It sounds kinda complicated. And I wonder if it's really possible."

"Oh, it's possible. We just need to be creative again," Martha says. "These are the types of hunts I really love. The challenging ones. It will be worth the complications when you are Mrs. Michael Warren."

*Mrs. Michael Warren.*

"Okay, everyone knows what their mission is. Are there any questions?" Miriam wraps things up. "Remember, if you haven't anted up for this round, you need to do so, please."

The next day at work, my mind is clearly not on pizzas. After the rush, when I'm waiting to check out a driver, I use my time productively. I take out a scratch piece of paper and a pen . . .

*Sandra Warren*
*Mrs. Sandra Warren*
*Mrs. Sandra Eileen Warren*
*Mrs. Sandra E. Warren*
*Sandra Greene-Warren*
*Mr. and Mrs. Michael E. Warren*

We share the same middle initial, at least.

# Chapter Fifteen
## Week Four

I sense something is different. Wrong. It's as if something is in the air that hits me the moment I enter Miriam's house. After slipping out of my shoes, I walk into the sitting room for the meeting. All of the members seem to be standing in a circle around one girl. Upon closer inspection, I realize it's Amber.

"Is she okay?" I ask Tammy, the closest one to me when I walk in the room.

"She still hasn't heard anything from Brantley," she whispers. "And Martha and Miriam are putting pressure on her to choose another guy."

"So, are we going to have two hunts going at the same time?"

"We can. But I doubt Amber is ready to go again. She's still got her hopes up that she can have Brantley."

"Okay, y'all, let's get started," Miriam says, and everyone sits down. Annette comes in, hugs Amber, and then sits down by me.

"It'll be okay, Amber," Rose says, touching her shoulder before taking her seat.

"I just don't want anyone else but him. And I don't know why we can't figure out a way to get him." She's trying not to cry, but it's obvious she's upset.

"Things haven't quite moved along at the pace we were hoping," Martha says. "But by next time, we'll know if she's ready to start a new hunt or not. And if you still want him, then remember, we can always Plan B him."

"No, way," Lexi says, almost standing up. "We're NOT doing that. Brantley is on a Senate advisory committee!"

"What is plan B?" I look over at Annette and then at Miriam. The other members are silent, which is almost eerie compared to how animated everyone usually is at these meetings.

"It's where we pull out all the stops, so to speak. Set up Brantley to be around Amber again," Liz explains carefully.

"I'm not sure what the problem is then. Why don't we just do that?"

"That could work," Tammy, sitting behind me, says, trying to sound optimistic.

"But, I can see where it could also not work." Liz is flipping through pages in her notes. "The edge is completely gone now. She could just as easily turn into the-Friend-He-Has-in-Dallas."

"This is all part of the game. I for one think the challenges make it all the more exciting," Martha says. "We'll know more at the next meeting."

"All right, then." Miriam nods and takes out her fancy pen and shifts in her seat. She turns to another chapter in her notebook before continuing. "Now, we should move on to Sandra's hunt."

"Congratulations, Sandra, on being selected as the next one." Amber smiles at me, and I quickly say thank you.

"Liz, let's get Sandra a mimosa." Rose gestures to the tray on the table behind Liz and then smiles at me. "Things are getting exciting for you." Liz hands my mimosa to Rose, who in turn hands it to me. I glance back at Amber as I reach for my notebook. I wonder if we should be getting her another drink, too. I finally hand Amber my mimosa, and another one is passed down for me.

"Week Four, everyone." Miriam opens her book, and the rest of us do the same. "Where are you, Team H?" Rose and several others wave. "What do you have for us?"

"Lots of good info from Jeremy and one of his associates in Malibu. Mike has won several 'World's Most Handsome Man' contests, which he hated. That, along with additional corroboration shows he really does hate publicity. I think he'd be doing plays in Peshtigo, Wisconsin, if he could, just to avoid the press," Rose says.

"Is he shy?"

"No, not shy. He just views himself as an artist and not a babe magnet the Hollywood press wants to make him into. That's why he's taken some strange roles in the past few years, playing drug lords and homeless people. He's also taken theater classes that focus more on classical acting. Shakespeare and that kind of thing."

"Oh, so he's a 'serious' actor now?" Tammy laughs.

"I thought he was pretty serious about it all along." Funny how I'm already protective of him.

"Lexi and Teresa will have to fill you in on how he spends

his time, but overall, he seems like a pretty good guy." Rose concludes her report as Miriam scribbles notes.

"Okay, so moving on to Team U. What have you got, Liz?"

"More personal info. Mike is five feet nine inches tall, and he runs five miles a day—as we mentioned last time. It looks like we're not going to be able to stake him out at the gym, since he doesn't seem to belong to one. That we can find, anyway. And, although the fan sites say his favorite food is popcorn . . ." She pauses as people laugh. "We actually discovered he loves seafood, especially Cajun-style. From what I've found out, Mike is actually a pretty smart guy, even though his acting roles usually are the opposite. He was accepted into the University of Houston his senior year in high school, as well as at the School of Visual Arts in Manhattan to study film and video."

"Get to the juicy stuff, Liz," Martha says from her corner throne. "We can read all that."

"Here, pass the sheets around, and we'll go over his medical records in just a second." She flips through one of the packets. "We also ran his credit. He has a pretty decent credit score, and you'll see his bank statements on pages seven and eight. You can see he's done well with his investments. Jeremy predicts the value is about 4.6 million."

"That's great news." Joyce and several others practically cheer.

"I don't see another house, though, besides the Malibu one," Amber says, catching up on where we are by looking through the documents that have been passed out so far.

"Let's hope he doesn't have an expensive drug habit or something." Miriam looks through the information from Liz. "You hear stories about those Hollywood actors."

"I don't think he does," Lexi says. "He's really big into health. He even eats organic foods and stuff."

"His medical records really don't indicate a drug problem either," Liz tells us. "He's not on antidepressants, so we don't have to concern ourselves about that this time around. In fact, he doesn't seem to take any maintenance meds at all."

"Have antidepressants been a problem in other hunts?" I ask to no one in particular.

"Well," Miriam says and winces a little. "Just being on antidepressants isn't a problem. In fact, it's better for them to be on them if they have suffered from depression than to not be on them. However we try to avoid guys with a history of mental illness in their families. Remember, we have the possibility of children that we have to consider."

"We're shooting for the ideal guy, after all. They aren't always perfect, but we have to at least try to eliminate potential obstacles," Rose adds.

"It's been interesting how common it is for the successful and good-looking guys to have problems with depression," Lexi points out. "That's says a lot about the pressure they are under, doesn't it?"

"You would think all the money would be a good enough antidepressant," Joyce says.

"It would certainly help me." Selma and several other ladies laugh. I have to agree with them in a way; I never thought of rich people as ever being depressed. Having money just seems like the answer to all of my problems.

"Liz, so what's the situation with all the antibiotics?" Martha asks, changing the subject as she is obviously scrutinizing his charts.

"If you'll see his doctor's diagnosis." Liz flips to the correct page and holds it up. "It is kind of hard to make out the handwriting, but apparently Mike gets several serious lung infections a year. It's from the pollution when he surfs, according to his doctor. I think it's a pretty common thing, though. Just difficult to get rid of sometimes because the bacteria are resistant to antibiotics."

"How can he keep from getting those infections? Is there anything he can take?" I ask, knowing that no one can probably answer me, since we're not medical people.

"The only thing his doctor told him—I'm paraphrasing what his doctor said on page five now—is he has to stay out of the water right after it rains. Everything gets stirred up during storms, I guess."

"But otherwise, our boy is healthy?" Martha taps her cane, and I almost want to go take it away from her.

"It appears so. He had all the usual childhood diseases— mono in high school, that kind of thing—but other than that, he's a healthy prospect."

"What about the N team?" Miriam asks. "Christine, did Monica get back with you?"

"Yes, and she was so nice. We arranged for her to meet Lexi and Teresa in L.A. and show them around. She also sent out a local hunt request for any info they could find on Michael Warren. Not much came back, but that may be good for Sandra, because at least he's not a major party animal who's going to be out every night."

"Good yes, unless Sandra wants to be partying with the Hollywood stars all night. Then she might be frustrated if she can't get shoes on him, and he won't go anywhere," Martha says.

"I'm fine with him barefoot and hanging out at the house." I laugh. "I'm not really into the big fancy all-nighters, anyway."

"Sounds like you two are a good match." Miriam smiles,

as if that is all there is to it to get us together. "Did you find anything else out about charity work he does? I would think he'd be pretty big into the environment, since the water pollution makes him sick."

"No, we really didn't find anything about that, other than the antismoking campaign we mentioned last time. He does like the local music scene, which seems to focus on the environment. Toad the Wet Sprocket. That kind of thing."

"Toad the Wet Sprocket?"

"It's a band." Christine says. I'm amazed at what we learn at these meetings.

"Did you confirm that he's between projects right now? That he's available if we set something up?" Miriam asks.

"Right, he's not working right now, although we did hear that he may be interested in producing an indie film. He just hasn't found the right one yet."

"Teresa, did you find out anything from Sammy?" Martha asks.

"Oh, our trip was so fun, I have to tell you. Lexi and I met up with Monica, you know, the leader of the L.A. Hunt Club, and she picked us up from the airport. We went straight to see where Mike lives. Sandra, you are going to LOVE it. It isn't right on the beach, but because of the hill, you can totally see the ocean." Teresa holds up a picture and then passes it around.

"That's all well and good, but did you get a chance to meet Sammy?" Miriam laughs.

"Yes, we went to a club called Catchum's or Catsup's or something."

"Basically a dive bar on the beach," Lexi says.

"And it wasn't hard to figure out who Sammy was, since he had his own Sammy Blankman T-shirt on. It was hilarious.

We hung out with him in the bar and just acted like tourists. After we bought him a couple rounds, he pretty much told us anything we wanted to know."

"And the best part is, I doubt he remembered the next day even talking to us."

"One thing we did find out, that I think we can use in a possible setup for Sandra, is scuba diving, which Mike loves to do. I mean LOVES it. And he goes several times a year on one of those Hawaiian minicruise things, just to scuba." Teresa is looking through her notes. "Here it is. He loves the night dives in Kona." She passes around the information.

"What the hell is that?" Liz holds up a picture of a flattened water creature that looks like it's just wings with eyes.

"That's the manta ray. It's what Mike is really into. Apparently, there are bunches of them, and they are huge. Like sixteen feet across. They are attracted to the lights from the scuba people. Or rather, the mantas are attracted to the little organisms or whatever that are attracted to the lights. They are completely docile and sweet animals, er, rather, creatures."

"That is bizarre." I laugh, studying the pictures. They look like aliens from another planet. "Mike likes these?"

"Oh, definitely. He spends most of his time on his trips sleeping days so he can dive at night with them."

"There's our core connection," Martha says from behind me.

"I was just thinking the exact same thing." Miriam turns pages in her notebook.

"What is a core connection?" I have to ask. I know I've heard it mentioned before and saw something about it in the game manual, but it wasn't really explained very well.

"It's what makes the hunt work," Annette tells me with a smile.

"It's a psychological theory. And Martha has expanded it

to help with the Hunt Club games we use. It involves finding out what is important to a person at the very deep core of his being. Every person has something. Finding what it is in Mike and then seeing if you match that can make all the difference in Mike's falling in love with you," Miriam says, not only talking with her hands but also with her pen.

"Sometimes it's obvious what is emotionally driving a guy, and other times you really have to search for it because even he may not know. But, if you can find what really influences him deep down, and if the girl has a similar interest, the bond can be quite powerful," Rose tells me.

"But, what they always fail to mention, Sandra, is that there is some serious controversy with doing this. Like when you find out what that core element is in the guy, but the girl doesn't share it or have a common connection whatsoever. What do we do then? Have her pretend she shares the same core element?" Lexi says, not looking up as she makes her point. "That's where we should be careful. I don't think it's right to manipulate a guy's heart and mind that way."

"Is it even possible to do that?" I ask. "I mean, how can there be a real strong connection if the girl is faking her side of it?"

"Yes, there still can be a connection, even then. Remember, it's not just personal preferences we're talking about here. If you can find a core injury to the guy's psychological or emotional development, you can have him latch on to a girl just by having her replicate the same event that caused it," Martha explains from behind us, and I wonder if she's a psychologist or something. "It's really quite fascinating. If you look at different relationships where you think 'oh my gosh, how did they end up together,' chances are there's a core connection."

"You see it a lot with people who can't let go of bad relationships," Lexi adds, and I notice that the reactions of the ladies seem mixed about this. "The guy manages to replicate the identical psychological injury that the girl suffered in the past, and she transfers all those deep emotions and feelings onto this new guy. Sometimes without even realizing it."

"It's true, that can happen," Miriam says, and several people nod. "But, it doesn't have to necessarily replicate an event that's negative. You know that, Lexi."

"It's been compared to imprinting on baby goslings. They get a mental attachment to the first thing they see when they're born, and they'll follow that thing everywhere. Likewise, if you trigger a person's core injury, you can really hook someone on a psychological level." Lexi looks down at the floor again, and I have to wonder if she's speaking from personal experience. It's pretty obvious she's not a fan of the core connection aspect of the game.

"I guess I'm still not getting it." I shake my head and try to find the pages in the Game Book that talk about it. "Is it just an intense emotional thing two people have in common?"

"Possibly. Sometimes you can arrange the core match, and it's obvious. And, sometimes it happens by accident where couples stumble onto the core connection without even realizing it," Rose tells me. "Especially in the case of when it happens unknowingly, it can create an impenetrable bond between the two of them."

"Remind me later to tell you about William's and my core connection," Annette leans over and whispers to me.

"I think I can give you a good example of an accidental one," Lexi says. "Do you remember the movie *Fatal Attraction*, with Glenn Close and Michael Douglas?" She pauses, and I nod. "She didn't get so hooked on Michael Douglas's character just because he was a powerful, good-looking law-yer. She, herself, was a well-respected acquisitions editor, but she turned into mush and couldn't stand the thought of los-ing Michael after that day in the park. Remember, Michael's character acted like he was having a heart attack, and it ended up being just like her father's heart attack. It was so vivid and real in her mind, that when she saw Michael fall, she instantly was back reliving that time when her father died."

"I do remember that scene from the movie," I tell her, nod-ding again.

"That was the core connection, and you could say that nei-ther of them really realized the depth of what occurred. And later, when Michael takes care of her when she cuts herself, you will notice it is more like a parent taking care of a child. That also solidified the core connection. And, it was obvious in the movie that, once Michael's character hit on her core injury, she felt a deep connection to him that she didn't want to lose no matter what," Lexi tells me. "In real life, the con-nection can be based on a core injury that happens when the person is a child or even as an adult. Or, it can be emotionally vital to the person for some other, deeply personal reason."

"That's kind of scary." I am finding the whole concept in-teresting. I've been wondering how the Hunt Club has man-aged to get those successful, good-looking guys to fall in love with girls like me. I'm guessing that this is it.

"It's kind of sick, you mean," Lexi says and looks at me.

I look over at Martha. "Is there really some way I could get to him that much? To where he'd be hooked on me like that?"

"Yes, it is possible." Martha smiles. "The core connections are what make our hubby-hunting game so successful. I think that's what we should focus on now for you. It sounds like the mantas that Mike loves so much might be exactly what we're looking for. For whatever reason, he seems really attached to them. Let's see if we can find out where the attachment comes from and have Sandra replicate that need in some way."

"And never mind that Sandra has never even heard of a manta before. Don't you think there is a line here we shouldn't cross?" Lexi sounds like she's getting angry again, but no one else seems to be saying anything. "It's wrong to manipulate Mike like that by having Sandra pretend she's into mantas to the degree he is."

"But maybe Sandra really does like mantas?" Amber says. "She just doesn't know it yet."

"That's exactly right," Miriam says. "You're overreacting, Lexi. It would be different if Sandra were going to make something up she didn't believe in at all. But, for all we know, Sandra could love those sea creatures just as much as Mike does."

"I do love all animals. Even ugly ones." I laugh, and I'm relieved when others do, too.

"So, who do we know in Hawaii?" Miriam looks over at Martha and then at Liz.

"Jackie is in Honolulu. But that's on Oahu, not the Big Island," Liz tells her, reviewing the notes about where the mantas are off the coast of Kona.

"Do we know what cruise company Mike uses?"

"He uses different ones, according to Sammy," Teresa says.

"Okay, that's no big deal. We wouldn't want to just have Sandra jump on one of his scheduled trips. We'll have to do a full setup, so several of us can be there to help."

"Miriam, be honest, you just want to go to Hawaii." Liz laughs and so does Miriam.

"Hey, anything for the cause."

"Do you scuba, Sandra?" Teresa asks me.

"No, never have." I'm studying the pictures of the manta rays.

"Do you have any problems with your ears?" Tammy asks.

"Ears? No."

"Can you swim? That should be the first question."

"Sure. I took years of lessons as a kid. Got my Red Cross certification to be a lifeguard at the Arlington YMCA."

"That's a great start," Martha says. "We'll need to get you scuba certified. I think there are places that will certify you in like three days. Plus home study. Miriam—"

"I'm already ahead of you, Martha. I'll contact Franklin after the meeting and see if he can make arrangements."

"We'll also need to help Sandra learn the background on the mantas. If Mike loves the marine stuff that much, then let's make Sandra an expert."

"Won't she have to move to Hawaii for that?"

"No, not necessarily," Miriam says. "Surely there are other creatures nearby that are similar to the mantas that Sandra can go look at. Mantas are in the ray family, right? Stingrays and that kind of thing?" It's obvious we're all novices when it comes to marine biology.

"Have you seen these pictures? They don't look like any stingray I've ever seen."

"We'll have Franklin look into that, too. Maybe have Sandra spend time at SeaWorld San Antonio. A few zoos, like the Dallas Aquarium at Fair Park." Miriam writes it all down.

"So, what do you think, Sandra? You look a little in shock or something?" Rose asks me.

"I'm fine. Just excited. Does this mean I'm going to Hawaii?"

"It's beginning to look that way, yes," Miriam says. "You have a lot of work to do, first. I know this isn't an easy subject, but how would you feel about leaving the pizza place? We really need your involvement twenty-four/seven if we want this to work."

I pause as if I need to think about this. *Humm.* How do I feel about leaving the pizza place? Can I quit YESTERDAY?

"That's fine with me." I laugh for a minute. "But, I still need to make my rent and stuff."

"Why don't we cover you? You can just include that for reimbursement after you're married," Martha suggests. "It's likely you'll be traveling a bit—to SeaWorld, marine sites, Galveston maybe. Places like that."

"That sounds great!" It's still hard for me to believe. I get to quit the pizza place. Learn to scuba. Study big-ass, freakish-looking rays. Go to Hawaii, meet Mike, and get married.

"Hey, y'all, aren't we forgetting one thing?" Liz asks.

"What? The plan sounds excellent to me," Teresa looks at her.

"What about Sofie, the girlfriend?"

"Sofia, you mean. Right, we need to take care of her, too," Miriam says. "Did we get a hold of Ronita in our N.Y. Hunt Club?"

"That's us. The T Team. We contacted Ronita, and she had the PI up there do a check on her. She's still struggling as a model. What I mean by 'struggling' is that she goes where they tell her to go. She's independent, yes, but to make the higher levels of modeling, you have to be competitive," Joyce tells us.

"So what are you saying? We should have Sandra compete or something?" Cheryl laughs.

"No, but I think we should try and find a way to send Sofia on an overseas job. Like to Paris or something?" Joyce asks.

"Do we even have Hunt Clubs in other countries?" Annette asks.

"No. Not yet, unfortunately. But someone is bound to have connections we can use." Miriam looks at Martha.

"Let me do some checking. I'll make sure Sofia has a six-month modeling contract somewhere far away. Maybe a movie . . . ?"

"Will that be enough, though? It looks like Mike has plenty of money. What's to keep him from going to see her?" I ask.

"We'll have to arrange for her to meet someone. Someone perfect for her."

"Like a reverse hunt or something."

"Right, Liz. Let's see who we know that can handle this for us. When you talk to Jeremy again, see who he knows in London or Paris."

"What type of timeline are we looking at?"

"Sandra, are you okay with quitting the pizza place?" Miriam practically whispers to me, sounding sensitive about the matter. They are all so considerate.

"Absolutely!" I laugh loudly.

"Will you need to give them notice, though?"

"I'd like to, yes, but I don't have to. What I'll do is tell them I'll work the hours I can for two weeks. And if my schedule's too sporadic, chances are they'll just let me go, anyway."

"Good, then the rest depends on the scuba training schedule, getting Sofia out of the way, getting Sandra up to speed on mantas." Miriam is checking off her list. "We'll know more at the Wednesday meeting, I think."

"Congratulations, Sandra, this one sounds exciting!"

"You deserve all of it," Selma tells me. "I hope you'll like mantas, though."

"They are kind of interesting. I'm sure I'll like them."

"Okay, teams, let's focus on the areas I just mentioned.

Also, narrow in on Mike's specific likes and dislikes," Miriam tells us.

"Like does he have a hair color fetish?" Tammy asks, and I guess she's remembering Brantley and his blond hair thing.

"No, he doesn't seem to. Just natural-looking, I think," Teresa says. "Which means a really good cut, styled to look natural. And long enough for him to run his fingers through."

"Of course." Liz smiles at me. "Should I set up a Daireds consultation?"

"Yes, let's go ahead and get things started, but with some flexibility while we see what Sandra's work schedule is going to look like." Miriam writes it down. My hair is about shoulder length, and I like it that way. I've never been to one of those expensive hair salons. I usually go to Supercuts or something, every couple of years. It should be interesting to see what this Darren or Daireds place can do for me.

"So, does this mean the movie thing is out?" Teresa asks.

"No, it's not out. Just on the back burner. Let's see how the plans go for the scuba setup first," Miriam says and turns her focus once again to the whole group. "Good job, ladies. Everyone know what they'll be doing for the next meeting? Great. Let's adjourn. Amber and the Relocation Committee, remember we'll meet in the dining room in a few minutes."

*I get to quit the pizza place! I get to quit the pizza place!* I'm practically singing and skipping as I make my way to the car.

# Chapter Sixteen
## Changes

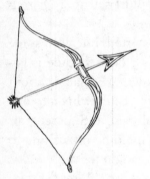

I really hate changes. Sitting on my couch, watching reruns of Mike's show and ignoring the sound of the semitrucks outside, I try to just stay completely focused. It's not like I'm going to miss making pizzas, so I don't know what I'm really worried about. I guess I feel like I'm going where no Greene has gone before. I love the idea of studying underwater creatures—even the weird ones. And going to Hawaii, being on a boat for a week. And learning to scuba, not to mention actually seeing Michael Warren. That beautiful face, those eyes, and that body. Up close. It's almost too much to take in all at once. Focus. Focus.

This may be my last all-nighter, I think to myself. Me, actually going to bed and getting up like a normal person. That, in itself, is almost too good to be true. No more smelling like pizza sauce. No more sweating and melting next to those ovens. No more flour everywhere and food under my poor nails. No more fighting with drivers over car-tops. No more damn teenagers.

If I never see another slice of pepperoni again, that'll be fine with me.


"Jerry?" I poke my head inside the office at work and notice my manager is checking out a driver. "Can I talk to you for a sec?"

"What are you doing here so early? You're closing tonight, remember? And don't you think for one minute you can get out of it either. I am SICK of you changing your schedule at the last minute, Sandra."

I smile and walk in the office. Ronald, the driver who is checking out, looks amused. How nice of Jerry to yell at me where everyone can hear him.

"When you have a second, can I talk to you alone?"

"Tell me now. I don't have time to play games. Just spit it out." He counts the stack of quarters and doesn't look up at me.

"Okay," I begin, noticing that people are still listening to us. "I need to give you my two weeks' notice."

He looks up at me. "You're joking." Ronald bursts out laughing.

"No, I'm not."

"Shit, Sandra. I figured you were out looking for another job. I guess you found one." He looks mad, and I really don't want to get into it with him.

"Sort of, but not really. I just need to quit. My last day will be two weeks from today." I look at the calendar on the wall, pick up a pen, and circle the date. "But, I probably will have to be in and out. So it'll be kind of hard to give you an exact schedule right now."

"What, do you think you can just walk in here and start giving me orders on scheduling?" He laughs, but I can tell he doesn't think it's funny. "I'll schedule you to work the same type of days you normally work. Or should have been working. If you're not here, then fine. But, I suggest you be here."

"Or what?" I laugh. "Are you going to fire me?"

"Yep, and then you won't get a good reference from me. Then what are you going to do?"

"Okay, I'll try to be here." It's not worth arguing, and I need to leave before I have a laughing fit. If these people only knew. Part of me wishes I could send Jerry a wedding invitation.

"Don't be late this evening," Jerry yells to me.

"I can't make it," I yell back. I've already arranged to meet Liz to get my hair cut and then later meet Franklin to discuss the scuba classes. "Tomorrow, maybe." And with that, I walk out the door, hoping that the Hunt Club can come through for me. If not, I'm out of a job.

"It's too short."

"No, it isn't"

"It's too flippy."

"No, it isn't. It's just perfect. You look darling," Liz says, staring at me in the mirror and running her fingers through the back of my now flippy haircut.

"It really does compliment your face," the hairdresser at Daireds Salon and Spa Pangéa tells me. "Brings out your blue eyes." My face and my eyes are the only positive things I have, and they are the only things people ever comment on. Usually.

"What do you think of the highlights?"

"They're okay, I guess." I'm being modest, because I do love the highlights. When I look in the mirror, I barely look like myself. I toss my hair back and forth and it seems to have a mind of its own. Or a body. Maybe that's where they get the whole "body" idea about hair.

"Let's do your makeup now." I'm led over to the Daireds makeup section. The makeup lady and Liz look over my face—they love my eyes again—and then they rip me to total shreds about the way I do my eyeliner. And blush. And what am I using as a cleanser.

"Now look at those eyes." The makeup lady sings, as she puts the final swings of mascara on me. They do look brighter. "And now the lips. This may burn just a little."

It actually burns a lot. "What the hell is that?"

"It's a plumper. It will make your lips look bigger."

"Do I want my lips bigger?" I ask them, and Liz laughs.

"Look how sexy they are now." She points at my face in the mirror. I guess it does look pretty cool. What will they think of next? "Okay, now you have your products. If you have any problems at all," she says, taking the cape off me, "call us. We're here to help."

The people at Daireds are nice; I'll give them that. It's just I don't like change. Especially change that will take six to eight weeks to grow out. The spa and salon personnel were nothing like I imagined them. I guess I anticipated complete snobbery or something. But the women there acted like my big sisters, there to show me how to do stuff.

"How do your lips feel now?" Liz asks and laughs, while she's driving me back from Arlington to Miriam's house so we can meet up with Franklin.

"Swollen. How long does this last?"

"Not very long. You do look very pretty, Sandra."

"Thanks. What about my weight, though?" I hesitate to ask her. The days of eating leftover remakes at the pizza place have taken their toll.

"What about it?"

"I thought Teresa said all Mike's girlfriends are skinny."

"Well, we haven't really looked into that too much. Are you interested in losing weight? Because that's something you should do for yourself, not for a guy."

"Sure, I guess."

"We have a nutritionist, and Miriam has a personal trainer she shares with us. If you want, I'll schedule an appointment for them to come by Miriam's in the morning?"

"That would be great." I would love the chance to work with Joseph.

When we arrive at Miriam's house back in Highland Park, Franklin is already there, eating cookies at the dining room table. Introductions are made, and I think Franklin looks like Santa. I like him instantly.

"Sandra, I LOVE your hair! It is gorgeous. And your make-up!" Miriam goes on and on.

"Thanks, I'm still getting used to it."

"I love it, too," Franklin joins in, just for the heck of it. He runs a private scuba school, and he's brought tanks and stuff to show me.

"We can get you certified pretty fast, but even with the training, you're going to want to get as many dives in as possible before you go on your trip," Franklin tells me. The scariest thing he's said so far involves compression and decompression. There's more to scuba than I thought, and I'm relieved when Miriam brings me a pad to take notes.

"Now, Liz and Miriam say you've been trained as a lifeguard?"

"Yes. Although I haven't worked professionally as a guard."

"That's fine. It's just good that you have the training. Y'all were also telling me we need to get her trained on some marine life and teach her about the creatures she'll be encountering."

"Right. The manta rays."

"They are funny looking, aren't they?" He laughs. "Tomorrow, can you meet me here in the morning? We can start your basic scuba training in Miriam's pool. Then I'll take you up to Lake Texoma later in the week."

"Yes, of course." I smile, wishing I had a pool. We wrap up our first scuba meeting, and Liz stops me as I'm walking out.

"If you want, you can take a run to the Aquarium at Fair Park. I'll go with you," Liz says. "I like underwater critters. And the seahorses over there are pretty bizarre." We leave to head over to check out the sea creatures. On the way to Fair Park, I get the chance to ask Liz questions about how the hunts usually go, and she asks me if I'm getting the e-mails that the Hunt Club sends out.

"Yes, but I haven't had a chance to read through all the hunt requests." There must be a hundred requests for jobs that can be filled with the girlfriends our members want to get rid of.

She laughs. "Oh, that's okay. Just skim them to see if any of them sound like something you can help with."

"How successful are all the Hunt Clubs at finding better jobs for all those girlfriends and female buddies so they'll move away?"

"Very successful. It's what makes or breaks a hunt, so we all do everything we can to help each other out. And it doesn't necessarily have to be forever that the girls have these jobs. Just long enough for the prospective bride and groom to get married. Then, after the marriage, if the girl isn't working out at her new high-paying job, she can always go back where she came from."

"Do they ever suspect anything?"

"No, we've pretty much got it down to a science now. The hunt requests come in, we all try to find job openings that will work, and the girlfriends get the offers. Often, the women end up in better circumstances, and everyone is happy. That's what we like to see happen."

# Chapter Seventeen
# New Direction

"Oh, I just love your hair!" Annette hugs me when I arrive at the meeting on Wednesday. "It looks amazing." I take off my shoes slowly. My arms are sore from the scuba lessons and the personal trainer from hell—Joseph.

*"Oweee."* I drop the shoes near the others.

"You're working out with Joseph, I see." She laughs as we walk to the sitting room. "How's it going so far?"

"Oh, you know, I'm in constant pain and agony, and I wish I could move my arms, but other than that, it's going okay." I walk over and pick up a glass of juice. No more banana-nut muffins for me, though. Joseph's orders.

"Sandra, we love your hair," people keep saying as Annette and I head to one of the couches. The compliments take some getting used to, and I actually have to stop myself from making sarcastic comebacks.

"Okay, let's get started everyone." Miriam opens her book and people stop talking. They all seem to be in a good mood.

"Sandra, we think we've come up with the perfect details for your setup," Martha says, her cane ready to start tapping at any moment.

"It's kind of a combination of ideas." Teresa leans forward in her chair, and I'm guessing part of the idea was hers. "It's combining Mike's love for underwater life—especially the manta thingies—with his love of acting and with his desire to produce."

"What we'll do is set you up as a researcher for an upcoming independent film project. We'll have you working for a director here in Texas who is interested in using mantas and other marine life in the film." Miriam is pointing at me with her pen.

Martha jumps in, "So, naturally, you'll have to go where the mantas are, observe them, research them for the film, work with your assistants, who will be on board with you—making you look all important—so you can give the information to your director."

"That sounds like fun." I'm a little concerned about the lying aspect of it, though, and I notice Lexi isn't at the meeting today.

"What a great idea." Annette smiles and writes it all down. "You'll have to learn some stuff, but it will be interesting stuff."

"We've done similar things like this before, only the idea was to do research for a book or other publication instead of a film," Miriam tells me. "It will also give Mike the incentive to be *reeeally* nice to you, so he can be a part of the movie project after the scuba trip. Get him here to Texas."

"But what about the film? Are we really going to make one?"

"The entertainment attorney, Herb, whom we know in Austin, says he has several possible scripts that can be adapted to include manta rays in it. Besides his law degree, Herb has a background in film, including a degree in mass communication from Texas Wesleyan University. He also has lots of connections with directors," Miriam tells me, and I'm relieved because maybe I won't be lying to Mike about researching for a film.

"We'll try to get you married before the film wraps. That way, if it works great, if it doesn't, well, you'll be married by then, and it won't matter," Liz says. "Film projects can take time. Snags develop with directors over which actor is going to do what and how a script will play out. So Mike won't be surprised if the film production is months away."

"Good work, y'all. I'm impressed," Rose says.

"Very impressed," Joyce adds from behind me.

"I have a question." Teresa raises her hand like we're in school or something. "How do we get Mike to take that particular scuba trip? We can't just randomly give him a prize and expect him to show up. He'll think the press is in on it as a publicity stunt or something."

"That's an interesting point. Even if we want to use the contest idea, we're probably going to have to have a legitimate entry from him into the contest," Martha says, and the cane tapping begins.

"Let's set it up to benefit a legitimate charity," Tammy says. "That way he'll have more incentive to enter."

"The question remains, though, how do we get that entry?"

"Who do we know out there that would be able to contact him?" Martha looks over at Miriam.

"I know!" Miriam has an epiphany. "Why not just contact his agent directly?"

"Sure, that should work." Liz looks through her notes.

"Liz, let's have Herb contact Mike's agent for us. She's bound to be more receptive to an attorney," Martha says.

"Okay, then, let's see if we can get the contest materials created. I'll contact the printer. Have an official entry form set up," Rose says, smiling. "I just love charity events. I'll be happy to check around and see whom we can donate the money to."

"When the official documents are ready, I'll send them over to Herb. He'll likely need to fax the agent some information." Miriam pulls out a yellow Post-it note, writes on it, then turns to look at me. "How are you doing, Sandra?"

"Fine. Relieved, now that we have a concrete plan."

"What do you think of the scuba lessons?"

"I think it's cool. I like it so far."

"She won't have to worry about being the champion diver, right?" Annette asks. "Since she's doing research, she'll have to go down and look around, but—"

"Right, there's no pressure to be a competitive diver or anything. You should still get as many dives in as you can before your trip, though. Just so you'll feel comfortable when the time comes and Mike is with you." Miriam smiles. I am feeling more and more excited by the minute, and I can actually see this working. Maybe.

"And Liz, you're helping her with the sims?" Rose asks.

"How does that work, exactly?" I hate to sound dumb, but all I really know is that it has something to do with a computer.

"It's a simple computer program that simulates different situations to predict the outcomes. Most people, including us, use it as part of a game. We've used it over the past several years to predict outcomes of some of our setups. So far, it's been reliable. It's like role-playing, only it's done on the computer," Liz tells me. "What I'll do is have you work with me on the different situations so you can see the best way to act to get the result you want."

"That actually sounds like fun."

"It is. And it lets you make mistakes here and now, instead of when you are actually with Mike." Liz turns again to the group. "Sandra and I are also working with Joseph to get her weight down before the trip. Those wet suits show everything."

"Everything? That's just great." My sarcastic side is suddenly showing.

"Don't worry. If you stick to what Joseph is telling you, you'll tone up and lose weight before the trip."

"But I need to lose like thirty pounds," I tell her, feeling somewhat proud of myself for losing ten pounds recently. Most likely due to the long walks back and forth to my car when I attend the meetings and no longer having pizza as my primary food group.

"What is the time frame now?" Rose asks.

"It depends. I guess we do need to set a date for the trip, especially if Mike is going to enter a contest," Miriam says.

"Let's give him two possible start dates for the trip. That way, he can decide which one is best for him." Liz looks at me. "How about a month? A month from this Saturday, I think, to get Sandra completely ready, mentally, physically, and scuba-ly."

"Okay, a month from Saturday. And then make two weeks

after that be the other option Mike can choose if he prefers." Miriam opens her pocket calendar. "Sound okay, Sandra?"

"Sounds fine to me. Can I lose weight that fast?"

"You can, if you're careful. And the toning will help, too," Annette tells me. "For my wedding I did that. Of course, you have to do everything Joseph says and watch what you eat the whole time. You can do it, though. Just don't overdo it. No guy is worth getting sick over."

"We really haven't found anything more that shows he only likes the skinny people," Teresa says. "I know he dates models and actresses, but Sammy told us Mike always insists the girls wear regular old T-shirts and shorts, like he does. I mean, it's not like he's obsessed with how they look or that he tries to make them look thin."

"That's good to know. You wouldn't want him if he's obsessed with skinny," Miriam says. "Just do the best you can, and I'm sure it will be fine."

"I guess I'll just see what happens." I'm embarrassed talking about my weight in a room full of people.

"I'll also reserve some time at Daireds for right before the trip. To get your hair done again, your nails and makeup, and to relax in their wonderful Spa Pangéa. Get rid of that stress," Liz tells me.

"I wonder if we should have Sandra learn about some film stuff?" Charlotte asks. "That way, she'll have more in common when she talks to Mike, and it will add legitimacy for when she does the research on the sea creatures."

"That's a good idea; who do we know locally who can give her a lesson in film studies?" Miriam looks at Martha again for the answer.

"Why not just contact Wesleyan or SMU? See if we can find

a student in TV and film who wants to make some money by tutoring her?"

"Believe me, Sandra, studying the movie industry is far more interesting—and easier—than trying to learn the marine biology stuff." Miriam laughs, and so do I. I can already tell I'll like the film stuff.

When I get back to my apartment, there is a message from Jerry, asking me if I'm coming to work tonight. I'm exhausted and in pain from Joseph's torture during our session after the meeting. I can't see going back to work there. For one thing, I can't break my diet. And if I'm around pizza all night, and there are slices available, I don't know if I can pass that up. Right now, Dawn, the nutritionist, has me eating three healthy small meals during the day, and a slightly larger meal, cooked by her, for dinner. Pizza is not on the menu.

I sit down on the couch and look at the schedule that Liz printed for me. Liz says there is flexibility if something comes up, but from where I sit, there's really no way I can work anymore, not with what I have to do: from scuba, to meeting with the nutritionist, to workouts with Joseph, meeting with Liz, working with the film student, and sleeping.

# Chapter Eighteen
# My Setup

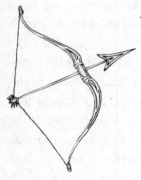

I park my car down the street out of habit; everyone knows what car I drive now, but the exercise from walking up the hill to Miriam's does me good. I'm no longer out of breath when I get there, and I'm relieved to have lost almost twenty pounds. Joseph is lucky to still be alive on some days, but overall, the workouts haven't been that terrible.

"Are you nervous?" Annette asks me as we walk to the sitting room.

"Yes, completely nervous."

"Where's Amber? Has anybody seen Amber?" Teresa asks, taking her seat.

"Martha and Miriam are in the dining room with her now. I guess they really want her to decide about Brantley," Liz says.

"Has she heard anything?"

"Not a word. If he was going to contact her, I'm afraid he would by now." Liz is whispering for some reason.

"So, what happens now?" I ask.

"It's up to Amber. She can always choose another guy from Week One, and we can start over."

"She sounded pretty sure she wanted Brantley, though. No matter what it takes." Annette sips her mimosa.

"Then, there's always plan B. I think that's what they're talking about now," Liz says with a sigh.

"What is plan B exactly? Where we set them up again, right?" I hate that I still don't know all the processes and procedures for the Hunt Club. But I figure, if I don't ask, how will I know?

No one says anything for a minute.

"It's where Brantley is offered a better job down here, and things are arranged so that he'll want to move here. That way, he'll be flung back into Amber's life. See if we can stir things back up between them," Liz says. "It's pretty drastic, but it has worked in the past."

"I can't imagine something like that happening. What kind of job would a Senate advisory guy find that's better in Dallas?" I ask, and no one really answers me.

"You'd be surprised." Annette and Liz both laugh.

"Tomorrow is the big day!" Rose walks across the room and hugs me. Miriam and Martha are right behind her. But no sign of Amber. "I'm so proud of you! You've accomplished a lot in the past month."

"Sorry for running a bit late, ladies." Miriam sits in her usual chair. "Liz, does everyone know what time to be at DFW this evening?" Miriam asks. We're flying to Hawaii at night, so hopefully the screaming babies will be asleep.

"Yes, we need to be there two hours early for check-in."

"Okay, I'll try to have my cell phone on, in case anyone here needs to reach me. Annette, are you and Christine ready to be Sandra's assistants?" Miriam begins going down a list, as usual.

"I'm ready."

"Me, too."

"Sandra, dear, are you all packed?"

"Liz is coming over after the meeting to make sure I have everything and to go shopping one last time. I had to practically buy a whole new wardrobe."

"Your hair looks fabulous," Rose says. "And you look fabulous. Mike is going to love you." I still have my doubts, but I hate to admit them to anybody. It makes me feel a little better knowing that Annette will be there.

"What about scuba gear?" Tammy asks.

"They let you use the stuff on the boat," Miriam tells her. "Do we want to go over Sandra's research again?"

"No, we've got it." Christine laughs, holding up the pages of our worn-out role-plays. We've got the conversations down perfectly.

"Miriam, you confirmed with Herb that he's spoken with Mike's agent? Mike's got his ticket and everything?" Martha asks.

"Yes. We were lucky that Mike's agent was so enthusiastic about our contest. Even if Mike isn't into saving the environment, apparently his agent is—she practically begged him to buy a chance to win the trip."

"And I also checked on Sabre," Liz tells us. "He's confirmed on the flight leaving this afternoon from LAX."

"Too bad you couldn't have ended up on the same plane," Rose says.

"No, that's too soon. We're going to just let things go according to plan," Miriam tells her. "We'll arrive in Honolulu tomorrow and take a flight to the Big Island to meet at the boat at five-thirty."

"What about the girlfriend? Sofia?" Teresa asks.

"She's already in Paris. Got a great gig there." Miriam laughs. "Looks like she'll be there for six months or more."

"I hear Paris is beautiful this time of year," Joyce says.

"Sandra, did you get your scuba certification taken care of?" Martha asks.

"Yes, and I've done about fifteen actual dives now. So, I'm excited."

"I wish we could have found a way to get to know him on a more personal level. To make sure he's as good a guy as we think he is." Miriam looks over at me.

"We've gotten some great info, Miriam. I think it's pretty obvious he's a good person. He's loyal to his friends. He takes his craft seriously. Loves animals. No restraining orders out against him or anything." Liz laughs.

"Just remember, Sandra, if you meet Mike and decide he's not right for you, that's okay," Martha says, and she sounds like she's giving a speech. "If he ends up being a jerk or something, we have no problem with you picking another prospect."

"That's true," Rose says and nods. "But, I wouldn't worry. I've got a good feeling about him."

"I think we all have done really well with this hunt," Joyce says. "And we all want to go to Hawaii with you!"

"Here's a toast to Sandra!" Miriam holds up her mimosa.

"To Sandra!"

Liz helps me get everything packed into my oversized *Barney*-purple suitcase. We arrive at DFW two hours early for check-in. Our flight stops in Houston before going on to Hawaii. The flight to Honolulu doesn't go as smoothly as I had hoped, and the turbulence makes it difficult to sleep. It's still hard for me to imagine how some place so far away can be a part of the United States. Annette, Christine, and I are exhausted by the time our flight lands in Honolulu, but the adrenaline has us all pumped up nevertheless. We're almost like giddy school girls as we walk through the airport.

"Miriam, do you think we'll have time to freshen up before we get to the boat?" I ask as we head to the gate for our flight to the Big Island.

"Yes, of course. We don't have to be at Kailua-Kona Bay until five thirty, and we'll take a limo from the airport. And if the Keahole Airport is as lovely as this one," she says, gesturing around Honolulu's open airport. "We can even stop and catch our breath."

"I just want to look okay, in case we run into Mike first thing."

"We arranged to get there about an hour before the other guests."

"Who else will be there?" Annette asks, and we finally arrive at the Hawaiian Airlines counter.

"Let's see, I have a list Liz gave me. Should be an older couple. And I think two married couples on their honeymoons. Sandra and Mike are the only single ones who will be on the boat with us."

We walk down the ramp to get on the small plane.

"Remember, Sandra," Miriam says, sitting in the seat next to me. "You don't know who Mike is. You have no idea he's an actor. And when you hear that he is, it really doesn't matter because you're not impressed with that kind of thing."

"Right. I'm there to work, dammit! And I'm around luscious blue-eyed actors all the time. They don't even faze me."

"They bore you, because you hate publicity and hype. You consider acting an art form." Miriam is trying not to laugh, I can tell.

"There's a captain's reception tonight, right?" Christine leans over the aisle to ask us.

"Yes, along with a buffet-style dinner. I think that is when we'll get to scope out Mike for the first time."

"I can't believe I'm actually going to see him." I've imagined it a hundred times in my mind, but it still seems surreal to think Mike Warren is going to be in the same room with me. Not to mention that it's us who have brought him here.

"Well, believe it, dear. You're about to spend a week with him."

As the plane lands, memories of how I've blown important events in the past seem to hit me all at once. I can't remember ever pulling something off successfully or having the good luck other people manage to have so easily. It would be wonderful for something good to happen, but I'm braced for things not to work. Part of me wishes for a second that I could back out. Maybe have some more time to prepare?

The warm sun and humidity greet us as we step outside of the Keahole Airport. Beautiful brightly colored flowers surround us, and the limo pulls into the passenger loading lane to pick us up. Taking a deep breath, I realize it's too late to turn back now.

"Now THAT is what I call a boat," Annette says, stepping out of the limo when we arrive at Kailua-Kona Bay. The stewards from the boat gather our suitcases for us, and we walk down the dock to the eighty-foot catamaran. All of a sudden,

I'm nervous and not feeling so well. Somehow, I have been the one to create all this. Me, the chubby pizza girl with the silver Hyundai.

The stewards show us to our staterooms. Annette and I are in one room, and Miriam and Christine are in the other. They both open out to a short hallway to the salon. I'm glad I ignored my initial impulse to ask if a hairdresser was on board. The salon has couches and a big screen TV, a wet bar, and a long formal dining table. I have a feeling this is one of the places where people will be hanging out when we're not in the water. The other area for hanging out is the upper deck, which has lounge chairs and a hot tub.

"I'll let you have the bottom, since you're the bride-to-be," Annette says, putting her rolling suitcase under the bottom queen-sized bed and then climbing on the single bunk above it. I open my bag and start hanging up some of my outfits. Somehow, Liz was able to pack everything in a way that prevents a lot of wrinkles. She also packed a note for me, telling me what I should wear on different occasions.

"I hope these plugs can handle my curling iron." I plug in the iron and turn it on. Next, I unpack my makeup. "I wonder if he's here yet?"

"Want me to go check?" Annette jumps down off the top bunk.

"Yes, that would be great." I'm washing off the old makeup to start applying the new as Annette walks out into the salon. I hear muffled voices, which means the other new arrivals must be in the salon, too.

After redoing my hair the way Liz and I practiced with the stylist at Daireds, along with my makeup, I walk to the tiny closet area. The reception is supposed to be formal, but apparently in Hawaii "formal" can mean your hair is brushed, and you're wearing flip-flops. I decide to put on one of my new sundresses for now. When it's time for the reception, I'll put on the strapless black dress.

There's a soft knock at the door. "Sandra, it's me," Annette whispers so loudly she might as well have just used her regular voice. I open the door for her, and she slips in. "HE'S HERE!"

"Really? Oh my gosh, here, zip me up!" My fingers are shaking now. "Where is he? How does he look?"

"He's on the back of the boat—I forget the name for that— anyway, he's looking over the scuba equipment and talking to the staff." Annette is talking really fast. "I only saw him for a split second, because you know I didn't want to seem obvious or anything, but oh my gosh, Sandra, he is so good-looking!" We're both laughing like junior high girls who just left a note in some cute boy's locker.

"Pinch me, Annette, I can't believe we're actually here."

"Miriam and Christine are already in the salon, and they said one of them would casually come let us know when he comes to the salon so you can make your grand entrance." Annette brushes her hair and changes into a cute shorts outfit, while I sit on the lower bunk and put on my strappy heels.

"Girls," Miriam's voice comes through the door when she knocks, and Annette lets her in. "Okay, Mike is in the salon, and so are the other arrivals. Everyone has made introductions, and they're getting drinks from the bar. So, Sandra, dear, whenever you're ready." She smiles at me. "You look absolutely beautiful."

"Thanks, I'm so nervous." I stand up and fluff out my sundress. It's amazing to think how much I've changed in just a matter of weeks. The old me would probably never have worn a sundress.

"Remember now, you don't want to make eye contact with him or anything that would indicate you know who he is. Just ignore him unless you're introduced, and then act like you don't know who he is."

"Right, no problem. I've been practicing my unimpressed look all day."

"Some of the other passengers have already mentioned that there's a director's assistant on board doing research for a movie, and he seemed really interested in that. It looks like things are going as we planned."

"What are the other passengers like?" Annette asks.

"They're nice. There will only be nine of us plus the crew, it turns out. You, me, Sandra, Christine, Mike, one newlywed couple in their twenties, and then one old couple celebrating an anniversary. Mike is the only one with his own room, but Sandra, you know the rules."

"Don't worry. At all. I have no intention of deviating from the plan like Amber did."

"You, Mike, the elderly couple, and maybe the groom are the only ones besides the crew who will be diving. The rest of us will be snorkeling," Miriam tells me, walking to the door and waiting for me.

"There's also snuba," I remind her. "Which is kind of snorkeling and scuba put together, only you don't go as deep and don't have to have all the equipment like scuba."

"We'll see. I'm not really big on sea creatures. But you're the boss, here."

"So if I say jump overboard, you WILL jump overboard."

"Exactly."

"Okay, I'm ready," I say finally, taking a deep breath.

"Me, too," Annette says.

"Don't forget to breathe," Miriam tells us as she opens the door. We follow her down the short hallway into the salon. It looks like your basic living room, only with windows that overlook the ocean and the decks. I glance casually around the room and smile at the people who look up at us. The married couple is intertwined on the leather couch. The elderly couple is talking to them, and then here comes Christine. Where is Mike?

"You look beautiful," Christine tells me and hands me a glass of champagne.

"Thanks," I smile and then lean toward her to whisper, "Where's Mike?"

"I guess he went to his stateroom. He'll probably be here any second."

"You must be Sandra?" A gray-haired gentleman wearing a bright orange-and-white-flowered shirt extends his hand to me.

"Yes, Sandra Greene." I shake his hand, firmly, just like Liz showed me.

"I'm George Waltman, and this is my wife Gloria Waltman." He gestures to his wife, who comes over. She has a nice smile, and I notice she is wearing really fun sunglasses.

"Well, hello. We hear you are in the movie business. I can't wait to hear all about that," Gloria tells me as she shakes my hand.

"Yes, and what do y'all do?"

"Oh, honey, we're retired." Gloria says, and they laugh. "George is a retired engineer, and my job is to chase our adorable grandchildren around. Would you like to see their pictures?"

"Yes," I tell her, "absolutely, but maybe a little later?"

"Oh, sure." Gloria looks disappointed. All I can think about is Mike right now. I glance over at the different doors to the salon, just aching for him to come through one of them.

"Hi, there, we're the Montecellos," the new husband greets me as I walk past. "I'm Dick, and this is Sherry." They have on matching shorts outfits, and it's very obvious they are newly-weds.

"Nice to meet you. I'm Sandra Greene."

"Is this your first time to the Big Island?"

"Yes, it is."

"We love it here. You must go to Volcanoes National Park," Sherry tells me. "Oh, and the coffee plantations."

I try to smile, but I am so nervous that I can barely stand still. I know that if I have to stand here and listen to descriptions of all the tourist attractions in Hawaii, I will scream. Then I glance over to the door leading to the staterooms, and I see a dark head of hair appear behind George and Gloria. Then the face. Then the rest of him. It's Mike. I quickly look over at Dick and Sherry, as if fascinated by their descriptions of lava flows.

"Have you already gone to see all that?" I ask, and I notice out of the corner of my eye that Miriam, Christine, and Annette have dispersed to find something to look at or do. I take a sip of champagne and try not to look over at Mike. Easier said than done.

"Oh, we've been here two weeks already. After this trip is when we'll head back home," Sherry tells me.

"Sandra, dear," Gloria says as she walks up behind me. I turn to see her and George standing there with Mike. I smile at Gloria, gluing my eyes to her. "Have you met Mike?"

"No, I haven't." I smile casually. "Is this your son?" I shake his hand, almost having to talk myself through it in my mind. He smiles at my comment; he has an amazing smile.

"No, no, this is Mike Warren," Gloria tells me, "from California."

"He's an actor," George says, and I nod as if I hear this kind of thing every day. I'm pretty much on automatic pilot, just going through the motions like Liz and I are practicing it back at Miriam's house.

"Well, it's nice to meet you, even if you aren't the son of George and Gloria." I laugh.

"You, too," Mike says and smiles as our eyes meet. He's just a little taller than I am in my heels. And standing there, larger than life, he is even better looking than on TV. His blue eyes, and his dark hair all kind of messy, with a few strands hanging in his eyes. Those lips . . . I have to tell myself to look away . . . to the side door that is opening, and other people are entering.

"Good evening, fellow passengers." A gray-haired couple, the man in a naval uniform, and the woman in shorts and a T-shirt, enters the salon. "May I present your captain? This is my husband, Captain Bobby. And I am Skipper Janis. We will be your hosts for the next seven days."

"We are just about to shove off in a few minutes. And then we'll have a reception to get to know each other. The buffet-style dinner will also be served," Captain Bobby tells us, as we each step forward to shake his hand and introduce ourselves. Then Captain Bobby turns to leave, probably to get our adventure started.

"I think I'll freshen up," I say to the group in general, not focusing on Mike. "Excuse me." I very slowly walk down the hall to our stateroom. A loud horn blasts suddenly, making me almost jump out of my shoes. Then I feel the boat moving slowly away from the dock.

There's a soft knock at the door, and then it opens and I'm joined by my coconspirators.

"You did so great!" Annette giggles once the door is closed. She walks over and bounces on the edge of the bottom bunk.

"It was perfect," Miriam tells me. "Better than rehearsal."

"He is sooo good-looking. I was afraid to look at him, like I'd melt or something."

"You did pick a great one," Christine tells me and sits down next to Annette.

"It's really hard not to gush, you know? It's hard not to be nice to him. I want to go hold his drink for him or something."

"Just be patient. He's used to the gushers," Miriam says.

"I'm trying." I put my hand over my heart as if trying to somehow slow down the beating. "It was like being outside of myself, watching. I could see myself throwing my arms around him. Tackle him, right in the middle of the salon."

"I don't blame you," Annette says. "Those eyes alone would be enough to make me pounce on him." We look at her for a second, and she blushes. "I mean, if I weren't married, of course."

"Of course," Christine and Miriam say at the same time.

"They've got to be colored contacts. I don't think normal eyes come in that color of blue, do they?" Annette asks.

"Did you see when the sun from the window hit them? They were like glowing almost." I laugh.

"That's his real eye color. We double-checked on that because it was hard to believe they were real back when we saw the video of the TV show he was in," Christine says and shakes her head in disbelief. "He's so good-looking, it makes you almost want to go call someone. Like *National Geographic* or something."

"Some of us should probably go out there and mingle," Miriam says.

"I'll go." Annette stands up. "I'm dying to get back out there."

"Me, too," Christine says. They leave the room while Miriam and I sit on the lower bunk bed. "We'll be back to let you know when the reception starts."

"This is a lovely bedspread," Miriam tells me, running her hand over the different bright colors. I can't believe she's focusing on the bedspread right now.

"I couldn't even tell you what the names of those other people are. I'm so nervous."

"There's plenty of time, so don't panic. You're doing great. As soon as the reception gets under way, we'll let you make another grand entrance in your strapless black dress."

When Christine and Annette come back to tell us the reception has started, Miriam and I make our way back to the salon. The black strapless dress fits perfectly, accenting the parts of me I want accented and concealing the parts I don't. I walk carefully in my heels and realize I can't really feel my feet because I'm so nervous. The smell of seafood and spices greets us when we enter the room.

"Wow, doesn't she look beautiful?" Gloria says when she sees me. She's sitting at the table with George and Mike. I notice Mike as he turns to look at me, and then I smile at Dick and Sherry, who don't appear to have moved since the last time we saw them. Captain Bobby and Janis are talking to the attendant at the buffet, and then they turn to greet me.

"Good evening." Captain Bobby shakes my hand again.

"Good evening." I smile at them. They lead Miriam and me over to the long formal table, while Annette and Christine speak to Dick and Sherry.

"Have you met everyone?"

"Yes, I believe so." I sit down next to Gloria, across from Mike. Liz coached me to always try to sit at an angle where Mike can still see my dress and my toned legs—thanks to Joseph. But, now that I'm actually here, it feels like I'm being too obvious. It's difficult to focus on what Liz has taught me when Mike is just a few feet away. I wonder if he can tell I'm shaking. I figure, if I have to, I'll go speak to Sherry again in a few minutes. That will make sure he notices me. I force myself to smile at Miriam as she sits down next to me.

"Can I get you something from our bar?" the steward asks me as Bobby and Janis move to greet the other guests.

"A glass of white wine, please," I say. I notice Mike is drinking a beer—but I remember from Liz's statistics that Mike hates it when women drink beer.

"You must try the fish buffet, Sandra," George tells me, placing an unidentified fish on his plate.

"I know. It smells wonderful. Almost like Cajun-style, which is my favorite." I stand up slowly to go look at the buffet.

"I love Cajun, too," Mike says. "But not the big chain restaurants."

"Right, you have to go to the Louisiana coast. Like where my relatives live." I'm looking over the buffet, and none of it really appeals to me.

"I didn't know you had relatives on the coast," Miriam says, and she's being truthful. I don't think I've ever mentioned it.

"Yes, in New Iberia." I turn and smile at the group, feeling like I'm performing in a play. "My uncle Buddy makes the best Cajun gumbo."

"Now that's what I'm talking about," Mike says in a Cajun accent. Sort of.

"Miriam, would you like something from the buffet?" It's my way of saying get your butt over here, and help me figure out what I should eat.

The first evening on the ship goes along pretty much as Liz predicted. Captain Bobby and Janis sit with us at the formal dining table, and my only real objective is to make sure I sound polite when I talk to everyone. I was given strict instructions not to get into heavy discussion with Mike yet. But it's difficult not to make him the center of attention.

Captain Bobby shows us DVDs his crew has made of the different diving locations we will be visiting. The underwater shots are beautiful, but I've looked at so many books and videos over the past few weeks showing the same kind of things, that it's hard to keep watching. Mike is shifting in his seat, and I know he's seen this kind of thing a hundred times as well.

"Sandra, I know you're going to like this next section on the manta rays," Captain Bobby tells us as video appears on the screen of the freaky-looking creatures swimming toward the camera. "You'll get to meet most of these."

"Has Lefty been seen around here lately?" I ask him, trying to sound like I know what I'm talking about. I practically memorized the Manta Pacific Research Foundation Web site.

"You might get to see her. You'll have to ask some of the guides," Bobby says over the tranquil music that accompanies the video. "What Sandra is talking about is one of the mantas named Lefty, because her left front fin has been damaged."

"Her cephalic fin just hangs limp, often blocking her mouth," I tell them.

"You've been diving here before?" Mike asks me.

"Not here, but I've been researching these mantas in particular."

"She's doing a film that will include them," Gloria tells him, and I almost laugh at how much she and her husband are helping our hunt.

"Using the mantas?" Mike asks and looks over at me.

"Yes, the water clarity here is perfect for our project. We are also shooting in Panama, but the manta rays here are my favorites and will likely be the ones I recommend for the movie. Depending on my research findings this trip." I almost get the practiced script verbatim.

"Those are amaaazing," Sherry says from the other side of the room. "I had no idea creatures like that existed."

"They look hollow," Dick observes. "Where does the food go?"

"They're pretty much wings with eyes," I say again. "When I first saw one, I remember thinking it looks like there's a piece missing—like its head." Several people laugh at my comments, including Mike.

"They're like big filters. Filtering out the plankton but letting the other stuff go right through," Mike says. I have to laugh. I never thought I'd be bonding with a guy over big-ass, freaky manta rays.

"What exactly is plankton?" Dick asks, "Is that like a plant?"

"No." Mike laughs a little. "Plankton is thumbnail-sized larval fish, octopus, lobsters, and microscopic mysids."

"Shrimplike animals," I add, and Mike nods.

Captain Bobby's video continues to show other dive sites and the fish we'll encounter. He also says there are plenty of videos they have for us to watch if we want to play "name that fish" before a dive so we'll know what we're looking at.

"Sandra, will your movie have other critters besides the ray in them?" George asks me.

"Sure, we'll have background cast—you know, the 'extras'—so to speak. We want to create the realistic environment," I tell him, noticing that Mike is listening. "One of the reasons we're here is so I can determine which 'critters,' as you call them, would be good in the movie."

"I'd be a good critter in the movie," Dick says and then turns to look at Sherry. "Don't you think?"

"You are a very good critter, honey." Sherry pats him on the head. You can certainly tell they're newlyweds.

After the video, the Captain and Skipper turn in for the night, leaving the rest of us to watch movies and play board games. When I walk to the bar for another glass of wine, Miriam catches up to me.

"You should say your good-nights pretty soon. Act like you have work to do. You don't want to give out too much information the first night," she whispers. "But don't worry, we'll talk about you while you're gone." I'm not thrilled with the idea of leaving, but everyone at the last meeting seemed to say the same thing about not sharing too much too soon.

"Well, good night everyone," I say casually, walking across the salon. "It was nice to meet all of you."

"You going to bed so soon?" Sherry asks me, sitting almost on top of Dick as they play Scrabble with Mike and George. I'm not sure where Gloria went.

"Yes, and I've got some work to do before our first dive tomorrow. This really isn't a vacation for me." I smile.

"Damn, I wish I had her job," I hear Sherry say.

I walk back to the stateroom and change out of my strapless black sundress into a pair of shorts and a T-shirt. It is torture having to sit in the stateroom while someone like Mike is in the next room playing Scrabble. We could be strolling on the upper deck right now. Or be in the hot tub.

I hang up my dress and sit down on my bed with a loud sigh. I was finally feeling more comfortable around Mike and could actually walk, talk, and breathe at the same time in front of him. The slow pace of the hunt is going to drive me crazy, but I know it would be a bad idea to get too close too fast. And I know we don't want him to spend time with me just because there aren't other single women here. The sims reports showed I have to let Mike make all the moves, and I have to appear to develop an interest in him over time. I know the Hunt Club would probably kill me if I made the mistakes Amber did. Not that I'm anywhere near that being an option. It seems impossible to imagine being that close to him.

Vic, our head scuba guide for the day, draws little pictures on a marker board to show the terrain for our first dive. We're all in our wet suits, getting our tanks ready. I have to admit that I like my wet suit now. At first, it was like death putting it on; it highlighted every bump and bulge. But, thanks to Joseph, my stomach is much flatter, and I have muscles where muscles should be. I can't help but notice Mike's muscles as well; he looks yummy in his wet suit.

Miriam is out here with me, keeping me company while we prepare our equipment and hear the safety speeches. I am pleased when I notice Mike checking me out. That never ever happens to me. I'm usually invisible when it comes to good-looking guys like him. It's an uncomfortable feeling, knowing that he is looking so closely at me. Not that I'm complaining. I just wonder how women get used to this.

"We're going to be filming another DVD of the dives. You

each will get one, and we'll use it to show the future passengers," Skipper Janis tells me.

That's my cue, I think to myself.

"Janis," I say softly, yet loud enough for Mike to hear. "I would prefer if they didn't film me."

"Oh, really?"

"Yes, if you don't mind. It's just being in the industry and everything."

"You'd think you'd be used to it." She laughs.

"Well, I am used to the filming. I just don't like . . ." I pause as if I'm trying to find the right words, ". . . the publicity."

"Well, okay, then. What about just not your face? We really need the rest of you."

I sigh. "I guess that's fine, like with my mask on or something. I just don't like to be used in the promotions."

"I'll tell Bobby and Shawn. That's not a problem."

"Skipper Janis," I hear Mike's sweet, deep voice behind me as I walk back to put my tank on as well as my bright yellow flippers. "I'd prefer the same thing."

"No face shots?" Janis asks. I guess Mike must have nodded back to her. "Well, okay. No faces filmed of Mike, either. Anyone else?" She laughs. "We'll make it a faceless video."

I'm given the thumbs-up from the guy, Joey, who is walking around checking everyone's equipment. I walk to the dive deck, where another crew member is waiting.

"This is so funny," I whisper to Miriam. "I never thought there'd be a time when people would be having to put weight *on* me." Terrance, one of the dive guides, fastens a weight belt on me.

"You look adorable." Miriam laughs loudly, and I notice that the other divers—Mike included—are now behind me. "Break a leg."

"No, Miriam, I don't think you say that in these situations." I laugh at her as Terrance checks my tanks for me again. There are several guides going with us, and two of them go in first, followed by me. I have it set in my mind that I won't swim around Mike. I'll just follow the guides and act like I'm checking stuff out—not touching, though. They're really big about that. You can't touch the coral or anything growing down there. And since I'm still not sure what is growing and what isn't, I fold my arms to keep from touching stuff.

The mantas aren't out during the day, but some of the other creatures are just as freaky looking. The water is so clear and blue that it almost feels fake—like I'm in an aquarium back in Fair Park. The dive is so beautiful that for a second I have to remind myself why I'm here—for Mike.

After the magnificent dive, which was uneventful as far as Mike is concerned, everyone changes out of their wet suits and heads to the upper deck. We'll wait at least forty-five minutes between dives, with most people getting in the hot tub or sunbathing. I walk back to our stateroom to redo my hair. This natural flippy, cute cut I have sure takes a lot of time to look "natural." I wrap a multicolored sarong around the bottom half of my one-piece bathing suit—the part untouched by the sun in years and years, making me thankful for self-tanners. I head back to the upper deck.

"Would you like a mimosa?" Christine asks me, from her spot on one of the lounge chairs where she is drinking one and enjoying the sunshine.

"No, thanks. They won't let you dive if you've been drinking."

"You become a snorkeler until the next day," Mike says, walking past us to the soft drink bar. He's wearing blue swim trunks and that's it. Except for his sunglasses. He is so hot with his wet hair and that body. He's like a magnet. I try not to watch him, instead sitting on the lounge chair next to Christine. Thankfully, when I put my sunglasses on, it's impossible to tell if I'm enjoying the beautiful ocean view or the beautiful Mike view.

With his Dr Pepper in hand, Mike walks over to the railing of the boat directly in our view and leans against it, facing away from us. If I didn't know better, I'd think he did that so we could study his perfect body.

"Where are Miriam and Annette?"

"Still snorkeling, I think," Christine tells me.

"You didn't want to go with them?"

"I snorkeled a little. Till I swallowed half the ocean. Then I decided to take a break."

"I don't think you're supposed to do that." I feel bad for laughing at her.

"Now you tell me," she says, leaning over toward me so the others can't hear us. "How are things going?"

"I feel like nothing is happening," I whisper to her. "I wish we could pick things up a little bit. I hate acting like he's a stranger."

"I know how you feel. I went through the same thing with my hunt for George. Believe me, the Hunt Club members are experts at this kind of thing. They practically have it down to a science. All you have to do is follow the plan. He'll come around. Don't worry."

The forty-five minutes go by fairly quickly, and we head back to the dive deck to watch Vic draw the terrain on his little marker board again. I'm back into my wet suit, adjusting my tank, when Annette comes out to check on me.

"How are things going?"

"Fine, and how are y'all doing? Getting any work done?" I casually glance over at Mike, who is helping George with his tank.

"A little. We're headed that way now. I'll have the laptop ready to go to record your notes."

"Thanks, great. I'll check in with you after the dive." I step back into my bright yellow fins.

"What are you looking for this dive, Sandra?" George asks me, and I have to think for a minute.

"I want to scout backdrops, mainly. Not that Vic isn't an excellent artist." I wave at Vic who is still over by his marker board. "We need to get some good marine scenes. Different types of coral formations, that kind of thing. I want to see for myself what the colorful creatures living in the coral look like."

"You'll get to see the lava tube today with the squirrel fish, frog fish, octopus, and reef sharks, but you'll probably really like tomorrow's dives," Vic says, smiling at me. "There are two caves you can swim through, Skull cave and Suck-'em-up cave. You'll probably see the white tip reef shark, trumpet fish, puffers, lobsters, and parrot fish."

"That sounds great. I can't wait," I tell him, thinking that if I were actually here to scuba, I'd be really happy right now.

# Chapter Nineteen
# Manta Madness

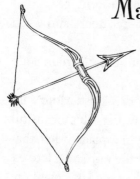

The following day is a picture-perfect replica of the day before. Same people hanging out, same types of dives, and still just brief, polite small talk with Mike. I feel like I am spinning my wheels here.

After dinner, a vote is taken, and we get to watch *Jaws* on DVD. The perfect movie when you're out on a boat, miles from shore. Not to mention how it sticks in the back of your mind while you're diving. As we are all saying good night at the end of the evening when the movie is finally over, Vic stops by the salon to see how everyone is doing.

"When is the manta ray dive?" Annette asks him as we walk to the hallway toward the staterooms.

"We'll do several, since that is what was requested for this trip. The first one is tomorrow night," Vic says. "We'll go north of Honokohau Harbor."

"It was ranked one of the top ten dives in the world by *National Geographic*," Mike says.

"Great, that's what we want." I turn to look at my "assistants" and try to sound businesslike. "Be sure y'all are ready after tomorrow night's dive. Miriam, see if we can schedule a meeting with the different dive guides the following morning."

"I'm on it," Annette tells me, turns on her heels, and walks into our stateroom.

"I'll set up the laptop for when you get back," Miriam adds.

The next morning, we go on a dive after breakfast. More coral formations, frog fish, squirrel fish, and puffers. It's beautiful, but I'm dying to spend time with Mike in a place other than underwater. After the dive, we gather on the upper deck to eat lunch. Mike and I are talking to each other, but so is everyone else. I feel frustrated that I'm not getting an opportunity to be alone with him so we can get to know each other.

"We'll I guess I'd better take a nap if I want to go on the dives later."

"Same here," Mike says. He follows me down the stairs to the salon.

"Have you been on this exact dive before?" My heart is pounding as I ask him when we're inside the salon.

"You mean the one we just finished?" He looks at me. He's actually several inches taller than I am, now that I'm not in heels.

I smile at him. "No, I mean the manta dive."

"Oh, yeah. Lots of times. If I can help answer questions or anything, just give me a yell." He smiles back at me, and all of a sudden the trip has been worth it.

"That would be great, thanks. I'll probably have questions after the dive."

"Anytime." He heads to his stateroom, and I go to mine.

Of course, I have a hard time falling asleep now.

Annette wakes me up for dinner, and I almost forget where I am. I take a quick shower in the world's smallest bathroom, then start the procedures for getting my hair to look 'natural' again.

"If anyone ever tells you that short hair is easy, and you can just wash and go, don't believe them," I tell Annette as she fills me in on Mike's activities this afternoon. He slept for several hours and then hung out on the top deck playing Scrabble.

"He's currently taking a shower before dinner."

"Is it formal tonight?"

"If you mean do we need to wear shoes, then yes. Otherwise, everyone seems pretty casual."

"Except me and my sundresses."

"Hey, don't get discouraged. You're doing great. Everything is going according to plan. You're here to work, remember?"

"At least we'll get to see the damn mantas tonight." I had no idea the waiting and timing of the hunt would be so painful. I put on my blue denim sundress with the short skirt and sandals. Looking casual, just like Mikey likes, at least according to his buddy Sammy. Tomorrow, Liz's schedule says I can start wearing shorts and T-shirts, which are Mike's favorites as well as mine.

The crew serves us a variety of seafood again, some of which I can't identify. I take the seat that Miriam saved me between her and George, as Mike comes in wearing khaki shorts and a T-shirt. The sun has made his face a nice tan color with just a touch of sunburn. He sits down across from George.

"Where are the honeymooners?" Christine asks.

"Do you really have to ask?" Miriam says. "I'm surprised we've seen as much of them as we have."

"So, what's on the agenda tonight?" George puts a bite of fish into his mouth.

"We've got the manta dive, remember?" I ask him.

"I'm not sure I can make another dive tonight. I'm pretty exhausted. How about a big game of Scrabble?"

"I'll play Scrabble," Christine says.

"Me, too," Annette raises her hand.

"We've got work to do, though," Miriam reminds them.

"No, that's fine. Play Scrabble. Just have the laptop ready for when the dive is over so I can enter my notes," I tell them.

"I'll also meet with Vic and get the oceanography descriptions."

"Good."

"Looks like it's just us, then," Mike tells me.

I smile at him for a second. "Yes, but we'll miss you, George. You'll get another chance tomorrow night, though. It's the mantas at the airport, right?"

"Not exactly *at* the airport." Mike laughs, and I love the way it sounds. "But, yes, near the airport. At a place called Garden Eel Cove."

"You'd think the noise from the planes would scare them off," Gloria says.

"Do they even have ears?" Annette asks.

"They don't exactly have heads," I say.

"I guess they might feel the vibrations, though." George is now eating the leftover fish from Gloria's plate. I'm determined I won't do that when I get married. When Mike and I get married, that is.

"The mantas can get used to anything." I smile at Gloria. "I also read that plankton are at the highest concentration out there."

"Aren't plankton really sea monkeys?" Annette asks, and we all just look at her. "I mean, I remember hearing that sea monkeys are those tiny shrimp things." She's embarrassed now.

"It's possible." Mike laughs at her. "I bet the mantas would eat your sea monkeys."

I can't help but wonder if Mike finds it strange that no one is asking him about his acting career or commenting on the shows or movies he's done. Instead, we're talking about sea monkeys.

"Okay, you both know the guidelines, right? No touching the mantas. They have a protective coating that will come off if you do, and then they'll be more susceptible to injury. Don't blow bubbles in their faces. Don't chase them or try to play with them. Let them come to you." We both nod.

"Ladies first." Mike gestures for me to go. One of our dive guides is already in the water waiting for us.

"Age before beauty." I laugh, gesturing for him to go.

He laughs. "So, how old are you, anyway?"

"Twenty-one. How old are you?"

"Twenty-seven."

"And I'm twenty-eight," Vic says from behind us. "Now, come on. Let's go already." Mike laughs and walks to the edge of the platform.

Underwater dives feel to me like it's just going down into one big room. The darkness makes the ocean seem to stop where the light stops. There are three divers with huge lights already down there, as well as our dive guide and two divers from another boat. One of the divers gestures for us to get into a semicircle. We give him the "okay" sign with our fingers.

Okaaay . . . , where are the monsters? Lights are on. Plankton is floating around. That's your cue, guys. I look over at Mike, who is next to me, and shrug my shoulders. He holds up one finger as if to say, wait a minute.

The shadows of the mantas arrive before they do. The divers holding the lights are now holding them over their heads—I remember Vic saying they have to do that or the mantas will run right into the divers. I guess they can't see that well.

I've never seen anything like it. They are huge. Hollow. Eyes on wings. That's what they look like. They like to do summersaults over our heads. I'm glad Vic reminded us not to touch them, because it's really tempting to play with them. They act like they're coming straight for you and then flip over. Mike is pointing to one manta in particular. I have to swim around him to get a better view. It's a manta with its front little fin all messed up. Suddenly I realize who I'm looking at: it's Lefty! Her left cephalic fin is just kind of hanging there. It's funny to be that close to a famous manta ray.

"I've never been on such an extraordinary dive," I say as Terrance helps me with my tank and sprays it off for me. "That was awesome." I can't seem to stop laughing.

"They are incredible, aren't they?" Mike is all excited, like he just got back from seeing friends he hasn't seen in a long time.

"I still can't believe we saw Lefty."

"Do you want to get something to drink?" Mike asks me.

"Sure. Let me get out of this wet suit, and I'll catch up with you in the salon."

*  *  *

I walk into the stateroom and quickly jump in the tiny shower again. Then it's the fastest hair preparation known to man. Makeup—just a little, since he doesn't like much.

"Where's that lip-plumper stuff?" I'm rummaging through my makeup case.

"Where are you going?" Annette asks me, still watching something on the TV.

"I'm meeting Mike in the salon. Here, find my lip plumper for me." I point to my makeup case, and she starts looking.

In the mirror, I run down the list. "Okay. Hair dry. Hair curled. Light makeup. Shorts and T-shirt, just like he likes. Slip on the sandals, okay. Put in the earrings."

"No, Sandra, no earrings. He wants casual."

"Take out the earrings. Perfume? *Mmm*, just a touch."

"Here it is," she sings. "Your lip plumper."

"Great." I smooth some on, and it starts to burn a little. But at least it looks good and tastes pretty decent, too. "How do I look?"

"Perfect. Good luck!"

And with that, I walk out the door and slowly pass through the entrance of the salon. Mike and I are the only ones in there—the only ones still up, probably.

"What can I fix you to drink?" Mike smiles at me. He has a beer in his hand.

"Do they have champagne over there?"

"Let's see here. Yep, little bottles."

"How about orange juice?"

"Orange juice? Check. Does that mean you'd like a mimosa?" He starts making it even before I say yes.

"Thank you, bartender," I take the glass from him. I walk over and sit on the tan leather couch. "So, what do you do when you're not bartending?" I take a sip of the mimosa.

He sits down next to me. "I'm an actor."

"No, really."

"Really." He laughs. "I'm an actor."

"Sorry." I laugh, too. "I thought George was joking when he said you were an actor. You just don't really seem like an actor."

"What does that mean?"

"I'm around actors all the time, and they just seem so, you know. Egotistical."

"And difficult to be around."

"Right. And you don't seem like that."

"I'm not. But I do know quite a few actors who are."

"So, is it Broadway or the big screen?"

"Both. Well, off-Broadway. A few movies. Sitcoms," he says. I try to look like I'm just being polite and that I'm not really wowed by him.

"I would have pegged you for the more intellectual type." I know by the look on his face that he's pleased.

"I know, actors aren't exactly intellectual."

"The craft has changed, I think. They used to be, but now, it's all about—"

"Appearances. Physical as well as whatever the press reports you're doing."

"Exactly! That's exactly the impression I've gotten, which is why I like working on indie films now. I'm more into the technical elements, the art of the acting, and the message of the film."

"I agree completely." He laughs loudly.

"What's so funny?"

"It usually takes me six hours of explanations and arguments to get someone to understand what you just said."

"I know what you mean. I have the same arguments with people," I tell him and sip my mimosa. The look on his face is similar to mine when I saw the manta up close. I can tell he's amazed. I've never had a guy look at me like that before.

Mike and I are still on the couch talking when George and Gloria come in looking for coffee the next morning. We stayed up all night laughing and talking about everything and anything. It turns out he loves cartoons, like I do, and we both agree that cartoons have influenced our sense of humor and how we view things. He's like a big kid at heart, who sees things in cool, creative, and simple ways. It's no wonder he loves the manta rays so much.

We eat breakfast with Gloria and George, and Miriam, Annette, and Christine join us. I'm sure they were panicked when Annette discovered my bed had not been slept in. They are impressively cool at breakfast, though. If they are concerned about anything, they are hiding it well.

"How were the mantas?" George asks.

"Beautiful," I say. "Amazing!"

"They were awesome." Mike uses my word. "We had a great time." He's talking more than he usually does, which I take as a compliment. Either that, or he's just tired.

"They are huge, George. The video doesn't do them justice."

"Well, you certainly seem excited about them. I hope I'll get to go tonight."

"We hope so, too," Mike says, and I love that he called us "we."

"I've got some great stuff to send back. I think the mantas here are the way to go." I turn to look at Miriam. "Everything is what we predicted. We even got to see Lefty."

"The one with the broken arm?" Gloria asks, sticking a piece of blueberry muffin in her mouth.

"She was pretty amazing, too. I can't believe someone hasn't tried to catch her to fix her fin somehow."

"They probably did. But I doubt there's much they can do for her. If they cut it off, she won't be able to block things from coming in her mouth on that side. And I don't know if they have artificial cephalic fins," Mike tells us.

"She doesn't look like she's in any pain, I guess."

"But the other mantas laugh at her behind her back," Annette says, jokingly from her spot next to me. "Can we see them if we go snorkeling there?"

"Sure, there were some snorkelers there last night, weren't there? Or did I just imagine it?" Mike looks at me.

"No, I saw them, too. They had their own light and everything."

"What time will the manta dive be tonight?" Miriam asks.

"Probably about the same time. I hope we can get in several dives this time, though," Mike says. "Which means, I need to get some sleep during this morning and afternoon."

"Just tell us when you want us to wake you up, and we'll come get you," Gloria tells him, and I can't help but smile. I need to get my sleep during the morning and afternoon, too.

When I get back to the stateroom, I lie down on the bottom bunk, completely sapped of energy. Annette, Miriam, and Christine quickly appear around the edge of the bed.

"What happened?"

"How did it go?"

"Don't worry, we just stayed up all night talking in the salon." I know what's on their minds.

"Oh, we know that," Annette says. "We spied on you several times."

"I'm glad you didn't see us. At one point, I couldn't get

Christine to stop laughing," Miriam says. "Y'all were so excited talking about those damn ray things. It was hilarious."

"We have a lot in common. And I mean A LOT. He is so funny and so sweet."

"Y'all were actually finishing each other's sentences." Christine is laughing again.

"I know. It felt really great."

"I can tell he likes you, too. He was like a completely different person this morning." Miriam sits down on the edge of the bed.

"I thought so, too, but maybe he was just tired?"

"He didn't look tired."

"You should see how his blue eyes light up when he laughs. And we were laughing most of the time. Like we've known each other for ages."

"That's great, Sandra."

"I owe y'all a big thank-you. I had my doubts. I never thought he'd like someone like me. But we talked about all kinds of stuff, not just the stuff we prepared in advance. We actually do have a lot in common."

"He just needed the right environment to get to know you," Miriam says.

"And I needed the confidence to be around him. I never would have been able to even talk to him if it wasn't for all of y'all."

I finally shoo them out of the room so I can get some sleep. I dream about mantas.


"Okay, now, you know the rules," Vic says to Mike and me as we stand on the dive platform. George couldn't make it again, and our snorkelers are inside watching movies. "Don't touch them. Don't blow bubbles in their faces," Vic continues, and Mike and I look at each other. We can almost say the words along with him. Looking out in the distance, it's no wonder the mantas like it here. The lights from the airport must bring in tons of plankton.

The underwater world is again magnificent. Mike and I swim together and point out interesting things along the rocks. The divers with the lights motion for us to come back with the others and make a semicircle. There are about a half dozen other divers besides us. Once again, the shadows of the manta rays appear before they actually do. There seem to be more mantas here than at the last location, and you can see why. The water is swarming with plankton.

Mike and I are laughing again as Terrance helps us remove our tanks. We love the mantas like they are little children or something.

"Do you want to go again, Sandra?" Mike asks me, and I love the way he says my name.

"Absolutely. In forty-five minutes, right?"

"Right. No alcohol if you want to do another dive," Terrance tells us.

"Want to go to the upper deck?" Mike leads me up there, and we sit on the edge of the hot tub.

"I wonder if we could put a manta in here?"

"He wouldn't fit. We'd have to get a bigger hot tub."

"Do they like hot water, though?" I love that Mike's sense of humor is like mine, and he'll discuss silly things.

"We could just get them a pool. Put salt water in it." He splashes his feet in the water. "Then we could feed them Annette's sea monkeys."

# Chapter Twenty
## Sticking to the Plan

We've been told that the mantas don't always show up, and I'm thrilled on the next dive when there are a whole lot of them. We arrive at the dive site after the other divers, so the lights are already in place. The first manta that we see we couldn't miss if we tried. She's a legend, and I remember reading about her on the Internet. With a wingspan of sixteen feet, Big Bertha starts swooping through the beams of light. Her mouth is a gigantic hole, and her cephalic fins form a scoop as she goes after the plankton.

The other mantas show up, too, and it is like watching a graceful ballet. Sort of. They are hilarious when they bump into each other—and into the divers holding the lights or one of the snorkelers. They do pretty well though, aiming to get as much plankton as possible without any major collisions. They love the food so much that they'll endure bumps and bruises to get it.

The videographer from our boat dives with us, and I act like I don't want to be near him. I think that impresses Mike the most. He must be relieved to be around someone who hates cameras as much as he does.

We complete the dive and clean off our equipment. Even though we'd planned on doing another dive, we end up telling Vic we're done for the night. Instead we hang out in the salon. I bring out the laptop for my "research," and Mike is lying on the couch, flipping channels.

"Anything I can help with?" he asks when he sees me walk in and put the laptop on the table. We're the only ones still up once again.

"Absolutely." I smile at him, thinking that I hope I can find the *Power* button on this thing. "I need to record my notes from the dive we just took." Where is that damn button . . . I'm reaching around the backside of it now. As I drag my fingers back to the front, I'm relieved to finally find the button on the side.

"Want some music while you work?" Mike scans the CD collection. "What do you like?"

"Oh, anything's fine. They probably don't have the kind of stuff I like."

"Such as?"

"Indie stuff, of course. And alternative retro, late eighties, early nineties. Pre-Nirvana." I remember the list Christine made for me and try not to look over at him. I can see him smiling out of the corner of my eye.

"Like what kind of bands?" He's testing me to see if I know my stuff. He walks over and sits next to me.

"The Cure, Material Issue, Natalie Merchant with and without 10,000 Maniacs, Dead or Alive, Psychedelic Furs, Lightning Seeds." I try not to list them alphabetically, since he might think that's weird.

"You must be the perfect woman!" He laughs. "First, you like Voltron. And now it turns out you like alternative edge retro music?"

"Don't tell me you actually like these bands, too?" I have to act surprised.

"Hell, yeah! In fact, a good friend of mine has a band that covers most of those bands." He's probably talking about Sammy, I'm guessing. Mike puts on a CD I don't recognize and adjusts the volume.

"That's great." I laugh, too, more out of nervousness than anything else. The program Miriam put on the laptop is just now loading. I go into Microsoft Word as they taught me. There are files on there already—Miriam has been busy—notes from Hawaii and other dive sites in the Caribbean we've supposedly visited, oceanography maps, and notes from the script. I open a file with today's date on it and discover a listing of the places we've been diving. I scan through the notes about the mantas and other critters.

"Is that for your notes?" He gestures to the computer screen. "If you don't mind me asking?"

"Oh no, that's fine. Actually, you can probably help me. I'm listing the mantas we've encountered so far. So I can recommend them to Herb for the movie." I scroll down the page, showing him the notes up to this point. Miriam has done a great job.

"You mean like their names? I think I only know a few of them by name."

"Let's see. We saw Lefty." I studied the different mantas on the Manta Pacific Research Foundation Web site before the trip. They have an identification system. I can only remember a couple of the names now, though.

"Yep, he's around a lot. I mean she is." Mike laughs. "And Big Bertha."

"Got her."

"Taz."

"Which one was Taz?" I ask him, already knowing the answer. The mantas have been named by different divers, mainly for physical characteristics or by the pattern of spots on their tummies.

"He was the little guy, who was doing all the excited flips in the lights. When he was a baby, they named him Taz after the Tasmanian Devil cartoon character. You can tell it's him by a *w* in the markings on his chest."

"Great. We have Taz."

"There's another one that has a big *w*, but it's a female. The *w* is much bigger, which is how you can tell she's not Taz."

"What's her name?"

"*W*."

"How appropriate." I type in the information.

"I think we saw Spatter. But since they all look spattered on the bottom, I can't be sure."

"I'll list him—her? Just in case."

"Her. Large female; I'd say about ten feet across. She actually got tangled in a boat's line once. Actually picked up the anchor and pulled the boat around."

"They're supposedly really strong." I smile at him and continue typing what he's telling me. The music creates the perfect ambiance. And it feels like we're the only ones on the boat.

"Elvis."

"Okay, now I remember someone—Vic maybe? Talking about him."

"Her."

"I mean *her*. She's got the four spots overlapping on her right chest." I type it in. "Where'd she get the name?"

"When she started playing guitar and singing Elvis songs." Mike laughs at his own joke. "No, actually, divers call her that because she actually goes to welcome the boats sometimes. She also gets real close to the divers."

"What was the one with the curled-up fins by her face?"

"Oh, that's Farrah."

"Farrah? You sure?"

"No, I made that up. She looked like a Farrah. I'm sure she has some other name." He laughs, and I go ahead and list her. Mike and I talk about the mantas we remember, but since we don't really know the other names, we just start making them up. Dumbo, Tinkerbell, Kitty, Greg Louganis.

"When you get back to work, if there's anything I can do to help with the film, just let me know," he says, smiling at me.

"Thanks, we might need you." I try to remain casual, like it's no big deal. But I'm extremely relieved he's finally talking about my film and possibly being a part of it. "Especially since you're so good with the mantas."

"Are you going to need any human actors?"

"Yes, of course. Would you be interested?"

"Sure. I'd really like to do an indie picture. I can even help produce if you need me to."

"We have a producer, but who knows? Anything is possible."

We end up staying awake all night talking again, and we're both surprised when George and Gloria come in for coffee. Time seems to fly by when we're together. We've gotten really good at playing off each other's jokes. We also share the same philosophy about wanting the way things were before everything was computerized, pre-Internet. He said we're Luddites. I had to wait until he wasn't paying attention so I could look the word up.

"We're going to end up in the friend zone if something doesn't happen," I tell Miriam when I'm back in the stateroom. "We've bonded over everything. Maybe too well?"

"Just stick to the plan. It's working. I promise. It's the way it has to be. He gets to know you and then makes his move, instead of the other way around. That way he's attracted to you from the inside out."

"I understand the theory. I'm just saying that I'm worried we're going to end up like brother and sister. Or like coworkers on the film. Maybe he's not really attracted to me?" I sit down on my bunk next to Annette.

"He is attracted to you. We can all tell," Christine says, leaning against the wall of the small room.

"Get some sleep, Sandra. We'll keep an eye on him. I'll wake you up before dinner so you'll have plenty of time to get ready for tonight's manta dives." Miriam leads the others out of the stateroom.

I wake up on my own, and I'm doing the hair thing again by the time Annette comes in to wake me up. Putting on a T-shirt and shorts, I'm relieved at least the sundress phase is completely over now.

"I have some good news," Annette tells me from the top bunk.

"What?" I ask, putting on makeup—but not too much.

"We were in playing Scrabble—me, Mike, George, and

Gloria—just a little bit ago, and Gloria asked Mike what he was doing staying up all night."

"I really like Gloria." I laugh.

"Mike said he stayed up with you. Made it sound like y'all were together. Or at least he didn't clarify it. And then Gloria said something like, 'You two make a lovely couple.' And Mike smiled and said he thought so, too."

"You're making that up."

"No, it's true. Gloria and George both think y'all are a great couple. George jumped in and was saying, 'You need a nice girl like Sandra.'"

"What did Mike say to that?" I put on the lip plumper.

"He agreed."

"I'm sure he was just being polite." I try to act like it's no big deal, but I'm actually having to resist the urge to jump up and down.

"We'll see. Just keep going like you are. You're doing really great, Sandra. And remember, he's lucky to be with you, too. Not just the other way around."

"It was funny. Because he did call me the perfect woman."

"He did? Well there you go! That's great." Annette jumps down off the bunk and walks over to look at herself in my mirror.

"It's because I like the same cartoons and music he does. That's why he said it."

"Well, maybe that's the clincher for guys nowadays?"

"Right, like he really went for that Sofia Elon girl because she liked cartoons. Had nothing to do with the fact she's a beautiful model or anything."

"But where is Ms. Sofia now?" She looks at me through the mirror. "Has he even mentioned her? They aren't that close, or he would have tried to bring her along."

"I wondered if he entered her on the entry sheet." I flip out my hair with my fingers.

"No, it was just him. Martha says Sofia got the Paris offer over two weeks ago, and she had to leave immediately. She's gone, Sandra. Time for you to swoop in."

"I want to swoop, but y'all won't let me." I decide I'm ready to go.

"He has to make the first move after he gets to know you. That's the plan." Annette shakes her finger at me like she's Supernanny. "C'mon, let's go eat."

Tonight's manta dives start with one just off the rocky coast near the Sheraton Keauhou Bay Hotel, in less than forty feet of water. The mantas are regulars here, and so there are more divers and snorkelers. Once again, our monster-sized friends flap around our heads and sweep past us like they're playing. Mike is great about pointing out the distinguishing features and marks on the mantas. Of course, we're not supposed to chase them, so we have to keep our distance while looking at their spots.

Later, Mike and I are laughing, putting away our tanks, while we try to come up with the names of the mantas we've seen on tonight's dives.

"Can you come to the hot tub for a while?" he asks me, as he hands off the last of his equipment to Terrance.

"Sure, be there in a few minutes." I head to my stateroom to freshen up. Annette, Miriam, and Christine are waiting for me with their words of wisdom.

"Don't get too close too fast."

"Don't be like Amber."

"Don't blow it."

They are driving me nuts as I put on my new blue and

green miracle bathing suit, which has all of modern science's latest technologies to make me appear slim and trim. I wrap a sarong around my waist.

"I'll be good. Don't worry, Moms," I tell them, thinking in the back of my mind that if I have a chance to pounce on Mike, I'm going to probably do it.

"You'd better. We'll be watching," Miriam warns me.

"Don't do that. I hate the idea of being observed."

"You won't even know we're there." Annette hands me my beach towel.

It's a little chilly with the wind on the upper deck, so Mike is already in the water with the bubbles turned on by the time I get up there. He's also poured me a drink and hands it to me.

"I hope you like Dr Pepper?"

"Love it," I lie. "Thanks, that was nice of you," I tell him as I drop my sarong and climb in the hot tub. I notice him checking me out, and I want to dive under the bubbles.

"That's a nice bathing suit."

"Thanks." I smile while wanting to ask, WHAT DO YOU THINK OF THE REST OF ME?

"You're kind of shy, aren't you?"

"Sometimes. I'm sure you're used to being around more aggressive women, huh?" I try to sound casual, but I'm not sure it's working.

"Yeah, but it's actually refreshing to be with you."

*Refreshing.*

"So, do you have a girlfriend back on the mainland?" Again, trying to be casual as I sip my Dr Pepper.

"I did." He drinks his Dr Pepper, too. "She broke it off a few weeks back. She had to leave the country."

I laugh. "You made her leave the country?"

"No." He laughs loudly. "She's a model, and she took a gig overseas."

"Wow, a model. I bet she's beautiful."

"I thought so, too, at first. But you know how when you're around someone for a long time? After a while, you no longer really see them. On the outside, anyway," he says. I love his views of the world, but sometimes he confuses me.

"Yeah, I know what you mean." I don't really know, but I say it anyway.

"What about you? Have you got a guy waiting in every port for you?"

"Well, of course." I smile, and he laughs again. "I have a group of friends I hang out with, and I date every once in a while, but I guess I'm kind of old-fashioned."

"How so?"

"I've been focusing on my career. And it takes me all over the place. I guess I'm more the type to hold out for that one special person than have a whole bunch of guys scattered around at every port." I'm not sure Liz would approve of my comments. It's not like I gestured to him or anything.

"I think that's good. I'm like that, too." He smiles at me. "My parents are divorced, so I've seen up close how relationships can fail. I don't usually get into one unless there is potential there."

*Potential.* I repeat the word to myself.

"My parents are divorced, too. Maybe that's why I'm so picky about who I want to marry. So I'll be sure not to put my kids through all that."

*Too much information! Too much information!* It's like a bell going off in my mind. I know the Hunt Club members would be screaming at the video screen if we were recording this one.

"The divorce was pretty tough on you, huh?" He finishes his Dr Pepper and scoots around on the seat so he's now sitting next to me.

I try to remember the version Liz and I drafted together before the trip, but my mind is completely focused on Mike sitting so close to me. The water glistening off his tan skin. His wet brown hair all tousled and some of it in his eyes. His big blue eyes. And those lips. . .

"Yeah, I think it's tough on all kids. The worst part was having to start over. Moving around all over Texas," I tell him, and it's not quite what I'd rehearsed, but it's the best I can do under the circumstances. I wish I could tell him about my mom and me and how my dad left us. But, I promised myself I would stick to the Hunt Club plan exactly.

"Did I tell you I'm from Texas originally? Houston actually," Mike says, looking at me.

"Wow, that's funny that we both are from Houston originally." I laugh, thinking I'm from Houston. Sort of. If Austin can be considered Houston.

"I loved living in Houston. Just close enough to go to the beach if I wanted but with all the cool stuff to do in the city. Plus, the warm weather and the whole Don't Mess with Texas attitude."

"That is kind of funny, isn't it? How much people make a big deal about being in Texas."

"I like the friendliness. In California, we have the beaches and the cities, but the attitude is different."

"Really? I thought Californians were supposed to be nice and easygoing?"

"Not the Californians I've been around."

"The thing I know I wouldn't like about California is the lack of privacy. When we've looked at doing films out there, it's been hard to plan things in advance because somehow the press always shows up." I'm starting to remember Liz's script once again.

"The paparazzi." Mike nods.

"We don't have that problem—at least not to that degree—in Texas. Plus, people tend to fight for privacy, and we frown on interfering with people's lives."

"That's what I love about Texas." He's laughing. "And you nailed it once again. Somehow you put what I'm thinking into words better than I do."

"How long did you live in Houston?"

"I was born in Houston, and then my parents lived just south of Houston. I lived there till I was out of high school. Then I came to L.A. What about you? You been in Texas all your life?"

"I was born in Houston. Then my parents got divorced, and my mom and I moved around a lot. She lives in Fort Worth now. We're not that close." I give him the short version.

"I don't see my mom much, either. My mom and dad divorced when I was ten."

"Did your mom get remarried?"

"Yeah. Yours?"

"No." Even though we're sitting almost right next to each other in the hot tub, our knees are the only things that touch every once in a while. So far, he's being a complete gentleman. I know he's supposed to make the first move, but he'd better hurry.

"I wish my mom hadn't remarried." He shakes his empty glass that still has some ice in it.

"Really? Is her husband a jerk?"

"Yes and no. It's just like you said, hard on little kids when everything changes so drastically. My stepdad actually wanted to adopt us. I thought that was terrible because I still loved my dad, you know? My dad finally gave up and took off. He didn't have the money for attorneys or courts, so he probably didn't have much choice."

"My dad left, too. I haven't seen him since I was eight." It comes out of my mouth before I realize it. Liz would absolutely kill me. "I'm sorry, I don't mean to bring stuff like that up."

"No, I'm glad you did." He looks into my eyes. "I haven't seen my dad since I was twelve."

"I know how bad that sucks." I try to smile.

"Yeah, it does." He reaches over under the water and holds my hand. "There are parts of Houston that are pretty poor, and that's where I spent my childhood."

"Yeah, I know. I probably lived near you." Near him meaning I was in Austin. I love holding his hand, fingers interlocked under the water.

"Only I don't think I knew I was poor at the time. Then when my mom got remarried, her new husband didn't want us kids going back to our dad's house. So, he tried to get my dad declared unfit or whatever." He stares at the bubbles in the hot tub. "Funny thing was I actually loved my dad's place, even when my stepdad called me and my brothers the shanty-shackers when we wanted to go there. Do you know what a shanty-shack is?"

"Yes," I say quietly. "More than you know."

"I didn't know shantytowns were bad until my stepdad made fun of us."

"We built forts all the time when we were kids. And I guess I just thought they were kind of like cool forts," I tell him, and he smiles at me. He looks at me for a long time before he finally leans over and kisses me.

"I don't think I've ever told anyone that I'm a shanty-shacker." He has his arm around me now. I wish I could tell him it doesn't matter, but in truth, I know it does. It's easy to dismiss it when you don't come from that. But when you've been there, you know how it stays with you.

Suddenly, I realize that the Hunt Club was wrong about the mantas being Mike's and my core connection. What we're sharing right now; THIS is our core connection. The mantas are just a way for him to deal with his life. It's like those sweet creatures accept him for who he is. And who he was.

"Do you have any idea where your dad is now?"

"No. I tried locating him, but when you're practically living on the street, there aren't a whole lot of records." He looks me right in the eyes. "What about you?"

"No, I have no idea. My mom tried to keep me from looking, which only made me more determined. I've even been all over the Internet. But with such a common name like 'Greene,' there's no way of knowing which one he is or even if he's still out there somewhere. I remember crying when we moved because I was scared he wouldn't be able to find us when he came back."

"I stuck around for that same reason. But then it just became too much shit. I wanted to act, and Hal wanted us all to go into his car repair business. So, I left for L.A. with only a backpack to my name."

"You've done really well for yourself." I smile.

"You, too." He hugs me from the side. "But it doesn't make that much of a difference does it?"

I know exactly what he means. "No, it doesn't."

"Hey, there y'all are!" Annette comes walking across the deck, and I wonder if they've been spying on us. "I've been looking everywhere." She sounds out of breath. "How was the dive?"

"Great," I tell her, thinking she already should know that since I was in the stateroom earlier. I hope the serious looks on our faces will give her the hint.

"Miriam wanted me to tell you she has the laptop program running. The maps are up, and she's already met with Vic. So, we're ready when you are."

"What time is it?"

"Almost one."

"Don't y'all want to just wait till the morning?"

"I would, but Miriam has been waiting up for you all this time." She kind of laughs.

"Duty calls." Mike smiles at me.

"I'm sorry. I keep forgetting I'm not on vacation." I look at his sweet face. He leans forward and kisses me again.

"Here's your towel." Annette is standing right behind me. I stand up and wrap a towel around me. He does the same thing.

"I completely understand. I've enjoyed talking to you. We can always continue tomorrow," he tells me. We three walk back downstairs and through the salon.

"Night," we whisper to each other as we walk into our separate staterooms. Miriam is lying on my bunk, and Christine is sitting in the chair.

"How did it go?"

"Fine. We were having a really serious discussion about our families."

"You seem sad. Is everything okay?" Miriam asks.

"Everything is fine. I'm just sorry we had to say good night so soon."

"It's the right thing to do, Sandra. It's okay to kiss him a few times, but it can't go beyond that. You don't want to end up like Amber did after the deaf conference," Miriam tells me for the hundredth time.

"It's no problem. Things are still right on track. He had a difficult childhood; that's what we were talking about. I feel bad for him. I guess I'm really starting to like him."

"Well, we're glad to hear that." Miriam laughs. "I'd hate it if you decided you didn't like him now."

"He's such a doll that I can't see that happening," Christine says, leaning back in the chair. Part of me wants to tell them what I've learned about Mike's past. About how I think what he went through actually is the core injury Martha was talking about. It almost seems too personal to discuss with them.

"Annette, I have been meaning to ask you for the longest time. You were going to tell me about your core connection with William," I say when I'm finished changing my clothes.

"Oh, with him it was really special." She smiles. "It turns out we share a common experience, especially when we were kids. We both had autism."

"You were autistic?"

"Yes, but they call it autism spectrum disorders now. And what Will and I were born with is considered Asperger's syndrome. It's the type on the spectrum where we can get by, but there are major interaction problems with other people. As kids, Will and I both were awkward and lacked coordination. We didn't respond to social cues or the regular grooming process kids go through," Annette explains as she opens her suitcase to get ready for bed.

"I've read about that," I tell her. "Is Will pretty difficult for people to get along with?"

"Yes and no," Miriam says. "He's an adult now, so he's had lots of schooling to help overcome some of the communication problems. But emotionally, people really get frustrated with him. There have been times when he didn't seem to fit in with anybody."

"Until Annette, that is," Christine says. "And once they found each other, it was like magic."

"When I told William that I had been through the exact same thing with my Asperger's, he finally felt like he could be himself. We formed an instant attachment. Oh, don't get me wrong. We still have our bumps with communicating sometimes, but I'm probably the only one that Will feels really understands him. And his parents and the rest of his family absolutely adore me." She laughs.

"There couldn't be a stronger core connection than that," Miriam says.

"That's really neat," I tell them as I brush out my hair. I'm trying to recall if Annette had mentioned the Asperger's to me earlier on in our friendship. We talked about so many things, especially about our childhood, but somehow she never said anything about it. "So you had all the awkwardness and communication problems he did when you were a kid?"

"Right. I was impossible to reach most of the time. Kind of like I was in my own little world. Very introverted and afraid of new things." Annette zips her suitcase and shoves it back under the bottom bunk.

I suddenly recall something Annette told me once about her childhood. When we had lunch together not too long ago, she said that she took all kinds of dance lessons when she was a kid. Years of dance lessons. I've never heard of an autistic child—one with Asperger's—being able to dance or take any kind of lessons like that. I'm tempted to ask her about it, but I don't want to bring it up in front of Miriam and Christine. Or do anything that might cause problems on the trip.

I also keep thinking about something Lexi was saying during the meetings, about how the core connection can be created even when the guy has the core element, and the girl fakes it. Lexi said she hated it when we manipulated the guys' minds so they'd marry us. I look over at Annette. I can't believe she'd lie to William in such a crucial way. But I know something is not right here.

They stay and chat with me to make it appear we're working. After Christine and Miriam finally leave, it's a long time before I can sleep. I keep thinking about Mike and the look in his eyes when he was talking about his dad. Talking to Mike tonight made me realize that I've never met anyone who understood what being poor as a child feels like until now. We don't know we have bad places to live. I thought I was a princess, just like any other girl. Until people made fun of me.

I can't help but wonder what Mike would think of the real me. The pizza employee, living in apartments with semitrucks idling all night outside. Driving an old Hyundai with 167,000 miles on it. Growing up with a mom living on food stamps and having to hide from the landlord. Would we be even closer?

I now have a lot better understanding of why Amber deviated from the plan with Brantley. As much as the Hunt Club excels at finding information about guys, they can't really know the person until they're alone with him.

# Chapter Twenty-one
## Good-byes

Mike and I are pretty much inseparable now—despite Miriam, Annette, and Christine's attempts to separate us. Not only do we stick together on the dives, but we eat at the same time, watch TV at the same time, hang out on the deck together, and sit in the hot tub together. The only thing we don't do is sleep together.

"You two are so wrapped up in each other's opinions that you don't even realize you're not including anyone else in your conversations," Annette tells me as I'm getting dressed after my usual nap.

"It's actually kind of rude," Miriam says and then laughs to let me know she doesn't mean it.

"You just look at each other, and it's like you don't know

anyone else is in the room." Christine is sitting on my bed, flipping through *Scuba* magazine.

"He just has a lot of important stuff to say." I put on some of the lip-plumper stuff, even though I'm going to wipe it off, anyway. I don't want Mike's lips to get plumped, too.

"Right. Important stuff like sharing memories of racing your Big Wheels when you were kids." Annette laughs at me.

"We raced bikes, not the Big Wheels." I flip my fingers through my freshly washed hair. "We turned the Big Wheels upside down to make ice cream." They laugh at me, and I know they can't possibly understand.

"I'm glad you and Mike are bonding so well," Miriam says. "We're just giving you a hard time because y'all are so wrapped up in each other, it's sickening."

"He's a great guy. Even beyond just his good looks. I've never met a guy I could totally be myself with. Ever."

When Saturday morning arrives, and we're sharing our last breakfast together as shipmates, I know if it wasn't for the three doting Mother Hens traveling with me, Mike and I would have been sharing a stateroom. I'm not really convinced that it's so vital for us not to sleep together; but I didn't dare risk it. All I can do is trust that the Hunt Club knows what its doing.

"Good morning, everyone," Sherry and Dick say as they walk in the salon.

"I'd almost forgot they were here," I say to Mike.

"I almost asked you who they were."

"Have y'all been here the whole time?" Miriam asks, finishing her scrambled eggs.

"Well, sure." They sit down at the table across from George and Gloria.

"Want to take a walk?" Mike whispers to me. I nod, and we

quickly slip out of the salon as Gloria is whipping out pictures of her grandchildren. Hand in hand, we walk up on the deck together and look over the railing. We're almost back at shore now.

"So, on your flight back? You have a layover in Honolulu, and then you have to stop in Houston before going to Dallas?" he asks me, putting his arm around my waist.

"Right." I try not to be sad. I had to listen to an hour of Miriam, Annette, and Christine telling me not to get too mushy. Stick to the plan.

"Is there any chance you could change your ticket to have your connection at LAX? At least then, we could fly back part of the way together." He kisses me.

"I don't see why not. We'll have to see what the airlines say."

"Well, let's call them." Mike leads me by the hand to use Captain Bobby's satellite phone. "Do you want to stop over for a few days? Let me show you around?"

My heart seems to be jumping up and down screaming "YES!" and I'm so tempted to do it. But Miriam warned me this could happen. She says it always does, and it can make or break the hunt. If I want to have a fling, then I can go home with him. If I want him to propose, I need to make him work for it.

"I really wish I could. But I have to be back in Dallas tomorrow to report on what we've done here," I say sadly. "Rain check?"

"Absolutely. Any time." He looks up the number for my airline. "And who knows? Maybe you'll need me in Texas sometime soon."

We say our good-byes to our other shipmates, including Sherry and Dick, whom we haven't seen that much of during the trip. When I turn to hug Gloria good-bye, I notice that she is wearing a beautiful brooch that has a number *five* made out of diamonds in the center of it. I can't help but laugh. Of course she's one of us. Her helpful comments this past week have not been a coincidence. I bet she's from the Hawaii Hunt Club.

We are escorted back onto the dock by Captain Bobby and his crew. It was hard to say good-bye to the mantas, but I know I'll be back at some point to see them again. Someday. Skipper Janis hands us each our DVD of the trip, with Mike's and my faces not showing up anywhere except through a mask or from a distance. The mantas are on the DVD too, so I'll have a way to watch the dives again.

Mike and I catch up with each other at Honolulu Airport, since our flights out of Keahole Airport left at different times. I find that I missed him, even just in the few hours we were separated. I can't imagine going back to Texas without him.

"Now, you come straight home," Miriam whispers, hugging me good-bye as she is about to get on her plane for Houston and then Dallas. "Remember the plan. No matter what."

Annette and Christine have similar advice for me, with Annette being the most direct, saying, "Don't screw this up." She laughed when she said it, but I know she's not joking.

Flying back to the mainland with Mike is so much more enjoyable than the flight down to Hawaii. We hold hands and snuggle against each other, talking about what we'll do together the next time we see each other. He wants to show me the little mom-and-pop shops along the beach. And how beautiful the ocean is. And take me to hear Sammy's band.

But the wise words of Miriam echo in my head, "Not yet, Sandra. It's too soon."

I guess I do want to go back to Dallas and see what can be

arranged for the film project. I know there is a lot of work to be done on a movie set and preparations. But, no matter what, the ball will technically be in Mike's court now. We're all counting on him calling me and wanting to come see me.

MAKE HIM WORK FOR IT.

That should be the Hunt Club's official motto.

"You sure I can't persuade you to come home with me?" Mike hugs me again.

"I really wish I could, but—"

"I know. It's okay," he tells me. I go with him to pick up his bags, and then we just hug each other until it's time for me to head to my gate. He kisses me one last time, and it's really difficult to let him go. I take my shoes off to go through security.

"I'll see you soon, Sandra."

"Okay, see you soon." One last kiss and a hug. He watches me go through security, and then he's gone. On the other side of the scanning machines, I'm trying not to cry as I sit down and put my tennis shoes back on.

"Excuse me," an airline employee—security it looks like— says to me. "Ms. Sandra Greene?"

"Yes?" I look up at the two security guards wearing black shirts and black pants, making them clash in the sea of brightly dressed tourists.

"Can you come with us please?" The shorter one gestures for me to stand up.

# Chapter Twenty-two
# FBI Meeting

"And that's pretty much everything that's happened and all I know about the Hunt Club," I tell Agent McFarland. I watch as he sits back in his chair, the yellow legal pad still in front of him with several pages turned back. He looks at me for a moment and then slides the black-and-white photo across the desk toward me again.

"And you're sure you don't recognize the woman in this picture?"

I lean forward to look at the picture and then pick up the page. I try to keep my face emotionless. It's a professional photo of Sofia Elon, Mike's ex-girlfriend. The model, who is supposed to be in Paris, on a big modeling gig.

"I can't really tell who that is." I try to keep my voice steady while my mind is racing all over the place. Was Sofia murdered? There's no way.

"Look at it closely. It's a picture of the model you mentioned to us a little while ago. A twenty-four-year-old woman named Sofia Elon. You sure you don't know her?" He asks again, and I can tell he already knows the answer.

"It's too hard to tell from the picture. I don't know."

"We think you can tell us why Ms. Elon was murdered."

I just sit there, not knowing what to say. I still can't believe she was murdered.

"And we think you can help us connect Ms. Elon's murder and the Hunt Club," Agent McFarland says. "You are aware that it is routine practice for the Hunt Club to kill young women?"

"I still think there's been a mistake. The ladies in this club would never hurt anyone." Maybe one of the other chapters in another state? Maybe the Hawaii chapter? But that would mean Gloria? No way.

"Okay. Then maybe you can explain why you, a member of the Hunt Club, were on a boat with Ms. Elon's ex-boyfriend the day after she was killed."

"Just because I was on a boat with her ex-boyfriend doesn't mean I know anything about her murder."

"Yet, we've discovered that is a familiar pattern with the Hunt Club girls. We find a murder victim, track down the people closest to them, and find that the boyfriends are all now dating—or married to—Hunt Club girls."

"That's bizarre. It can't possibly be true." The murder victims' boyfriends are all dating Hunt Club members? I run the words over and over in my mind.

"Do you know a girl named Brenda Bain?" Agent McFarland continues with his questioning.

I have to think for a minute, and then I almost laugh. Brenda Bain is the bubble-blowing, neon-lip-gloss wearing, nitwit teenager who worked for me at the pizza place.

"Yes, I know Brenda Bain. Why?"

"She was in a car accident a little over a month ago."

"Right, I remember that."

"We have reason to believe that one of the Hunt Club members was responsible for running Brenda Bain off the road, almost killing her."

"That's crazy. She ended up with like a broken arm or something. And the Hunt Club doesn't even know her. And if you think it was me, you're even crazier."

"We know it wasn't you. There was a witness at the scene who we believe was responsible. The witness's name is Martha Roberts."

Martha was the witness at Brenda's accident? It must be a coincidence. Did I ever even mention Brenda's name to Martha? Or to anyone at the club?

"You know Martha Roberts?"

"Of course. She's a very nice lady. Who's like in her seventies or something. Why would she hurt a sixteen-year-old kid?"

"Do you know a woman by the name of Camille—or Cami—Terrell?"

"The name sounds familiar." Then it hits me. Cami is Brantley's best friend. The journalist in D.C.

"She was murdered a little over a month ago. Attacked in her driveway at her home in Maryland." McFarland stares at me, looking for a reaction indicating I know something.

"Oh no way. I can't believe that."

"So, you did know her?"

"I've never met her or anything. I've just heard of her. A journalist, right?"

"Do you know a woman named Jodee Margaret Orkester?" He's going down a list in the file folder that the little man brought in with him. Did something happen to Jodee, too? The fresh from the farm White House intern?

"I've just heard her name. Did something happen to her?"

"She was in a fatal car accident while driving in Washington, D.C. We believe she was run off the road." I shake my head. It's got to be a coincidence. They would never actually hurt anyone.

"I'm sorry to hear she was in an accident, but I don't see how a ladies' group in Dallas, Texas, could possibly have anything to do with it."

"And then we're up to Sofia Elon. She was murdered outside of her hotel in Paris a week ago." McFarland closes the file folder and shifts the legal pad back in front of him.

My heart sinks, and I can't breathe. I know that is way too many people to be a coincidence.

"But, the Hunt Clubs are only in the United States right now," I tell them. "How could they be responsible?"

"We have reason to believe it was orchestrated by one or more Hunt Clubs within the United States," Agent McFarland says without missing a beat.

Sofia was murdered because of me. Because I wanted Mike for myself. And Jodee and Cami were murdered because Amber wanted Brantley. And Brenda. Oh my gosh, what did I do to that poor kid? I remember talking to Miriam when I brought my membership application back to her. I remember saying how horrible the teenagers were—no, telling her it was just one in particular—Brenda.

"What else can I do to help you?" I say finally.

"We are willing to grant you full immunity from prosecution if you cooperate with us," he tells me. I open my purse and pull out a tissue.

"I guess I've seen too many cop shows. Will you still grant me the immunity if I talk to an attorney?"

"Of course." He laughs. "Or, if you want, you can wait until you hear what we need to know first. It's up to you."

I ask him if I can go to the restroom, and he shows me where it is. I am so tempted to call Mike. But what would I even say? Maybe I should call the L.A. Hunt Club? But if these people are murderers, I don't really want them pissed off at me.

"Can you put your immunity offer in some kind of writing for me?" I ask the agents when I return to the office.

"Sure, we can do that. Jackson," he says as he turns to the little man behind the desk—his partner, I guess—who stands up and leaves the room. We wait while a form is typed up for me.

"During the course of our investigation, we've discovered the number *five* seems to be associated with the Hunt Club. For example, several of your members have brooches with a diamond number *five* in the center. What does the number *five* stand for?" McFarland asks me after the immunity agreement is signed and a copy given to me.

"It's weird, because I've heard different answers every time the topic has come up. Some people say the *five* stands for the number of new girls the senior members recruit. Like you get the pin when you bring in five new people. Then, other times, they said it was the number of months of courting before marriage. Or the number of rules in the Game Book. The number *five* seems to be on everything."

"Do you think it could be the number of women each one

has had murdered? Let me rephrase. Do you think it could be the number of women each one has *relocated*? Like they get their diamond *five* pin when they've successfully relocated five girlfriends?"

"I don't know. It's possible, I guess."

"How do the Hunt Clubs interact with each other?"

"They all seem to know each other. I think they use the same private investigator. Some guy named Jeremy."

"Do you know Jeremy's last name?" Agent Jackson writes down what I'm saying.

"No, they just always called him Jeremy. They also said something about other PIs, too. They help all the Hunt Clubs."

"How do they help?"

"Oh, shit!" It finally dawns on me how the system within Hunt Club has been working. "The different Hunt Clubs contact each other any time there's a girlfriend who needs to be relocated. They have Relocation Committees. They help each other make sure the girls are out of the way."

"How do they do that?"

"Supposedly by offering them great jobs in other cities. The members know about the jobs or even create the jobs, or the members convince their successful husbands to help find the girls jobs. Then, the girlfriend is offered more money, and she of course transfers to start a new, better job."

"We do have records indicating that is what happened in some of the circumstances." McFarland tells me, nodding. "Are the husbands involved with all the Hunt Club activities?"

"No, I don't think so. The Hunt Club has a rule about making sure we keep information from the husbands." I think back over the past few months and the different husbands I have heard about. What about Tammy? She is always so quick to volunteer the services of her husband, Jeff-the-almighty-lawyer. And there's Christine's husband, George. "Then again, there are a few of the husbands who have been around for a while that the Hunt Club seems to trust. They get asked to help with some of the stuff. They are the exceptions, though."

"I believe you mentioned three husbands. Let's see . . . there's Gloria Waltman's husband on the boat." McFarland flips back through the pages of his yellow pad. "And you mentioned Tammy's husband, Jeff, and another man named George who's married to Christine. Do you know their last names?"

"I don't know how involved they are, I mean . . ." I hate to think I'm getting people in trouble when I don't know for sure what they've done. "Tammy and Jeff's last name is Essler. And Christine and George's last name is Leto. Christine and George, you know, are really nice and—"

"Are there any others?"

"No, not that I can think of. Overall, we try to keep the husbands in the dark about what really goes on, and I'd say most don't know. Or really care, for that matter. The only thing all the husbands know about is the relocation stuff—the hunt requests. And the ones who do that are just trying to help their wives, not to help the Hunt Club in particular." I look down at McFarland's legal pad to see if I can tell what he's writing. It's difficult to read his scribbles upside down, and the only thing I can make out is something about relocations. "How long ago did they stop actually relocating the girls?"

"You mean, when did the murders start? The first one we suspect was about five years ago, but they've increased in numbers gradually."

"Why would they do that?" I still can't believe it.

"We're the ones supposed to be asking the questions," Agent Jackson says, and they kind of laugh.

"I'm just really surprised. If you knew these women. They are just your average girls. Nothing special about them."

"Yet, they all marry very wealthy men."

"We're a matchmaking club. We help average girls who normally are invisible to the nice, successful good-looking guys."

"How do you help them?" McFarland asks, and he's beginning to frustrate me because I've already explained what we do.

"It's a game called hubby hunting. We'll find out as much as we can about the guy the girl wants, and then figure out a way to set the circumstances so they can meet. And hopefully, eventually, get married. We have a Game Book and everything."

"I think we have a copy of one of the books. I'd like to show it to you and ask some questions about it."

"That's fine."

The questioning continues through most of the night. I can't believe I didn't suspect something about the Hunt Club or get the feeling something was wrong. I was so caught up in it all—in the Cinderella story of helping an average girl like me meet the perfect Mr. Right.

"So, what happens now?"

"I'm afraid we need you to get us more information."

"How?" I take another sip of the Coke they bought me.

"Go back to Dallas. Act naturally. Find out as much as you can about who the private investigators are and how the different Hunt Clubs interact with each other."

"You think I can actually be around these people? And act naturally?" I'm not sure I can keep such a big secret quiet. Or spy on them. "If they find out what I'm up to? Won't they want to hurt me, too?"

"You'll have to be careful."

"Isn't there some other way?"

"Yes, we could always arrest all of the Hunt Club members, including you, and let the courts sort it all out."

I sigh. "I'll try getting the details for you."

"If you want the immunity, that's what you will need to do, Ms. Greene," Agent McFarland sits up straight in his chair. "For the safety of the other girlfriends out there, as well as your own, I recommend that you get us the information as soon as possible. The Hunt Clubs are dangerous. As long as they continue to operate, you and the other people involved in the matchmaking are likely to be in danger."

Which means not just me. But also Mike.

The agents arrange for me to catch the first direct flight from L.A. to Dallas in the morning. I haven't had any sleep, and I feel like I'm about to lose it any second. I call Annette to pick me up from the airport. I don't know how to explain all this to the Hunt Club. What if they've called me or something and know I didn't come back on the flight yesterday?

"Sandra!" She waves to me, with a big smile on her face. "We were so worried."

"Don't worry, I didn't spend the night with Mike or anything."

"Oh, we know you wouldn't do that." She laughs. I wonder for a second HOW they know? Just how much surveillance do they do? Do they know I was detained by the FBI? She and I head down to baggage claim. Supposedly, my bags were pulled off the plane yesterday, and they made it on the right flight today.

"My ears were really bad when I got off the flight from

Hawaii. I bought some decongestants, but I was afraid to fly again until the pressure in my ears went back to normal. I spent the night at the airport. I have the names of the airport security guards I talked to if you want to verify it."

"Geez, Sandra, I believe you. Besides, if you were going to spend the night with Mike, I'm sure you'd stay longer than you did."

"I'm sorry if I sound snappy. I just have a headache. And my ears are still bothering me."

"Hey, it's okay. I know I was pretty punchy when I had to leave Will after my setup was over. The waiting is the hardest part, believe me, I know."

Poor Mike. I wonder if he knows about Sofia yet. I tried to watch the news at the airport, but I didn't see anything about her. Maybe they're keeping it quiet for some reason? To my surprise, my suitcases come sailing around on the baggage treadmill.

"I think I'll probably sleep for a week," I tell Annette.

"You're not coming to the meeting tonight? Amber is supposed to report on how plan B is going so far with Brantley. Should be pretty exciting," she tells me as she drives me home to my apartment.

"I forgot about the Sunday night meeting." Shit. If I miss it, will that look suspicious? "Of course I'll be there," I say with as much enthusiasm as I can muster.

# Chapter Twenty-three
# Report

I park my silver Hyundai down the street and start walking to Miriam's house. I'm a few minutes early, but I think it's a good idea. Arriving early is what I would have done if the whole FBI thing hadn't happened, and I was excited to be back.

"Sandra, you made it!" Annette waves at me from where she parks her BMW. "Did you get some rest?"

"A little. But I wanted to be here." Big fake smile. I walk over to her car.

"I know what you mean. I'm dying to hear what happened with Amber and Brantley." She throws her designer bag over her shoulder, and we make our way up the hill.

"So, where are they with the plan exactly? Is Brantley here now?"

"Yes, I guess he's already come down here. Miriam just gave me a few details a little while ago. Brantley got himself into some kind of trouble at his job in D.C. He actually called Amber because he was worried about what she would think of him if she heard about it on the news. She told him about a job—the one too good for him to pass up, of course—down here and suggested he move here. They were going to have some big dinner with Brantley to discuss the job. Amber is supposed to fill us all in tonight on how that went."

"Do you know what kind of trouble he got into at his job in D.C.?"

Annette laughs. "Apparently, Jeremy set up a Hugh Grant–Divine Brown type of thing. Poor Brantley went for it, and he was caught with his pants down. Literally. With a hooker. I guess she made him an offer he couldn't pass up, either."

"That's really sad," I tell her. "I can't believe Amber went along with that." I'd never do that to Mike. I can't even imagine manipulating his life the way they've done to Brantley. Then, I start thinking about the film project. I really have been manipulating Mike. How far was I really going to take it? It's amazing how caught up in this I have been.

"Well, Amber didn't exactly have much choice in the matter." Annette half laughs.

"What do you mean she didn't have a choice? I would have just quit the Hunt Club completely."

"Oh, no one ever quits the Hunt Club, Sandra." Annette stops walking and turns to look at me. "I mean, what crazy person would quit and give up the chance to get the perfect man of her dreams? Of course Amber is still going after a husband, whether Brantley or someone else. And she wants to get Brantley." She sounds like a devoted cult member all of a sudden, just rattling off phrases she's supposed to say. But the serious look in her eyes tells me there's more here than she's letting on. She starts walking again. "Plus, if you quit, you have to pay them back every cent you owe them. Including the percentage they would get if you had gotten married. And we're talking thousands and thousands of dollars. It's in the contract they had us sign, remember?"

I follow her up the hill slowly. "It's all about the money. Setting homely girls up to trick rich guys and then taking a percentage of their income."

"That's not true, at all. It's more than just about money. Hunt Club is our family now. We can't leave it. How can you of all people not understand that?"

"There you are!" Rose walks quickly toward us in her high-heeled pumps, and my conversation with Annette comes to an abrupt halt. We're practically in front of Miriam's house now. Rose gives me a big hug. "I heard you did great."

"Thanks. But I miss him already." I decide to play up the whole missing Mike thing to help explain my mood. I change out of my tennis shoes and follow Rose and Annette into the sitting room.

"Congratulations," Amber says and hugs me. She looks especially happy, I guess because things are moving along so well with her and Brantley. I wonder what she'll say when she hears Brantley's friends have been murdered. Isn't it weird that she doesn't know? Wouldn't Brantley know if his friends were killed? I sit down on the couch next to Annette.

What if the FBI is lying?

What if they were really Hunt Club people? Testing me?

"So glad to see you, dear." Joyce and a few other members hug me. "Miriam says the trip was a success?"

"Yes, it was wonderful. Now, we start the waiting game." I notice there are about a dozen women here already, and some of them are in the dining room. Another Relocation Committee meeting or something.

"Oh, you'll hear from him. Don't worry." Rose sits down on the other side of me as Annette jumps up to get us drinks real fast. Looking at Rose, I just can't imagine her killing someone. She wouldn't hurt a fly.

Miriam and the other ladies come into the sitting room a few minutes later, and after everyone has said hello to me and heard I'm waiting for Mike's call, the focus then shifts to Amber.

"The dinner went well?" Tammy asks Amber from her usual seat behind me. The atmosphere in the room is jubilant. I've never seen so many smiling faces. Annette walks over with a mimosa and hands it to me before sitting down next to me again on the couch.

Amber is laughing. "The dinner was fabulous. They kind of grilled Brantley about the scandal in D.C., and they made him sweat a little bit about that, which I felt bad about."

"Oh, you shouldn't feel bad, Amber. Brantley is going to be much better off," Rose tells her, and the others agree. I feel sick when I think about what these ladies are doing to him.

"I know. It was just hard to watch him have to explain it. Especially when I don't think he fully understands what happened to him. Like with the confidential documents they said he showed that hooker."

"They said on the news that they actually have the documents he supposedly showed her," Martha says. "So he didn't do anything he didn't want to do. We just gave him options, and he took them." There is silence in the room as no one really knows what to say. I don't think any of us know all the details of what happened.

"The important thing is, everything is set up for the job,

and Brantley is very thankful to me and for my family connections he thinks I have. Of course, he wouldn't dare risk making my family angry. So, when the topic came up later about how long he could stay with me, I told him how my family felt about that kind of thing. That he should find a place nearby."

"And the poor guy doesn't know anything about Dallas or the housing here. He doesn't even know anyone besides Amber and her wonderful family," Miriam says, beaming with a smile. "And Brantley's parents have been distancing themselves from him."

"Brantley wasn't really interested in finding his own place. I guess he already knows he'll have a hard time, since he was just fired, under investigation, and everything. He's been so beaten down by the whole scandal, he's been absolutely clinging to me. And sweet to me about everything."

"That's wonderful, Amber," Charlotte says. "I'm so glad to hear things are back on track for you two."

"Wait, it gets even better." Miriam laughs.

"Right." Amber is laughing, too. "So, when I told Brantley that he really can't stay with me, that I can't live with anyone till I'm married, he really didn't know what to say. He can't go back to D.C. He doesn't really have any money, and people are kind of staying away from him because of the scandal and stuff. So in the very next breath he said, 'Okay, let's get married, then.'"

"You're kidding? Isn't that kind of fast?"

"Wasn't he just joking, Amber? Y'all barely know each other. Well, he barely knows you anyway," Teresa says.

"I acted like he was joking." Amber turns to look at Martha. "Just like y'all said to do. I even acted like I wasn't really interested in the idea."

"I'm guessing that since we screwed up his credit, he thinks he needs to be married?" Tammy suggests from behind me.

"Y'all messed with his credit?" I ask, and no one answers me.

"Exactly," Martha says. "We made sure, thanks to Jeremy, that he's been notified about his credit. He knows it will take months and months—if not years or even longer—to fix the problems with the government charge accounts that are suddenly over the limit. He can't buy a house or rent anything because of his credit history. Not only does he have no where else to go, he would also no doubt love to get married and be able to use Amber's credit. Hers is pristine."

"Won't getting married hurt her credit, since his is messed up?"

"Not necessarily," Martha says, "and it won't matter, anyway. As soon as they are married, we'll make sure his credit is cleared up."

"Wow, y'all managed to pull off a miracle, here," Annette says, laughing. "Amazing!"

*They got him fired, tricked him into moving here, destroyed his credit. So he would jump at the chance to marry Amber.* I feel like I'm in shock.

"Now listen, Amber. It is very important that you let Brantley talk you into marrying him. Don't make it too easy for him because we want him to really want it." Martha is sitting on the edge of her seat, pointing at Amber with her cane.

"Okay, okay, I know." Amber is obviously losing patience with Martha. "It's driving me nuts, but I'll play everything by the book. I don't want to blow it."

"You're sooo close, Amber. Time to really focus," Charlotte says.

"Just tell him you want to think about it. Wait twenty-four hours, and then you can tell him," Miriam says.

"Right, and then act like you think it's a little fast, but you can see being very happy married to him," Martha continues. I glance over at Amber, who is actually writing the directions down.

The rest of the evening is spent celebrating Amber's news. No one seems the least bit concerned that we tricked this poor guy into proposing to Amber. Not even Annette, who I thought was so much like me.

"You look really tired, Sandra. You need a vacation from your vacation," Martha tells me, her cane already tapping away. I look at her, and I just don't see it. They may play psychological games to trick men, but for my life, I can't imagine her being involved with hurting Brenda or killing someone.

Walking down the steps and over to my car after the meeting, I feel defeated. How can I possibly get the information the FBI wants? The only information I found out tonight was that Gloria from the boat was, as I suspected, from the Honolulu Hunt Club. They don't seem to give out the full names of the private investigators they use. And how do I find out how the clubs contact each other? I just get e-mails from Miriam and the others. And sometimes from clubs around the country. But I don't know who else gets the e-mails or who starts them most of the time.

Feeling lost, alone, and exhausted, I pull into my old parking spot in front of my apartment building. It seems like years since I've been here. The semitrucks are already parked for the night, and a group of men—truckers, I assume—are gathered at the far end of the lot. Staring at the men, I wonder if the Hunt Club would have its PI investigate me. I decide to be careful about what I do, even in my own parking lot at home.

I climb out of my Hyundai and walk inside my apartment. I know I need to go to sleep, but I want to see if there's anything on CNN about the murders. Nothing. No word. Could the FBI be wrong? I push the button on the answering machine as I lounge on the couch, too tired to make it to the bedroom.

"Hi, Sandra." I sit up when I hear Mike's sweet voice. "It's Mike. I wanted to call and tell you again how much fun I had with you. Please give me a call back. Bye."

I want to call him back immediately. To just hear his voice. I also want to tell him what is going on, but I know I can't. There's no reason to involve him in this, for his own safety. Instead of calling Mike, I check the lock on my front door and then get on the Internet to look up the names of the people who the FBI said were murdered.

*Jodee Margaret Orkester.* Sure enough, there are news reports and her obituary. She was killed in a car accident in Washington, D.C.

*Cami Terrell.* Under the name *Camille Terrell*, there are news reports about her being murdered in her driveway, and they think it has something to do with a story she had been investigating in a bad part of Maryland.

*Sofia Elon.* Tons of pictures, promotional materials, and modeling pages. I finally discover some news reports in London and Paris about her being "missing." Is the FBI or whatever agency works in Paris keeping it a secret that she was murdered? Wouldn't someone contact Mike even if they heard she was missing? Maybe if I continue searching, I'll find something about her murder, but I'm too tired to do this right now.

I lie down on my bed and close my eyes. With everything the Hunt Club is involved with, I am worried about how this is going to play out with Mike. I don't want him associated with these people. He didn't ask for this, and I wouldn't be able to live with myself if something ever happened to him. Then there's the whole issue of marriage and paying Hunt Club back. What the hell was I thinking? Would I really trick Mike to give the Hunt Club 10 percent of his income?

Mike hates publicity. He fights for his privacy. What is he going to think when he finds out I'm responsible for private investigators digging for stuff on him? That we have his dental records and medical records and financial records. And we know every girlfriend he's ever had.

My mom always tells me I'm at my best when I'm pissed off because that's when I'm forced to actually use my brain. She may be right in this situation. I've got to protect Mike no matter what. And as far as the FBI goes, I know there must be a way to get the information they need.

"Sandra, so nice to see you!" Rose greets me at Miriam's door at the Wednesday morning meeting. She and the other ladies are smiling and jovial again. No doubt there's more good news to be announced about Amber. I sit at the small bench and remove my shoes. I'm a girl on a mission. In a way, the Hunt Club has created a monster, and now they are about to be bitten by the monster they created.

"Heard anything about Amber?" I ask Annette when she walks over to me.

"No one is saying anything about it. I get the feeling, though, that a wedding is definitely in the works." Annette giggles as we join the other ladies in the sitting room.

"Hey, Sandra, any word yet?" Liz asks, looking up from her notebook.

I sigh heavily just for dramatic effect. "No, nothing. I don't know why he hasn't called." I lie gracefully.

"He will. It's just been a few days," Liz says and smiles.

"You did everything right, honey. It's just a matter of time," Miriam tells me as she brings in a tray. There is champagne on it, poured into tall crystal flutes. Annette and I sit on the couch across from Liz. I pretend to look sad—it doesn't take much effort.

In a burst of noise and energy, the doors to the dining room open, and Amber skips into the sitting room. Martha, Joyce, and a few other ladies follow her. The smiles on their faces say it all. The room falls completely silent as all eyes are on Amber.

"I'm ENGAGED!" Amber announces gleefully and holds out her left hand to show us the ring. Cheers go up in the room as people jump forward to hug Amber. The diamond must be several karats, and it's marquis shaped.

"That's so WONDERFUL!" Everyone seems to be saying at the same time.

"Champagne for everyone." Miriam makes her rounds to all the ladies.

"Sit down, honey, and tell us all about it." Charlotte takes her hand and sits next to her on the couch.

"I let him talk me into it, which was really hard because I was so happy. But I knew what y'all said, to wait twenty-four hours." She pauses to smile at Martha. "As soon as twenty-four hours was up, I sat down with him, acted like I thought it was a little fast, but that I could see us being very happy together as husband and wife. He was thrilled. We went shopping together for my ring. His parents are delighted at the news, and in spite of everything, they insisted on paying for the ring since, you know, Brantley's bank accounts are frozen for now." She's giggling and holding out her hand again for people to admire the ring. "I just LOVE it!"

"Now that's an example of good parents!" Joyce holds up her champagne glass. "I'm sure the news of the engagement and his new job has made things better for the whole family."

Several of the women stand up and hug Amber once again. No one seems to have a problem with what has been done to Brantley. I feel sick and almost have to leave the room.

"Amazing," Christine says from the other side of the room. "I really was worried there for a while."

"I love it that she made him think the whole thing was all his idea," Martha says.

"Let's get her down the aisle." Liz sighs. "Then I'll be happy."

"We're looking at the end of the month. The last Saturday," Amber announces. "Joyce told me she belongs to that big, beautiful Highland Park Presbyterian Church, and we can have it there."

"I'll get back with you and Miriam later today, after I confirm with the church that there is a time available that afternoon," Joyce says, sounding almost as excited as Amber.

"The end of the month? That doesn't leave us much time," Annette points out.

"I know it seems like short notice."

"No, it's okay. We'll pull strings if we have to. What can we do to help?"

"Brantley and I want to have a small quiet service, you know, try to avoid the press and everything," Amber says, and I almost have to hold my breath to keep from laughing. She wants a small quiet service, but it's going to be at one of the biggest churches in the Dallas–Fort Worth Metroplex. "Everyone here is invited, of course. And Brantley talked to his folks last night. They will be here, I guess."

"Let us take care of all that for you," Rose says, taking notes. "Do you want the reception at a country club?"

"I asked Brantley, and he said it would be great. He's worried about bad publicity, though. He doesn't want it to upset me."

"Don't worry about that." Martha laughs. "This is Texas, for goodness' sakes. We love a good scandal. We're proud of a good scandal. The bigger, the better."

"Gleneagles Country Club? Or, something smaller?" Rose asks.

"Why don't we check several of the country clubs to see what's available on that Saturday, Rose," Joyce says. "I'll check with Ronda at the church about the time for the wedding, shooting for before six for good luck."

"Reception at seven thirty," Rose writes in her notebook.

"Thank you all so much. I can't believe how wonderful Brantley is." Amber is glowing.

"Just wait till you see how happy he is when he gets his life back on track and starts his new high-paying job," Annette says.

"Absolutely." Miriam laughs. "We'll give you the wedding and the honeymoon, so don't worry about money before the wedding. Liz, can you find some time this week to show her our wedding gowns?"

"Y'all have wedding gowns?" I ask.

"You bet. Really beautiful ones. Our older members buy gowns from all over the world. That way the brides can have the very best."

"Is that how you got yours?" I whisper to Annette.

"Yes. I love that dress."

"It was gorgeous."

Time passes quickly, as everyone wants to be a part of Amber's plans. It's fine with me if the focus is on her; the last thing I want is my new hunt to get into full swing. I have to focus on hiding my disappointment when Miriam calls the meeting to order.

"Have you heard anything at all, Sandra?" Martha asks me.

"No." I shake my head. The way Martha is looking at me makes me wonder if she knows I'm lying. For the first time I realize how creepy Martha is. She's sitting in that huge chair like she's the ruler over all of us.

"What can we do to make sure Mike takes the next step?" Christine asks. "Y'all should have seen the way he was looking at Sandra on the boat. I just don't get what the problem is. Why hasn't he called?"

"Maybe it was because I was the only single girl there?" I suggest quietly. "I kind of got the feeling the connection wasn't as strong as it could be."

"How's that?" Miriam asks. "You two were inseparable by the time we docked."

"It's just," I say, having to think quickly. "When we were saying good-bye at the airport, you know. It was just a feeling I got. He asked me to stay a few days with him in Malibu. And I had to say no, so—"

"No, you couldn't stay with him, because it would have made things too easy. He never would propose under those conditions," Miriam interrupts me.

"Well, it doesn't look like he's going to be proposing, anyway," I tell her, sounding sad. "I think he took the situation wrong. Or something." I know it's not a perfect explanation, but it is all I can come up with under the circumstances.

"I still think you did everything right, Sandra," Annette touches my arm.

"I can't believe there isn't something we can do at this point," Christine says.

"We've done everything. We need to let him make the move. Let him indicate he misses her first," Charlotte reminds her.

"But it's been three days," Tammy says from a chair behind me.

"What are your thoughts on what to do next, Sandra, dear?" Rose asks.

"I'm worried. I'm guessing once he got home that maybe he considered me and the trip just another vacation. And that's that. We're done."

"I'll never understand guys," Annette says. "By the way Mike was looking at you, I was just sure you had a connection with him that was solid. I would have bet anything that he would have called by now."

"Some men are impossible to understand." Miriam nods. "We knew going into this that, as an actor, he's had a really easy life. He's used to girls just throwing themselves at him and never having to emotionally commit."

I struggle to keep from defending Mike, but it's hard to keep my mouth shut.

"Don't forget, now. We always have the option to plan B him," Martha says from her corner.

I literally have to hold my breath to keep from biting her head off.

"How? He's not in an industry that would frown on him being with a hooker," Teresa says. "In fact, it could only help his career."

"I thought we were going to get him here with the whole movie thing?" Christine asks.

"We are. But he's got to make the move by calling Sandra about it. Then, we'll arrange with Herb to organize the film project and likely move Sandra to Austin. Otherwise, if she just calls him, it greatly increases the chances that he'll say no," Miriam tells us. "Statistically speaking, if we want them to have a relationship, then we have to wait and see if he makes a move. The man always makes the move," she says, and I'm not sure I agree with her old-fashioned tactics anymore. It doesn't matter, anyway, since I'm not going to pursue anything with Mike.

Liz nods. "If he likes her enough for a relationship, then he'll call her."

"I say we plan B him." Martha is like a broken record.

"I agree, let's do it," Charlotte says. I remember she said she's gone on hunts for four different husbands. I wonder how many she had to plan B?

"I don't think there's a way to do that." I turn to look at Martha. "He's not going to have a reason to stay with me. If something bad happens, he has thousands of people who will take him in. If anything, it may make him less likely to call me because he won't want me involved in it."

"Oh, I can think of a way."

"So can I." Miriam and Martha seem to be cooking something.

"Such as?" I ask.

"We've been wanting to try out a plan B involving the new Homeland Security problems," Martha begins. "All we have to do is have his money and other assets frozen due to questionable donations made to known terrorist groups."

"Wait a second," I say more harshly than I probably should.

"You want Mike to appear to have connections to terrorists?"

"Wonderful, Martha," Rose says.

"That's a great idea!" Charlotte says.

"Exactly. Then he will be cut off from his money, and those thousands of people you're talking about helping him? You can pretty much forget that." Martha laughs, and Miriam joins her. I look around the room filled with women. No one else is against the idea.

"I'm not sure I want to go that far." I pause for a moment to think about the most persuasive thing I can possibly say that will get them off of this plan. "I would never want to be married to an alleged terrorist. Ever. I just couldn't do it." I shake my head.

"It would be kind of hard to fix his reputation afterward. People don't tend to forget that kind of thing, even if it is a mistake," Liz says.

"I'd almost rather move on to someone else," I tell them.

"Well, you always have that as an option, Sandra," Martha tells me. "Is that what you want to do?"

"I don't know. I really, really like Mike." I fake a tearful moment before I continue. "But if he doesn't like me enough to even call me. . . ?"

"He may not be the right one for you." Annette finishes my thought.

"I'm afraid if he goes much longer, I'm actually going to be ticked off when he finally does call." I look over at Martha again. "We all worked so hard for this. I'm just sorry that he obviously doesn't want me."

"There are plenty of guys out there who would love to be with you," Teresa says, and the other women jump in.

"That's exactly right, Sandra."

"He's not worthy of you."

"You deserve better."

"He's from California."

The women are so sweet, although I don't quite understand Christine's California comment.

"Do you want to start looking at Week One again? Just in case," Miriam suggests.

"I hate to give up too soon. And I don't know if I should do another one after all I've put y'all through."

"Don't be silly," Charlotte says. "We've enjoyed it."

"It's all part of the game," Miriam tells me. "We want you to find your perfect man. And it's important that it happens now more than ever."

"Sandra, you should pick yourself out a nice doctor or lawyer. They're always easier to hunt and are suckers for marriage," Martha says.

"Oh, Rose, who was that DARLING doctor you had? The one at Harvard Medical School?" Miriam asks, and Rose starts flipping through her notebook.

"He is gorgeous, remember, Sandra?"

"Here he is! David Allen Hopwood Jr." Rose holds up an eight by ten of the good-looking doctor.

"Wasn't he the one with a lot of school left?" Annette asks.

"I checked on him after the Week One meeting. He's beginning his residency this semester."

"Where is he doing his residency?"

"Johns Hopkins, I think. And that usually takes what? Two years?"

"I think so. And Johns Hopkins is an excellent school. He will do well as a doctor," Martha tells us, as if she knows the future. "Sandra, what about having Jeremy look into him for us?"

"Don't you think we should wait just a little longer on

Mike, just in case?" Christine asks. "I mean, come on. You saw the way they were together."

"It's Sandra's call," Miriam says and looks over at me. "If you want to wait a little while before deciding, then that's okay, too. We can pick a new bride and start another hunt in the meantime."

"Great, I'm ready to draw for the new hunt," Cheryl says from behind me. Poor thing is always the bridesmaid.

"Let's hold off on a new hunt for a bit. I'm still betting we hear from Mike shortly, and then we'll need to get the film project under way." Martha taps out the syllables with her cane. "I read the reports carefully. Sandra did everything in accordance with the sims. We should hear from him any moment now. And if we don't hear from him, well, we can always take a stronger approach."

If she says we'll plan B him one more time, I will scream.

"It probably wouldn't hurt to have David's background checked. If not for Sandra, then maybe one of the other girls will want him in the next hunt," Miriam says, and Martha nods at her.

"I guess it does make me feel better to know there is another option out there," I say quietly, hoping I sound convincing.

"Well, of course there is," Rose pats my arm. "There are lots of men out there who would be lucky to have you as their wife."

"Okay, Liz, let's get Jeremy going on David's background check. If he's starting his residency at Johns Hopkins, we need to look into the environment up there." Miriam is writing it all down.

"Where is that, anyway?" Amber asks.

"It's in Baltimore," Rose tells us. Great, more convenient to the FBI offices.

"How fabulous. Not too far from D.C. or New York," Tammy says.

"Harvard and Johns Hopkins are the very top medical schools." Martha is still hung up on his schools. "You can't do better than that."

"Won't he be completely poor when he gets finished, though?" And Joyce is obviously concerned about his financial-aid situation.

"The money isn't a big deal to me anymore; that's one thing I've learned. I'm sure we'll have enough." I glance up at Miriam who gives me a disapproving look. Obviously, Miriam thinks marrying someone with less money would never work because it would mean less money for the Hunt Club. "In fact," I glance over at Martha, "if I need to start over and pick a new husband, I think I might go for that good-looking fireman. Do we still have his picture?"

"*Oooh*, yeah! He was hot!" Teresa laughs. "Get it? Fireman? Hot?"

I'm glad Teresa makes a joke. It allows me to laugh at Miriam and Martha's reaction to my wanting to marry a fireman instead of a doctor.

"Here he is!" Cheryl passes down the eight-by-ten picture to me. He has dark hair and a tremendously well-sculpted body. "He works for the Grand Prairie Fire Department, and he's a real sweetie. His name is Dwayne Daubert."

"Du-wayne Daubert?" Joyce says from behind me. "You've got to be kidding? Come on, Sandra. Don't you want a good-looking doctor? Someone who can take care of you financially? That fireman probably only makes what? Thirty thousand a year?"

I'm trying not to laugh. Ten percent of Dwayne's thirty thousand would go to the Hunt Club. You can practically see the calculators going off in Miriam's and Martha's heads. Martha looks like she's about to have a stroke.

"But what's the difference if the doctor is going to be financially struggling, too, with all the school loans and stuff?" I ask finally.

"It may not even be a problem," Rose tells us. "His father is a doctor, too. It's possible his parents are paying for his medical school."

"With his credentials, David will never struggle financially," Martha tells us.

"We can have Jeremy check on both of them," Liz says.

"Sandra, if you don't hear from Mike for some reason, you can't go wrong with either David or Dwayne." Selma smiles at me.

"Where's that doctor's picture?" Joyce asks, standing up and looking around the room. "Show her his picture again."

"I have it," I pretend to be mesmerized by the eight-by-ten photo of the doctor. "He is very good-looking."

"Your children will be beautiful."

"And healthy."

Everyone is so enthusiastic about Dr. David Whatshisface. But, I'm even more tickled that they appear ready to let go of Mike so easily. I am going to throw myself into the hunt process for this medical school guy or the fireman, and hopefully, everyone will forget about Mike completely. I doubt there will be time to complete another hunt anyway. The FBI is going to break this whole thing up. It's just a matter of time.

When the meeting is over, and everyone is heading into the dining room for more celebration of Amber's engagement, I stop to talk to Miriam in the kitchen.

"I wanted to ask you something." My heart is racing.

"Sure, Sandra. Anything."

"With all the talk about weddings and everything, I've been thinking a lot about my dad and how I would really like him to be at mine. I know there's still time yet before a wedding, but I would still like to find him. Do you know of a good private investigator I might be able to use?"

"Well, of course. You can use Jeremy. He is great. Fast, too." Miriam sets the mimosa glasses on the counter for the maids to wash later.

"I don't have much money, though."

"That is not a problem. Don't even worry about it." She puts her hand on my arm. "Liz?"

"Yes?"

"Would you hook Sandra up with Jeremy, please? She needs him to locate someone for her."

"Of course. I'll get his number and e-mail address for you," Liz says and walks into the other room to get her notebook.

"Thank you, Miriam." I smile at her and touch her hand in typical Hunt Club fashion.

"Here you go." She gives me Jeremy's business card. "He's a really nice guy, but he can be a little hard to reach. You might try e-mailing him first."

"Thanks, that's a good idea."

Feeling a little triumphant, I join Annette at the table where she's been saving me a seat.

"Here's to Amber!" Martha makes a toast. "The future Mrs. Brantley Garnier!"

I feel bad for Amber because she has no idea what has happened to Brantley's friends or what she is getting herself into. The Hunt Club now will expect 10 percent of his income. They are also probably hoping the marriage won't work—or Brantley will get hit by a bus—so they can have half his assets.

And Brantley's political career has already been ruined, and he can likely never go back home to D.C.

After the formal dinner, we change back into our shoes, and Annette and I walk out to our cars together.

"If you ever need to talk or anything. You know you can always call me," Annette says, as she arrives at her white BMW. "I know what you're going through."

"Thanks, Annette." I open the door to my Hyundai. Part of me is still tempted to ask her about what she said on the boat regarding the core connection between her and William. I'm dying of curiosity to know how she could tell William and everyone else she was born with Asperger's syndrome when she told me she took years of dance lessons—ballet, tap, and jazz—when she was a child. I watch her unlock her BMW and decide I don't want to bring it up. I'm not sure she would tell me the truth, anyway. I think she's been in Hunt Club too long.

Once I'm on Central Expressway—which is congested as always—I look more closely at Jeremy's business card. Jeremy's last name is Lambert, and his office is in D.C. This is the man who is arranging the murders. Mr. Jeremy R. Lambert. It makes me nervous just holding his card.

Finding out how the different Hunt Clubs contact each other about the relocation requests turns out to be much harder. When I get home, I search through the e-mail messages I have received. I don't know exactly who is sending them. Some are from Miriam, but some come from just "Hunt Club."

# Chapter Twenty-four
## New Beginnings

I can't keep my hands off of my answering machine as I finish getting dressed. I press the message button to hear Mike's latest message again. This makes a total of five messages he has left, and each one breaks my heart.

"Sandra, I hope you're okay. Please give me a call. I just finished watching the DVD from our dives, and I miss you."

I want to call him so badly. But it's better that I don't make contact, because my resolve is too weak at this point. I know I'll cave. Or worse, I'll start blurting out all the stuff I've been doing with the Hunt Club to get him. Not to even mention the FBI and the fact I inadvertently played a role in his ex-girlfriend's death. He's better off moving on and forgetting about me.

I walk over to the counter and pull out the DVD copy I have of the dives we took. I know I shouldn't, but I can't help it. I want to be back on the boat right now with Mike. I want to be back in the world of mantas, where our only concern is figuring out what their names are. I put the DVD in the machine and turn it on.

I watch about twenty seconds of it and turn it off again. Just seeing Mike's scuba-masked face as we're underwater at the lava shoot. Him making the "okay" sign with his fingers. I'm glad we told them not to record our faces, because actually seeing his would be torture. I don't know how to get over this guy.

A knock at my front door interrupts my thoughts.

"Ready to go?" It's Annette, and she looks beautiful.

"Yes, let's go," I tell her, thinking the last thing I need is to go to a wedding right now.

"This is the Maryland-style mini crab cakes, with dilled remoulade sauce," Rose announces before putting a bite in her mouth. Amber's wedding reception is smaller than Annette's was, but I actually like it better. It was a beautiful ceremony, too, in the chapel. Members of Brantley's family were there, and the rest were pretty much Hunt Club people and their husbands.

Amber looks stunning in her flowing wedding gown and train. Her colors are blue and white, and the bridesmaids were thrilled with her choice of dresses. Even with the lovely ceremony and Amber looking like a model, I still think Brantley steals the spotlight in his tux. That is one handsome man.

Some of Brantley's college buddies are here, as well as a few friends I remember seeing at the birthday party. Brantley looks happy and relaxed, and his parents are wonderful. Amber's "parents" are picture-perfect, of course, handpicked by Miriam and Martha. The bridesmaids were eight of Amber's friends from the Hunt Club, and the flower girls were daughters of other members.

The wedding just screamed major society event, and it's a shame that the press wants to be so negative about Brantley. Amber doesn't seem to care, though. She's absolutely on cloud nine.

"This is blackened jumbo shrimp with avocado and lemon crème." Annette takes a bite, and Will laughs at her. I'm not sure he's caught on to our silly wedding traditions by now or not. Rose and Charlotte are also sitting with us, and of course Joyce, who is always the life of any party. It's hard to believe that just a few months ago I was sitting here wondering who all these people were and how the women ended up with such breathtakingly gorgeous men.

"I finally found out what happened to Brantley with the whole scandal," Joyce tells us in almost a whisper. She is the best when it comes to finding out information. "The undercover cop came walking into his office dressed and acting like a hooker—she said she was solicited by him, which is also how she got past his receptionist and secretary. At the time, Brantley thought maybe his friends sent him a hooker as a gag or something. Anyway, next thing he realizes, the woman is unbuckling his pants and is all over him. One of the senators comes in right at that moment, and all hell breaks loose. Security is called, and the police, and the FBI."

"*Eeek*, I hate when that happens," Annette says, laughing.

"He doesn't know what the deal is with the documents they think he showed to the girl," Joyce says, acting innocent, too, most likely for Will's sake and anyone else who isn't in on it.

"The poor guy." I turn to look at him, and he's smiling

and joking with Amber. "He seems to have come out okay, though. I guess."

"I would like to propose a toast," Brantley's dad—who was also Brantley's best man—says. Amber told us that his parents are now standing by him through the scandal, and they believe he must have been set up by someone. Democrats, they said.

After spending the day psyching myself up, I head for the Sunday night meeting. I must appear enthusiastic about firefighter Dwayne and Dr. David Whatshisface. I walk up the steps to Miriam's house, where I'm greeted by Annette. She's been waiting for me to see how I'm doing.

"I told Will that I needed to come to the meeting tonight to see you. He said to tell you that we've got broad shoulders if you ever need one."

"Thanks, I really appreciate it. I'm doing okay, though." I change out of my shoes. "I'm determined to put Mike behind me." I can't look at her, because I know she can probably tell I'm lying.

"I think you'll really like David." She tries to be optimistic.

"I'm really okay, don't worry." I smile at her. "And why David and not Dwayne? He is really cute. And it would be nice to be with someone so heroic and caring."

"But, he'd be gone a lot," Annette insists, and I get the feeling that Miriam or Martha must have gotten to her to try and change my mind about Dwayne.

"Yes, but a doctor would be gone a lot, too, wouldn't he?" I ask her as we walk into the sitting room. I should probably stop toying with them about it. The main thing is to get them off of Mike; I don't care who we end up going after.

"Okay, we're on Week Two, everyone." Miriam gets the

meeting started. There is excitement in the air again as a new hunt is under way. For some reason, it doesn't feel like a game to me anymore.

"How are you, Sandra?" Rose asks me, cocking her head slightly to one side.

"I'm okay. I'm focusing on the future. On finding the RIGHT guy for me."

"That's great, Sandra."

"We have some bad news, I'm afraid, about the fireman, Dwayne." Miriam sighs melodramatically.

"I'm sorry, Sandra," Cheryl says. "I went by the station to see Dwayne, and he no longer works for the Grand Prairie Fire Department. He got a better job offer to fight wildfires in, like, Wyoming. Or some place like that. I'm still trying to get a forwarding address or other contact info."

Well, gee, what a surprise. He received a better job offer that's thousands of miles away, and he had to leave so suddenly. I almost comment about it but decide not to. I know it would come off as sarcastic.

"Don't bother with the contact info, honey." Joyce laughs. "I can't imagine Sandra wanting to live in Wyoming, of all places."

"That's probably true." I try to sound disappointed. I decide to stop pushing for Dwayne. If they would go to the trouble to relocate him to Wyoming, there's no way they'd let us really go after him in the hunt.

"Oh, what a shame. He was so darling," Rose says.

"That's terrible," Annette whispers to me. "I'm sorry, Sandra."

"Not to worry," Joyce says enthusiastically from where she sits behind me near Martha. "We still have Dr. David Allen Hopwood. Junior."

"He's a good one."

"Liz, do we have information from Jeremy?" Miriam asks, pen in hand and ready to go.

"Oh yeah. David is a nice prospect." She starts passing out the statistic sheets. "I think you'll really do well as his wife, Sandra. He's twenty-six years old, five foot eleven, wears glasses only when he reads. He is originally from Boston, where his dad is a doctor—a surgeon. They also own land out in the country, a farm that has been in their family for generations. His mom doesn't work. He has two older sisters and a younger brother. He's Methodist. Goes to church every Sunday. He is still really close to his family."

"Any information about his financial aid?" Joyce asks, and Miriam shoots her a funny look. "I'm just asking."

"David's parents are wealthy and are paying for his schooling. We did a check on school loans, and so far, he doesn't have any. Now, that doesn't mean he won't have to pay his parents back, but as far as the information I've found on him, he is fine financially. Good credit score. He has investments of over three-hundred thousand, and with his attendance at the top-ranked schools, he'll have more than enough in terms of money and other assets."

"I'm glad his parents aren't divorced," I try to sound pleased.

"Yes, it increases the chance that you and he won't get divorced if at least one set of parents isn't divorced," Miriam tells me. It's all about trends in statistical data to her, the numbers.

"What's he like in person? Do we know?" Teresa leans forward to pick up a mini muffin off the silver tray on the coffee table. "I hope he's not snotty, being from Boston money and everything."

"That's a good point. As soon as we can, we'll have to go check him out." Miriam looks over at Cheryl and Teresa. "Do you two feel like a trip to Baltimore?"

"Well, it's not Hawaii or anything, but sure. It should still be fun." Teresa tries to make a joke, and no one laughs.

"Okay, why don't you fly up later in the week? See what you can find out." Miriam writes the information down.

"Wait," Christine says. "Has it been officially decided then that Sandra is off of hunting Mike? I mean, we don't want to jump too fast here."

"How are you feeling about this, Sandra?" Martha asks. A wave of fear flashes through me. I must get her off of Mike and her thoughts away from any kind of plan B.

"I think it's the right thing to do." I nod at Martha. "I need to move on. He's not going to call, since it's already been so long."

"Just as long as you're sure, honey," Charlotte says.

"I'm sure." I smile at her. "I can't take the waiting anymore. I want to move on."

"That's great, because I really like David." Rose laughs. "I can see you two having a long, happy life." Rose is probably the sweetest one in the room. I know she can't possibly have anything to do with the murders. I wish she wasn't wearing the number *five* diamond pin, though.

"Do we have his medical records yet?" someone asks, and I'm not really paying attention.

"Yes, he's in great shape. Doesn't smoke. Doesn't do drugs or anything. No maintenance meds of any kind. No history of any major medical conditions. He had the usual childhood diseases, but otherwise, he's healthy," Liz tells us. "And as far as his dental records, same thing. Although, he did have braces for two years."

"He has a gorgeous smile," Charlotte tells me, as she stares at the eight-by-ten photo. "Nice eyes, too."

"What about a girlfriend?" Christine asks, and I hold my breath. This may be the next person to have a fatal car accident, compliments of Martha, Miriam, and Jeremy.

"Right now he's dating a girl named Kate. But it's not too serious. Jeremy says Kate is dating other people. So, no big deal as far as we can tell."

"Is Kate a medical student, too, Liz?" Martha asks.

"Yes, which means they also don't have much time for each other. That, and she dated him while they were both at Harvard. I don't have any information about where she's doing her residency. I doubt it's Johns Hopkins, though, or Jeremy would have found it."

"That's good news."

"He's so busy. Does he even have time for a serious relationship?" Annette asks.

"He does if she is the patient, understanding type of girl who understands how hard he has to work," Martha tells us. "I think it's time for Sandra to start reading up on the medical profession."

"Great idea. Who is available for her to work with?" Miriam asks. "What do y'all think of Marcus?"

"*Ooh*, yes. Marcus would be good." Charlotte jumps in. "You'll really like him." Which means that Charlotte really likes him.

Miriam writes it down. "Marcus is the husband of another one of our members. But they recently moved to San Antonio. He still comes up to the Metroplex every so often to visit UT Southwestern, so I'm sure I can arrange for you two to meet. He'll be able to give you a feel for doctors and the medical profession."

"His wife, too, Staci. She is so sweet. She can be a help for her, too," Tammy says.

"Oh, definitely. Let's arrange for Staci and Marcus to meet Sandra." Miriam writes that down, too. "Next weekend, perhaps?"

"Sounds good to me." I smile.

"I'm really impressed with how well you're handling everything," Annette tells me after the meeting when we're walking out to our cars. "I know how much you liked Mike."

"Some days I handle it better than others." I wish I could tell her what's going on. "That David guy is a hottie, though, don't you think?"

"Yeah, he is." We arrive at her white BMW.

"Hey, Annette, I wanted to ask you about something."

"Sure, what's up?"

"I've been reading over all the hunt requests, you know, on the e-mail?"

"Sure, they're kind of fun to read, aren't they?"

"Yes, interesting, too. Anyway, I notice some are from Miriam, but then some of them just say Hunt Club. Do you know where those come from? Are they from Miriam, too?"

"Oh, those are off the listserv. All the members are put onto a computerized e-mail list, and we get all the messages that are posted on there. So you're getting the e-mails from a central computer."

"Do you know who sets that all up?"

"I'm guessing it's the New York office, since they originally started the e-mails. Ronita? I think that's her name. She's a computer wiz. And any time we have a posting to the listserv, we have to send it to her, so I'm guessing she set it up."

"So, if I wanted to send something out to everyone, I'd have to send it to her first?"

"Yeah, but really all you have to do is hit REPLY on the e-mail. It will automatically go back to her."

"Okay, that makes sense. Thanks, you know I'm not really up on computers." I try to laugh it off.

"Yeah, I remember Mike saying y'all were Luddites," she says and then freezes. "I'm sorry, Sandra. I didn't mean to mention him again."

"No, it's okay, really. Thanks for your help," I tell her and start walking toward my Hyundai.

When I get in the house, I grab a pen and try to remember what Annette just told me. My heart is beating a mile a minute as I get my thoughts together to call Agent McFarland. Hopefully, this is the information he needs, and I can start getting this mess behind me.

"Agent McFarland." He answers his own line.

"Hi, this is Sandra Greene."

"Yes, Ms. Greene. Do you have some information for us?"

"I think so." I give him the contact information for Jeremy and explain what Annette told me about the e-mail listserv.

"Good." I can tell he's writing it all down. "That's really great, Sandra. Do you have that address?"

"The e-mail address? Um, let me check." I turn on my computer and go to my e-mail. I open the last hunt request and give him the e-mail address. "I also get other e-mails, you know, from Miriam and the other members. But that listserv is how the Hunt Clubs interact with each other."

"That's good work. The FBI thanks you."

"I also wanted to mention something else the Hunt Club is doing. Have you heard of plan B?" I give him the details about what happened with Brantley in D.C.

"Yes, we are aware of that kind of thing happening with the Hunt Clubs. It's very similar to the relocations of the girlfriends they were doing before the murders began. It's all a part of our same ongoing investigation."

"So, what happens next?"

"Well, we'll research the people involved, such as this Ronita person. As well as Jeremy Lambert and his colleagues. Then, we'll get warrants issued and start making arrests."

"How long will this all take?"

"It depends on what we find."

"Is there any way they can find out it was me who gave you the information? I'd really hate to have these people mad at me, if you know what I mean."

"If you run into any problems, be sure to contact us and your local police department. The FBI will try to keep you out of it until arrests are made. Our investigation will be confidential until the grand jury proceedings, and we'll do our best to protect you as our source. We're pretty good at making it look like people didn't cooperate with us when they really did."

"There's something else I wanted to ask you about. There was a member named Lexi Donaldson in the Dallas Hunt Club. She seemed to be a strong member, but then she all of a sudden disappeared several weeks ago. The main reason I bring it up is because I remember right before she disappeared, she was complaining very loudly about some of the stuff that was going on."

"What kind of stuff going on?"

"The whole core connection thing I told you about, and how it's used to manipulate the guys into marrying us."

"We'll do a check on her." It sounds like he's typing it into a computer. "We'll see what turns up."

"What should I do now?"

"Just keep going like you have been. Go with the flow, and just act like the Hunt Club would expect you to act. This is very important, not only for your own safety, but also for the successful outcome of the investigation. The Hunt Clubs will likely be shut down when arrests start being made. Then you can go back to life as normal. In the meantime, let us know if anyone threatens you or if you receive other information."

"Right now, the group has started looking at a doctor they want me to meet. And I was wondering if we should be worried about the girl he might be dating."

"What is the doctor's name?"

"He's a medical student starting his residency at Johns Hopkins. David Allen Hopwood."

"Do you know the girl's name?"

"It's Kate something. I'm not sure they're still dating, but her name came up."

"The FBI will look into it." He is speaking in the third person again, saying "the FBI" instead of "we" or "I."

"Should I try to stop the whole matchmaking thing with David?"

"That's up to you. For your own safety, though, remember the more you can just proceed like they would expect you would, the less likely they will be to suspect you reported anything. Time to keep a low profile."

"I have just one more question." It's a fear that has been lingering in the back of my mind. "The Hunt Club has been helping me out. Financially."

"We're prepared to grant you immunity in exchange for you helping us, remember? It doesn't look good for you to take any kind of payment from the Hunt Club."

"Right. It's just that, they've been helping me with my bills. Once the Hunt Club is closed down—"

"The Hunt Club assets will be frozen, Sandra, and you really can't be taking any money from them now that you know where that money is coming from." McFarland's voice is getting louder. The last thing I want to do is get myself in criminal trouble.

"I understand. I just don't know what to do about money."

"Get a job, Sandra. Do it as soon as possible where it won't raise too much suspicion with the Hunt Club. Tell the Hunt Club you want to make your own money—that you want to show them you aren't mooching off of them."

I get off the phone feeling a little sick. I'm relieved that the FBI will be closing the Hunt Clubs soon, but, at the same time, disappointed that I still have to act like I'm pursuing Dr. David. Agent McFarland also brought up an interesting point. When all this is over, my life is supposed to resume to normal. I don't know what "normal" is anymore, and I can't imagine life without the Hunt Club. Not much is left.

I glance at my kitchen counter at the stack of bills that has accumulated there, waiting to be turned over to Liz so the Hunt Club can pay them. I have no savings and no way I can even make those bills, much less the ones that will be coming in for next month. McFarland is right that I need to get a job, but what? It's not like I have gained marketable job skills beyond the knowledge of manta rays and stalking men. How will I even survive? Go back to making pizzas?

# Chapter Twenty-five
## Waiting

I have been hoping that the FBI would step in and start closing the Hunt Clubs in a matter of days, but it hasn't worked out that way. I'm finding it difficult to pretend to be interested in Dr. David. Meeting with Dr. Marcus and his too-happy wife, Staci, hasn't helped much, either. I'm now being groomed on how to be a doctor's wife.

Arriving early for one of the meetings, I step out of my shoes quickly and wait for Liz as she finishes her small talk with several of the other ladies. She smiles when she looks up at me.

"Liz, I wanted to give you these." I pull a big brown envelope out of my Hunt Club Game Book, which is now decorated with medical emblems and other doctor stuff that I cut out from magazines. By all accounts, I now appear to love doctors.

"Oh, okay. Thank you," Liz says, taking the brown envelope and putting it with her stack of papers for the meeting. She knows exactly what is in it.

"No, really, thank you." For months, the Hunt Club has been paying my bills for me, and I figure this one more batch of bills will be okay for them to pay. It will make it more believable than to just stop asking for their help all of a sudden. At least that is what I tell myself. In truth, I have no choice but to let them take care of this month's bills because I have absolutely no money. It is almost painful to think this will be the last time I can turn over my bills to Liz.

"It's not a problem. At all." Liz is looking at me, probably wondering why I'm still standing there hesitating.

"I wanted to ask you, Liz, um, about the money and stuff." I take a step closer toward the kitchen, hoping she'll follow me so our voices are out of earshot of the other ladies who are arriving and removing their shoes. Cheerful greetings echo from all around us.

"Sure, Sandra. Is there something wrong?" she whispers, touching my arm. I notice they all do that—act all touchy-feely when they talk about something serious.

"Well, I was wondering if I haven't been, you know," I say, trying to word things carefully. "I don't want to take advantage of the Hunt Club generousness—er, generosity. I hate that y'all keep paying my bills when I'm nowhere close to getting married. I mean, it's not like I married Mike, and really, we set up for my bills to be paid back when Mike was the target, and now with Dr. David—I mean, David—well, you know, I'm still so far from anything really being set up and stuff." I hate it when I'm nervous, and I just keep rambling on and on. Liz is so polite. She just stands there, smiling sweetly, trying to figure out what the heck I'm saying. "I was wondering if I might get a job, or something, until things really get close to an engagement?"

"Don't worry, Sandra, it's fine." Liz is touching my arm again. "I know you were hurt by Mike, and it's only natural to feel discouraged. But really, don't worry. I'm sure things will work out with David."

"Oh, right, I know. It's just that I have so much time on my hands, and I really think I miss working. I need to feel like I am being responsible. This is very important to me." Lies, lies, lies.

"Are you saying you want us to help you find a job? We can do that, no problem. Let's talk to Miriam—" Liz starts looking around for Miriam.

"No, not really." I stop her. I don't want a job that the Hunt Club finds for me. Once the FBI makes arrests, the last thing I want to do is be stuck in a job with Hunt Club people or their husbands. I want to stay clear from the Hunt Club. "I don't want to get into anything major. Just something until we're ready to do the setup with David or whatever."

"So, what do you have in mind?" Liz's smile is gone now. She probably thinks I'm nuts. "Are you saying you want to go back to the pizza place?"

"I don't know. I guess so. If they'll take me back. I didn't exactly leave on good terms."

"Oh, no, Sandra, no. That place is beneath you. You've come so far since then. You are no longer the same girl who worked there."

I feel tears sting my eyes because I know she's right. But where else can I go? Without help from Hunt Club, I have no real options. For a second, I wonder if I'm doing the right thing by helping the FBI shut down the Hunt Clubs. I am giving up the chance to change my life.

"Yeah, but it won't be for long, and I'm already trained there and everything. I really think it's the best thing," I tell her, almost choking it out of me. "Just temporarily."

"Okay, honey. If that's what you want to do. I admire your desire to want to be responsible. You're a good person."

"Thanks, Liz."

"In the meantime, we need to get things rolling for your setup with David. I don't want to undo all the good things we've done so far."

"I won't undo anything. I promise." I am sliding toward the door to the sitting room now, dying to get lost in the crowd of ladies who have already gathered and are taking their seats for the meeting.

"What did you and Teresa find out in Baltimore?" Miriam asks Cheryl once the meeting is under way. The women are completely focused on setting me up with David now. No one even mentions Mike anymore.

"Oh, he is a good one, Sandra!" Cheryl gushes, taking out her notes from her trip.

"If you don't want him, I'll take him," Teresa says and laughs.

"Not only is he gorgeous in person, but he is the biggest sweetheart. He never complains about the long hours, and he makes time to joke with the little kids he runs into at the hospital. Lots of energy and enthusiasm. Great sense of humor," Cheryl adds.

"And he is so smart. We talked to some of the other residents at Johns Hopkins Hospital, and everyone raves about how intelligent and sharp he is," Teresa tells us.

"That's wonderful," Charlotte says, looking over at me. "Good looks and a great personality. How often does that come around?"

"And money. Let's not forget that." Joyce jokes, but it's clear she's not really kidding.

"Oh, and Sandra, Rose and the H team have some great news for you." Miriam extends her arm, as if she's Vanna White showing the puzzle. "Rose, if you please."

"We found out he loves animals, like you do. We also discovered more information about his family's farm. David absolutely loves it there. Any time he has a free second, he goes to the farm to hang out with his animals. In fact, one of his former classmates said David was actually accepted into vet school and was going to go until his dad talked him out of it."

"You know, that may be the core connection right there," Miriam says, pointing her pen at Rose.

"Yes, I agree. Do we have any more details about his interest in animals and veterinary medicine? Like any specific breeds or anything?" Martha asks.

"Tammy, wasn't there something animal related in the information we received about his social and charitable activities?" Rose asks.

"Actually," Tammy says as she starts passing around several sheets of paper. "We found some really good information. Here is a list of the activities he's into. You can tell he's really into human medicine, but there are a few animal charities and events he's been involved with. Some of it may be because of his family's farm, though."

"What is this MEA group, Rose?" Martha asks.

"Where are you looking, dear?"

"Bottom of the second page," Martha says, and papers start flipping.

"Oh, that's right. He's been heavily involved with the Medical Equestrian Association."

"Equestrian? As in horses?" Selma asks.

"Equestrian medicine," Martha repeats. "Is that group involved with medicine for the horse itself? Or is it medicine for the people who ride horses?"

"We'll have to look it up," Miriam says, which translates into Liz needing to go in the other room and check on her computer.

"Can I get anyone anything while I'm up?" Liz calls out. She sets her books down in her chair and steps out of the room.

"Another glass of wine for me?"

"I'll take another mimosa."

"Miriam, when is that wonderful cheesecake scheduled to make an appearance?"

"I'll check on that." Miriam stands up, too, and heads for the kitchen.

Rose turns the attention back on to me. "How do you feel about horses, Sandra?"

"I LOVE them!" I blurt out, and the ladies all smile at me. In truth, I have no idea if I like them or not. I've never been on a horse in my life, and frankly, would be happy never being on a horse. Let them think this would work as a core connection, though. I'd hate for them to dig up something else that affects David deeply that we can then use to screw with his mind.

"Over on the fourth page," Tammy points out, then pauses to let people catch up. "There are some other references to equestrian groups. It looks like he's spoken at several Equine Medical Symposiums. Says here that he's even involved with the American Association of Equine Practitioners."

"Wonderful!" Rose writes it down. Liz walks back in and takes her seat.

"It will be a few more minutes on the cheesecake." Miriam appears with a tray of drinks, and the ladies step forward to get them. "Likely after the meeting, it should be ready for us."

"Okay," Liz says, back to business now, "It appears that the Medical Equestrian Association deals with horse-riding safety. Preventing human accidents on horses it looks like, plus the law and court cases," she tells us.

"That's fine. From Tammy's information, it is pretty obvious that he is interested in the actual health and treatment of the horse itself," Martha says.

"Oh yeah, he's definitely interested in horses," Liz says, laughs for a second, then takes out a stack of paper, and plops it in her lap. "This morning, Jeremy faxed over several pages of information about the research David has been into. If y'all would pass these around."

"It says here," Martha reads through the materials, not even waiting until everyone has a copy. "David actually enrolled in a vet school. University of Kentucky."

"Kentucky?" Joyce nearly spits her mimosa out of her mouth.

"It shows he was enrolled in their Equine Protozoal Myeloencephalitis Research Program." Liz is reading from Jeremy's notes. "But for whatever reason, he never actually attended there."

"His dad probably insisted he go into human medicine instead," Joyce says.

"So what is Equine Proto-whatever?" Annette asks.

"I'd have to research it some more, but according to Jeremy, it looks like some kind of horse neurological disease. They get it from being around possums or something."

"Opossums?" Martha asks.

"What's the difference between a possum and an opossum?" Annette asks and then looks over at me. "I never did get that."

"Same thing."

"I didn't know horses liked to hang out with possums all that much," Tammy marvels as she drinks her glass of wine. "Amazing what we learn at these meetings."

"So, he's into neurological diseases of horses, huh?" Charlotte repeats. "Is there any way we can set Sandra up to have the same research interests?"

"What about just setting Sandra up as someone with a horse that has a neurological disease?" Martha looks over at Miriam.

"Anyone know where we can get one of those?" Tammy laughs again from behind me.

"Great idea, Martha. We need to get Sandra trained on horses and then have her meet up with David. Through a common friend, perhaps? Then have her ask David for help with her dear, beloved sick horse. Who do we know who owns a ranch around here?" Miriam asks.

"There are those riding stables that Becky and her husband own. Remember? South of Fort Worth toward Granbury?" Rose is on the edge of her seat now.

"Right. We used them for that hunt for Jennifer and Lance." Liz points at Miriam with her pen.

Tammy taps me on the shoulder from behind. "Have you spent a lot of time around horses, Sandra?"

"Not too much, really. But I like them a lot."

"If you can learn to scuba with mantas, I'm sure you can learn to ride a horse." Annette elbows me in the side. It's obvious that the ladies are getting excited about the horse connection.

"Go ahead and see about getting Sandra set up for lessons, then, Liz. The sooner she can start, the better." Martha dictates with her cane tapping away.

"Wasn't Becky's ranch the one that sells horses, too?" Liz asks.

"I'm sure they do, but I'm not too sure we'll actually need to buy a horse," Miriam says and looks over at Martha. I am getting the feeling Miriam doesn't like horses very much.

"It's probably most effective if we actually buy the horse and use it in the hunt. It will give David and Sandra something tangible to bond over, rather than some hypothetical horse and disease," Martha says. "Besides, the Hunt Club can always use a horse, anyway. The difficulty arises in having to find a way to make our horse neurologically sick."

"That is the key," Miriam says, nodding.

"Hey, I've got it. What is that disease where they stumble around all crazy?" Annette asks.

"You mean mad cow disease?" Teresa laughs. "I don't know if horses get mad cow disease."

"Maybe there's a mad horse disease?"

"Can't we give a horse mad cow disease?"

"The cows get it from eating contaminated cow products. I doubt we could get a horse to eat cow meat," Liz says. "We might be able to inject it, I suppose. I'll do some digging to see what I can come up with." She writes notes down in the notebook on her lap. "Maybe see how the equine protozoal disease is transmitted exactly."

"What we really need to do is contact a veterinarian," Martha says.

"Well, doesn't Hunt Club have an official veterinarian we can consult with on this kind of thing?" Christine asks, laughing. "We seem to have everything else."

"Who was that vet we used when we set up the greyhound rescue during that one hunt?" Martha asks. "Roger Somethingorother?"

"Dr. Roger Collier, wasn't it?" Miriam says, flipping through her notebook.

"That's it!" Martha snaps her fingers. "Let's get a hold of him."

"Team H," Miriam turns to look at Rose. "See if you can locate him. Let's set up a consultation with him for sometime this week, if possible. He owes us, anyway. I know he'd be helpful if we need to make a horse sick."

"Fabulous!" Rose says, and several of the other ladies agree.

"Wait a sec. Can't we just like rent a horse that's already got a disease? I mean, do we really need to make a horse sick? That's kind of really twisted, don't you think?" I am completely shocked that no one is objecting to hurting a horse. Even Annette. What is wrong with these people?

There is silence in the room; no one agrees with me.

"If we want to get a core connection for you and David, then there will obviously have to be certain sacrifices," Miriam says matter-of-factly.

Joyce sighs loudly. "It's all part of the game."

"Sandra, don't you think this is the perfect connection for you and David?" Teresa asks me.

"Well, sure. It's just I really love animals, and I . . . ," I hesitate when I notice Martha and Miriam exchanging agitated glances. Now is not the time to make waves. "I just want to make sure David will actually like me. I'd hate to go to all that trouble and have it end up like Mike."

"Oh, he will like you, dear, don't worry," Rose says.

"Mike just wasn't the right one. David is so much better. I am sure he'll like you." Charlotte and several of the other ladies tell me. Out of the corner of my eye, I can see Martha is calmer now. I really need to be careful what I say.

"U Team, let's everyone focus on getting more information on David's interest in equine medicine. Maybe find out what drew him into that in the first place. Perhaps he had a sick horse who had that disease Liz mentioned." Miriam is writing in her book again.

"The more information about David's personal experiences with horses, the more intimate core connection we can create with Sandra," Martha tells us.

I can already picture where this is heading. I'm going to have to learn how to take care of and ride horses. Then, they are going to buy a horse and purposely make it sick, so I can take it to Dr. David. It's hard to imagine anyone harming an animal like that, but with the Hunt Club, I've learned that anything is possible.

*The FBI needs to hurry.*

"N Team? Let's have y'all work with Sandra on becoming more experienced with the world of horses. It's like a whole other culture, almost. See if several of you can take the lessons with her and help her along with that," Miriam says.

"I took horseback riding lessons a few summers as a kid," Annette says. "I'll try to tell you what I can remember." Annette smiles at me, and I force myself to smile back. She sure did have an active childhood for someone who supposedly suffered with Asperger's syndrome.

"And T Team." Miriam looks over at Liz. "Liz, get them to help you with researching the neurological diseases. I'm sure Dr. Collier can help with this, but you never know what ideas might come to you once you've looked into what is out there." Liz nods, and I notice everyone is taking notes. Except for me. I feel like I am sitting in a room full of crazy people.

"Oh, and Liz, have Jeremy find out if David has close friends who are into horses, will you?" Martha adds. "We need to start getting some contacts and leads established."

"My question is does David even have any free time to deal with horses?" Christine asks.

"He has some time to do what's really a priority. If he still loves horses as much as it sounds as if he does, then he'll make time for that. But, one thing I do know. He doesn't have a lot of time to spend getting to know people outside the medical circles," Cheryl says. "Sandra is going to have to jump into his world."

"We might have her work with Dr. Collier for a while," Rose suggests.

"Good idea. Sandra has already been working with Marcus and Staci Boxbinder to learn how to shine around doctors," Miriam tells everyone. "They are, of course, quite impressed with our Sandra." Everyone seems so pleased, and they all stare at me. I want to roll my eyes and say something sarcastic, but instead, I just smile.

*The FBI needs to hurry.*

After the meeting, I don't even wait for Annette when I get up to leave. I am making my way toward my shoes when Liz stops me.

"Sandra, about what you said earlier? You are now going to be so busy with the horses and preparing to meet David. Do you think you still want to work? I spoke with Miriam, and she agreed with me. We'd be happy to continue helping you."

"Well," I say, trying to make my hesitation sound like I'm thinking it over. My heart is racing in my chest. "Yeah, I want to go back to work. I think it's the right thing to do. Just in case something happens this time, and it doesn't work out with the Hunt Club and with David and stuff."

"Why wouldn't it work out?" Liz is looking at me with a strange expression on her face.

"Oh, you know. Like what happened with Mike." I put on one of my sandals, wanting to kick myself with it, as Rose approaches us.

"Not to worry, Sandra. David is different. I know you two will be perfect together." Rose reaches for her designer pumps.

"Absolutely!" Joyce joins in. Suddenly, Liz and I are surrounded by Dr. David–loving well-wishers. Luckily, it is enough for Liz to give up on her questioning. I quickly make my good-byes and leave.

Once in the door at home, I can't help it; I immediately rush to check my answering machine for a call from Mike. It's been several weeks, and he has finally stopped calling. I thought it would be easier this way, but I have found it's even worse now that he's no longer leaving messages on my machine. I still check though. I really miss him. But for his safety, I know I'm doing the right thing.

I feel like I'm waiting for the plane to crash. I scrutinize the people I run into on the street. Could they be FBI? Or a private investigator hired by the Hunt Club? It's obvious the Hunt Club members will do anything and not hesitate when it comes to hurting people. Or animals, for that matter. It would be easy for them to have people hang around my apartment complex, pretending to live here. I can see Martha setting me up for some type of plan B without giving it a second thought. I've got to be even more careful about whom I talk to and how I'm acting.

I check my e-mail several times a day. I figure when the hunt requests stop coming in, it will be some kind of indication that the FBI has taken action. So far, the hunt requests show no sign of slowing down. I must get ten to fifteen a day from the listserv. Everyone wanting to know if there are jobs we can fill with the girlfriend of the guy they are hunting. How many of these girlfriends are going to end up dead?

I try to calm my nerves, but nothing seems to work. Flipping through some magazines, I find some pictures of horses. They are perfect for the cover of my Hunt Club Game Book. I find my scissors and glue. My hands are shaking as I begin cutting out horse pictures.

# Chapter Twenty-six
## Déjà Vu

"We're having a rush for some reason," Jerry, my flour-covered manager says when I walk in the door. I hate that I actually had to beg for my old job at the pizza place. Jerry finally gave in, but it was mostly because he was still having a difficult time finding someone else who would put up with all of the crap an assistant manager has to put up with. He agreed to hire me back, under the condition that I'm brought in as an MIT—manager in training—again, until I "prove" myself.

Jerry quickly shovels a pizza out of the oven, throws it on the cutting board, and chops it into eight pieces. "Driver up!"

Nothing ever changes around here.

"Thirty-seven," a driver yells, running out the door with a pizza carrier held out in front of him.

"Forty-three." Another one goes.

"Get these times down, people," Jerry yells to the bright-lip-glossed teenagers on the food line who are giggling and sticking pieces of ham into their mouths.

"Hey, girls, why isn't someone slapping?" I tie my orange apron around my waist and hurry past the ovens to help on the pizza line.

"Pull your pinks!" Jerry yells from the cutting board on the upper level, hovering over us. Nicole and Erin pull their pink order slips off the small rack in front of them and stick each one under a different pizza.

"What do you need?" I ask, washing my hands before I begin slapping.

"Two sixteen inches and three twelve," Nicole tells me, with the hat on her head almost falling off.

"Is Chris working tonight?" Brenda asks me from her spot at the phone counter. She can't make pizzas until the cast comes off her arm, but she still asked to work here as a phone person, since her mother is making her pay for a new car.

"I haven't seen him yet, Brenda," I tell her. She and I are getting along much better now, mostly because I'm cutting her a lot of slack. I guess I still feel responsible for Martha causing her accident. I'm not cutting the others slack, though. I am trying to use my experiences—good and bad—with the Hunt Club, almost as if I don't want to lose myself in the pizza place. Compared to dealing with the upcoming Dr. David setup, learning how to ride horses, and trying to act "natural," pizza place problems no longer seem like a big deal. Waiting for the FBI to complete their investigations and close down the Hunt Clubs—that is the big deal.

"Thirty-nine," another driver yells as he runs out of the

store with his pizza. I can't believe the pizzas are still going out the door over thirty minutes old.

"I NEED A REMAKE!" Jerry practically sings. "It's a twelve-inch, pepperoni and extra cheese. Y'all forgot the extra cheese again!" Jerry hollers at us.

The phones are still ringing off the wall.

"First ring!" I yell to the phone people. "Get them on hold!" I turn to check on the pizza makers and can't help but laugh at the pizza chaos. "Nicole? Which pizza are you making? Here, why don't we slide this one to Erin. Then, you can make the pepperoni and extra cheese from that one. And Erin, you have waaaay too much sausage on that one."

"Remake in!" Nicole slides the remade pizza in the oven.

"Sandra," Brenda yells at me from the phone counter. "We've got a walk-in customer at the counter. He says he wants to talk to you."

"Can you take a message, please, Brenda? We're in the middle of a rush here."

Brenda walks around the ovens and over to where I'm saucing the next pizza.

"He says it's really important." She has a big goofy grin on her face, which usually means it's a pissed-off customer who wants to chop my head off.

"I'll be right there." I hand the pizza crust to Nicole and wash my hands real fast. Dusting the flour off the front of my apron, I sigh as I make my away around the ovens and over to the takeout counter. "Can I help you?"

"Sandra."

I look up to see Mike's sweet face, standing on the other side of the takeout counter.

"Oh no!" I blurt out, immediately ducking down behind

the counter. "I don't want you to see me like this." I can't believe he's here . . . Part of me wants to jump up and down, screaming with excitement. The other part of me wishes the floor would open up and swallow me whole.

"It's okay, Sandra." He laughs at me. "I think you look cute." I poke my head up.

"I can't believe you're here." Tears are stinging my eyes. My stomach hurts—I've missed him so much.

"Can I talk to you for a second?" He asks. I look around the store. The phones are ringing off the wall. Drivers are leaving with pizzas over thirty minutes old. The pizza makers are waiting for me to slap more crust. Then I look at Jerry.

"Five minutes," Jerry tells me.

"Let's go outside." I gesture to the door as I quickly take off my sauce and flour-covered apron.

"I'm sorry, I—" I'm interrupted by Mike kissing me. All of a sudden, I forgot what I was going to say.

"Are you okay? I've been worried as hell." He still has his arms around me as he looks me in the eyes. I wish I wasn't wearing this dorky pizza outfit.

"Yes, are you okay?"

"Yes." He hugs me again. "The FBI said they spoke to you, too. I'm so sorry, Sandra. I hate that you had to be involved in all that."

"What? Wait, what do you mean?"

"About Sofia, my ex-girlfriend. She was killed in Paris. The FBI stopped me as I was leaving LAX when your flight left. They told me about Sofia. And all about the Hunt Club."

"I am so sorry, Mike!"

"It's not your fault, Sandra. I know you were not involved in her death."

"The FBI stopped me at LAX, too, and I've been scared to death about everything that has been going on." I look into his blue eyes. "You really shouldn't be here. It's not safe."

"It's okay. The FBI said they are investigating the Hunt Clubs. I'm sure it's just a matter of time before they start making arrests."

"I know, they said the same thing to me. But in the meantime, I'm supposed to lie low and just go with the usual flow of everything." I look around the parking lot. Most of the cars belong to the drivers and have lit neon signs on their roofs. It is the one or two cars without the car-top signs that I'm worried about.

"Shit, Sandra," Mike reaches up and touches my cheek. "When I couldn't get hold of you, I was so worried something had happened. Thankfully, the FBI finally told me where you were."

I nod for a moment. "I've been here. I just didn't know what to do about everything. The Hunt Club was supposed to be a matchmaking club, you know? But, then I talked to the FBI, and I found out what they really do. I was afraid of what would happen if I continued to see you. I thought it would be safer this way. I am so sorry," I keep saying over and over as I hug him. "You have no idea."

"It's okay. The only thing that matters is that you're safe."

"We still have to be careful," I warn him. "I get a strong feeling there are people watching me."

"That's because there are people watching you." Mike points behind me. The front windows of the store are lined with pizza employees watching us, their fingertips and noses pressed against the glass. "Let's go somewhere and talk." He takes my hand.

"But what about work?" I gesture over my shoulder to the pizza place, embarrassed.

"I was kind of hoping I could convince you to leave it and come back to Malibu with me. So we can spend some time together."

"Just let me grab my purse."

"Wait." Mike grabs my hand again as he's laughing. It's so good to hear his laugh and to see his smile. "You're supposed to maintain the status quo, right? Then you probably can't just leave so fast. We need to come up with something."

"I can't believe I have to go back in there and work. After seeing you—" I wrap my arms around him again, and I don't want to let go.

"Can I go wait for you at your apartment?"

"I don't know." I look up at his face. "It's a dive, Mike. Really."

"You know I don't care about that."

"Okay, I'll get you my keys, and I'll meet you there as soon as I can get off." I rush toward the store, and as soon as I step inside, I'm greeted by a chorus of "*Whooa*, Sandra's got a boyfriend!" And the girls all want to know how I know THE Michael Warren.

Once I finish work, I rush home to meet up with Mike at my apartment. After I take a shower to wash off tonight's pizza mess and change into casual clothes, I return to the living room. I just stand there, watching him for a few seconds. The lights are off except in the kitchen, and Mike's blue eyes are highlighted by the glow from the TV. "I still can't believe you're actually here."

"Me, either." Mike smiles at me from the couch. When I

walk closer to him, he stands up and slips his hands around my waist to hug me again. I try not to cry, telling myself it would ruin the makeup I just so carefully applied.

"You're watching the DVD that the dive crew made for us on our trip," I say finally, and we sit down on the couch together. "There's Big Bertha," I point out to him. "It's funny how much I've missed the mantas."

"The DVD doesn't do them justice. Big Bertha has got to be sixteen feet across." He laughs, looking at me closely, like he's memorizing my face.

"Would you like something to drink? Dr Pepper?"

"Sure." He squeezes my hand as I stand up and head for the kitchen. "You know, it was hell for me when I first watched that DVD they gave us. Watching you swim around, pointing and waving at the mantas."

"I could only get through about twenty seconds of it before I had to turn it off." I pour the Dr Pepper into glasses with ice and laugh to myself because I only started to like Dr Pepper when we were on our Hawaii trip. Returning to the living room, I hand him his glass and sit down on the couch again next to him. "I was so afraid I'd never see you again."

"I wasn't about to let that happen." He puts his arm around me.

"I'm also sorry we won't be seeing them again." I gesture toward the mantas that are doing somersaults on the screen. "Or making a movie with them."

"Yeah, I know what you mean." We watch the video in silence for a few minutes. Mike suddenly smiles. "Although, we really could make a movie with the mantas."

"We could?" I laugh. "How?"

"We just put together a script, hire a crew, hire some other actors, and make an independent film." He brushes the bangs out of my eyes with his fingers. "I've been looking for a project to produce for a while now."

"It would be amazing to work with them, wouldn't it?" I watch the mantas gracefully swoop and flip around us on the video. "I don't think most people have ever seen or heard of a manta ray."

"What were you thinking the film was going to be about, when you talked to me before?" He leans back against the couch.

"We hadn't really planned it yet, but while we were on the boat, I kind of came up with some ideas. Promise you won't laugh." I pause to look over at him, and he nods. "I was thinking of a family-oriented movie, you know, like the ones that were out when we were kids? Have a loner kid who's unhappy with his parents' divorce and having to move because of his mom's new husband. He has a difficult time fitting in, and the only thing he really likes to do is snorkel with the mantas. They become like his little friends, and then one day something happens. Like one of the mantas finds a diamond or something, and of course the little boy has to find out where it came from."

"Kids love those kind of movies." He nods with a big smile on his face. "Throw in an old pirate-ship sunken treasure or something. I see a lot of possibilities, and there are probably scripts out there already that we can modify. And you're right to make it a family film, geared toward kids, because it would be hard to incorporate the mantas into a film targeted to an older audience. Not as the primary focus, anyway. Unless we made them like evil mantas or something."

I laugh. "But how mean can a manta be? They don't even really have teeth."

"We could have them grow big teeth as part of the story, maybe? And then have some teeth artificially made for the film." He laughs, too, making his blue eyes almost light up.

"Can you imagine someone putting them in the manta's mouth, though? Like getting Lefty to hold still long enough?" It is beginning to feel like no time has passed since the last time Mike and I were together. And I love the idea of making an indie film together—for real!

"I think our first step is to get hold of some buddies of mine in Hollywood. See if we can get them interested, too, and get the script under way. You still interested in coming back to Malibu with me?"

"Of course. But, what about the whole Hunt Club mess?"

"All the more reason for me to get you to Malibu as quickly as possible. Like you said, it's not safe for you here, Sandra. I don't want to spend any more time here than we absolutely have to."

"How can we just leave, though? You know what they're capable of. They will know where to find us, and there are Hunt Clubs in California, too."

We're both quiet for a minute.

"Wouldn't it be logical to them for me to come after you? After all the time they saw us together on the boat. Would they really think it was weird if I showed up here?" Mike finally asks.

"You're right; I bet they would be thrilled to know you came here looking for me. But they have no idea that you tried to call me. They think you weren't really that interested, so they have pushed me in other directions."

Mike laughs that adorable laugh of his. "What does that mean?"

"They're trying to set me up with someone else."

"You're kidding. So fast? Gee, thanks a lot."

"No no, it's not like that. When the FBI told me about what had happened, I wanted you to stay as far away from us as possible for your own sake. So, I told them I thought you gave up on me. And that I gave up on you, too. I wanted them to set me up with someone else."

"Can you tell them you changed your mind?"

"I think so. Once I tell them you're here, I can't imagine them trying to set me up with someone else." He has no idea how much I would love to blow off the whole Dr. David fiasco. Or how the lives of one or more horses may be saved from opossum neurological diseases. "I just hope I can pull it off."

"You don't think you can pull off having feelings for me? Gee, thanks a lot." He teases again, obviously trying to make me feel better by injecting humor.

"No, I'm not talking about my feelings for you! I'm just kind of freaked out about everything. My nerves are completely shot. What if I blow it?"

"You won't blow it, Sandra. I'll be right there with you. Just tell them we're together, and I want you in my life."

"There's more to it than that, I'm afraid." How do I tell Mike about the engagement requirement? That they may not want me living with him unless we're engaged, like it was with Amber and Brantley?

"Whatever it is, we can do it. Make it as simple as possible."

"They will want to know that we're serious about each other first, before they'll let me go off to Malibu with you."

He's holding my hand again. "Okay, so how serious do we need to be? More serious than, say, me tracking you down, flying cross-country, and showing up at your job? Doesn't that show I'm serious about you? Tell them we're talking about our future. That I want you to meet the people closest to me because we're making plans on a life together out there. Would that work? I mean, it is pretty much the truth, anyway."

I feel tears in my eyes when I think about what he went through just to be here with me. I really never thought I'd see him again, much less be talking about going to Malibu together.

"I think it would work. They should be ecstatic."

"Then that's what we'll do. When is the next meeting?"

"Day after tomorrow."

"Good, then you'll have time to pack, quit your job, and make whatever arrangements we need to." He seems pleased.

Mike has no idea how happy I am to be leaving Dallas and the Hunt Club. We arrange for airline tickets the next day, I quit my job—again—at the pizza place, and start packing. Everything is falling into place for my performance at the Hunt Club meeting.

"Should I go in alone?"

"Is that what you would normally do?" Mike asks me, as he sits next to me at my kitchen table, going over our itinerary.

"Yeah. And, I think I'd probably call someone like Miriam ahead of time. Probably Annette, too."

"Great. Good idea. I don't really like you going back to that place alone. See if I can come with you. If you call ahead of time, maybe they'll be more likely to let me in?"

"I hope so. I should probably also call Agent McFarland, the guy I've been talking to at the FBI. Fill him in on what's going on." I reach for the phone, deciding to call McFarland first. He usually answers his own phone, but this time a woman answers.

"FBI, how may I direct your call?" The female voice asks.

"Officer—I mean, Agent McFarland?"

"He's out of the office. Would you like his voice mail?"

"No, well, is there any other way I can reach him?"

"Who's calling, please?"

"This is Sandra Greene. I am helping with an investigation he is working on." I can hear her typing something into a computer on the other end of the line.

"The information has been sent to him."

"Thank you." I don't know what else to do, so I just hang up.

"He wasn't there?" Mike asks.

"No. I left a message, though. I think." I look up at him. "It was kind of weird."

"It's the FBI. They're kind of weird." Mike puts his hand over mine on the table. "Do you want to try calling Miriam or Annette?" His smile always seems to make me feel better.

To my relief, Miriam is home and answers her phone.

"Oh, Miriam, guess what! I have the most exciting news; guess who came to see me, Mike—he's here, right now standing in my kitchen, and we've talked about everything, and I'm so happy because we've been making all kinds of plans, and I can't believe it, but he has serious feelings for me, and he says he wants us to have a future together!" In my typical nervous fashion, I blurt out the story about Mike to her, practically all in one sentence.

"That is wonderful!" Miriam replies. "I'm so happy for you, dear. When did this all happen?"

"Last night. He showed up at the pizza place. I could have just died." The enthusiasm in my voice is sincere.

"Well, to tell you the truth, I always thought that boy would come to his senses. I think it's just wonderful!"

"We are anxious to get to Malibu, so I can meet the people closest to him, and we can make concrete plans about our future. What do you think? Is it, like, okay for me to do that?" It feels weird to ask her permission so bluntly, but I don't know any other way.

"Well, of course, Sandra. You must come to the meeting tomorrow night so we can tell everyone. We'll want to hear all the details. You will wait and leave for Malibu after the meeting tomorrow?"

"Sure, but, um, I think our flight leaves shortly after that. Is there any way I could possibly bring Mike with me to the meeting?"

"*Humm.*" Miriam pauses for a few seconds, and I hold my breath. "I know everyone would love to meet Mike. But, that would mean you would have to explain who we all are. Have you said anything to him?"

"No. He still only knows about you, Christine, and Annette, and how y'all are helping me with the film. He doesn't know about anyone else," I lie, and I'm afraid she can tell because I'm talking so fast.

"Good. I think it will work. You should just tell him we are your colleagues and friends supporting you and your film. And it's only natural that all of us would want to get to know him since he's so important to you and may be in the film down the road. Does that sound like something you can do?"

"That sounds perfect. I think he'll really like that." I glance over at Mike.

"I'll prepare everyone ahead of time. I CAN'T WAIT to tell Martha! And Joycee and Rose. They'll be so happy."

"Not as happy as I am," I tell her. "And I have all of you to thank."

"This has turned out to be one of the most special hunts we've had yet. Martha! Martha! Come in here, I've got some wonderful news!" Miriam is practically yelling. "I must let you go, now, Sandra. We will see y'all tomorrow. Congratulations!"

"How did it go?" Mike asks me when I finally hang up the phone.

"Wonderful." I laugh. "She kept saying 'wonderful.'"

"Makes you think she didn't believe you?"

"I can't tell. Maybe I'm just being paranoid. She did seem really happy," I tell him. "It just was easier than I thought. Maybe too easy?"

"Tell me exactly what she said." His face is just inches from mine. His hair is in his eyes again, and it's hard to keep from brushing it from his face with my fingers. I play with it for a few seconds before reviewing Miriam's conversation with him again, word by word.

"It sounds like to me she was surprised and excited, but you know her better than I do. We do need to be cautious," Mike concludes.

"I wish we could get hold of Agent McFarland. He was the one who said it was important to my safety and to the investigation that I act natural, to just do what Hunt Club would expect me to do." I stand up and walk in the living room. There are two empty boxes waiting to be packed. "I'm afraid if we just leave that they really will figure out something is up and come after us. They know where we're going, after all."

"I agree that leaving right now, especially when they are expecting us at the meeting, will raise a red flag." Mike is looking at the boxes now, too. "I still think it's safer if we let them see us completely wrapped up in being together. Like we don't have a care in the world about anyone or anything else but each other. If they see you're preoccupied with me, they'll assume you'd never have time to think about causing them any trouble. They'd see you are no threat to them."

"Okay." I nod and smile at him, thinking it won't be that difficult to portray. If not for fearing for my life, or his life, and the lives of other people, I really would be completely consumed by him.

"We'd better get you packed, then."

"I have so much stuff I'm not sure what to do with." I put my foot in the box closest to me, looking around the living room and into the bedroom at all my stuff.

"I'll help you. And whatever we can't get on the plane, we'll pack up and just have it shipped once you're safe with me in Malibu."

It feels weird to have a guy, especially Mike, going through my stuff with me to see what I need to take on our trip. At the same time, it's nice when he discovers something of mine, and we realize we have even more in common.

"Do you want to bring your copy of our dive DVD?" Mike asks me as the afternoon wears on. He's flipping through my DVDs and VHS tapes stacked on the TV, in the cabinet next to it, and on the floor.

"Sure. You never know when we might need to have my copy for some reason." I know Mike has his own DVD of our dives, but it somehow seems right to bring my copy, too. Part of me feels as if I'm not ever coming back here. It's strange how that thought doesn't bother me. I head to the kitchen to start packing the dishes.

Familiar music comes from the living room, and I find myself humming to it. I freeze with a plate in my hand when I realize what Mike is watching on the VCR.

*It's My Life.*

It's the tape of the TV show Mike was on. Somehow, I put the plate in the sink and walk quickly into the living room, where Mike is kneeling on the floor, glued to the TV.

"Mike," I begin but don't really know what to say. I turned most of my Hunt Club stuff about Mike over to the FBI. But I couldn't part with these VHS tapes of his show. I needed them in case I never saw Mike again.

"You've got all the episodes," he says, almost in a monotone. I can't tell if he's asking me or telling me.

I kneel down next to him on the floor. "I'm so sorry."

"The FBI told me how the Hunt Club operated. I knew you and I were set up." He looks over at me. "I guess I just didn't realize how much planning went into it. How much *you* planned it."

Several possible responses go through my mind all at once. Maybe I could say something like, "Oh, is that YOU?" Like I didn't realize it was him on the video. Or maybe I could say I didn't get the episodes until after our trip to Hawaii?

*This can't be happening.*

"Mike, I'm sorry," I say again. "I don't blame you for being mad. You have every right to hate me for this." I have to tell him the truth. I can't lie anymore. "The Hunt Club let us choose who we wanted. Who I wanted them to set me up with."

He doesn't say anything. We watch as the video shows Mike in his character of "Jake" walking through a classroom. Past the homely girl who has a crush on him. He sits down in the seat in the back row. All the other students have books and papers on their desks, but Jake doesn't even have a pen.

"I guess I should be flattered that you chose me when you could have chosen anyone?" He half laughs. My stomach hurts, and I'm afraid to move. I can literally feel what it would be like for him to get up and walk to the door and just leave me. I start to cry—the ugly cry.

"I knew who you were before we met on the boat. We researched you, and they told me how to approach you. How I should act with you. I was afraid you—" I hold my breath for a second. Visions of me flopping on the living room floor hysterically go through my mind. Must not do that.

"Afraid I would what?"

"I was afraid you'd never be interested in me if I didn't follow their plan."

"Sandra." Mike sits back on his heels and shakes his head.

"I didn't know what else to do. I really wanted to meet you."

"Sandra," he says again and looks at me for a second. "You could have come on board that boat in your pizza uniform, covered in flour and whatever else all over you, and I would have still been interested in you."

I look at him, wondering what the catch is. When he doesn't include a "but" at the end of the sentence, I lean my head against his shoulder. I can finally breathe again when he puts his arm around me.

"I feel like that homely girl on the show," I tell him, more into his shoulder than out loud. We both look up at the TV screen. The homely girl is writing a note to her friend about how cute Jake is. "Just like her. I thought you would never notice me."

"You do realize who that actress is, don't you? She's been the lead in other films and on the cover of fashion magazines. She's beautiful. On this show, she was just cast as a homely girl, but she's really far from it." He hugs me from the side for a second. "Like you."

I look up at his face to try and figure out what he is saying.

"It's like you were cast in this role you're trying to escape.

Working at the pizza place, dealing with your past and the difficult people in your life. But that's not really who you are. Not any more than that actress is a homely girl."

"You are the only one who has ever thought that way."

"I doubt that," he laughs. "You just need to see yourself in a more realistic light."

The next morning, as I finish packing my suitcases, Mike takes them out to the rental car. Watching him leave with the latest load, I think about how much we have in common. We may be from different worlds, but at the same time, we are from the same background and the same roots. Mike is no more a shanty-shacker than I am a homely girl. We both have taken extreme measures to try and outrun the memories of our childhood. It's not who we are. Who people are is not determined by their past but by their future.

"Sandra, there's someone here to see you outside," Mike says, as he comes back in from the rental car. All of a sudden a screeching and screaming Annette comes running by him and throws her arms around me.

"Sandra! I'm soooo happy!" She's still jumping up and down.

"I know!" I'm jumping up and down with her, screaming.

"I'm so happy for you!" She's hugging Mike now. He jumps up and down with her, too. He's such a good sport. "I was literally crying when Miriam called me this morning. I just couldn't believe it. What a miracle!"

"I was going to call you, Annette—"

"That's okay, that's okay. Miriam said you were bringing Mike to the meeting tonight." She pauses to take a breath. "I was going to wait to see you then, but then I couldn't wait, so here I am! Oh, Mike, I am so glad to see you!"

"I'm glad to see you, too." He laughs. "Sandra, I'm going to go make sure the car is locked up. I'll be right back."

"So, tell me everything. What happened?" Annette grabs my hand and pulls me toward the couch. She's dressed up in fancy clothes and designer sunglasses, and it makes me sick now that I know how the Hunt Club made its money. I also hate what the Hunt Club has done to her personality.

"He just showed up night before last. While I was at work—"

"Did he say where he's been? Why didn't he get ahold of you right away?" She rolls her eyes. "I could just kill him! What took him so long to get here?"

"It's kind of complicated. I don't know," I say in a whisper, not knowing how to answer her. I hope that by whispering she'll think I just can't talk about it because Mike will overhear us.

"Oh, I bet he had to make sure things were really over with Sofia. Is that it?" She's whispering now.

"Maybe. It could be," I say, looking up at the door and wishing Mike would hurry up. "Yeah, I bet that's it." I'm so glad Annette has a creative imagination. I want to change the subject. "Hey, what happens now with David?"

"David?"

"Yeah, you know, my other hunt? What will happen now?"

"Oh, don't give him another thought," Annette says, touching my hand. "It will be like that hunt never happened. Martha and Miriam will make sure of that. We haven't even gotten the horse yet. So, it's fine. All it means is you've learned some horseback riding stuff. You never know when that might come in handy."

"I just didn't know if it would be a big deal."

"No, not at all. Everyone is so happy about Mike. Except

for Rose, maybe. She's the only one, I think, who had her whole heart set on you being Mrs. David Hopwood. Junior. The others will be glad you and Mike are together. All you have to do now is meet the Five-Month Rule."

"Oh, that's right. How does the five-month thing work exactly?"

"I'm sure Miriam and Rose are planning on pulling you aside to go over all of that with you again at the meeting. According to the rule book, Mike has to ask you to marry him within five months of when you first met him. So you still have what? Over three months?"

"Annette," I whisper again and pause for effect. "There's no reason to worry about that. We're already talking about our future."

Annette hugs me. "I am so relieved!"

We both look up when Mike comes back in. "Can we get you something to drink?" I am up, off the couch, getting Dr Peppers for everyone.

"Mike, you have no idea how happy I am to see you," Annette sounds calmer now, almost tearful. "I knew when we met you on the boat that you and Sandra were soul mates. Just like lobsters."

"Lobsters?"

"They mate for life, you know."

"That's him. He's my lobster," I tell her, feeling tears well up in my eyes, too.

We finish our Dr Peppers, and Annette leaves to run errands for William. Mike walks over and sits next to me on the couch. "Everything go okay?"

"Yes, she's really happy for us. And I know it's real; I've never known Annette to be a very good liar. I have been able to see through stuff with her." I tell him about the Asperger's syndrome core connection and how I caught on to it. "She's really a good person. She just got all caught up in the excitement."

"Maybe she doesn't know about the murders?" Mike asks, intertwining his fingers with mine.

"But, she does know they plan B people. Wouldn't she know about all of it?"

"You didn't know until the FBI told you. It's possible Annette and the others really are innocent in all this. Maybe only the top ones, like Miriam and that Martha woman you told me about, have a part in the criminal stuff."

"You're probably right. In fact, now that I think about it, the Hunt Club has been really careful to make sure Jeremy handles everything. We don't know any details at all, even about what goes into the plan B stuff, until it's over." I tell him about the situation with Brantley and how we didn't know what really happened with the hooker until Joyce was able to find out and tell us.

"That would never work on me." Mike laughs out loud at what happened with Brantley. "What an idiot."

I don't have the heart to tell Mike about what Martha's idea was to plan B him.

"Maybe McFarland is right, and things will be fine as long as we act natural." I smile at him, and he kisses me.

"It will be fine," he says. "We'll just go to the meeting, say our hellos and good-byes, and get the hell out of Texas."

# Chapter Twenty-seven
## The Meeting

Everybody has that one shoebox tucked away in his or her closet somewhere. It's a box no one else is ever supposed to see, and a great deal can be learned about a person by what they have inside of it. For some people, that box contains money or something romantic, such as old love letters. For me, that box contains a special collection from my childhood.

"You've got about fifty little Matchbox cars in here!" Mike is laughing from where he sits on the floor of my tiny bedroom closet. "But, every one of them is the exact same car. The Mach Five?"

"I know. I kind of had a crush."

"A crush? On Speed Racer?"

"Yeah. He was my first love," I tell him about my crush

on the cartoon character and sit down next to him. I get the feeling Mike would be rolling around on the floor laughing if there were enough room in the closet. He's picked up two of the Mach Fives out of the box and is racing them along one of my legs, complete with *vroom-vroom* sounds.

"I used to pretend I was Speed Racer. I had a little Mach Five, too," he says. "But only one. I remember getting into fights with kids on the playground over whether it was called the 'Mach Five' or the 'Mark Five.'"

"It's the Mach Five." I grin at him.

He runs one of the cars up my back. "I also had a soapbox-size one my dad and I built when I was about five or so."

"Did you race it?"

"Nah, but Dad and I rolled it down the muddy hill in our backyard several times."

I smile at him, and our eyes meet. Mike knows what it's like to not know where Dad is. He is one of the few people I have met in my life who truly understands the hole that's been left without my dad. I stand up in my closet that is now empty of all my clothes.

"This pretty much wraps up everything, doesn't it? The last box." He puts the lid back on my Mach Five collection. "You sad to be leaving here?"

"No, not really." I look down at him. "Not at all." In truth, I can't wait to go to California and start over with my life with Mike. I want to leave all this behind, like it's in a big shoebox I can fasten the lid to and store somewhere in the back of my mind.

As Mike tapes up the last boxes, I double-check to make sure I have everything.

"I wish we didn't have to go to the Hunt Club meeting. I want to be on the plane. Right now."

"I know what you mean," Mike says and puts his arm around me. "I'm not exactly looking forward to seeing these people." He hasn't said much about Sofia, but her death must weigh heavily on his mind. It must be difficult for him to think he'll be standing in a room full of people who contributed to her death. Spending the afternoon reminiscing about our childhoods while going through all my belongings has gotten both of our minds off of the meeting. It has also helped to finally squelch the fear that has pretty much taken over me these past few weeks. The fear is resurfacing, however, as we leave for the final Hunt Club meeting.

Dressed in casual shorts and T-shirts, the kind you never see on anyone in Miriam's fancy home, Mike and I head to Highland Park in his rental car. I decided to leave my car with one of my neighbors, who has agreed to help ship my stuff out to me once I get set up at Mike's house in Malibu. She acted like it was a Mercedes or something, hugging me and thanking me, when I gave her the keys to my Hyundai.

"You're really good at driving in traffic," I tell Mike, holding his right hand while he steers with his left. Without me having to say anything, he moves in and out of the appearing and disappearing lanes on Central Expressway without getting caught in the backup.

"Must be my innate pizza-delivery-driver skills." He tries to make me laugh while not taking his eyes off the road. "Either that, or it's because I'm used to driving the Five in L.A. It's much worse than this."

"Really?"

"Oh yeah, you'll see when we get out there. You can get stuck sitting there for hours on it if you don't know what you're doing."

Mike's calmness seems contagious, but I still feel a sense of doom as we turn onto Miriam's street. I no longer have any faith or trust in the Hunt Club. There have been too many innocent people who have been hurt, like Brenda, and Cami and Jodee, and Sofia. So many lives have been changed, and so many men have been tricked. I'm glad it is almost over because I can't take much more of wondering if I'm being followed or if the cars in the parking lot belong to Jeremy and his friends. I smile for a second, realizing that my days of paranoia are almost over.

"You doing okay?" Mike glances over at me. It suddenly dawns on me that my grip on his hand has tightened.

"I think so. The house is just up the hill, there. Where all the cars are." The BMWs, Mercedes, and other fancy cars that I don't know the names of are all parked in and around Miriam's driveway. "Now, remember, Mike, you don't know anything about what the Hunt Club really does. Okay? Nothing about the setups or anything. They are just my friends and colleagues from the film project."

"Right." Mike looks for a place to park. "What about the husbands? How much do they know?"

"The Hunt Club makes sure to keep most of the husbands in the dark. The guys know we're a women's club, but they think the primary focus of the club is charity stuff and community service. I think it's like with any typical expensive women's club; I don't think men really want to know what goes on here. The men just help out whenever they're asked, and that's pretty much it."

Mike slows the car and parks down the block. As he turns off the engine, I take a deep breath.

"Hey, look at me," he says, taking off his seat belt and turning to face me. "Things are going to be fine. Okay? I promise I won't ever let anything happen to you."

I smile at him. He leans forward and kisses me. Looking up into his blue eyes, I believe in him, and I trust him. I feel like I can accomplish anything if he's with me. "Okay."

We start walking up the familiar hill near Miriam's house. Poor sweet Mike; he doesn't have a clue how these Hunt Club ladies can be when they all get together. I thought about warning him about all the questions he'll likely get from people like Joyce and Rose, but I decide he can take it. I notice Mike doesn't seem affected at all by the huge homes and beautiful landscaped lawns. He's used to this life. And I can't wait to be used to it, too.

"We'll just play it cool." Mike squeezes my hand as we start up the steps to Miriam's house. "Thirty minutes. Then, we're out of here."

I laugh for a second, thinking there has never been a time when Hunt Club ladies could end any type of meeting in just thirty minutes. They won't be done hugging him in that amount of time.

"We have to take our shoes off," I tell him quietly as I ring the bell, and we hear the chimes.

"Okay. I'm not wearing socks. But, hey, at least my feet are clean." He and I laugh, looking down at his sandaled feet.

"Sandra and Mike!" Miriam greets us at the door. "So wonderful to see you!" Miriam opens the giant-sized door, hugs each of us, and lets us in the foyer. We remove our shoes and follow Miriam. Familiar voices echo from the sitting room. "Charlotte is running late with the mimosas." She smiles awkwardly. "But, she should be here any moment." Mike and I are still holding hands as she leads us through the living room and on in toward the sitting room. The room gets strangely quiet as we walk in.

"Mike," Joyce says in her lyrical voice as she stands up to

greet him. Mike shakes her diamond-covered hand. I look around the room filled with ladies—my friends. No one is making eye contact with me.

Amber?

Teresa?

Rose?

Are they mad about my hunt for David being over? I glace over at Annette, sitting on the familiar couch we always sit on. Her face is red. She's been crying, and it doesn't appear to be tears of happiness. Something is definitely wrong. I glace over at Martha's chair in the corner, which is uncharacteristically empty. Has something happened to Martha? Liz is missing, too. Miriam is still standing next to us. No one says anything. There is a tray of mini muffins and sandwiches on the coffee table, but the usual party atmosphere is missing.

"Something is wrong," I say quietly to Mike.

"Maybe it's because Charlotte is late with the mimosas?" he whispers back.

Suddenly the door to the dining room opens. Liz appears, followed by a large bearded man, and Martha. With her cane.

"You must be Sandra." The man looks a little like Dr. Phil as he extends his hand to me. "I'm Jeremy Lambert." His southern accent even sounds a little like Dr. Phil.

"Oh. Hi, nice to meet you." I glance down and notice he is still wearing his shoes.

"I had been looking forward to speaking to you about finding your father," Jeremy says. "But then, I never heard from you." I completely forgot about telling Miriam and Liz that I wanted to contact him about finding my dad.

I smile, embarrassed, and start doing the mumbling thing. "Oh, I wasn't sure if I could bother you." Things feel weird all of a sudden, and I don't know what else to say. I look over at Annette, who is not looking at us and appears to be crying again. Amber is sitting next to her now.

"And Mike," Jeremy says, turning to face Mike with a smile on his face. "Nice work." Jeremy suddenly pats Mike on the back.

They shake hands, a little too enthusiastically.

"Well, I got the information you were looking for," Mike tells them, laughing.

"Yes, you did. And we appreciate it." Jeremy is still shaking his hand.

"And your suspicions were right. She is helping the FBI." Mike's smile has faded now. The room is silent except for Annette's quiet sobbing. "I'll give you that information, but first, I believe there's still the small matter of my fee?"

"Of course. I believe Elizabeth can help you with that." Jeremy nods to Liz, who leads Mike back toward the dining room.

"Thank you, Mike. You've done a fabulous job." Martha shakes his hand as he passes by her.

"Wait," I say quickly, stepping toward them. "Mike? What's going on?"

"I don't have anything to say to you," Mike yells back over his shoulder as he follows Liz.

"No no. You get to stay out here with us, Sandra." Jeremy holds up his hand, halting my thoughts of chasing after Mike. I look at Miriam, then at Martha. Their faces are expressionless. Joyce is sitting back down in her chair. Other than that, no one has moved.

I want to go with Mike. That's all I can focus on. Mike.

"Why don't you have a seat?" Jeremy points to the chair in which Miriam usually sits. My feet can't move. "Go ahead,

Sandra." He gestures to the chair again. I make my way slowly and sit down across from Annette.

"You knew about this?" I ask Annette, but I don't know exactly what it is she knew or what is really going on myself. She won't make eye contact with me.

"So," Jeremy says, pulling a chair from against the wall and sitting down right next to me. He's sitting a little too close. "You have been helping the FBI."

"I want to talk to Mike."

"Mike is busy right now."

I look up toward the front door to think about making a run for it. But Jeremy is blocking my path, along with several of the ladies. Why aren't any of the ladies saying anything?

"What happened with Mike?" I ask, feeling total panic wash over me.

"He's been helping us." Jeremy laughs. "Surprised?"

I really shouldn't be surprised, I guess. The Hunt Club does things like this all the time. Secrets. Setups. Pretending. Was this some kind of plan B? I just never expected Mike could ever betray me.

"He contacted us when he was unable to reach you," Martha tells me matter-of-factly. She's leaning on her cane, hovering above us like a big old black bird. "Why didn't you tell us that Mike had been calling you, Sandra? You LIED to us."

"He said he called you every day for weeks. He couldn't understand why you wouldn't take his calls," Miriam says. "He finally contacted the charter boat company we used for your hunt to see if they would give him the contact information for Annette, Christine, and me. Of course they wouldn't give out our information, but they did take a message. When they contacted me, that's when I called Mike."

"He was more than eager to find out what was going on. We told him we wanted to help y'all get together—for your best interest," Martha continues.

"Amazing how interested he became in helping us, once he got to know everyone," Joyce adds, sounding like she's Mike's best friend or something.

"Not to mention when he got to know so many of our Ben Franklins really well," Martha says, laughing.

"Ben Franklin is on the one-hundred-dollar bill, in case you didn't know," Jeremy says, mockingly. I don't know which bothers me more, the fact he's in my face or how his tone makes me sound like I'm some poor girl who only knows what a hundred-dollar-bill looks like because I hustle people.

It's hard for me to believe that Mike would betray me like this. Especially for money. I thought he had feelings for me. What happened to the core-connection theory? Isn't it supposed to be unbreakable?

"We knew something was up when you went back to that awful pizza place," Miriam says. "Especially after all we did to help you. That made even less sense to us than you not taking Mike's calls."

"Did you contact the FBI, or did they contact you?" Jeremy asks. I glance at his face, but only for a second. Up close, it looks like leather, and his breath is a combination of Jack Daniels and cigarette smoke. My heart sinks, and I don't know what to say. I glare at Annette, my eyes begging her to do something. She just sits there across from me, crying.

"You really failed me." Martha starts tapping the floor with her cane. "You failed all of us."

"Martha and Miriam, if I could speak to you." Jeremy wiggles his finger in their direction, and they walk to the edge of the sitting room. "Everybody just hang tight. Charlotte should be here any minute." They make sure they are blocking the only way out of the room. I wonder for a moment if it is to stop me or some of the other ladies, as well.

"What are they going to do, kill me now?" I ask as quietly as I can, trying not to cry, but not doing a very good job of it. No one says anything, which gives me the answer to my question. I glance around the room at the blank faces. "I just want to know why."

Annette looks up at me, and I continue in a whisper. "Why the murders? Why running people off the road? Like what happened with Brenda, for example, the teenager from my work. Why in the world would Martha want to hurt an innocent sixteen year old?"

"She wasn't that innocent, was she?" Annette is staring at me, looking hurt. Betrayed. I know how much the Hunt Club means to her. I'm sure that hearing I'm working with the FBI had to hurt her.

"You just don't get it, do you? Martha helped you. Everyone did," Tammy says from where she sits behind Annette and Amber.

"How does hurting Brenda help me? And what about the murders?" I can tell when no one looks shocked that everyone here knows about the murders. I lean forward so Annette, Amber, and Rose are the only ones who can hear me. "The murders just made it possible for more marriages and divorces to exist, and that was all for one reason only. So the Hunt Club could make its money. It's all about the money."

"Yes, hurting the girls like Brenda helped you," Rose says, and it surprises me. I never would have guessed Rose would support such a thing. "It helped all of us, really. Don't you see? Hunt Club is all about giving us power, Sandra. It's not about money, not about stature, not even about the men. It's about us not being invisible anymore. Girls like Brenda—" she pauses as if there are no words could accurately describe her "—they are the ones who make us invisible."

I know she's right. Girls like Brenda absolutely destroy any hopes and dreams for the invisible girls, like who I was—and like who I am afraid I still am. "But, that doesn't mean we have the right to hurt them, does it?" I ask her. "You can't really sit there and expect me to believe y'all think it's okay what the Hunt Club has done?"

Rose lowers her voice. "Like Martha always says, those beautiful women are, in essence, killing us—making women like us invisible and nonexistent."

"I am not saying I support the murders and all that stuff," Annette says. "I'm just saying that I UNDERSTAND it."

"And the situation with Brenda," Rose continues, "Martha was just showing you that you don't have to take it anymore. None of us do. All along, what we have been doing is helping you get your power back, Sandra. Letting you know that you won't ever be invisible ever again."

"There's got to be a better way."

Several of the ladies shake their heads slowly. It's Amber who finally asks the question: "What if there isn't?"

We're silent again as we wait for Jeremy, Miriam, and Martha to decide what they want to do with me now. Liz walks out of the dining room and joins in their discussion. She looks at me for a moment, but her face is emotionless. There is no sign of Mike, and I'm guessing he's still in the dining room. My strongest impulse is to try and get out of here. I can just envision jumping over Joyce. Or Rose in her chair. And making a run for the front door.

My attention is diverted back to the group at the edge of the room. Martha must be reading my mind; she is looking straight at me, her face scrunched up, and her eyes are squinted. I can't make out what she is saying to Jeremy, but when she points her bony finger at me, all eyes turn in my direction.

"Sandra, you see my hand in my pocket? That means you'd better be braver or faster." Jeremy glares at me with his right hand prominently in his jacket pocket, making it clear that he has a weapon on him. When I lean back in my chair, he pauses for a few more seconds and goes back to the conversation.

I take a deep breath and try to exhale slowly. As I look around the room, no one will make eye contact with me. It's sinking in that, in a room filled with people who are supposed to be my friends, no one is going to help me. Then, I look over at Annette again. As much as I'm surprised about Mike, I'm shocked and angry about Annette. How can she just sit there and go along with what the Hunt Club is doing?

"Annette," I whisper to her, my disappointment obvious. "You really didn't have Asperger's syndrome when you were a kid. Did you?"

"How can you even ask me that?" Annette shoots me a wounded look. "That was the basis for Will's and my core connection."

"But, you told me about your childhood, remember? The years and years of dance lessons—ballet, tap, and jazz? Horse-back riding lessons? I think you also told me before about how you took baton lessons and sang in the church choir. You know kids suffering with Asperger's wouldn't do any of that."

Annette stares at the other ladies in the room, unsure of who can hear us and who can't. She looks toward the door-way, and I wonder if she is thinking like I am—how to escape. We watch as Jeremy continues his conversation with Miriam, Martha, and Liz.

"What do you want me to say, Sandra? That I tricked my husband into marrying me? I have been there for him like no one else in his life ever has. Doesn't that count for something?"

"I think it's terrible that the Hunt Club stooped so low to trick guys into marriage." I have to remind myself to keep my voice down.

"How in the hell else can girls like us ever have a chance at getting a guy like William?"

"You underestimate the guys." I shake my head, feeling more disgusted. "And you underestimate yourself."

"You sound just like Lexi," Amber comments.

"Yes, but Lexi was lucky enough to get out of the Hunt Club, wasn't she?" I ask gingerly, hoping for some information on what happened to Lexi.

"I told you before, Sandra, no one gets out of Hunt Club," Annette says. "And before you judge me and the rest of us so harshly, you need to take a look in the mirror. You did the same damn thing to Mike. If you hadn't, he wouldn't even be here."

I can't keep from crying now. "Really? Why exactly is Mike here, Annette? Tell me, because I have no idea. It certainly isn't for me, now is it?"

She finally looks me straight in the eye. "I'm sorry, I didn't know about Mike's involvement with Jeremy until today. Until a few minutes before you got here. Just like I didn't know about your involvement with the FBI."

"I didn't have any choice."

"Neither do I," Annette mouths the words to me as we notice Jeremy walking back in our direction.

"That's enough chitchat," Jeremy interrupts us. Miriam and Martha are still talking at the edge of the room, and Liz has gone back in the dining room. There is still no sign of Mike. Miriam and Martha take a few steps into the room, but neither of them sits down.

Jeremy is looking me over from head to toe, and it is making me very nervous. "What happens now?" I ask in a voice that doesn't sound like my own. I quit my job, and my neighbors think I have left for California. Anything could happen to me now, and no one would notice. My mom and I haven't spoken in months. She won't even know what's been going on if something happens to me. Oh, why haven't I called my mom?

"You answer our questions, for starters." Jeremy is just inches from my face now. "Then, if you don't mind me sounding cliché . . ." he pauses and laughs harshly, "you and me, we'll go for a little ride."

Tears are rolling down my cheeks, and I wipe them off before crossing my arms. I've never felt more afraid or helpless in my life. I don't know where I would go, anyway, even if I could get away.

Jeremy begins yelling. "Now let's try this one more time. When did you start working with the FBI?" I notice his hand is in his jacket pocket again.

"It wasn't like I went looking for them. I really—I didn't have any choice."

"I strongly suggest you start giving us details. Right now." He's shouting just inches from my face with his pungent breath punctuating every syllable. I hear Annette sob quietly. Jeremy's yelling practically drowns out the sudden sound of doorbell chimes. He doesn't move from where he hovers over me.

"Finally, there's Charlotte with the car. Miriam, go let her in," Martha says quickly, as if to make sure she's not interrupting Jeremy.

"And you thought she was bringing mimosas, didn't you?" Jeremy laughs in my face, and I try to avoid looking directly in his eyes.

Miriam is already heading toward the door. Before she reaches it, the front door bursts open. Men wearing black quickly fill the foyer.

"Excuse me!" We hear Miriam yell. "Can I help y'all?"

"FBI! We have a search warrant!" The first man yells. They're suddenly in the sitting room, and I don't know whether to be happy or scared to see them. "Stay right where you are. No one move. Ladies, I need you to keep your hands where I can see them. Sir! Your hands out of your pockets!" The men are dressed in black pants, black shirts, vests with big "FBI" letters on them, and they're wearing helmets. The first agent has a gun in one arm and is lifting Jeremy to his feet with the other. In one swift motion, he has Jeremy turned around and leaning across the chair next to me.

"Excuse me!" I hear Miriam scream. "I'm sorry, but you men are going to have to show me some identification. And I need you to remove those filthy boots at the door, PLEASE!"

A group of other FBI agents walk in right past Miriam. They scatter throughout the house. Loud noises from outside instantly radiate into the room, and it sounds like a huge truck is trying to make it up the hill in front of Miriam's home.

"Is this really necessary?" Martha asks, as one of the FBI agents with a big black gun stands right next to her and aims the gun at her. It's obvious she's trying to sound frail and helpless. "I'm a seventy-six-year-old lady, for goodness' sakes!"

"Let's all just calm down now, shall we?" Rose says. Always the gracious hostess, she gestures with her hands for the men to sit down with us. "Won't you have a seat, please? There's been some kind of misunderstanding, I'm sure."

"What is the nature of your visit?" Joyce asks in her usual sweet voice. "May I offer you gentlemen a muffin?" She reaches toward the silver tray on the table.

"Ladies, I say it again: I need for you all to remain completely still!" One of the agents stops Joyce before she can pick up the muffins.

"Jeremy Lambert, you have the right to remain silent—" The FBI agent removes a handgun from Jeremy's jacket pocket and begins reading him his rights. I don't know what to do besides freeze where I am. The look on Annette's face is one of utter fear. I've never seen her like this before.

"What is going on?" Joyce asks again, this time not so sweetly. "We are simply trying to have a quiet little women's meeting. Is there some kind of problem?" She has playing blonde down to a science.

"Listen up!" Agent McFarland steps forward with a clipboard, and I finally breathe a sigh of relief when I see him. "No body moves. No body talks. I am going to read off a list of names, and I need to have these people identified."

Silence fills the room. The only noise is the FBI agent with Jeremy. He helps him stand up, and they move quickly through the sitting room. The agent is still finishing the Miranda warning as he shoves Jeremy out the front door.

"Where is Martha Roberts?" Agent McFarland asks. No one says anything.

"I am Martha Roberts. Why do you want to know?"

"Go ahead," McFarland gestures to the FBI agent who is standing next to Martha. He takes her by the upper arm and starts pulling her through the room.

"Now you wait just one damn minute!" Martha looks like she is about to hit him with her cane. "This is my daughter's home, and I am not going anywhere."

"Yes, you are, ma'am." The FBI agent pulls her arm harshly. He takes her cane out of her hand. "We have a warrant for your arrest."

"You have made a big mistake. Just you wait until I call my attorney!" Martha is practically growling at the men. "I guarantee! You will be sorry."

"Martha Roberts, you have the right to remain SILENT!" And within a few seconds, Martha is out the front door. They don't even stop for her shoes.

"Miriam Roberts Ellington."

"I'm Miriam," Miriam says hesitantly from where an agent has her standing near the wall to the sitting room. McFarland nods, and Miriam is escorted out. It's happening so fast that I'm having a difficult time registering it all.

"Miriam Roberts Ellington?" I whisper in Annette and Amber's direction. "Is she really Martha's daughter?"

"I said silence!" McFarland yells at me. He is showing no indication on his face that he knows me. He moves on to the next name. "Rose Baker."

"I am Rose Baker. What is this about, gentlemen?" Rose turns sideways to look at McFarland. Her number *five* diamond pin is glimmering in the soft lighting of the sitting room.

"You need to come with us, ma'am." An agent steps forward and grabs her arm above her elbow.

"Well . . ." Rose acts completely insulted. "I never!"

"Let's go."

"It's the Membership Committee," someone whispers. Several agents turn around and look in the direction of where Teresa and Selma are sitting. The girls freeze, trying to look like it wasn't them.

"Joyce Yardling." McFarland is moving steadily down his list. No one moves. No one says anything. I glance over at Joyce, who is looking down at her feet. "Joyce Yardling," McFarland says again. He looks around the room. "No one is getting out of here without going through us, so you might as well cooperate."

"Oh my goodness me, I'm sorry." Joyce says in her sweetest lyrical voice. "Did you say Joyce Yardling?"

"Yes."

"That would be me," she says, lightly tapping her bright red nails on the arms of the chair.

"Come with me, ma'am." An agent pulls Joyce up.

"Elizabeth Gray-Milner," McFarland says.

"She's right in there," Teresa points behind her. She seems to be almost enjoying this now. "In the dining room."

"How many people are in there?"

"It should be just Liz and one other guy, Mike Warren," Teresa says.

McFarland gestures to the room behind where Teresa and Selma are sitting. Two agents quickly raise their guns and storm the dining room, breaking the door off its hinges. In seconds, Liz and Mike are walking toward the front door, escorted by FBI agents.

It's when I see Mike that I really start crying. The ugly cry.

When the FBI wants to search a home, they are like a bunch of Africanized bees. They are relentless, everywhere, working quickly, and highly organized. They turn over or go through everything in their path. The agents questioned every one of us separately. The rest of the Hunt Club members who are not on Agent McFarland's list are eventually allowed to leave, but we are directed not to leave town without notifying the FBI.

I purposely wait around outside the yellow police tape that is strewn across the front of Miriam's house and landscaped lawn. I want to catch Agent McFarland before he leaves to see if he can tell me what is going to happen to Mike. Where is he being held? What are all the charges? How much involvement has he really had with Jeremy? I really don't know what else to do or where to go. It is difficult for me to comprehend how Mike could hurt me after all we've shared.

Sitting on the lawn watching the FBI agents remove items from Miriam's house, I finally see McFarland appear with a circle of other agents still buzzing around him.

"Agent McFarland, can I speak to you for a minute?" I stop him on the steps.

"Yes, of course." The other agents keep walking, carrying black cases of information they retrieved from Miriam's house and garage. McFarland is carrying a stack of yellow notebooks.

"The FBI thanks you again for your assistance with the investigation." McFarland is speaking in third person again.

"I'm just relieved it's over," I tell him, trying to remember the questions I had wanted to ask him. "Are you going to need anything else from me?"

"You will likely be called to testify as a witness in court. That will be up to the prosecutors. You may also be asked to testify before the grand jury."

"Did you find out anything about Lexi Donaldson?"

"No, we haven't been able to locate her, but we did question Martha Roberts about her." He quickly flips through one of the notebooks he's carrying. "She said Lexi was having some sort of affair with a married man, which goes against the rules of the Hunt Club. According to Ms. Roberts, Lexi was no longer morally fit to be a member."

"Oh, like Martha is all moral all of a sudden."

"Right. Exactly." McFarland smiles. "They said the married guy set Lexi up in an apartment and is supporting her. So, she's kicked out of Hunt Club, and that's why she disappeared."

"You don't actually believe that?"

"No, we don't believe it. According to what we found, Lexi works for a clothing store in the Galleria, and they haven't heard from her or seen her. Neither have her parents. I'm afraid it doesn't look good, Sandra. I'll let you know if we get anything concrete about the married boyfriend, though."

"Okay. Thanks," I say, sharing in the bad feeling he has about what's happened to Lexi. "What happens now with the Hunt Club?"

He sighs. "Let me tell you, these ladies had a good racket going. Any time one of the husbands died or they got divorced, the Hunt Club got half of the wife's assets. The FBI has disbanded all Hunt Clubs nationwide, effective immediately, and frozen all bank accounts. Our biggest concern was Jeremy Lambert. We tracked him from D.C. to Atlanta, but then he didn't surface until today. He was the key player in the murders."

"I am really thankful y'all came in when you did." My eyes start to tear up again. "I don't know what I would have done if—"

"It was thanks to Mr. Warren that we found out Jeremy was here today. He called us from his cell phone to tell us Jeremy was holding you hostage inside. You should really be thanking him."

"Mike?"

"Yes, he's been assisting us like you have. In fact, we stopped him at the airport on his way back from Hawaii at the same time we stopped you. His work to get information on Jeremy Lambert was integral to Mr. Lambert's arrest."

"So, Mike's been working with the FBI all this time?"

"We regret we couldn't tell you. It was necessary for the investigation. We had to make sure Jeremy and the Hunt Club trusted him completely. The FBI couldn't take the risk of telling you."

"Does that mean Mike's not arrested?"

"No, he's not arrested." McFarland laughs. "He's in the mobile unit, over there." McFarland points at one of the black vans. "As soon as he's finished giving his statement, I'm sure he'll want to talk to you."

I'm so relieved to hear his words that I have to sit down on the steps.

"Are you okay, Sandra?"

"Yes." I laugh and cry at the same time. "I was just so worried, you know, about Mike and everything."

"He's been worried about you, too. He was upset when he heard his ex-girlfriend was murdered. Which is why he was so willing to help us. But at the same time, he has been insistent on making sure you were safe, especially if you were going to be in the Hunt Club and helping the FBI, too."

"I didn't know what was going on."

"He'll be able to tell you about it now that his assistance is no longer needed. You both will need to testify, but other than that, your roles in the investigation are complete."

"Hey!" We look up and see Mike walking over toward us. "Anybody need a ride?"

"Mike!" I stand up, run over to him, and jump in his arms. "Why didn't you say something?"

"I couldn't. We were trying to flush out Jeremy, and they wouldn't let me tell you anything." He mumbles into my shoulder as he hugs me. "I promised you I would never let anything happen to you, remember?"

"I'm so glad you're okay, too." We're standing there, in the middle of the street, kissing and not about to let go of each other.

"I was just telling Sandra, you will need to appear before the grand jury and to testify at the court proceedings," McFarland says, walking over to us. "But other than that, you are free to go anywhere you want as long as we can reach you."

"How about Malibu?"

"Sounds great to me." My arms are still wrapped around him.

"You shouldn't have any problems. We were able to make all the arrests, except one. Charlotte Nichols," McFarland tells us. "She somehow must have seen the FBI vans or otherwise found out about us. She's disappeared."

"Hey, if you want to find her, all you have to do is look for her diamond number *five* pin," I joke. "It's the biggest one I've seen."

"Did you ever find out what the number *five* stands for?" Mike asks as he shakes McFarland's hand.

"We aren't sure yet, although we did get some type of an answer from Jeremy Lambert. He said the number *five* is 'a reminder of what they are.' Does that mean anything to you?"

A reminder of what we are, that we're really fives—that on a one-to-ten scale, we're average. I guess the Hunt Club chose the number *five* because they want to highlight where we've come from and whom they were trying to help. I understand why they wear the number *five* in huge, bright, shiny, diamond pins. "It's to make the point that fives are not invisible," I tell McFarland.

And they never will be again.

A+

AUTHOR
INSIGHTS,
EXTRAS, &
MORE...

FROM

**LISA
LANDOLT**

AND

**AVON A**

# Creation of GOOD MAN HUNTING

*Good Man Hunting* only took about ten days to write, but I played with ideas for writing it over the course of several years as different elements inspired me. Media such as current television shows and the Internet have influenced the underlying concept of how far people will go for the sake of matchmaking. Television shows like *The Bachelor* and other dating reality shows help to create a sense of satire and irony about dating and the drive to "get" a guy at any price. The popularity of shows such as *Desperate Housewives* further illustrate society's interest in the fantasy of finding Mr. Right or Ms. Right. Matchmaking has become big business on TV, in movies, and services on the Internet. *Good Man Hunting* just takes the phenomenon one step farther and shows what could happen if the obsession for getting anyone a person wants is taken to the extreme.

Over the years, I have been influenced by the literary works of authors such as Joyce Carol Oates, Charlotte Perkins Gilman, and Shirley Jackson. Their use of satire and irony, as well as the psychological dynamics of their characters, inspired the elements now found in *Good Man Hunting*.

Another influence for the book was the growing recognition of the problems faced by people who feel, and are often treated as if, they are invisible, especially women. Law school and the practice of law have allowed me to see how the legal system and society treat people who are uneducated and right at or below the poverty line. Working with victims of consumer scams, women who have been sexually harassed, and people otherwise discriminated against has presented the same circumstances of people feeling invisible or being treated as if they "don't matter." The same women who are taken advantage of by consumer scams and discrimination are often the same women who feel invisible to men. Often without a college education or the financial means to make positive changes, they tend to feel stuck in their positions in life.

All of these influences came together to create the character of Sandra Greene. I wanted to show what might happen to an average young woman with little education or money when she is given the opportunity to create her own station in life, go after and get any man she wants to have, and explore what she can accomplish. The book developed into a modern-day Cinderella story—with a twist or two.

—Lisa Landolt

# Hunt Club Membership Questionnaire

If you were interested in joining the Hunt Club, you would need to fill out the following Prospective Husband Questionnaire. What type of man would you choose if you could have any man you want?

The following questions involve characteristics that will help you develop a connection with the right man for you. Don't be afraid to be honest. The more honest you are, the more help we can be to you.

*I. Rank in the order of most important (number 1 would be the most important, and 12 would be the least important) for your potential husband:*

\_\_\_Love of Children and Family  \_\_\_Time to Spend with Me
\_\_\_Physical Appearance  \_\_\_Movies, Music, Tastes
\_\_\_Financial Wealth      in Entertainment
\_\_\_Education  \_\_\_Love of Sex
\_\_\_Career & Ambition  \_\_\_Sense of Humor and
\_\_\_Kindness      Friendliness
\_\_\_Charity  \_\_\_Religion

*II. Describe how you would build Your Ideal Man from scratch.*

1. Head and hair (hair color, long or short, etc.):

_____

_____

2. Face (consider eye color, glasses, mustache, beard, etc.):

_____

_____

3. Shoulders:

_____

_____

4. Arms and hands:

_____

_____

5. Back:

_____

_____

6. Chest:

_____

_____

7. Stomach:

_____

_____

8. Belly button (inny or outty?):

_____

_____

9. Waist:

_____

_____

10. Rear end:

_____

_____

11. Sexual instrument [a polite Hunt Club term]:

_____

_____

12. Legs:

_____

_____

13. Feet:

_____

_____

14. What is your Ideal Man's wardrobe?
    (a) Suits and ties all the time. You rarely see him without
        a tie.
    (b) Suits and ties if he has to, but he prefers nice pants and
        a button down shirt.
    (c) He hates having to wear suits and ties, preferring to
        wear jeans and T-shirts if he can get away with it.
    (d) He doesn't own a tie and wouldn't know how to tie
        one.

15. To help us better understand what you prefer in physical
    characteristics for your Ideal Man, please name one or more
    famous men who reasonably resemble him.

_____

_____

_____

16. How would you describe your Ideal Man emotionally?
    (a) He's your rock. He's a pretty tough guy and not really emotional at all.
    (b) Very emotional on the inside and shows it when you're alone, but otherwise he appears and acts strong on the outside.
    (c) He's emotional. He shares his open and honest thoughts and feelings all the time.
    (d) He's very logical, even about serious emotional matters. He understands emotions and articulates them rationally, but he does not act them out and encourages you not to, either.

17. If you and your Ideal Man were in an argument, which emotional reaction would be closest to the reaction you would prefer:
    (a) He avoids confrontation and leaves the room until you both calm down.
    (b) He shares all of his emotions openly and honestly, holding nothing back.
    (c) He picks his words carefully, cautious of hurting your feelings but also not completely honest about what he is thinking.
    (d) He shares his emotions but backs down when you get upset and does anything he can to make peace with you.

18. You married your Ideal Man, and he is with you at the time you give birth to your first child. Which of the following most closely describes how he reacts?
    (a) He's emotional and teary-eyed, is there every minute, empathically feeling your pain of contractions, and crying openly when your child is born.

(b) He's strong and encouraging, holding your hand and coaching you, spending time with family members in the waiting room to let them know how things are going, and when the baby is born, he is happy and joyful, eager to celebrate with you and family members.

(c) Your best friend is there to coach you, and your husband shows up just as the baby is being born. He's busy with work and making money, and it's fine with you if he can't be with you the entire time. When the baby is born, he is happy and lets the hospital take care of your needs, trying to stay out of the way.

(d) He can't wait to meet his child and spends the entire time videotaping the contractions and birth, making jokes to keep you calm.

19. Your Ideal Man becomes your husband and has a beautiful boss who requires he work overtime on nights and weekends.

(a) Your husband tries to avoid overtime, doing anything he can to get out of it, even if it means losing his job.

(b) Your husband is eager to make as much money as possible and will do anything he can for his boss because it means more money.

(c) Your husband doesn't discuss the matter with you because he will work overtime if he needs to.

(d) Your husband works the overtime and welcomes you to come with him and help him if you want.

20. You are out at a restaurant with your Ideal Man, and an attractive woman comes up to say hi. He obviously knows her. Which describes how he would likely act?

(a) Your Ideal Man is always very friendly with people, so he introduces her and asks her to join the two of you.

(b) He says hello, introduces her to you, says good-bye to her, and encourages her to go on her way. When she's gone he will explain briefly she's just a friend and drop the issue.

(c) He says hello, introduces you to her, and encourages her to go on her way. He then tells you exactly who she is, every detail about how he knows her, and he expects you to do the same with every man in your life.

(d) He talks to her for a few seconds and turns his focus back to you, letting her know the conversation is over. Nothing is explained about her.

21. Your Ideal Man is your husband, and he's having a stressful time at work that is making him irritable at home. Which of the following most closely describes how he handles it.

(a) He starts taking antidepressants and seeing a therapist to deal with his problems.

(b) He starts looking for another job immediately, and he leaves the situation.

(c) He suffers through it for as long as it takes, without medication or therapy.

(d) He wants to go out every night with you or his buddies to take his mind off his problems.

22. Your Ideal Man is your husband and he

(a) has lots of friends, both male and female.

(b) has no female friends or women in his life besides you.

(c) has other females in his life but treats them as incidental and unimportant in his life.

(d) shares your female friends with you.

23. Your Ideal Man is your husband and he

(a) wants to know every single detail about your day.

(b) doesn't ask you about your day, and you don't ask him about his. Work stays at work.

(c) listens to you about whatever you want to share but doesn't ask questions about your day. You do the same with him; you listen to whatever he wants to share, but you don't question him about it.

(d) you work with your husband, so you and he already know about the details of your day.

24. Your Ideal Man is your husband, and someone is giving you a hard time at your job. What best describes what your husband will do?

(a) Your husband stays out of it and encourages you to not worry about it.

(b) Your husband worries about it with you, spending hours going over it all and calling you at work to see how it's going.

(c) Your husband wants to know who this person is and goes and confronts him or her, telling that person to leave you alone or else.

(d) Your husband won't get involved beyond listening to you if you want to talk because he knows work is your business, and you will handle it.

25. Your husband's idea of the perfect dog:

(a) no pets

(b) a puppy

(c) a German shepherd

(d) a mutt at the pound that is so ugly and scraggly that no one else is even looking at him, and he has only one day left before he's put to sleep

26. Describe your Ideal Man's relationship with his parents:

(a) Calls and sees them as often as possible; they are an important part of his life.

(b) Tries to remember to call once a week and sees them when they need something.

(c) Sees them on holidays and calls once a month or so, sending e-mails occasionally.

(d) Doesn't really have much to do with his parents.

27. Describe your Ideal Man's religious beliefs:
    (a) He attends church every Sunday, reads the Bible often, and prays every day.
    (b) Doesn't go to church that often, but he believes in God, and tries to live his life the way God wants him to.
    (c) Considers himself a good person but isn't religious at all.
    (d) Doesn't like going to church, but otherwise he believes in God even though he doesn't want to talk about it.

28. Truthfully, if your Ideal Man accidentally hit a vacant car in a parking lot, no one saw him, and there's no damage to his own car, what would he do?
    (a) Stop and leave a note with an apology, his contact information, and his insurance information.
    (b) Look around to make sure no one saw him, and then get the heck out of there, never mentioning it to anyone but worrying if anyone saw him.
    (c) Drive off without even worrying about it.
    (d) Drive off and later joke about it with you and his friends about how he did it and drove off.

29. Which of the following most closely describes your Ideal Man's tastes:
    (a) champagne and caviar
    (b) cocktails and dancing
    (c) beer and pizza
    (d) iced tea and barbecue

30. At a social gathering, you would likely find your Ideal Man
    (a) at the center of attention; the life of the party
    (b) talking in a small group off to one side
    (c) talking to one person at a time and not being a real party-person
    (d) standing back and just watching, not really talking to anyone

*IV: Your Ideal Man's Intelligence and Education*

31. How would you describe your Ideal Man's education?
    (a) He's very well educated; he went to college and probably graduate school of some kind.
    (b) He's very intelligent, but he's very easygoing and doesn't flaunt it at all, so a person wouldn't know it unless you really grill him about his educational history.
    (c) He's very proud of his educational accomplishments, and everyone knows how intelligent he is.
    (d) It doesn't really matter how intelligent he is as long as he has street smarts.

32. Your Ideal Man must be
    (a) more intelligent than you are so you can look up to him
    (b) more intelligent than you are, but he doesn't make you feel less intelligent
    (c) the same level of intelligence as you
    (d) not as intelligent as you

33. To help us understand your intelligence preference for your Ideal Man, name one or more famous men who reasonably resemble your intellectually perfect man.

_____

_____

*V. Marital Status*

34. Which of the following most closely describes your preference. Your Ideal Man must be
    (a) never married
    (b) never married or divorced with no kids
    (c) never married or divorced with or without kids is fine
    (d) never married or divorced with kids under 10
    (e) never married or divorced with kids over 10

35. What is your Ideal Man's relationship with his ex-wife:
    (a) Very good; they are still friends.
    (b) They are out of each other's lives completely.
    (c) They remain polite for the sake of the kids.
    (d) They don't talk unless they have to, and then it's about the kids only and is very brief.

*VI. Your Ideal Man's Financial Status*

Remember our Hunt Club Motto: "You can fall in love with a rich man just as easily as a poor man!"

36. The financial status of your Ideal Man would most closely be described as follows:
    (a) Makes enough money for us to live on and be comfortable.
    (b) Makes over $200,000 a year, including investments.
    (c) Makes over $500,000 a year, including investments.
    (d) Is at least a millionaire.

37. Name one or more famous men who reasonably resemble your financially perfect man.

    _____

    _____

38. Which of the following most closely describes your Ideal Man's type of hobbies:
    (a) Likes working around the house and the yard.
    (b) Likes adventurous activities like white-water rafting, skydiving, or race car driving.
    (c) Likes museums, lectures, reading, and other intellectual activities.
    (d) Likes to travel.
    (e) Likes leisure activities such as boating, spending time at the beach or the pool, or just hanging out with friends.

39. How does your Ideal Man feel about kids?
    (a) Likes kids but doesn't have to have them if I don't want to.
    (b) Hates kids and doesn't want any.
    (c) Loves kids and wants a big family
    (d) Wants one kid.
    (d) Wants one or more kids but wants to have a nanny or other help.

*VIII. The following questions involve Deal Breakers a potential husband may have that would absolutely disqualify a man from being someone you would choose as your Ideal Man.*

40. What are the physical appearance deal breakers about your Ideal Man?

_____

_____

_____

41. What are the personality deal breakers about your Perfect Man?

_____

_____

42. What are the location deal breakers?

_____

_____

43. Family issues deal breakers?

_____

_____

44. What are the other deal breakers about your Ideal Man?

_____

_____

45. How old is your Ideal Man?
   (a) 18–25
   (b) 21–29
   (c) 30–39
   (d) 21–40
   (e) 21–50
   (f) 35–50
   (g) 21 and up

IX. *If You Already Know Who Your Ideal Man Might Be*

46. Who do you have in mind as your Ideal Man?

_____

_____

47. Where is he located? What are the details about where he lives (house, apartment, roommates, etc.).

_____

_____

48. Does he have a girlfriend? If so, how serious are they?

_____

_____

49. What is his profession? Where does he work?

_____

_____

50. Approximately how much money does he make per year?

_____

_____

51. What do you know about his family and friends?

_____

_____

52. Where does he hang out most of the time?

_____

_____

53. What are his hobbies and interests? At what locations?

_____

_____

54. Do you have initial ideas for a possible setup?

_____

_____

55. How well do you know him?

_____

_____

56. What common interests, friends, or possible common elements do you share with him?

_____

_____

57. What obstacles do you anticipate if he is selected for the hunt?

_____

_____

This concludes the Prospective Husband Questionnaire. You have just completed the first step toward joining the Hunt Club. Your life is about to change forever.

_____

Visit www.goodmanhunting.com for more information about the Hunt Club.

Photo courtesy of Lisa Landolt

**LISA LANDOLT** is an attorney and mediator in Dallas/Fort Worth, Texas. Her law practice involves literary representation, and she enjoys working with new and established authors. While still hunting for her own good man, Lisa lives in Arlington with her six-year-old cat named Haylie. Visit her website at www.goodmanhunting.com.

Lisa Landolt